D1510153

HIGHLAND

A Novel

WARRIOR

Also by Monica McCarty

Highlander Untamed
Highlander Unmasked
Highlander Unchained

HIGHLAND
WARRIOR

A Novel

MONICA McCARTY

BALLANTINE BOOKS • NEW YORK

A Ballantine Books Mass Market Original

Published in the United States by Ballantine Books, an imprint of The Random House Publishing Group, a division of Random House, Inc., New York.

BALLANTINE and colophon are registered trademarks of Random House, Inc.

This book contains an excerpt from the forthcoming mass market edition of *Highland Outlaw* by Monica McCarty. This excerpt has been set for this edition only and may not reflect the final content of the forthcoming edition.

ISBN-13: 978-1-60751-730-6

Cover illustration: Aleta Rafton

Printed in the United States of America

To Dave, my very own big, strapping lad.
Hmm . . . I wonder how you'd look in a kilt?

Acknowledgments

From the first spark of an idea, to the time the final page proofs leave my hand, there are many people who provide invaluable help and guidance along the way. A special thanks to my editor Kate Collins whose return to Ballantine happened to coincide with the due date for this book and who, despite being inundated, nonetheless managed to read it in record time. Nothing like hitting the ground running is there, Kate? Thanks also to Charlotte for her early guidance on this project and to Kelli Fillingim for keeping everything going. As always, thanks to my agents Kelly Harms and Andrea Cirillo, my cp's Nyree and Jami, the Fog City Divas and brainstorming buddies, the production team at Ballantine, and the Web design team at Wax Creative—you guys are the best!

My brother-in-law Sean for answering my medical questions (see, I told you you'd get some ink!). Hope I didn't screw anything up. If so, the errors are mine. Who would have thought that when my sister married, I'd gain not only a brother, but also a doctor with an interest in historical battle injuries? I really should play the lottery more often . . .

Thanks to Tracy Anne Warren and Allison Brennan—two authors who've "been there" and helped me navigate the maze of writing *two* back-to-back trilogies.

Finally, to my kids, Reid and Maxine. You might not be old enough to read these books yet, but I hope someday you'll appreciate that by choking down all those leftovers (especially the beloved "mommy's pasta") you helped mommy do something she loves.

Chapter 1

"A law is no justice."

—Scottish Proverb

Ascog Castle, Isle of Bute, Scotland, June 1608

Caitrina Lamont peered into the looking glass as the young maid pinned the last section of lace ruff in place behind her neck. The delicate points, embellished with tiny jewels, framed her face like a sparkling halo. She bit back a mischievous smile, having no illusions in that regard. As her brothers so often delighted in pointing out, she was far too bold and opinionated to ever be confused with an angel. "A man wants a biddable, demure lass for a wife," they'd tease, knowing full well they were only encouraging her to do the opposite.

Finished at last, she stepped back to get a better view of her new gown in the small mirror. Excitement sparkled in her eyes. The dress was truly magnificent. She met the reflected gaze of her beloved nursemaid in the looking glass. "Oh, Mor, isn't it the most gorgeous gown you've ever seen?"

Mor had been watching the proceedings with the brooding consternation of a mother sending her son into battle for the first time. The analogy wasn't too far off. Tonight, there would be a great feast to celebrate the opening of the Highland gathering being held this year at Ascog. But Caitrina was well aware that her father had every hope of securing her betrothal to one of the many Highlanders who would be descending on their keep to test their strength and skill. Quickly, before it could spoil the excitement of her gift, she pushed away the disagreeable thought.

"Gorgeous?" The older woman snorted her disapproval, staring meaningfully at the low-cut square bodice where Caitrina's bosom strained to near bursting against the tight confines of stays and satin. Mor shuffled the young maid-servant out of the room and then resumed her diatribe. "Immodest is more like it. And I don't know what's wrong with the twenty other 'gorgeous' gowns you have hanging in the ambry."

Caitrina scrunched her nose. "Oh, Mor, you know I have nothing like this." She glanced down at the swell of flesh rising high over the edge of her gown. The neckline *was* rather low. She could practically see the pink edge of her . . . She fought the blush, knowing that it would only give Mor further cause for argument. "This gown is quite proper," she said firmly. "All the fashionable courtiers are wearing dresses just like this at Whitehall."

Mor muttered something that sounded suspiciously like "damn fool English," which Caitrina chose to ignore. Centuries of enmity would not be forgotten simply because Scotland's king had also become England's. She lifted the pale gold silk in her hand, allowing the light from the window to catch in iridescent waves, and sighed dreamily. "I feel like a princess in this dress."

The old woman snorted. "Well, it certainly cost a king's ransom to have such a gown sent all the way from London to the Isle of Bute." Mor paused and shook her head. " 'Tis sheer foolishness when there are perfectly capable dressmakers in Edinburgh."

"But they are woefully out-of-date with the most recent styles," Caitrina protested. Still, something Mor said bothered her. She bit her lip, not having considered the cost of her father's largesse. "Do you really think it was too costly?"

Mor lifted a sardonic brow, unable to hide her amusement. "Blackmail doesn't usually come cheap."

Caitrina's mouth twitched, fighting another smile. "It wasn't blackmail. The gown was Father's idea. No doubt he was feeling guilty for forcing me to endure the attentions of the endless parade of peacocks he struts across our hall. I think he agreed to have the gathering at Ascog with the hope that with so many 'braw lads' to choose from, I would find one to my liking—as if I were picking a bull at market."

In truth, her father's insistence that Caitrina begin a search for a husband worried her more than she wanted to let on. It wasn't like him to be so stubborn. That was Mor's domain.

Mor assiduously avoided the subject of marriage and returned to the gown. "That man would have offered you the moon to see your tears dried. I suppose it could have been worse than one dress." She shook her finger at Caitrina. "But one of these days someone is going to come around who you can't twist around that pretty little finger of yours."

Caitrina grinned. "They already have." She leaned over and pressed a kiss on the wizened cheek. "You."

"Ha." Mor chortled. "Incorrigible scamp."

Caitrina wrapped her arms around the old woman, resting her cheek against the scratchy wool of her *arisaidh,* savoring the warm, familiar scent of peat and heather—of hearth and home. "Do you really not like the gown, Mor? I won't wear it if you don't."

Mor held her back by the shoulders and looked into her eyes. "Don't listen to me, lass. I'm just a silly old woman who's worried about what the wolves may do to my wee lamb." Her gaze softened. "You've been so sheltered, with no inkling of the wickedness of men." The back of her finger smoothed Caitrina's cheek. "That gown simply reminds me that you are a woman full grown." Caitrina was surprised to see tears misting in Mor's troubled eyes. "You look so much like your mother. She was the most beautiful lass in the Highlands when she ran off with your father."

Caitrina's chest squeezed; though her mother had been gone for over ten years now, the pull of emotion was still strong. She'd been eleven when her mother succumbed to the wasting ailment, and the memories of the laughing, beautiful woman who'd held her in her arms grew fuzzier with each year that passed. But there would always be an empty place in her heart and the knowledge that a vital piece of her was missing.

"Tell me again, Mor." She never tired of hearing the story of how her father had caught one glimpse of his enemy's daughter and fallen in love. Of how her parents had met secretly for months, until her father finally convinced her mother to run away with him.

But before Mor could respond, Caitrina's younger brother came bursting into her room. "Caiti! Caiti Rose, come quick!"

Her heart plummeted, thinking the worst. Who was hurt, and how badly? She grabbed Brian by the shoulders and with a calmness she didn't feel—but with three brothers to take care of, she'd unfortunately become used to—said, "What's happened?"

He eyed her warily. "Promise you won't be angry?"

"How can I promise when I don't know what it is?"

At only two and ten, Brian had yet to develop firm negotiating skills. He gave up bargaining and started with excuses. "It wasn't my fault," he hedged. "I told Una—"

At the mention of the little girl's name, Caitrina guessed what was wrong. "Oh, Brian! How many times have I told you to keep those beastly dogs away from the kittens?"

He looked down at his feet, shamefaced. "I told Una that I was taking the lads out, but she forgot to close the door to the stables, and then, well, it happened so fast. Boru was just playing, but the silly cat ran up the tree."

Caitrina groaned. "What tree?"

Brian grimaced. "The old oak. Caiti, please, you have to help me get the kitten down before Una finds out. She'll cry." He kicked at the wooden floor uncomfortably. "I hate it when she cries."

Caitrina met Mor's gaze. Una was her granddaughter, and Mor had a soft spot for the little girl.

"I'll see if I can keep her occupied while you," Mor said, stabbing her finger at Brian's lanky chest, "get that kitten out of the tree."

"Come, Caiti, hurry," he said, dragging her by the hand from her solar.

It wasn't until they'd stepped outside the keep and started toward the gate in the *barmkin* wall that the curious stares of her clansmen reminded her that she was still wearing her new gown—and no shoes. Though the skies were blue, the ground was damp from this morning's rain, and mud squished between her toes. Knowing there was nothing she could do about it now, she lifted her skirts as best she could to keep from soiling the hem.

"You might have given me a moment to change my gown," she grumbled.

Brian spared her a hurried glance. "Why? You look fine."

She rolled her eyes. *Brothers.* She could be wearing a sackcloth and they wouldn't notice.

After passing through the gate, they headed down the path, taking the right fork that led toward the woodlands—the left led down to Loch Ascog. On the eve of the games, the outbuildings along the banks of the loch were bustling with activity, but as she and Brian hurried toward the trees it was surprisingly quiet, except for Boru's barking, which grew louder as they neared the great old oak. The Lamonts descended from the great kings of Éire, and Brian had named the dog after his namesake—Brian Boru, the famed high king of centuries past.

"You left the dog here?"

Her brother reddened. "I told him to go home, but he wouldn't listen. Since the silly cat was already stuck in the tree, I figured it wouldn't matter."

"He's probably scared the poor thing half to death." She turned to the dog and said sharply, "Boru!" He stopped barking and looked at her, head cocked at an inquisitive angle. She pointed in the direction of the castle, no longer visible through the trees. "Home."

With a soft whimper, Boru nuzzled her skirts and gave her an apologetic look with his soulful brown eyes. She shook her head, refusing to be moved. The dog certainly had a gift for the dramatics. "Home, Boru." Whimpering again, this one even more pathetic, the great deerhound hung his head low and trotted back toward the castle.

"I don't know how you do that," Brian said, amazed. "You're the only one he listens to."

Caitrina pursed her lips, biting back the quick retort that sprang to mind: Because she was the only one who gave him commands. Without her, the dogs would be as wild as wolves. Though she supposed much the same could be said about her brothers.

Gazing up through the maze of branches, she gasped, just able to make out the tiny bundle of orange-and-white fur. "How did he get way up there?"

"When I tried to climb up after him, he just kept going higher, which is why I ran to get you. He's scared of me."

She turned to her brother with a start. "You can't expect me to climb up there?"

"Why did you think I brought you out here?" He appeared genuinely perplexed. "The cat won't come to me. He likes you, and you've climbed this tree a hundred times."

"Years ago," she said with exasperation. "If you haven't noticed, I'm long past the age for tree climbing."

"Why? You're not all *that* old."

Caitrina was going to have to work on his flattery skills if Brian was going to have any hope of ever wooing a lass. Although with his face, it probably wouldn't matter. What her brothers lacked in gallantry and manners, they made up for in countenance. They were rogues, the lot of them, but she loved them beyond measure. How could her father think she would ever want to leave them? They *needed* her . . . and she them. Whatever it took, she intended to stay right here.

Attempting to reason with Brian was getting her nowhere. "I'm not going up there. I'll help boost you up or you'll have to find someone else."

He wore an expression of dejection that rivaled Boru's moments earlier. "But why?"

"This dress, for one."

"Please, Caiti, there's no one else. Father, Malcolm, and Niall are hunting with the men, and the others are busy with the preparations for the feast."

That's strange. "I thought they finished hunting."

Brian frowned. "I did, too, but they all ran out of here in a hurry this morning. Father looked worried, and when I asked him where they were going he said hunting. So you see, there is no one else. Please, Caiti. . . ."

As if on cue, the kitten began to mewl. The frightened plea tugged at her heartstrings. *God save her from man and beast.* Furious, she turned her back to her brother. "Oh, very well, but help me out of this thing." Even if the fates appeared to be conspiring against her, she had no intention of ruining her new dress.

He threw his long, gangly arms around her. "You're the best sister in the whole world! I knew I could count on you."

She sighed; it was impossible to stay angry with him for long. No longer a boy and not yet a man, Brian was that odd age in between. Already taller than she, in a few years she knew he would add the muscle and bulk of a warrior like Malcolm and Niall—her two older brothers. Brian had been only a bairn when their mother died, and Caitrina had always taken care of him. Though he hadn't been sent away to be fostered as most young boys were, he would leave soon to become a squire for a neighboring chief. She felt a pang in her chest, wishing she could hold time in a bottle.

After giving him a short squeeze, she hurried him about the business of removing her gown—which wasn't a simple proposition. Overskirt, farthingale, underskirt, forepart, and sleeves were peeled away, layer by layer, until all she wore was her sark and stays. As she was going to have to lift her arms above her head, the stays would also have to be removed, but Brian was having a difficult time working the ties. She could hear him mutter with frustration, until eventually he gave up and started yanking and pulling.

"Ouch!" she said. "Be careful."

"I'm trying, but this isn't easy. Why do you wear all this stuff, anyway?"

Good question. One ripe for a nonanswer. "Because that's what ladies wear."

Once he'd finally extracted her from the linen and whalebone, the stays joined her gown across the fallen log. Though the linen sark she wore covered her well enough, she wanted to get this over with before anyone happened upon them. Although it would be unlikely, since this part of the woods was some distance from the main road, it would be embarrassing to be caught in her underclothes.

She studied the tree appraisingly, plotting her course. It *had* been quite a few years. It was the tallest tree in these parts, and the kitten had managed to climb near the top. "I'll need a boost."

Brian bent down on one knee, and she used his leg as a step to reach the lowest branch. The bark scratched the bottoms of her feet as she climbed from branch to branch, slowly working her way up as though on an uneven ladder.

"Ouch!" she yelped when her foot snagged on a sharp piece of bark. Her feet and hands were going to be torn to shreds by the time she was done.

The kitten watched her approach with wide, anxious eyes, meowing plaintively. She could see him shaking as she neared his precarious perch, so she made soft, soothing noises to calm him. The branches thinned as she climbed higher, and she had to stop and test each one before moving on. Finally, she reached the kitten, who had climbed about five feet out on a thin branch that she knew wouldn't be able to hold her weight. Instead, she used it to balance and carefully eased out sideways along the lower branch, gripping tightly with her feet.

"Be careful," Brian warned.

She resisted the urge to shoot him a glare, not wanting to look down. As if she needed a reminder. Her heart thumped with each step. It was slow work. She had to stop to get her balance with foot forward as the lower branch swayed to accommodate her weight. One more . . .

Her fingers grasped soft fur.

"You've got him!" she heard Brian shout from below.

A burst of accomplishment surged through her. She gathered the tiny ball to her chest and felt the race of the heartbeat that surely matched her own. His little claws poked her through the thin fabric of her sark as he clung to her for dear life.

Now for the hard part. She had only one hand this time to keep her balance as she slowly made her way back along the branch. When she was safely near the trunk, she breathed a sigh of relief. Glancing down, she saw that Brian had climbed up a few branches below her.

"Here, I'll take him," he offered.

Knowing that she wouldn't be able to climb down with one hand, she carefully lowered the kitten into her brother's outstretched hands. He tucked the small bundle behind his leather jerkin, ambled down a few branches, and dropped easily to the ground.

She took a moment to catch her breath and steady her heartbeat, then started to work her way down.

"Thanks, Caiti," he shouted, "you're the best."

She turned at the sound of his fading voice, but it was already too late.

"Wait, Brian, I need your . . ." Her voice dropped off. *Help*. She could just make out his back as he turned the corner out of earshot, running back toward the castle.

"Brothers," she muttered. "Some thanks. When I get hold of him . . ."

She looked down, realizing she was still too far off the ground. A few more branches and she should be able to drop just like Brian. Carefully, she grasped a branch with her hands and lowered one foot and then the other—

The sound of a loud crack signaled disaster. For a moment her stomach rose to her chin, body weightless as she dropped. She grasped the branch above her head just as the one under her feet cracked at the trunk and bent at a perilous angle to the ground. Her brother's weight must have weakened it. If she let go now, the branch would probably give way entirely and she'd go crashing to the ground. She wasn't quite hanging by her fingertips, but almost.

She was also stuck. She looked down past her toes. The ground was at least fifteen feet below—still too far to attempt a drop.

She'd have to wait until Brian remembered. She groaned, realizing she might be here all night.

When I get hold of him . . .

"I think you already said that."

Caitrina gasped at the sound of a deep voice—a deep *male* voice. She looked down and her eyes locked on the steely gaze of a stranger who stood a few feet away, watching her with an amused glint in his eyes. How long he'd been standing there she didn't know, but it had been long enough for him to dismount from the massive destrier at his side.

She didn't know whether to be relieved or embarrassed—probably a little of both. She had need of a rescuer but would have preferred him not to be so—she frowned, searching for the right word—*masculine*. Blatantly so.

From her current position hanging so far from the ground, it was difficult to gauge precisely, but she would guess he stood at least a handful of inches over six feet. A giant by any standard—even a Highland one.

If he was a Highlander.

He'd spoken in Scots and not in the Highland tongue, but she thought she'd detected a hint of brogue in his voice. It was difficult to tell from his clothing. He wasn't wearing the *breacan feile* of the Highlands, but that wasn't unusual for a man of wealth and position. And on that account she had no doubt. Even from a distance she could see that the black leather doublet and trews he wore were of exceptional quality.

But the fine clothing did little to camouflage the savage beauty of his broad chest and powerfully muscled arms and legs. His impressive build coupled with the enormous *claidheamhmór* sword he wore slung across his back left no doubt in her mind that he was a warrior. And she'd wager an impressive one at that.

But it was more than his size that bothered her. She would also have preferred a rescuer who wasn't quite so dominating. It was everything about him: his wide commanding stance, the stamp of absolute authority on his face, and the bold way he looked at her. His manner unsettled her so much that it took her a moment to realize how handsome he was. Arrogantly so—as if his expertly chiseled features were a mere afterthought to the force of his overpowering masculinity.

She wasn't alone in her perusal.

Her body prickled with awareness. Dear God, the way

he was looking at her . . . at *all* of her. His gaze roamed her body from head to toe, lingering at her breasts long enough for a blush to rise in her cheeks. Suddenly she became very conscious of her nearly undressed state. The sark that had seemed a suitable covering a short while ago now felt as insubstantial as gossamer silk under his penetrating stare. It felt as though he could see right through the linen to her bare skin.

She'd always been protected by her father and brothers; no man had ever dared to look at her like this—as if she were a juicy plum ripe for the picking.

And Caitrina didn't like it one bit. She might not be dressed as one right now, but any man of sense could see that she was a lady—even if he didn't notice the fancy gown that was plain as day right under his nose.

Who was this bold warrior who held himself like a king?

She would swear she'd never seen him before. From his clothing and weaponry, he was obviously not an outlaw. He was probably a chief from distant lands come for the games—which meant he was owed the sacred obligation of Highland hospitality. But if he was a chief, where were his guardsmen?

Well, chief or not, he shouldn't be looking at her that way. "Your name, my lord?" she demanded. "You are on Lamont lands."

"Ah, then I have reached my destination."

"You are here for the gathering?"

He gave her a long look, one that made her feel he knew something she did not. "Among other things."

He hadn't told her his name, but at the moment she didn't care who he was. She would welcome the devil himself—or, God forbid, one of his Campbell minions—if he would help her down. Her arms were starting to ache from trying to hold most of her weight as to not put too much weight on the fragile branch. Her rescuer certainly was taking his time. "Well, are you just going to stand there watching me all day?" she asked impatiently.

His mouth lifted at one corner. "I might just do that. It's not very often that a man happens upon a half-naked wood nymph climbing a tree."

Caitrina's cheeks flamed. "I'm not half-naked, and if you could spare a glance upward"—*away from my chest*— "you would see that I'm not climbing, but stuck and in need of some assistance."

Her blustery response seemed only to increase his amusement. Though he wasn't precisely smiling, his steely blue eyes twinkled as radiantly as the shards of sunlight streaming through the trees.

The wretched brute was laughing at her.

Caitrina narrowed her gaze, not used to being laughed at—particularly by a man. She supposed there was something amusing about the entire situation, but he should have the courtesy not to show it. It left her feeling at a distinct disadvantage, which was silly given her circumstances. She *was* at a disadvantage. But not for long. When he got her down from here, she would give him a piece of her mind.

She bristled and in her most haughty voice—the one she used with her brothers when she wanted them to do something—said, "Just hurry up and help me down . . . now!"

She realized immediately that issuing demands might not have been the best tactic when the smile that had temporarily lightened his hard expression vanished and his lips thinned into a straight line. He gave her a long stare, then crossed his arms over his broad chest. Her breath caught, confronted with the impressive bulge of muscle. Good gracious, he was strong.

"No," he said lazily. "I don't think I shall."

Chapter 2

❖ ❖ ❖

Caitrina gasped, more shocked than angry—at first. "No? You can't say no."

He lifted a brow, begging to differ.

"But why not?" she sputtered inanely, finding it impossible to comprehend a refusal.

His gaze slid over her body. "I'm rather enjoying the view from here."

"How dare you!" She gave him a withering stare, which was easier said than done from her position. "You are a vile man."

The smile that curved his mouth sent a shiver running through her. "If I were in your position, I think I'd be praying that you were wrong about that."

She ignored the warning. "But I will fall," she protested.

He eyed the distance from her feet to the ground. "I wouldn't advise it."

"You can't be serious." Caitrina was at a loss—never having encountered a situation like this. In truth, she wasn't used to being told no—particularly by men. Was he in earnest or merely toying with her? His expression was infuriatingly unreadable.

She'd gone about this all wrong. But he'd irritated her with his amusement at her predicament and his bold appraisal of her body. Taking a deep breath, she forced a broad, playful smile to her face and batted her lashes for good measure. "For a moment I thought you were serious, but I know a gallant knight such as yourself would never refuse a lady in peril."

Gallant knight, ha! He wasn't likely to be confused with a knight in shining armor anytime soon.

He arched a brow. It was obvious he knew exactly what she was up to. He gave her another long, penetrating look, one that she felt all the way to her toes. "Perhaps we can come to some sort of arrangement."

Something in his voice caused the hair to prickle at the back of her neck. "What sort of arrangement?"

"I believe it is customary in such situations to offer a boon." Their eyes met, and she could see the unspoken challenge in his gaze. "A kiss, perhaps?"

Her eyes widened. Of all the arrogant . . . Outrage coursed through her body, but somehow she held her temper in check. "I believe it is customary in such situations for a gentleman to offer to help a woman without condition."

He turned back to his horse, gathered the reins, and started to lead it away. "Suit yourself."

She gaped at his retreating back. "Where are you going? You can't just leave me here."

He turned and gave an infuriating lift of his brow. He didn't need to say anything, the gesture said it all: He could indeed.

The branch under her feet cracked and sagged a few more inches. He might have made a movement toward her, but she couldn't be sure. Her arms had begun to ache from the strain of supporting most of her weight; she didn't know how much longer she could hold on. Her face was hot with anger and indignation. She would argue with him later. "Very well. Just get me down."

He gave a mocking bow. "As you wish, my lady."

For such a tall, muscular man, he negotiated the branches of the tree with surprising agility and speed, stopping a few branches below the weakened branch that was partially supporting her. In the span of only a few seconds, his hands circled her waist. She sucked in her breath at the unfamiliar sensation. His hands were big and strong, and she was acutely aware of his thumbs positioned under her breasts.

Their eyes met. Shock reverberated through her. Up close, he was even more handsome that she'd realized: piercing slate blue eyes, dark brown hair that in the sunlight contained hints of the red it had probably been in his youth, a wide mouth, and a hard, square jaw. It was a harshly masculine face, but also an incredibly attractive one. Given his abominable behavior, it shouldn't affect her, but she found herself flushing nonetheless. Though his expression betrayed nothing, somehow she knew that he was not as indifferent as he seemed.

His hold was firm and sure as he plucked her from the cracked branch and lowered her toward him, bringing her to rest securely against the hard length of his body.

Relieved, she sagged against him. Her arms felt like jelly, and for a moment she allowed herself to take refuge against his warm, solid strength. Solid was perhaps an understatement. His chest and arms were like granite. But rather than intimidate, the powerful evidence of his strength made her flush with a strange, heavy heat.

She'd never been this close to a man, where it seemed as if every inch of her body were melded to his. It felt . . . exciting—disturbingly so. One of her legs was caught between his powerful thighs, and her breasts were crushed against his chest. She could feel the steady pounding of his heart, all the more disconcerting because of the erratic beat of hers. He was so warm and smelled incredible—clean and soapy, with the faint hint of an exotic spice.

She had to tilt her chin to meet his gaze and realized he was every bit as tall as she'd imagined. The top of her head barely reached his shoulders. "You can let go of me," she said unevenly. "I can get down from here."

At first she thought he would refuse, but after a moment he released her.

Thankfully, the feeling had returned in her arms and she was able to follow his lead the rest of the way down. He dropped to the ground from the lowest branch and reached for her. She stared at his outstretched hand and hesitated. It seemed somehow significant. Cautiously, she slipped her hand into his and jumped. He caught her by the waist and lowered her down as if she weighed no more than that kitten she'd just rescued.

When her feet touched the ground, she wanted to sigh with relief. Instead she found herself unable to breathe, caught in the web of his magnetic gaze—and the strange sensations wrought by the realization that only a very thin piece of linen separated her nakedness from him.

What if he wasn't a gentleman? It was probably something she should have thought of earlier, but she'd never been in such a vulnerable predicament. And she'd never met anyone like him.

Her heart fluttered like the wings of a bird trapped in a cage. His arms were still around her. She should pull away—he was a stranger, a man who hadn't even told her his name—but her body seemed to have a will of its own. She stood there, transfixed by a connection that was unlike anything she'd ever experienced.

But its strength frightened her, enough to give her the sense to jerk away.

"Thank you," she said quickly, her voice unsteady. She tucked a stray lock of hair behind her ear nervously. He watched the movement with an intensity that unnerved her. Actually, everything about him unnerved her. "I can manage from here." But all six-foot-plus, heavily muscled inch of him stayed exactly where he was—too close. If she weren't feeling so strangely vulnerable and unsettled, she might have admired the impressive physique she'd just been plastered to. "You can go now."

Again she'd taken the wrong tone, she realized.

"Dismissed, my lady? Aren't you forgetting something?"

Her cheeks burned. "You can't mean to hold me to your ridiculous condition. I agreed only under duress."

"It's a debt of honor." He paused. "Is the word of a Lamont worth nothing?"

She gasped. "You know my name!"

He laughed again with that knowing look. "An educated guess. 'Tis said the Lamont has a very beautiful daughter." He frowned, giving her face great scrutiny. "But maybe I'm wrong. They didn't say anything about a crooked nose."

"What!" Her hand went immediately to her nose. "I don't have a—" She stopped, heat staining her cheeks, seeing his grin. The arrogant lout was teasing her again. Well, not exactly arrogant, she supposed. More like confident in his authority and strength. She flushed at the memory of his hard body stretched against hers.

And now he wanted her to kiss him.

Caitrina bit her lip, debating what to do. She owed him nothing, but she had agreed to his "bargain." His attack had been well aimed, striking in the one place every Highlander was vulnerable—their pride.

Her struggle seemed only to amuse him. "What is it to be, my lady?"

A long, slow smile spread across her face; she had the answer. "Very well. You shall have your kiss."

She thought a flicker of surprise crossed his face. When she held out her hand, he looked puzzled for a moment before comprehension settled in that cool, steely gaze.

She thought she'd won when he took her proffered hand, but then she saw the determined glint spark in his eyes. Determination that made a shiver of alarm slide down her spine.

Her fingers seemed to be swallowed by his big warrior's hand. It was warm and hard with calluses—and strong. He could crush her without effort, but instead his thumb caressed her palm and the hair on her arms stood straight up. He turned her hand over, revealing the jagged scratches on her palm.

A frown settled over his handsome features. "You're hurt. Why didn't you say you were hurt?"

Self-conscious, she tried to pull her hand away, but he held firm. "It's nothing," she dismissed.

Holding her gaze, he slowly lifted her hand to his mouth.

She couldn't turn away. She couldn't breathe. All she could do was wait and anticipate, her pulse as frantic as the wings of a hummingbird.

She felt the warmth of his breath on her hand right before he pressed his lips against her injured palm. She sucked in a short gasp of air. The shock of his kiss was like a lightning bolt, a brand upon her skin.

His lips moved along her palm to the sensitive skin at her wrist. Her heart pounded faster, realizing what he intended. This would be no simple kiss of the hand. It was a seduction.

And it was working. Something strange was happening to her body. Her legs felt suddenly weak as a heaviness descended over her. His mouth trailed from her wrist to the bend of her arm. The press of his soft lips and warm mouth on her bare skin sent tiny shivers sweeping up her arm. The gentle scratch of his chin on her skin made every nerve ending stand on edge and prickle with awareness.

Her lips parted and her breath hitched. He lifted his eyes to her face, and something changed. In one movement, his hand slid around her waist and he pulled her to him.

His handsome features were drawn in a hard line, but there was no mistaking the heat in his gaze. His eyes fell to her mouth. The pulse at his jaw quickened.

She knew what he was going to do.

She could have stopped him.

But she didn't want to. She'd never wanted a man to kiss her before . . . until now.

He cupped her chin, stroking her skin with a sweep of his callused fingertips. It seemed impossible that such a physically powerful man could touch so gently. He tilted her mouth to his. She sucked in her breath, anticipation crackling inside her like wildfire on dry leaves. Her nipples tightened against his chest, pressing against him, straining. Her entire body felt so sensitive, as if with one touch she could dissolve into a pool of liquid heat.

The warmth of his breath brushed her skin, the subtle hint of spice sweet temptation. Finally, when she didn't think she could wait a moment longer, his lips touched hers.

She felt a sharp tug in her chest, then a shock of surprise and a moment of blissful awakening like the petals of a flower blossoming under the hot sun. His lips were warm and velvety soft. She could taste him. The hint of spice she'd detected earlier—cinnamon—but made deeper and more mysterious by his heat.

His hand moved from her chin to behind her neck, his fingers wrapped around the sensitive skin, sliding through her hair to bring her lips more firmly against his.

His kiss was bold and possessive—like the man—and nothing like the chaste peck she'd imagined.

She sank against him, savoring the sensation of his mouth on hers, wanting to taste him deeper. Excitement pulsed inside her. He moved his mouth against hers, urging her lips apart. His hard muscles bulged under her fingertips with restraint, and she could feel him struggle with something.

With a soft groan he released her, leaving her senses reeling. Leaving her disappointed. But most of all leaving her wanting more.

That realization shattered the haze that had surrounded her since he'd first taken her hand. A flush rose in her cheeks in mortification over the liberties she'd allowed him to take. A stranger. Her father and brothers would kill him if they knew what he'd done.

"You've taken your payment," she said shakily, turning away so he couldn't see how he'd affected her. "Now if you please, leave me in peace."

He caught her arm and forced her gaze to his. "I didn't *take* anything, my sweet." She could see the anger in his gaze. "Care for me to remind you?"

Eyes wide, she shook her head. He dropped her arm and moved to his horse. She wondered if he was just going to leave her without another word. The thought was strangely disappointing.

Instead, she was surprised when he retrieved a plaid from the leather bag attached to his saddle. He strode back toward her. "Here," he said, holding it out to her. "You can wear this."

The thoughtful gesture couldn't have surprised her more than if he'd just sprouted wings and a halo instead of the horns and trident she'd attributed to him. She had only just realized herself how hopeless it would have been to try to put her gown on by herself. With his plaid wrapped around her, she could prevent the embarrassment and awkward explanations of returning to the keep in her sark. "Thank you," she whispered. He nodded his head in acknowledgment and turned to leave, but she stopped him. "Who are you?"

A wry smile hovered around the edges of his mouth. "A simple knight, my lady." Without another word, he mounted his horse and rode off toward the castle.

She watched him go, wondering if perhaps his armor wasn't shining in the sunlight after all.

Damn. That hadn't gone at all as he'd planned.

Jamie Campbell wasn't often taken by surprise, but the Lamont lass had managed to do just that. She'd been like a warm, sugary confection in his arms. Soft and sweet, dissolving against him in a delicious pool of heat. He drew a deep breath, trying to tamp the fire still simmering in his blood, but the surge of lust that had taken hold of him from that kiss was proving unusually tenacious. It had been a long time since he'd experienced that kind of hunger—hunger that would take a whole lot more than a kiss to satisfy.

It certainly had been an inauspicious introduction to the lass he was supposed to be here to court.

He'd been in the woods searching for something far different when he'd happened upon the tail end of what appeared to be the successful rescue of a kitten. The lad had just scampered off when he caught sight of her—or he should say her nicely rounded backside—just as she was about to fall and break her pretty wee neck.

He'd noticed the fine gown strewn over the log, but it wasn't until he'd seen her face that he'd realized who she was: Caitrina Lamont. It had to be her; the resemblance to her mother was uncanny. He'd seen Marion Campbell once when he was a child, and she was hard to forget. Marion's father, the Laird of Cawdor, had never forgiven his beautiful daughter for running off with his sworn enemy, the Lamont chief, all those years ago. The feud between the clans lived on. An all too common occurrence for neighboring clans where land was scarce and its possession subject to dispute.

Jamie had heard tales of Caitrina Lamont's beauty sung far and wide, and for once rumor wasn't exaggerated. Usually, he preferred a quieter, more reserved beauty, but something about the chit called to him with her striking combination of black hair, fair skin, blue eyes, and red lips. And that body . . . Hell, she had a body to make a man weep with desire—long, shapely limbs, a curvy backside, and lush, round breasts. His body stirred, remembering all too well how all those delectable curves had felt pressed up against him . . . it had been heaven—and hell, because he couldn't touch her. The naïve chit should be glad that it was he who'd discovered her.

Though he doubted she saw it that way.

He'd had every intention of helping her down from the tree, but something in her tone had provoked him—as if it never occurred to her that someone would refuse. And he'd felt an unexpected urge to tease her. The expression on her face when he'd told her no was priceless: utter bewilderment and confusion. Caitrina Lamont was obviously a lass used to getting her own way.

He'd thought to teach the haughty minx a lesson by demanding a kiss. He'd had no intention of holding her to their bargain—until she'd tried to outmaneuver him by offering her hand instead. Still, he'd intended only to make her *desire* a kiss—not to actually kiss her. But the sweet taste of her skin, and the even sweeter tremble of innocent passion when his lips pressed against her wrist and arm, had proved too tempting to resist.

Leaving the shelter of the trees, Jamie slowed his mount as the castle came into view. Ascog Castle, the stronghold of the Lamonts of Ascog, was a simple rectangular tower house of four stories and a garret surrounded by a sturdy *barmkin* wall situated on a small rise on the northern edge of the loch. With the loch to the south, woodlands to the west, and hills to the north, there were plenty of potential hiding places. It was his mission to discover whether anyone was using them.

Alasdair MacGregor and his men were on the run, and Jamie had the letters of fire and sword that gave him the authority to find them and bring them to justice for the dark deeds done on the day that had become known as the massacre of Glenfruin—the glen of sorrow.

It wasn't the first time the MacGregors had been outlawed. The clan had been in trouble with the law off and on for the last eighty years, but for King James, Glenfruin—where over one hundred forty Colquhouns were killed and every house and barn in Luss burned—had been the last straw. The Privy Council proscribed the clan— forbidden on pain of death even to call themselves MacGregor—and gave orders to hunt down and extirpate them. The commission of doing so had been given to Jamie's cousin the Earl of Argyll.

Jamie had followed the trail of rumor, stolen livestock, and burned-out farms throughout Argyll and the borders for the past month. Though all signs pointed to MacGregor heading to his former lands near the Lomond Hills, Jamie thought it was too obvious. Alasdair MacGregor was smarter than that.

Despite their outlaw status, the MacGregors still had plenty of friends in the Highlands who might be willing to give them shelter—friends like the Lamonts. An old tale of Highland hospitality—the most revered of Highland customs—and a hunch had led Jamie to Ascog instead.

When he reached the gate, one of the Lamont's guardsmen stopped him. "Your name, sir."

Jamie met his friendly gaze. "James Campbell, captain of Castleswene."

All signs of welcome fled, replaced by barely concealed hatred and a healthy dose of fear. It was a reaction that Jamie had grown accustomed to over the past few years. It was also why he'd hesitated to identify himself to the lass. Once again, it appeared that his reputation—exaggerated, no doubt—had preceded him.

The guardsman tightened his hand on the grip of his sword. "I'll advise the chief that he has a . . . guest." He said the word as if his mouth was full of dung.

Jamie dismounted and tossed the reins to the surprised guardsman. "I'll tell him myself," he said, motioning toward the man who'd just appeared from the armory.

The guardsman tried to block him. "But you can't—"

"Yes," Jamie cut him off in a low voice, one that augured no argument. "I can." He stepped around the younger man. "Lamont." His voice rang out with authority across the *barmkin.*

The chief turned toward him. Recognition flared in his gaze, and he quickly said something to the two younger men at his side. The Lamont was a seasoned warrior who hid his reactions well, but the younger of the two men at his side was not. Jamie was watching them closely, so he noticed a flash of alarm that was quickly covered up. Was it simply because a Campbell had entered their keep, or were they hiding something? He would find out soon enough.

The Lamont strode toward him. For a man who must be past fifty years, he wore his age well and moved with the strength and agility of a formidable warrior.

"Campbell," he said. "I would have been here to greet you myself had I known you were coming."

Jamie smiled. They both knew the lapse had been intentional. Alerting the Lamonts of his arrival would hardly have served his purpose. If Lamont was hiding the MacGregor and his men, as Jamie believed, he wouldn't give him a chance to spirit them away. With Jamie and his men watching, they would be forced to stay put.

The Lamont looked behind him, and his brows drew together. "You've come alone?"

In a time when a man's power was equated to the number of *luchd-taighe* guardsmen who surrounded him, it was unusual to travel without a retinue—not to mention dangerous. But Jamie didn't need an army of men to protect him. He preferred to work alone or, in this case, with only a few handpicked men. "My men will arrive later." After they'd finished scouting and establishing a perimeter. Jamie gestured toward the two men who stood protectively beside their chief. "Your sons, I presume?"

The Lamont nodded. "My *tanaiste,* Malcolm, and my second son, Niall." The elder resembled his father, with fair hair and green eyes, but the second—Niall—made

Jamie even more confident that the lass in the tree had been Caitrina Lamont. In coloring they might have been twins, though Niall was a few years older. "Come," the Lamont added. "Join us in the hall for a drink. The feasting will not begin for a few hours yet."

Jamie agreed and followed the men up the wooden forestairs into the keep. As with most tower houses, the entry was on the first floor, above the vaulted ground level. In an attack, the wooden stairs could be easily removed or, if necessary, burned.

It was considerably cooler and darker inside. The thick stone walls were an effective barrier to both man and sun. They passed through the small entry into the great hall. The castle was well tended and comfortably furnished: Colorful woven rugs adorned the floors, paintings and tapestries lined the walls, and several silver candelabra were spread around the room. The Lamont was not a wealthy man, but neither was he a poor one. Still, everything had a well-worn appearance—the years of feuding with the Campbells had taken their toll.

They sat at the high table, and the Lamont instructed a serving woman to bring them some refreshment, which arrived promptly in carved silver goblets engraved with the crest and motto of Lamont—*Ne Parcas Nec Spernas*, Neither Spare Nor Dispose. When she'd gone, the Lamont turned to him and without preamble said, "Why are you here? What does the Earl of Argyll want with me?"

Jamie took a long drink of ale, watching the other man over the rim of his goblet. Directness was a trait he admired. He put the drink on the table and deliberately took his time in answering. But all three men sat perfectly still, betraying nothing.

"You are hosting the games, are you not?"

"You can't mean to enter the competition?" Niall blurted out, unable to hide his astonishment.

Jamie gave him a hard look, guessing the reason for his

reaction. The Campbells were an old and proud Highland clan, yet because of their connection with the king, too many saw them as akin to Lowlanders. "I *am* a Highlander," he said, a warning edged in his voice.

Niall looked as though he wanted to argue the point, but he wisely held his tongue.

The chief moved to defuse the brewing tension. "I wouldn't think Argyll would find the gathering worthy of the attentions of his most trusted hench"—he cleared his throat—"captain."

Jamie raised a brow, well aware of what he'd been about to say. Henchman was one of the nicer names he was called. "My cousin takes a keen interest in all that happens in Argyll and Bute," he said pointedly. He drew his finger over the heavy engraving of his goblet. "But there's also the matter of your daughter."

All three men tensed, looking as though they wanted to reach for their swords. The old chief recovered first. His eyes were hard and flat. "Why would my daughter concern you?"

"I've come to see for myself whether the rumors are true."

The old man studied him carefully. Jamie watched him struggle with the implications. Although he might not like it, the Lamont was shrewd enough to realize that an alliance with the Campbells—particularly the trusted cousin of the most powerful Campbell of all—could not be summarily dismissed.

"And she is of interest to you?" the chief asked with surprising calm, though Jamie could see from the whiteness of his knuckles gripping the goblet that he was anything but.

"Perhaps." He shrugged noncommittally, pleased that his ruse had worked. The Lamonts were suspicious about the purpose of his visit, but now they were also worried, and some of their focus would be directed on the lass.

Chapter 3

❖ ❖ ❖

By midday, Caitrina was restored to her former state of dress, if not her prior good spirits. She'd put the episode in the forest out of her mind as best she could, but the memory of that kiss seemed permanently imprinted on her consciousness, leaving her unsettled.

She hurried down the stairs toward the great hall, hearing the sounds of revelry, knowing she was late. A fact that was sure to annoy her father. He would undoubtedly interpret her tardiness as another attempt to avoid her "duty."

It just wasn't fair. She was being paraded before a bunch of hungry vultures, and her two brothers, her two *older* brothers, were left alone to do as well they pleased. Malcolm was almost five years her senior and he'd yet to take a wife. While her brothers dallied with every unsuitable lass on Bute, for the last year she'd been forced to fend off the steady stream of suitors who had presented themselves at the castle gate.

She knew her father thought he was doing what was best for her by forcing the issue of her marriage. He worried that she would grow weary and eventually resent caring for him and her brothers and that they'd kept her too sheltered. She'd never been beyond Bute, except to visit her uncle, the Lamont of Toward. But her father was wrong. She had no desire to go to court—or anywhere else, for that matter. Everything she wanted was right here.

She loved her family and had no intention of leaving Ascog anytime soon. And certainly not for one of the overbearing oafs who leered at her across the dining table night after night as if she were some prize to be won, or for one of the stammering youths who proclaimed their undying love not five minutes after meeting her. No, Caitrina was quite content where she was. She smiled. Even if she had to reject every man in the Highlands to ensure that it stayed that way.

This time, however, she wasn't trying to avoid her suitors by being late; it had taken longer than she thought to bathe and have someone help her with her gown for the second time in one day. Actually, she was rather looking forward to the feast. Even if she didn't like her father's ulterior motive—namely to find her a husband—when he'd offered to hold the gathering at Ascog, it was an honor, not to mention exciting. And she could admit to a certain curiosity in discovering the identity of her bold warrior.

She paused in the stairwell just outside the great hall to catch her breath, sneaking a peek inside. The large, cavernous room was filled to capacity with the colorfully clad clansmen, boisterously celebrating the opening of the games with plenty of the Lamont's best ale. Although the sun shone brightly through the four windows, the gentle heat of a late spring day did not have the strength to warm the lingering chill of an unusually persistent winter, and the smoky smell of peat from the enormous fireplace situated behind the dais filled her nose.

Caitrina's gaze immediately sought out her father, trying to gauge his temper. Seated at the high table, he looked resplendent in his fine silk doublet. She couldn't see his plate from here, but she hoped he'd followed the healer's advice about staying away from the rich French foods that her mother had introduced him to long ago. He'd been experiencing pains in his chest lately, and Caitrina was worried.

She was just about to step into the room when she felt a familiar presence behind her.

"I think you forgot your crown."

She turned to find herself looking into the laughing blue eyes of her brother Niall. Lifting her chin, she feigned obtuseness, quite used to her brothers' teasing. "I don't know what you mean."

He did a quick once-over of her gown and made a soft whistling sound of amazement. "My, my, would you look at that. One might think you were on your way to Whitehall to tarry with the damned English." He shook his head. "But have care; Queen Anne might not wish for a rival."

"Oh, shut up, Niall," she said with a sisterly shove.

He laughed and caught her up in his strong embrace, lifting her feet off the ground and spinning her around. "Ah, Caitrina, lass, you're a bonny sight."

She giggled. "Put me down, you overbearing oaf!"

"Overbearing oaf?" he said, spinning her again.

She was laughing and out of breath by the time her feet finally touched the ground. Not to mention dizzy. He had to hold her upright for a few moments until she steadied herself. Unable to help herself, she asked, "Niall?"

"Yes, puss."

"Is there anything wrong with my nose?"

His brows wrinkled as he studied her face. "Why do you ask?"

She hid the flush that crept up her cheeks. "I thought it looked a little crooked."

He grinned. "Isn't it supposed to be?"

Seeing the laughter in his gaze, she hit him again. "Wretch. I don't know why I bother asking you anything serious."

He took her nose between his fingers and gave it a little wiggle. "There is nothing wrong with your nose. Now," he said, turning his gaze back into the hall, "whose unfortunate heart will be served up on a platter tonight?" He pointed to a handsome young man seated near the door. "Young MacDonald over there, or perhaps a Graham"—

his finger moved around the room—"or maybe it shall be a Murray."

She pushed him away, unable to prevent herself from smiling. "You know I have no interest in any of them."

Niall arched his brow, eyes twinkling. "Well, dressed like that, they'll be interested in you."

Caitrina didn't give one whit about that, but unconsciously her gaze shifted back into the room, searching for her unknown rescuer. She glanced again at the high table, seeing her father seated at the dais with Malcolm on his left. On his right was her empty seat, and next to that . . . Her breath caught. It was him, seated in a place of honor at the high table. So she'd been right in guessing that he was a man of wealth and position.

"Niall"—she fought to control the breathlessness that had suddenly crept into her voice—"who's that man next to Father?"

Niall's face darkened, all signs of humor fled. "James Campbell," he spat.

A strangled sound caught in her throat, and the blood drained from her face. *A Campbell.* Her fingers instinctively went to her lips in horror. *Dear God, she'd kissed a Campbell.*

She didn't know what was worse—realizing that she'd kissed the devil's spawn . . .

Or that she'd liked it.

Jamie's presence had not gone unnoticed among the revelers. But despite the general chill of his reception, he was enjoying himself. The Lamont's pipers filled the hall with song, the food was plentiful and well prepared, and the ale flowed fast and free. Only one thing was missing: There was still no sign of the Lamont's daughter.

A rueful smile curved his mouth. He wouldn't be surprised if the wily chief had secreted her away to keep her safe from his clutches. Hell, Jamie didn't blame him. Cai-trina Lamont was a jewel any man would covet.

Despite the absence of the lady of the keep, he had to ad-mire Lamont for his skills as host. The chief had seated his unexpected guest next to the only person in the room who likely did not object to sitting beside him: Margaret MacLeod. Margaret—Meg—was one of Jamie's sister Eliz-abeth's closest friends.

There was a time not that long ago when Jamie had thought to make Meg his wife. But she'd chosen to marry Alex MacLeod—brother to Chief Rory MacLeod—instead. Though Jamie had been angry at the time, with al-most three years' perspective he knew she was right. He'd loved Meg to the best of his capabilities, and he cared for her enough to know that she deserved more.

"I'm so happy you are here, Jamie," Meg repeated, a wide smile on her face. "We see so little of you."

Jamie lifted his head in the direction of her husband, seated farther down the table and engaged in a conversa-tion with the Maclean of Coll, husband to Alex's half-sister Flora—who also happened to be Jamie's cousin. Flora was too heavy with child to travel, so her husband of less than a year had come alone.

"I don't think your husband shares the sentiment," he pointed out.

Alex and Rory MacLeod had both offered Jamie a cor-dial but reserved greeting. Not that it surprised him. In the three years since Jamie had fought alongside Alex at the battle of Stornoway Castle, Jamie's interests and those of his former childhood friend had diverged to the point of discord. Though bound to the Earl of Argyll through manrent—contracts that bound clans together like kin by providing protection in return for feudal duties—Alex and Rory still clung to the past, resenting the king's increasing authority in the Highlands. They were sympathetic toward the MacGregors and didn't like Jamie's part in subduing them. But then again, the MacLeods, like the Lamonts, had not been on the receiving end of the MacGregors' reiving and pillaging.

Jamie missed the easy camaraderie he'd shared with the MacLeods in his youth, but he realized such friendships were in his past. Though they still respected one another, as Jamie's responsibility and power increased, so too did the complexity of friendships. He worked alone; it was simpler that way.

Meg wrinkled her nose. "Don't pay Alex any mind. He hasn't forgotten what you did for him," she said warmly, putting her hand over his and giving it a gentle squeeze. "And neither have I."

Jamie acknowledged the unspoken gratitude with a nod. After the MacLeods' victory at Stornoway against the king's men, Jamie had used his influence with Argyll to prevent Alex from being put to the horn or charged with treason.

"Are you happy, Meg?"

Her gaze immediately slid down the table to her husband, and the soft expression on her face said it all. He'd always thought Meg pretty, but when she looked at her husband she transcended mere physical beauty. Alex MacLeod was a fortunate man.

"Yes," she said. "I've never been happier."

"Then I'm happy for you," he said, and meant it.

"And what of you, Jamie? Are you happy?"

Her questions took him aback. Happiness wasn't something he thought of. As a younger son twice over, he'd been driven by other considerations. Happiness—a woman's sentiment—wasn't one of them. Justice, the rule of law, authority, land, the ability to provide for his men—those were what mattered to him. "I'm content."

Meg studied him keenly. "You've certainly made quite a name for yourself."

He laughed. That was Meg, putting it baldly, to say the least. "I take it you do not approve."

She shrugged. "I don't believe half of what they say."

He smiled wryly. "You do not fear I will crawl through your windows at night and steal away your babe?" he mocked, referring to the warnings given by mothers to their children to behave, "else the Campbell Henchman will make off with you."

Meg grinned and shook her head. "No, but the earl relies upon you too much. Elizabeth writes that she hardly sees you anymore."

"Lizzie exaggerates." He gave Meg a long look. Though many in this room chose to stick their head in a bog and ignore what was happening around them, Meg understood the change facing the Highlanders. The age of the unfettered authority of the chiefs was gone—and frankly, since the dissolution of the Lordship of the Isles, they'd proved unequal to the task. Like King James, Jamie was determined to see the Highlands tamed of its lawlessness and unrest. At one time, he thought she'd understood. But perhaps Meg's marriage had changed her more than he realized. The increasing power and authority of Argyll, and Jamie in turn, had created widespread resentment and distrust—impacting many of his friendships. He'd hoped it wouldn't extend to Meg.

"She's only worried about you," Meg said, seeming to sense the turn of his thoughts. "As I am."

"It's unwarranted," he said flatly. Then more kindly, "I'll see Lizzie at Dunoon soon enough. She'll see there is nothing to worry about."

Another tray of food arrived, and he welcomed the lapse in conversation that ensued.

He knew the moment the Lamont lass entered the hall. A sudden hush descended over the crowd, and every male eye in the room fastened on her as she slowly made her way to her father's table as regal as any queen—*a princess,* he corrected. She looked far too fresh and innocent to be a queen.

She took his breath away. Her glossy black hair was swept up high on her head, and long curly strands tumbled down her long neck. Her features were classical in their beauty, but made all the more striking by the vivid contrast of her snow white skin, bright blue eyes, and ruby red lips. *Hell,* he thought with a shake. He sounded like a damn bard.

As she drew closer, Jamie felt his entire body turn rigid. *What in Hades was she wearing?* The flash of anger that gripped him was as intense as it was irrational. He had no claim on the chit, but every instinct flared with the sharp blade of possessiveness. His hand squeezed around his goblet as he fought to control the primitive urge to swing her over his shoulder and carry her upstairs so she could change into something decent. Though the wide skirts of her gown did not reveal her curvaceous figure with the nearly transparent detail of her earlier attire, the same could not be said of the bodice. What little fabric there was seemed stretched to the point of bursting and barely covered the pink of her nipples. The lush, youthful roundness of her breasts were displayed for all to see.

His hand squeezed until he thought the silver would bend. What was she trying to do, incite a riot?

He waited for the swell of anger to abate, but the bold and admiring stares of some of the men in the hall didn't help.

She was the center of attention, yet she seemed completely oblivious. If Jamie expected the Lamont to send her back to her room, he was to be disappointed. Pride showed in the old man's face, and he seemed blissfully unaware of the tantalizing morsel she presented.

She greeted her father with a kiss on the cheek and whispered something in his ear—from her contrite expression,

Jamie assumed it was an apology for her tardiness. Her father gave her a few stern words but softened at the first sign of unhappiness, as if he couldn't bear to see her sad.

"She's very beautiful, isn't she?"

Jamie frowned at Meg's tone, which contained a healthy tinge of amusement. "Yes. But young."

"Not *too* young."

He was about to set her straight—that he had no interest in the lass—until he remembered his ruse. "Perhaps."

The concession surprised Meg, and she lifted her brow in a silent question.

He chose not to answer and turned his attention back to Caitrina as she greeted a few of the other men at the table. Though it was not a raised dais, the Lamonts still had a high table reserved for the highest-ranking guests—the chiefs or chieftains of the clan.

Even though all feuds would be put aside for the duration of the gathering, much could be told about the current hostilities by the seating arrangement. On one side of the Lamont were MacDonald and Mackenzie, and on the other were MacLeod, Mackinnon, and Maclean of Coll. Jamie also recognized a smattering of Murrays, McNeils, MacAllisters, and Grahams around the hall. Noticeably absent, however, were the proscribed MacGregors.

Jamie knew that even if his hunch was correct, the bold Alasdair MacGregor wouldn't be foolish enough to risk participating in the games—not after his narrow escape two years ago.

Caitrina had yet to acknowledge him, clearly avoiding his gaze, but when she finished greeting the other guests and moved around to take her seat beside him, she could no longer avoid him. By the time her father made the introductions, he'd managed to bring his anger under control.

"James Campbell, my daughter, Caitrina."

He could tell by her reaction—or lack thereof—that his identity had not come as a surprise. Had she made inquiries? The thought pleased him more than it should. He took her hand and bowed. Her fingers felt so dainty and soft in his big callused hands. "Mistress Lamont."

Her smile could have frozen a loch in midsummer. "My laird."

Her father shot her a glare, obviously a reminder of her duty to be a good hostess.

"I apologize for the delay," she said, forcing out the words as if there were rusty nails in her mouth.

His gaze slid over her appreciatively. "Beauty such as yours is worth any wait." But his compliment was ignored, and she sat down and gave him a superior view of the back of her head as she spoke to her father.

Her reaction intrigued him. Most beautiful women he'd observed seemed to feed on compliments as their due, but Caitrina made him feel as if he'd just failed some unwritten test.

She did not engage him directly in conversation, responding to her father, her brother Malcolm, or Meg when necessary. Most of the time, however, she spent fending off the steady stream of admirers who appeared before her throughout the meal under one pretense or another.

If Jamie hoped to hear anything of interest to his mission, he was to be disappointed. Whenever the talk at the table turned to politics, feuds, or outlaws, her nose would scrunch up and she would get an extremely bored look on her face. At one point, an interesting—albeit heated—conversation arose next to her among her father, her brother Malcolm, and a Mackenzie chieftain about the spate of raids in Argyll and what was being done about it. Jamie listened with increasing interest as tempers rose.

"Father," Caitrina said, reaching over and putting a staying hand on his arm, "you know how this talk of feuding makes my head spin."

At first, her interruption seemed to startle the Lamont. When the heat of the argument had faded, and no doubt realizing she might have unintentionally saved him from saying something he didn't wish Jamie to hear, the Lamont gave her an indulgent smile and a small pat on her hand. "Ah, Caiti! You are right. 'Tis the time for celebration, not for talk of war."

She turned a charming smile on the young Mackenzie laird, who appeared dazzled by the attention. "I sometimes think war is nothing but an excuse for men to show off their prowess with a blade and put all those impressive muscles to use. What do you think, my laird?"

Preening like a peacock with the compliment, the Mackenzie mumbled something unintelligible while Jamie felt an inexplicable urge to smash something.

Her attention shifted subtly to him. "Though there are those who are too ready to wage war on their neighbors under any pretense, and will never be satisfied until they've seized every inch of land they can."

A sudden hush descended over the table, and she feigned obtuseness. "Oh, dear!" she exclaimed, covering her mouth with her hand. "Generally speaking, of course."

Jamie lifted his goblet to her in mock salute. "Of course."

Conversation resumed in a nervous burst, and she resumed ignoring him. He, in turn, observed the interactions with increasing admiration. Her skill at avoiding the promise of a dance or future conversation was both deft and subtle. There was nothing that could be construed as flirtatious or coy in her manner, but the result was all the more intriguing. Cosseted and indulged by the men in her keep, she was brash, slightly spoiled, completely without artifice—and utterly charming.

She didn't understand that her very disinterest made her all the more irresistible. She was like a hothouse flower in a garden of wild bramble.

She might be doing her best to avoid talking to him, but he could tell she was just as aware of him as he was of her:

the way she'd pull her arm away quickly when they happened to touch; the way her hand shook and she spilled a drop of claret when his thigh pressed against hers; the way the heat rose in her cheeks when she knew he was watching her.

It seemed he couldn't help watching her.

But every time she leaned forward, he fought the urge to smash something—usually another man's face.

If she were his, he'd rip that dress in two. After he ravaged her senseless for making him half-crazed.

But something puzzled him. He noticed her reach over on her father's platter—as she'd done numerous times throughout the meal—and exchange portions of his beef slathered in dark gravy with turnips or parsnips when he wasn't looking. When her father turned back to his plate, he would frown and look at Caitrina with a questioning glance, but she just smiled innocently and asked him how he was enjoying the feast.

When the Lamont resumed his conversation on his left, Jamie could no longer contain his curiosity. "Does your father have a particular fondness for root vegetables?"

She bit her lip and her cheeks turned an adorable shade of pink. "Unfortunately, no," she said wryly. "I'd hoped no one would notice."

"I assume there is a reason why you have waved off all the sauces as well?"

Her blush deepened and she nodded. She seemed disinclined to explain further, but Jamie had an idea what she was about. Apparently, her father wasn't supposed to be eating rich foods, and Caitrina had taken it upon herself to ensure that he didn't. The Lamont was well aware of what she was doing but was content to let her have her way. Something he realized probably happened all too often.

After a moment, she looked at him again. "Why did you not tell me who you were?"

"Would it have made a difference?"

Anger sparked in her deep blue eyes. "Of course!"

His eyes dropped to her mouth, knowing that she was referring to their kiss. Her lips clamped tightly together, as if she could stave off the memory he roused. But it was there, hanging in the air between them—heavy and hot and full of promise.

God, he could almost taste her on his lips. Heat pooled in his groin as he thickened with the thought. The uncharacteristic loss of control annoyed him, and he shifted his gaze. "I don't think so," he said. "You needed help, and as there was no one else around to come to your rescue, knowing my name wouldn't have changed anything."

"You have an unusual concept of rescue," she said dryly.

He chuckled, and the sound drew the attention—and concerned frowns—of her father and brother. Hell, it had surprised him.

"The dancing will begin soon," the Lamont said. "Although not the court dances that you are used to at Inveraray or Dunoon."

Jamie didn't take the bait. He knew the Highland dances as well as anyone in this room. He realized that there was more behind this subtle dig when Caitrina frowned. "But those are the strongholds of Argyll."

Apparently, she knew he was a Campbell—but not which one. He held her gaze. "The earl is my cousin."

"James Campbell . . . ," she murmured. He could see the moment she put it together. Her eyes widened and she blurted: "You're Argyll's Henchman."

"Caitrina!" her father reprimanded sternly.

Jamie lifted his hand, holding him off. "There's no need. The moniker is common enough." He gave the horror-struck lass a hard look. "I am the captain of the Earl of Argyll's guardsmen. If by 'henchman' you mean that I enforce the law and see to it that justice is done, then yes." He used physical force only when necessary. His usual method of enforcing was persuasion, and when that didn't work . . .

well, Highlanders were a stubborn lot, and sometimes the traditional method of solving disputes was the only way.

Caitrina blanched. "I see."

But of course she didn't. Her reaction bothered him more than he wanted to acknowledge. He was used to hatred and fear—his reputation had its uses—but never before had he wanted to explain and make someone understand. To make her see that envy and ignorance were behind the exaggerated rumors.

Why the opinion of this wisp of a girl mattered, he didn't know. But it did.

Chapter 4

❖❖❖

In a fitting tribute to the opening of the games, the next day dawned bright and clear, but Caitrina was still mired in the fog of the revelations of the night before.

Jamie Campbell. The Highland Enforcer. The Scourge of the Highlands. The Campbell Henchman. By whatever name, he was the most feared man in the Highlands—more feared, perhaps, than even his cousin. Argyll did not dirty his hands with warfare, but plenty of blood had been shed by the hands of his henchman.

And she'd kissed him.

Her father and brothers rarely discussed feuds or Highland politics with her—subjects that usually didn't interest her—but for once she wished they didn't stop talking when she entered the room. Occasionally she would hear things from the servants, and she'd heard of Argyll's fearsome cousin. 'Twas said Jamie Campbell had never been defeated in battle. That he was ruthless in his pursuit of any who opposed him. That any man who got in his way was a dead one. That he had more power than the king in the Highlands because he had the ear of "King Campbell"—the Earl of Argyll.

Yet he was nothing like the monster she'd expected; he seemed so . . . civilized. Not a ruthless, bloodthirsty ogre, but a man who looked as though he would be just as commanding at court as he was on a battlefield. His calm authority seemed at odds with his merciless reputation. Though she did not doubt that he was a formidable warrior—his physical stature alone was proof enough of that—there was far more to him than brawn.

Yet admittedly, as she'd sensed from the first, there was something hard—almost ruthless—about him. She'd never met a man who was so controlled, who never gave a hint of what he was thinking.

More than once throughout the evening, she'd felt his unwavering gaze on her—cool, steady, and utterly unreadable. She, on the other hand, was a mass of nerves. Ignoring him had proved impossible; she was aware of every move he made. They might as well have been tied together, so deeply did she feel it.

He flustered her. She would like to dismiss it as fear, but the truth was far more unsettling: She was attracted to the vile brute. He was handsome enough to make her breath catch. Of all the men in the Highlands to be attracted to, it had to be a Campbell. There was irony there, but she was too disturbed to see it. She didn't know what to do about it, except try to avoid him as much as she could.

Caitrina spent the morning busy attending to her duties as hostess, but after the midday meal she welcomed the chance to escape to the stables for a while before the games resumed for the afternoon. It was cool, and the pungent, earthy smells were oddly calming. She dragged a bench from one of the stalls to sit on and picked up the kitten that had caused so many problems yesterday.

Caitrina sighed contentedly and stroked its soft fur while the cat purred and nuzzled against her hand, savoring the moment of peace. Usually she would sit by the loch, but with so many people about for the games, the stables were about the only place she could find some solitude.

Or so she'd thought.

"Here you are."

She stifled a groan, turning to find Torquil MacNeil, one of her more persistent suitors, beside her. If she were inclined to pick a man by the appeal of his countenance, the young laird would be the perfect choice. He was tall and lean, with dark blond hair and brilliant green eyes. Not much older than she, he'd already made a name for himself as a skilled warrior. She could do worse, *if* she were looking for a husband.

Remembering her duty as hostess, she forced a smile to her face. "Did you want something, my laird?"

His eyes slid over her. There was nothing overtly threatening in the movement, but it made her uncomfortable nonetheless. It wasn't admiration she detected in his gaze, but possession.

"I wished to speak with you. It was so crowded and noisy last night at the feast, I did not have the opportunity."

Caitrina put down the kitten, stood up, and shook out her skirts. She didn't like the way of this conversation. She took pains to make sure private opportunities like this did not arise—it was easier that way. Half the men she rejected didn't even realize it. But she sensed that MacNeil would not be so easily put off. There was a streak of youthful arrogance in him that promised stubbornness.

"I intend to speak to your father," he said as if he were dangling a meaty bone to a dog.

Caitrina feigned obtuseness—one of her favorite ploys. "Of course. I shall take you to him."

He grabbed her arm and swung her back toward him. "Don't you want to know what about?"

One by one, she carefully pried his fingers from her arm and then smiled. "Oh, I haven't the faintest interest in the talk of men."

"You'll be interested in this," he proclaimed, looking her over once more. "You're beautiful, but not too small around the hips—which is good. We will make fine braw sons." Drawing up his chest, he expounded with the confidence of a king, "I've decided to make you my wife."

Caitrina gritted her teeth and bit back a sarcastic retort.

There was nothing as romantic as being compared to a beautiful brood mare. "You are too kind," she said sweetly. "It is an honor indeed to be considered for such an illustrious position. But you speak precipitously. We barely know each other."

He took a step closer. "There is time enough for that when we are married."

Caitrina swallowed. As she'd suspected, this would not be easy. She needed to think of something . . . fast. "I hardly know what kind of man you are," she said, and then hesitated, an idea forming. "And you are still *so* young."

He bristled. "I'm man enough for you, my sweet." He pulled her closer. "Care for me to prove it?"

There it was. Her way out. "What a brilliant suggestion! Prove to me that you can protect me as a husband ought by winning the archery challenge at the end of the week and we will discuss this marriage further."

He had no chance. Rory MacLeod was the best archer in the Highlands. The MacLeod chief had won for ten years straight—challenged only once two years ago by Alasdair MacGregor on one of the rare occasions when the outlaw made an appearance at the games.

MacNeil looked momentarily confused, but she could see the moment he realized what he'd done. How his arrogance had been twisted against him. His expression shifted from cocksure to enraged. She'd tricked him, and he knew it.

Eyes blazing, he bowed stiffly. "Until the end of the contest, then"—he gave her a calculated look that was just short of menacing—"when I shall come to claim my prize."

She watched him storm away, feeling a prickle of discomfort. Discomfort that only worsened a few moments later.

"Morning, Princess."

Caitrina startled, recognizing that deep, husky tone immediately. The man could melt a frozen loch with the heat of that sultry voice. So much for avoiding him. She looked over to see Jamie Campbell standing in the doorway, holding the reins of his horse.

Princess indeed. "It's well past morning, and don't call me Princess." He grinned, and Caitrina berated herself for letting him bother her. Her eyes narrowed suspiciously. "Don't you have something better to do than spy on me? Frighten a few helpless old women or children, perhaps—"

He led his destrier inside a stall, gave instructions to one of the stable lads, and strode toward her. Her insides seemed to toss about like a rudderless *birlinn* in a storm as he neared. He might be a devil, but he had the face of an archangel. Handsome enough to make her wish he weren't a Campbell. The intense slate blue eyes, the aquiline nose, the hard sculpted cheekbones and wide mouth above a strong square jaw. She couldn't seem to look away, drawn to his dark masculinity in a way that she could not explain. Except that it resonated, she felt it in every inch, every pore, of her body. His size, his expression, his fearsome reputation, should urge danger. But it wasn't fear that set off bells of alarm—it was the intensity of her reaction to him. Unconsciously she took a step back.

"Spying wasn't necessary," he said, pointing to the open shutters opposite the door where hay for the horses was tossed in. He gave her a long, thoughtful look. "Your ability to rid yourself of a suitor is to be commended, but your delivery lacks finesse. Have care for the pride of a young man, my sweet. From the look on that one's face, his was badly bruised and he'll not soon forget it."

"I don't recall asking for your advice," she said with an angry toss of her chin. It was none of his blasted business.

The infuriating beast only laughed. "You shall have it all

the same. It's about time someone around here spoke the truth."

The hair at the back of her neck rose in full affront. "I have no idea what you are talking about."

"Not all men will be led around by their—" He stopped. "Not all men will bow to your bidding."

"Like you, for one?" she said, not bothering to hide her sarcasm.

He moved a little closer. Close enough for her to smell the sun and sweat from his ride. The primitive scent was oddly arousing, swarming her senses with wicked yearnings. He stood so close, she could see the dark stubble that shadowed the hard lines of his jaw. She remembered how it had felt rubbing against the tender skin of her cheek when he'd kissed her, and something fluttered low in her belly.

"Aye, like me," he said huskily, almost as if he knew what she was thinking.

"I'll keep that in mind." She turned away, not wanting him to see how deeply he rattled her. When he didn't leave as she hoped, she asked, "Why were you out riding? I thought you were taking part in the games."

"I hadn't decided, but now that I've heard the prize to be won, I think I shall enter the archery contest."

It took her a moment to realize what he meant. Her eyes flew to his face, thinking he was jesting, but his expression was implacable. "You can't be serious." He couldn't intend to court her.

His eyes met hers, and the intensity shook her to her toes. "And what if I am?"

She ignored the sudden race of her heart. Despite her confounding attraction to him, the idea of marrying a Campbell, let alone *this* Campbell, was so far-fetched that she didn't know how to respond. The misery of her mother cast out from her clan was never far from her mind. She'd avoid that fate at all costs. "You're wasting your time." She tried to breeze by him, but he blocked her path. Her shoulder collided with the steely shield of his chest, and she sucked in her breath at the shock of physical awareness. The strange sensations he'd wrought in her yesterday came flooding back: the warmth, the fluttering in her stomach, the race of her heart, the prickle of awareness that chilled her skin.

"Am I?" he said in a low voice, and the warmth of his breath tickled her ear, making her shudder. "You didn't seem to think so yesterday."

Caitrina flushed. *How dare he bring up that kiss!* The kiss she couldn't forget when he was standing so close to her, his powerful body radiating heat that seemed to entrap her. "You had no right to kiss me." She dared not look up. He was standing too close. She felt this strange pull . . . as though someone were sliding the floor mat out from beneath her feet. As though she wanted him to kiss her again. She could turn her head and feel his mouth on her cheek, sliding along her jaw, on her lips . . .

Her heart thumped wildly, and she felt as if she were drowning in something more powerful than she could control.

But she couldn't forget who he was.

She forced her eyes to his and said with all sincerity, "I'd sooner marry a toad than a Campbell."

Jamie might just make her eat those words. He could lean down, cover her lips with his, and kiss her until he proved her wrong. And God, he was tempted.

He'd had no intention of actually finding a wife when he came here, but taming this brazen girl with her strange mix of haughtiness and innocence might damn well be worth it. It was rare that he met a woman he didn't have to tiptoe around for fear of overwhelming or intimidating her. He smiled. Nay, Caitrina Lamont was decidedly *not* intimidated by him.

He was returning from meeting with his men, who'd

scoured the caves in the hills beyond but had found nothing, when he'd overheard the conversation between Caitrina and Torquil MacNeil. She was clever, he'd give her that. As she'd proved many times over last night, she had an uncanny way of ridding herself of suitors—but there was a dangerous naïveté to her boldness. And one day it was going to land her in a heap of trouble.

The lass seemed to have every available man within a hundred miles under her spell. Even now, with her hair tumbling freely around her shoulders, straw on her ridiculously fine skirts for sitting in a barn, and looking adorably mussed, her allure was undeniable. For all her pristine beauty, there was an unmistakable air of sexual promise that surrounded her, hinting at far more earthy delights. A rose waiting to be plucked.

He wanted her with an intensity that defied reason. He wanted her in a primal way that he'd never felt before with any woman. And when Jamie wanted something, he got it.

Yet she seemed entirely unaware of what a temptation she presented or how close he was to tossing her down in the hay and kissing her senseless. His blood heated at the thought of her under him, his hands stroking her soft skin, his mouth . . .

Disgusted, he fought back the haze of lust. He was a man of prodigious control when it came to keeping his desire in check, but never had he met a lass who so aroused such primitive impulses in him. Or, for that matter, one who could provoke him so easily by casting her careless aspersions on his clan.

He stood back and crossed his arms. "So it's my name that bothers you?"

"Isn't it enough? Our clans are enemies, and have been for decades."

"What better way to end a feud? Besides, your mother was a Campbell."

She flushed with anger. "And she was disowned by her

Campbell father, the Laird of Cawdor. I have no familial love for the Campbells, and your cousin is the worst of the bad lot."

"For someone so obviously disinterested in politics, you certainly seem to have strong opinions."

"Everyone knows that Argyll is a despot who steals land and then, when the clansmen are broken with nowhere left to go, hunts them like dogs."

"I assume you are referring to the MacGregors?" Jamie said idly, feeling anything but. What did she know of the MacGregors? Of the massacre of the Colquhouns at the battle of Glenfruin? Of the countless Campbells who'd been victims of their reiving and pillaging? He cupped her chin, running his thumb over the frantic pulse in her neck. "The MacGregors are brigands and outlaws who would slit your pretty neck without a second thought. Remember that when you condemn my cousin."

Her eyes widened with alarm. "You're just trying to frighten me. You forget the MacGregors are allies of the Lamonts."

He hadn't forgotten that at all. In fact, it's what had brought him here. "I suggest you choose your friends more wisely."

She pursed her mouth defiantly. "If they're outlaws, it's because they have no other choice, since Campbells have taken their land. And you make them sound worse than they are. It's what Argyll wants people to believe to justify his actions."

Jamie fought to keep his temper in check, knowing that she spoke out of ignorance and didn't understand the complexity of the issues facing the Highlands or the centuries-long dispute between the MacGregors and the Campbells over lands—lands to which the MacGregors had no legal claim. But he felt a strange urge to explain. "My cousin seeks to put an end to the lawlessness that has plagued the Highlands and protect the innocent, and believe me, the

MacGregors are not innocent. Do not romanticize their plight; they are not the Robin Hood and Merry Men of legend. Nor have they been blameless in what has happened to them."

She wrenched free, breathing hard, eyes flashing. "So they deserve to be hunted and butchered?"

His gaze hardened. "They deserve to be brought to justice for their considerable crimes."

Her voice dripped with mockery. "What about your crimes? Have the Campbells not been accused of similar injustices? Has your cousin not burned people off their land?"

"Unlike the MacGregors, we do not break the law."

"How convenient, since you *are* the law."

His mouth tightened. "I am the man who wants to make it so that you can ride the countryside without fear of attack."

"By fear, force, and intimidation."

He took a step closer, resisting the urge to pull her into his arms and quiet her ridiculous accusations. His patience stretched taut by this brazen lass with her flashing eyes and red lips that begged to be kissed, a lass who said things to him that no one had dared before—no one. "By whatever means the law provides," he said tightly.

"Does that include cutting off heads for a bounty?"

He knew she referred to the recent enactment by the Privy Council giving not just a reward, but the dead man's possessions to the bearer of a MacGregor head. "I've seen grisly things on both sides that would give you nightmares for years. You are a woman. Men are not so squeamish about such things—'tis the Highland way."

"And that makes it right?"

"The government has found it effective."

"Don't you mean your cousin has found it effective, since he is the government? Or would like to make himself so."

"My cousin seeks to unify the Highlands—*with* the support of most of the chiefs through bonds of manrent. Without authority, the alternative is a return to the fractious feuding of clans. Is that what you want?" If it wasn't the Campbells, it would be the Mackenzies or Gordons, but there was no doubt it would be someone.

She thrust up that adorable chin and boldly met his gaze. "It's not what is good for the Highlands, but greed that motivates King Campbell."

Jamie clenched his jaw, furious to be taken to task by a sheltered, pampered girl with little understanding of the harsh realities of the world. "You spout rumor and hyperbole as if it were fact. But what do you really know, Caitrina? You are a cosseted girl who lives in a glass castle, protected by your father and brothers. Somehow I doubt your father takes you into his confidence." Her flush proved the truth of his observation. "But beyond the gates of your keep is the real world, a world that is not black and white as you would make it, but much more complicated. Before you are so quick to judge, make sure you know the facts."

She turned away from him, a stubborn set to her slim shoulders. "I know everything I need to know."

Her unqualified rejection shouldn't bother him, but it did. Condemnation such as hers was common enough, but somehow coming from this lass it felt different. He took her arm and spun her back toward him, catching her against his legs and chest. His body surged with heat and anger. She struggled against him, but he held fast. One way or another, she would listen. "And what of you, Caitrina? What do you want? More men to fawn over your beauty? More jewels and costly gowns?"

She gasped with outrage. "You know nothing of what you speak."

"I know that your father can deny you nothing, that you traipse around here dressed like a queen—even in the stables—but that the feuding has taken its toll on your clan." His gaze passed from her fine silks to the rusty tools lined up against the faded, lime-washed walls of the barn, and he could see her sudden realization. "I know that you reject every man who comes before you so you don't have to leave the comfort and safety of your little kingdom. I know that your father was widowed many years ago and yet has never remarried. Why do you think that is, Caitrina? Is it because he worries that it would upset you and the position you have claimed in the household?"

She flinched as if he'd slapped her. It was clear no one had ever talked this way to her. "You're wrong!" she seethed, her cheeks crimson and lovely breasts heaving. But he saw the flicker of uncertainty.

He released her, knowing he'd said enough. Stepping back, he dragged a hand through his hair, giving his body a chance to calm. He hadn't meant to speak so harshly, but her curt dismissal of his suit—a suit he'd never intended to actually pursue—had pricked his anger. Her prejudice against the Campbells was all too common throughout the Highlands, but this lass with her bold tongue and naïve accusations had penetrated his armor like no other.

He strode toward the door and turned to look at her one more time. She stood stone still, her face pale and hands clenched at her side. Strong and proud, but surprisingly fragile. His words had left their mark. He felt a twinge of guilt, an urge to comfort, but quickly forced it aside. He'd spoken the truth; it was time Caitrina Lamont heard it. Her father was doing her no favors in keeping her ignorant of the problems and unrest in the Highlands. If Jamie's suspicions about Alasdair MacGregor proved true, the real world would rain down on her soon enough.

Chapter 5

❖ ❖ ❖

Edgy after his confrontation with Caitrina, Jamie decided to return to the keep rather than join the others at the loch for the races. He'd ridden out early that morning, and except for a few oatcakes and a bit of dried beef to break his fast, he hadn't eaten all day. As he passed across the yard, he was surprised to see the Lamont chief walking toward him, having just descended the stairs from the keep.

Jamie nodded in greeting. "Lamont. I thought you would be down at the races."

"I had other matters to attend to." The older man gave him an appraising stare, taking in Jamie's dusty, windblown appearance. "You left early this morning."

"My men and I decided to do a bit of hunting."

"And were you successful?"

Though innocuous on its surface, Jamie was aware of the subtle undercurrent to the question. The Lamont was wary of his presence, and though Jamie's expressed interest in the lass had deflected some of the suspicion—it hadn't deflected all of it.

"Not this time." But he would be. He knew the MacGregors were here. He could feel it. Though for the Lamont's sake he hoped he was wrong.

His cousin had wanted to send troops immediately, but Jamie had convinced Argyll to wait until they had more to go on than an old tale of Highland hospitality—although the story itself provided a compelling explanation for why the Lamonts would risk so much in sheltering the outlawed MacGregors. There was nothing more sacred in the Highlands than the age-old custom of Highland hospitality. When it was invoked, a clan was obligated to shelter even its worst enemy. The well-known tale between the Lamonts and the MacGregors was proof of its force.

Years ago, a Lamont chief had gone hunting with the son of a MacGregor chief. An argument broke out, and the Lamont took a dirk to the MacGregor's son, killing him. The Lamont escaped but was pursued. He was forced to seek shelter at Glenstrae—the stronghold of the very man whose son he'd killed. Not knowing that the Lamont had just murdered his son, the MacGregor chief agreed to shelter the Lamont from his pursuers.

When the MacGregor clansmen showed up and told the old chief about the murder of his son, the chief—despite his grief and fury over the death of his son—according to the custom of Highland hospitality, refused to turn the Lamont over to them. Fearing that his enraged men would harm the man, the MacGregor personally escorted his son's murderer back to Cowal.

Despite this heartbreaking loss, the bond between the two clans had been unbreakable ever since, and Jamie suspected that the time might have come for the Lamonts to pay back the MacGregor's hospitality.

But a hunch wasn't good enough; he needed proof.

Jamie had been watching the Lamont closely, and so far there had been no signs of anything unusual. Not that he would have expected otherwise. If the Lamont suspected Jamie's true purpose, he would know he was being watched. Jamie's men had the perimeter secured: No one was getting in or out of Ascog without them knowing it.

It was clear that the other man had something else on his mind as well. The look he fixed on Jamie was hard and calculating. "And what of the purpose for your visit, Campbell?"

Jamie didn't pretend to misunderstand. He respected the other man's challenge. "Your daughter is very beautiful."

The old chief's eyes narrowed. "You are in earnest, then?"

"I am." It should have been a lie, but Jamie was surprised to realize by the vehemence in his voice and the deep sensation in his gut that he actually meant it. It was a visceral reaction, a snap decision for a man who otherwise planned everything carefully. Sometime between that first kiss and now, the ruse had become reality. He wanted her.

His tone must have impressed the Lamont as well, because he looked as though he believed him. "Why would Argyll's cousin seek an alliance with a Lamont? As you said, my daughter is very beautiful, but her tocher is modest. I would think that your cousin would see a more lucrative connection."

His cousin would be just as surprised as Jamie was. "My cousin wants an end to the feuding. It is something I would assume you want as well."

"Aye," the Lamont said reluctantly. The enmity between the two clans ran deep. Jamie admired the control of the other man, who showed little reaction when inside he must be seething at the prospect of seeing his beloved daughter married to a Campbell. But no matter how much he loved the lass, the good of the clan would come first. And an alliance with Jamie would help the Lamonts—they both knew that. "And there is no other reason?" he asked suspiciously.

"I want her."

The Lamont gave him a long look, making Jamie wonder how much he'd revealed by the fierceness of his tone. "The lass has a way of penetrating even the most hardened heart," he observed. "But I'd not see her harmed."

Jamie's jaw hardened. "I would never hurt a woman— despite what my enemies would claim. You and I may have been on opposite sides all these years, but have I given you

cause to believe otherwise?" He paused, hearing the Lamont's silent assent. "Your daughter would want for nothing. I would protect her with my life."

The chief nodded slowly, stroking his chin. "I will consider it."

Jamie gave the other man a pointed look. "Of course,
my cousin will want some assurances."

The Lamont tensed. "What kind of assurances?"

"Your loyalty, for one." He held the other man's stare,
watching his reaction carefully. "There have been rumors."

"What kind of rumors?"

"The kind that could get a man killed." The punishment
for harboring the proscribed MacGregors was death, and
that's what the Lamont would be facing for hiding the
fugitives—the obligation of Highland hospitality or not.
Jamie wasn't without sympathy for the Lamont's plight,
choosing between his honor and the law, but he wanted to
make sure the old man knew exactly what he risked.

The old chief's expression betrayed nothing, but he
nodded. "I hope you don't always believe what you hear."

"Not always."

Jamie started to walk toward the stairs, knowing that he
might have just given himself away. But something had
compelled him to give the Lamont a warning.

Hell, was he growing soft? Jamie realized that he liked
the Lamont . . . and his daughter.

"Campbell."

He stopped and turned.

"I'll not force her to wed. If you want the lass, you'll
have to convince her."

Aye, Jamie thought, there was the rub.

Caitrina waited in the stables long after he'd left, unable
to breathe, her hands fisted tightly at her side. It was all she
could do to hold back the tears. No one had ever talked to
her like that.

His accusations rang in her ears. Jamie Campbell had a way of making her feel foolish and frivolous. There was nothing wrong with her gown. She gazed down at the pink silk. It was one of her favorites, and she'd wanted to look her best. For him? She was a fool. She looked around; the rusty tools and chipped lime taunted her. She felt sick to her stomach.

No. He was wrong. He didn't even know her, yet he accused her of—

She stopped, realizing that she'd accused him of the same. Of not knowing him before passing judgment.

But this was different. Jamie Campbell knew nothing of her family.

Still, after leaving the stables, Caitrina found herself searching desperately for her father—not a simple prospect in the crowds that had descended upon Ascog for the games. She passed through the gate and started down the path to the loch. There must have been a hundred people milling about the thin strip of muddy shoreline and slightly wider patch of moorland.

She put her hand to her forehead, shielding her eyes from the bright light of the sun. The swimming races were set to begin. The competitors had lined up for the start, including her brothers Malcolm and Niall, but her father was nowhere to be seen.

He should be here. Brian tried to run past her in a pack of young boys, but she caught him by the arm. "Brian, have you seen Father?"

He shook his head. "Not since this morning, why?"

"I need to see him."

"Have you checked the keep?"

She shook her head. "No. He should have been here for the races."

"I'm sure it's nothing," Brian said impatiently. "Can I go now?"

She could see his friends disappearing into the woods. She let go of his arm. "Go. I'll look for him inside."

It wasn't like her father to disappear like this. What was going on around here?

Caitrina rushed up the path and passed through the gate, stopping midstep when she caught sight of her father speaking with Jamie Campbell across the *barmkin*. From the tense expressions on both men's faces, she could tell it was not a friendly conversation.

When Jamie disappeared into the keep, her father seemed to sag a little, his face visibly distressed.

She ran toward him and hurled herself into his strong embrace, feeling like a child again. How many times had she done the same after a scrape or bruise or some particularly cruel brotherly teasing? Her father had always been there to wipe her tears and soothe the hurt.

Unbidden, another of Jamie's accusations came back to her. He was wrong. She had never prevented her father from remarrying. He had loved her mother so desperately. . . . But her father was still a handsome man, and she knew there were many women who would be eager to take her mother's place. *My place.*

Her chest tightened, and she rested her cheek against the warm, scratchy wool of his plaid, feeling precariously close to tears.

She hated Jamie Campbell for making her feel like this. For making her fear that she was the most selfish daughter in the whole world. "I'm sorry, Father."

"What's this, lass? What has upset you?"

"I saw you talking with that horrible man."

Her father pushed her back so he could look at her, his face as fierce as she'd ever seen it. "Has Campbell done anything to offend you?"

She shook her head. "No, nothing like that," she said, putting the kiss out of her mind. "Everything about him offends me. He's a Campbell. And Argyll's bloodthirsty cousin to boot."

Her father sighed and shook his head. "You've been listening to gossip, Caiti Rose."

She pushed up her chin, hearing the censure in his voice. "It's the only way to find out anything around here since you and Malcolm and Niall never tell me anything."

"There's no reason for you to worry." He patted her on the head as he always did, but this time it bothered her.

Jamie Campbell had made her feel foolish, made her feel as if she didn't know what she was talking about. "I know all I need to know about Jamie Campbell. He's Argyll's Henchman, no better than a hired killer." But even as she made the accusation, she knew it rang false.

"Hush, child," her father said harshly. "Have care for what you say. Jamie Campbell is not just a hired thug or Argyll's strong arm. He's far more dangerous: a man of great physical strength coupled with cunning political acumen. He is a powerful and influential man in his own right. And a dangerous man to cross." He gave her a long look. "He has spoken to me about you."

Caitrina's cheeks flamed at the man's arrogance. "He had no cause. I told him as much not half an hour ago."

"Well, whatever you said did not dissuade him."

"But I'm sure you did."

When he didn't say anything, her eyes widened. "You can't seriously expect me to consider him," she said, aghast.

"Aye, lass, I do." He cut off her protest. "I did not say wed him, but consider him."

"But he's a Campbell."

"Aye, and Campbells are no friends of ours. But I can't ignore the benefit of an alliance with such a powerful man. It would be an end to the feuding."

She didn't miss the twinge of anxiousness in her father's voice. Again, Jamie's words came back to her, and the squeezing in her chest grew a little tighter. The feuding was taking its toll. How could she have been so unaware of what was going on around her? Her father didn't want her to see, but that was no excuse. "Has it been so very bad, Father?"

He pulled her against him and stroked her hair. "Ah, lass, it's nothing for you to worry about. I'd never force you to wed a Campbell, but I want you to consider him. Make your own judgment of the man."

"But—"

He staved off her protest. "That is all I ask. Jamie Campbell is a fierce warrior and a hard man, but not cruel. Despite what you may have heard, he is not a monster. Even though we might not like it, he acts within the law. I can't like the man, but he has always been fair in our dealings." His gaze softened. "He's not the man I would have chosen for you, but there would be much benefit to our clan. As his wife, none could ever harm you. And there are some things—" He stopped and sighed, the deep sound of a man burdened with the heavy weight of responsibility. "There may come a time when we are in need of his friendship."

Duty. She heard the unspoken admonition, and it felt like a betrayal. Why was her father doing this? He hated Campbells as much as she did. Why did she get the feeling that he wasn't telling her something . . . something important?

"It is time for you to wed, Caitrina. If not to Campbell, then to someone else."

He meant it. Caitrina felt an acute moment of panic, lost in the uncertainty of the future that had just been thrust upon her. Where she would be ripped away from everything she knew and loved. She remembered that horrible emptiness when her mother died, but then there had been her father and brothers to fill the sense of loss. Without them . . .

"I know you think so, but I'm not ready, Father. I can't

bear the thought of leaving you and my brothers." Life at Ascog with her family was all she had ever known. It would be like tearing her heart in two to be forced from them.

He brought her into his arms again, and for a moment she thought he would relent. But her time, it seemed, had run out.

"And it will cause me great pain to see you go, my love. But go you must."

Caitrina nodded, tears streaming down her face. The ache in her heart was unbearable.

She wished she'd never set eyes on Jamie Campbell. This was all his fault.

Chapter 6

No matter how much she cajoled, her father would not be swayed. The knowledge that she soon must wed was like an ax hanging over Caitrina's head. It tainted her enjoyment of the next few days and forced her to look at each prospective suitor with eyes that were, if not exactly open, then not exactly closed, either. It also forced her to acknowledge that compared with the boring, fawning attentions of the other men, Jamie Campbell's confident command stood out. *He* stood out. Not just for his handsome face and impressive build, but for the aura of power and authority that emanated from him. But whether by intent or effect, she also noticed that it served to keep him distant from the rest. He was one of them, but apart.

Why it should bother her that he was alone, she didn't know. But it did.

As much as she wanted to ignore him, wanted to hate him, something about the man drew her. Throughout the week, she found herself watching him and his interactions with the other Highlanders. For the most part, he kept to himself or with the handful of guardsmen he'd brought with him, though occasionally she would see him speaking with the various chiefs. She supposed it wasn't surprising; as his cousin's right-hand man, he would have had dealings with most of the Highland elite. But the guardsmen and lower-ranking men of the clan tended to avoid him, looking at him with a mixture of fear and hatred—particularly the Murrays and the Lamonts, who were both allies of the outlawed MacGregors.

Despite Jamie's admonition, she knew not all MacGregors were thieves and brigands. Many, including Alasdair MacGregor and his close relations, had dined in this very hall before they were proscribed. Her father disapproved of their wild ways but sympathized with their plight. Blame for which many in the hall obviously put on Jamie and his cousin.

Quite a few times, she noticed Jamie standing with Rory and Alex MacLeod. The three men presented an impressive picture: tall, broad-shouldered, well-muscled, and uncommonly handsome. Jamie had the height of Rory MacLeod but was slightly leaner in build—more like Alex MacLeod, who stood a few inches shorter than the other two, albeit still well over six feet. She sensed a history among the three men that was different from the rest. Over the course of the week, she'd noticed a distinct warming among them. She'd even caught Jamie laughing once or twice. Perhaps it was because he usually held himself so apart, but the effect was devastating, providing a glimpse into an entirely different side of him—an approachable side.

It intrigued her.

He intrigued her, blast him.

But the person Jamie was most comfortable with was Margaret MacLeod, Alex's wife. Seeing them together, watching the easy banter between the two, made something pinch hard inside Caitrina's chest. It was a feeling unlike anything she'd ever experienced before—almost irrational in its intensity. Even the knowledge that Margaret MacLeod was so obviously in love with her husband did not lessen it any. Why their easy camaraderie should bother her, she didn't know . . . except that it did.

Which was ridiculous, since nothing would ever persuade her to consider Jamie Campbell—her father's half-hearted request notwithstanding.

Her hatred of clan Campbell had been fed since birth and would not be easily cast aside. It was part of who she was: Lamonts hated Campbells. Too much blood had been shed between the two clans. But her reasons were also personal. She'd seen what they'd done to her mother, how much it had hurt her to be disowned by her father and cut off from everyone in her family. She would never repeat her misery. Her father couldn't seriously expect her to look at Jamie Campbell as anything other than the enemy. If she married a Campbell, she might as well be banished; the effect would be the same. She would be cut off from her clan by years of hatred.

But it wasn't simply who he was—though that was cause enough—it was how he made her feel. He watched her with those steely blue eyes that seemed to bore right through her. It was a look of possession and desire that threatened her in a way no man ever had before—that just because he'd kissed her, he had some kind of claim on her. It made her feel trapped by feelings she didn't understand and longings that made her yearn to escape.

She could not deny the strange connection between them: a heightened awareness that left her feeling warm and prickly, her skin strangely tight and sensitive. At meals when his leg or arm would accidentally brush against hers, it felt as if she were jumping out of her skin. He seemed to delight in tormenting her. As if he knew what his touch did to her and how much he unnerved her. But nothing she did or said seemed to get through to him. Her attempt to treat him with cool disdain was met with wry amusement.

The incident in the barn had not been broached, but it was there, hanging between them—as was the memory of his mouth on hers. It was a memory she yearned to forget, but it seemed the harder she attempted to push it away, the more she could think of nothing else. She tried to think of other men kissing her, but the only face she could visualize was his.

What kept her sane was the knowledge that her discomfort soon would be at an end. Tomorrow the gathering would be over. Jamie Campbell would leave with the rest of the guests, and her life would return to normal.

But for how long? Her father had laid down the law about her marriage.

She fought the spark of panic, refusing to think of that now. When everyone left, she would find a way to dissuade him.

Caitrina sat on a rock under the shade of an old birch tree along the edge of the woods. In the moors beyond, the final competition—archery—was just about to get under way.

She stiffened, sensing his presence even before the mocking words had left his mouth.

"Miss me, Princess?"

She hated that he called her that, but after the first time she had refused to let him know how much it bothered her.

"Like the plague," she replied sweetly.

He chuckled. "Stubborn lass. But as much as I'd love to sit here and spar with you, my sweet, you'll have to forgive me." He gave her an amused look and nodded toward the field of play. "I have a contest to win."

She noticed the bow slung over his muscled shoulder and felt a prickle of disquiet. "But you haven't participated in any of the games. With such an unusual affinity for hunting, I thought you'd be off on another ride."

"Keeping track of me, Caitrina? I'm flattered. But I couldn't resist the prize for this event."

Her cheeks burned. She hated how she could never tell whether he was teasing or in earnest. "You know very well that was not meant for your ears. Even if you could best Rory MacLeod, which you can't, it wouldn't matter. My offer did not extend to you. Besides, I've already told you I'm not interested."

He gave her a long, dark look. One that made butterflies dance low in her belly.

"I know what you've told me, but your eyes say differently."

She turned away from him in a huff. "You are blind and arrogant."

"Have care, lass. You might hurt your neck tossing your hair around like that." He twisted a long tress around his finger like a ribbon and then let it spring free. "Though it is lovely." Laughing at the outraged look on her face, he bowed. "I'll be back soon to collect my prize."

He infuriated her, but her gaze followed him as he walked toward the other men, mesmerized by the flex of muscle in his long, powerful stride. She jerked her head away with a start.

He is wrong. He means nothing to me. It was simply that he'd dared what no man had before. She was inexperienced in her intimate relations with men (he'd been right about that). His had been her first kiss. But Caitrina intended for that to change. Soon.

Perhaps she'd been too hasty in rejecting Torquil MacNeil. He was young and boastful, but seemingly suitable. And certainly more appealing than some of the other men brought before her.

Her gaze slid down the line of contestants. There were about twenty men set to start. Sacks stuffed with straw and grass had been set up at about fifty paces. Each sack was marked with white concentric circles. After each round, the targets would be moved back another ten paces.

Mindful of her duties as hostess, Caitrina left her solitary position on the rock and joined a group of women who'd gathered to watch the contest. With each round that passed, the hammering in her heart increased. Jamie Campbell was holding his own. And so, surprisingly, was MacNeil.

"He's an excellent bowman."

Transfixed by the contest before her, Caitrina suddenly realized that Margaret MacLeod had been speaking to her. She blushed. "I'm sorry?"

Margaret smiled and repeated her comment.

"Who?" Caitrina said nonchalantly, plastering an innocent look on her face.

"Jamie. I saw you watching him."

The blunt observation brought a guilty flush to her cheeks. The other woman was studying her carefully and no doubt noticed the reaction. "Perhaps," Caitrina conceded. "But not good enough to best the MacLeod chief."

Meg grinned. "Oh, I don't know about that. Jamie's beaten my brother by marriage countless times before."

Caitrina's heart raced, and her voice, which she tried to hold steady, came out like a squeak. "Really?"

Meg nodded. "It's been a fierce rivalry for years. Rory and Alex were fostered with the old earl, and Jamie spent most of his youth at Inveraray."

Caitrina's gaze shot to Jamie. He drew back the arrow and released; it flew to the center of the target. "I didn't realize . . ." She looked back to Meg, silently asking for more.

"After the death of Jamie's father, he and his sister, Elizabeth, went to live with the earl."

She could no longer hide her curiosity. "He had no other relations?"

"Two older brothers. His elder brother Colin, who was only a lad himself on the death of their father, became Campbell of Auchinbreck. Their mother had passed the year before, and Argyll held their father in the highest esteem. Like Jamie, his father was a trusted captain. He fell at the battle at Glenlivet, taking a shot meant for Argyll, and the earl will never forget it. Jamie is like a brother to him. Argyll values his opinion above all others."

The bond between Jamie and his cousin went far deeper

than she'd realized. "From what I've heard, I'm surprised that the earl takes advice from anyone."

Meg grinned. "Oh, he's not that bad."

Caitrina lifted her brow skeptically.

Meg chuckled at her expression. "He's better than the alternatives of Mackenzie or Huntly."

Jamie had said much the same thing. Listening to Meg, Caitrina realized just how little she knew of the issues plaguing the Highlands. Embarrassed by her ignorance, she changed the subject. "You said there were two brothers. What of the other?"

Meg's face clouded. "Jamie doesn't talk about him much. Though you might have heard of him." She gave Caitrina a hard stare, as if debating whether to say more. She looked around, making sure they would not be heard, but everyone else was focused on the contest. Only four men remained: Rory MacLeod, Jamie Campbell, Torquil MacNeil, and Robbie Graham. Nerves too frayed to watch, Caitrina was glad of the distraction. Meg continued in a low voice. "His eldest brother, Duncan, is a bastard born. He was their father's favorite and despite his birth had been named a captain, but he was disgraced after the battle of Glenlivet years ago. His treachery was blamed for Argyll's defeat, and he was forced to flee Scotland. He's called Duncan Dubh." *Duncan the Black*. Her eyes widened. The Black Highlander? Meg smiled wryly. "Aye, he's made quite a name for himself on the continent. But the scandal hit Jamie particularly hard; from what I hear, they were very close." Meg's expression lightened with amusement. "But no one will ever confuse Jamie with his brother."

"What do you mean?"

"Whether you agree with him or not, no one can say he doesn't follow the law."

Though she'd said it jokingly, Caitrina wondered if there was more truth to Meg's comment than she realized. Was that what drove him? "And his sister? She is married?"

Meg smiled and shook her head. "Not yet. It will be an impressive man who can please both her brothers and her cousin. Jamie mentioned that Elizabeth will be joining him at Dunoon soon with the earl."

Argyll, she knew, was the keeper of the royal castle of Dunoon. The earl had numerous castles, including his Lowland stronghold, Castle Campbell, and his Highland stronghold of Inveraray Castle.

Embarrassed by how much she'd revealed by her questions, Caitrina fell silent, her attention returned again to the field—just in time to see MacNeil's arrow land wide of the mark. He was the farthest away, but she could see the anger and bitter disappointment on his face. He'd acquitted himself well, dangerously well for her comfort, but clearly he'd intended to win. Caitrina felt a twinge of guilt, realizing that perhaps she'd been unfair. She'd treated MacNeil's offer lightly, but it had obviously meant a great deal to him. Later, she'd find him and apologize.

Robbie Graham shot next, and his arrow landed on the lower right edge of the target. A superb shot from that distance, which was probably at least one hundred paces by now. Rory MacLeod stepped forward. It was clear the crowd sided with him. They swayed as he drew the arrow back, holding their collective breath as he released and . . .

Thump. A great cheer rang out. The arrow had landed in the center circle near the middle of the target. It would take a perfect shot to beat him.

Caitrina could feel the restless tension build around her as Jamie raised his bow and took aim. She couldn't breathe. It was almost as if she knew what was going to happen. His confidence left no room for failure. The arrow flew, and she didn't even look. Her eyes were fastened on Jamie. The gasp of the crowd would have been enough, but at the moment of victory he turned and looked right at her, his eyes pinning her to the ground. Her heart jumped to her throat. The deep, penetrating stare seemed to see everything, seeing her turmoil, seeing things that she didn't want him to see.

Only after his men and the MacLeods had moved to congratulate him did she glance at the target. He'd hit a perfect bull's-eye.

While he was occupied with his men, Caitrina took the opportunity to make her escape. She knew he'd come looking for her, and it might be cowardly, but her nerves were so raw that she didn't think she could take one more confrontation with Jamie Campbell.

Why couldn't he just leave her alone?

Tomorrow couldn't come soon enough.

Not ready to return to the castle and wanting to avoid the crowd, she veered off the path and wandered through the trees toward the loch. There was a small inlet on the eastern edge that was a favorite fishing spot of her brothers. She would relax there for a while until she could sort through the jumble of emotions twisting her stomach in knots.

She was so rattled by what had just happened that it took her a moment to realize someone was following her. She heard a noise, the crush of a branch underfoot, and spun around to look behind her—but didn't see anyone. Her pulse spiked and the hair at the back of her neck rose.

"Who's there?" she asked, her voice wavering as she scanned the trees.

But there was no answer. Icy droplets of fear trickled down her spine. Something didn't feel right. She hadn't gone that far, but with all the noise, would someone hear her? Jamie's warning about outlaws came back to her.

She had opened her mouth to cry for help when a man stepped out from behind a tree in a ray of sunlight not five feet away.

She exhaled with relief, recognizing Torquil MacNeil right away.

"My laird, you startled me."

The sun was behind him and she couldn't see his face clearly, but anger seemed to radiate from him. "I trust you found the competition entertaining," he said, his voice holding the edge of a sneer.

"No, I—" She twisted her hands, not knowing what to say. He stepped closer, close enough for her to see the fury marring his handsome features. She'd hurt his pride; she must try to soothe it. "I want to apologize—"

"You tricked me."

Though he sounded somewhat like a petulant child, Caitrina reached out and put her hand on his arm. "It was wrong of me, and I deeply regret doing so."

He gave her an uncertain look. "You do?"

She nodded and smiled up at him encouragingly. "You acquitted yourself extremely well today."

For a moment he puffed up a bit under her obvious admiration, then he frowned. "But I didn't win." His face darkened. "That Campbell bastard did."

Jamie Campbell, Jamie Campbell . . . If she never heard his name again, it would be too soon. She studied MacNeil's face; he was undeniably handsome, yet for some reason he did not rouse the same fluttering in her stomach or make every nerve ending stand on edge—a fact that only served to irritate her further. A streak of recklessness that she didn't even know she possessed took hold. There was nothing special about Jamie Campbell, and she was going to prove it.

She put her hand on his shoulders, lifted up on her tiptoes, and pressed her mouth against his in a light kiss. And felt precisely . . . nothing. Not the merest stirring or faintest yearning or anything. His lips were soft and he tasted pleasant enough, but he did not drown her senses in heat or make her body heavy and sensitive.

Furious, she pressed a little closer, trying to find the spark. He groaned, sliding his arm around her waist and pulling her against him. She felt the power of his body, the muscles and the strength, but she did not feel like melting into him at all. Being pressed against him only filled her with unease. It was nothing like she'd felt in Jamie's arms.

Damn him.

This wee experiment had failed miserably.

MacNeil pulled her tighter, and his mouth grew demanding as he tried to ply her lips apart. She felt a flash of alarm. Somehow she'd lost control of the kiss.

She pulled her mouth from his, gasping for air. "Please let go of me."

His eyes were dark with lust. "I don't think so, my sweet. I'm not a man to be made the butt of some silly chit's jest."

Too late, she realized she'd miscalculated. Jamie's warning came back to her. Perhaps this had been MacNeil's intention all along. Foolishly, she'd just helped him to it.

She tried to wrench free, but he was too strong. He might be young, but he had the physical strength of a seasoned warrior, a fact that was only now impressed upon her. His mouth descended on hers again, and his kiss turned brutal and punishing. Revulsion crawled up the back of her throat, and fear unlike anything she'd ever experienced crashed over her.

Dear God, what have I done?

She struggled against him, using every ounce of her strength, but it wasn't enough.

Panic had started to set in when she suddenly found herself free, staring into the steely blue eyes of Jamie Campbell. Except that his eyes weren't steely at all, but ice cold with rage. Her heart skipped a long beat, realizing what she was seeing. Danger. Rage. Fierceness to make her blood run cold. *This* was the man who struck fear across the Highlands.

Jamie was out of control. Possessed by a black rage that was unlike anything he'd ever experienced. The sight of

Caitrina in another man's arms had unleashed something primitive in him; the sight of her struggling had unleashed something murderous.

It was only by chance that Jamie had caught sight of MacNeil as he'd stalked away from the field of play. He had a hungry, predatory look in his eyes that made Jamie's instincts flare. He'd followed the young warrior at a distance, not surprised to see him confront Caitrina. Jamie had been about to intervene when he'd seen her slide her arms around MacNeil's neck and press her lips to his.

It stopped Jamie cold. Everything went black as he fought to absorb the crushing blow. It felt as if he'd been walloped by a heavy taber across the chest.

Mine. The visceral claim resounded through him, permeating every fiber of his being.

What the hell did she think she was doing? Caitrina was his, but she was kissing another man. Then it changed. He saw her try to push him away, saw the look of determination on the other man's face, and Jamie saw red, the roar in his ears deafening. He closed the distance between them in a matter of seconds and tore her from MacNeil's arms, striking his fist into the other man's jaw with the force of a smith's hammer, hearing the satisfying crunch. The next blow landed in MacNeil's stomach, making him keel over.

"What are you doing?" MacNeil said, gasping for breath.

"You damn bastard! The lass is not willing."

MacNeil wiped the back of his hand over his mouth, trying to stay the gush of blood from Jamie's first blow. "She was willing enough. She kissed me, or didn't you see?" He gave Caitrina a leering glance. "I was only giving her what she begged for—"

Jamie's fist cut off the offending words. But the other man was ready. When he'd been bent over, he'd managed to slide a dirk from his side and now plunged the blade toward Jamie's gut. Jamie spun to the side, avoiding the blow, and caught the other man's wrist in his hand, turning until he heard bone crunch and the blade slipped from his grasp. After kicking it out of the way, he hit him again, and this time MacNeil dropped to the ground.

Slowly, he tried to pull himself up. Jamie made a move toward him, intent on finishing him off, when Caitrina stepped in front of him.

"Don't." She put her hand on his arm, forcing him to look at her. Bloodlust still pounded through his veins, and it took a moment for his gaze to clear. "You'll kill him."

"It's no more than he deserves," Jamie said through clenched teeth.

"Please." She stepped closer, her sweet floral perfume drowning out the primitive stench of battle. She looked as if she were about to cry; unshed tears sparkled in her eyes, and her mouth trembled. "Not for me."

Jamie stood stone still, muscles clenched, every instinct clamoring to finish what he'd started. He gazed down at her face, and the gentle plea worked its soothing magic.

He drew back, raking his hand through his hair. What the hell had just come over him? He'd never felt like that. He was always under control. *Always.*

He turned to MacNeil, who'd managed to right himself again. "Get out of here. If I see you near her again, I'll kill you."

Realizing how close he'd just come to suffering that fate, MacNeil mustered what dignity he could manage and ran, disappearing through the trees.

Caitrina collapsed against him, and his chest squeezed so tightly that it felt as if it were burning. Just for a moment, he let himself savor the sensation of her gratitude, of her need for him. "Thank you." She lifted her watery gaze to his. "I was so scared."

His temper had cooled, but not completely. He wanted

to kiss her senseless and punish her for tormenting him like this. When he thought of what could have happened . . . It made him ill.

"He deserved worse for what he attempted. What if I hadn't arrived when I did?"

The color slid from her face.

At least she realized how close she'd come to rape. He took her by the shoulders and forced her gaze to his. "What did you think you were doing, toying with him like that?"

"I didn't mean . . ."

"Then what did you mean?" The odd tightness in his chest returned. "God's wounds, Caitrina, I saw you kiss him."

Her eyes flashed and she lifted her chin to meet his gaze. After what had just happened, he had to admire her spirit.

"It's all your fault."

His jaw slackened. "My fault?"

"You should never have kissed me."

All of a sudden, he understood. He couldn't believe she could be that naïve. "So this was some damn experiment?" When he thought of how she could have been hurt . . . "Don't you know what might have happened?"

Her face burned with humiliation. "I just wanted to stop seeing your face."

Her voice broke, and it did something to him. His anger slid away. He could understand her confusion—hell, he felt it, too. She was innocent. Too young. With little knowledge of what happened between a man and a woman. She couldn't realize that this passion and fierce attraction between them was different. But he would show her.

He lowered his mouth, his lips hovering only inches from hers. He could feel the quickening of her breath against his and the quiver of anticipation that ran through her.

She wanted this as badly as he did. Her lips parted . . .

But he did not kiss her mouth. His lips dropped to her jaw and neck, tasting the honey of her skin. He burrowed into the warm, soft skin of her neck, inhaling the floral perfume of her silky hair. He devoured her skin, kissing, sucking, licking, until she shuddered against him.

He was hot and hard, desire pulled tautly in his groin.

But he would not press his claim. He needed her to acknowledge her desire. He lifted his head and took her chin in his fingers, forcing her half-lidded gaze to his. "Is this what you want, Caitrina?" His voice was rough with passion.

He slid his thumb over the soft pad of her plump lower lip. He couldn't wait to taste her again. But he would hear it from her own mouth.

She gasped and nodded.

It wasn't enough. "Tell me."

"Yes," she whispered. "I want this."

A primitive heat surged through him in a rush of pure masculine satisfaction. With a groan, he gave her what she wanted—what they both wanted—and covered her mouth with his.

So this was desire. This all-consuming need. The heat. The feeling that if he didn't kiss her right now, she would die. Nothing could have prepared Caitrina for the conflagration of emotions surging through her body. She was on fire, her skin hot and sensitive to the touch.

When his lips finally touched hers, she sighed against his mouth. It was the same as before, only stronger, more intense. How could something so new and unfamiliar feel so right? It was as if she'd been waiting for this her whole life.

His lips were firm and soft, entreating but not demanding. His hand cupped her chin, the rough pads of his fingers caressing with such tenderness that she felt her heart squeeze with longing. It didn't seem possible that a man known for his ruthlessness could be so gentle.

Everything about this kiss was tender and sweet, but it wasn't enough. Not to quiet this strange yearning burgeoning inside her.

As if he could sense her need, he kissed her again, this time using his mouth and fingers to deftly urge her lips apart.

At the first sweep of his tongue, she gasped. But her shock was quickly forgotten in the maelstrom of new sensations rippling through her. He tasted her again, stroking deeper and deeper with his tongue. It was exquisite, this joining, the dark, carnal taste of him; the melding of their mouths and tongues. He parried and feinted with long, slow strokes, the gentle teasing sending a wild fluttering to her stomach and driving her mad with longing.

She couldn't seem to get close enough. She wrapped her hands around his neck, stretching her body more fully against his. He felt incredible, so warm and hard, she just wanted to dissolve against him. There was something undeniably rousing about the power of his hard warrior's body. She ran her hands over the heavy bunch of muscles at his shoulders, savoring the strength harnessed under her fingertips. Her nipples hardened, straining against the muscled wall of his chest.

He was magnificent. And he wanted her, she could feel it drumming inside him. But he kept a tight rein on his passion. She knew he didn't want to frighten her given what had just happened. But Jamie was nothing like Torquil MacNeil. Instinctively, she knew that he would never hurt her. His control was admirable, but perversely it egged her on—she wanted him falling apart, as she was.

Tentatively, she reached her tongue out to meet his. He groaned, tightening his hold around her waist, molding her body more firmly against his. More intimately. She felt the evidence of his desire hard and powerful against her stomach, and heat pooled between her legs.

The excited beat of his heart against hers urged her on.

She gave herself over to the kiss, meeting every stroke with one of her own. The heat between them was building to explosion. Her skin felt tight and sensitive, aching for his touch. Unconsciously, she rubbed against him, seeking the relief that only friction could bring.

This was madness, but she couldn't get enough. The kiss turned more frantic, deeper, wetter, hungrier. She felt the imprint of his hand on her waist, on her ribs, sliding up to cup her breast.

She trembled, never imagining that she could so crave a man's touch. His mouth dropped to her jaw, to her neck, and down her chest. The scrape of his jaw blazed a path of fire along her skin. She shivered as the warmth of his breath and the wetness of his tongue made her skin prickle. But nothing prepared her for the sensations that took hold when his tongue slid below the edge of her bodice. She gasped with surprise and then pleasure to feel the wet heat of his tongue sliding over her nipple. He'd loosened the laces of her bodice and gently scooped her breasts over her stays.

His voice was rough and husky as he ran his thumb over the hardened tip of her nipple.

"God, you're beautiful."

For a moment, reality intruded. Embarrassed, she felt the heat of a blush spread over her skin. But it was forgotten an instant later when he covered her taut peak with his mouth, scraping her lightly with his teeth. She sank against his mouth, bolts of pleasure striking straight to her heart.

Jamie knew he was playing with fire. His control had been stretched to the breaking point by her enthusiastic response.

He'd taken it slowly, having care for her innocence, but he sensed that with Caitrina he would learn the limits of his own endurance. Never had he been so filled with lust and yet so unfocused on relief.

He wanted this to be perfect for her.

He scooped her lush breasts in his hands, lifting them to his mouth but pausing to admire the soft ivory skin and delicate pink tips. He wanted to rub his face in the deep cleft, inhaling the soft floral perfume of her skin. But first he had to taste her. His mouth closed over one delicate tip, and he took her deep in his mouth with a long, delicious pull.

His cock jerked hard at her moan.

She was so responsive to his touch, he couldn't hold back. He sucked her harder, circling her with his tongue and pulling her gently between his teeth. The honey sweet taste of her was more potent than ambrosia. He could feel her tremble, feel the race of her pulse and the harsh quickening of her breath.

He felt her urgency and knew the restlessness was building inside her. Knew how badly she needed relief. If he touched her, he knew she would be hot and deliciously wet.

God, he could make her come.

Once the thought was in place, it would not be dislodged. It was all he could think of. Being the first to show her pleasure. Binding her to him, making her his.

He worked her breast with his mouth as his hand skimmed over her hip and bottom—resisting the urge to bring her more firmly against him—and down the long length of her leg to slide under the edge of her skirt.

At the first touch of her skin, he felt her stiffen with shock. He soothed her skittishness with soft murmurs whispered against her damp skin as he continued to kiss and suck her breasts. "Don't be scared, my sweet. I only wish to give you pleasure. I will stop whenever you wish."

He released her breast and kissed her mouth again, stroking her with his tongue, mimicking the movements he would make with his finger. He felt her body relax.

His hand slid up the delicate curve of her leg; her skin was as soft as velvet.

His erection strained against the leather of his breeches. Lust pounded in his ears, but he quieted it, focusing solely on the beautiful woman about to come apart in his arms. His fingers caressed the soft skin of her inner thighs.

Her breath caught and he broke the kiss, lifting his head so he could look at her when he touched her. Her eyes were hazy with passion, but also hesitant.

He swept his finger over her, and her eyes widened with shock.

He fought the groan that racked his body, feeling her dampness. He'd never been so aroused by anything as the slick evidence of her desire. *For me.*

He touched her again, teasing, coming achingly close to her core, to the place she so desperately wanted him to touch.

She shuddered against him, growing heavier in his arms as her legs weakened. He brushed her again and again, until her back arched and her hips started to move against his hand in innocent frustration. When he couldn't stand it any longer, he took her breast in his mouth again and sucked just as he slid his finger inside her. The sound of pleasure she made nearly unmanned him. She was so wet, he had to fight the shudder of his own desire. He was hot and hard and ready to explode. He wanted nothing more than to slide inside her, feeling her tightness clamp around him and draw him in.

But first it was for her.

He sucked and stroked, his hand and mouth working in perfect tandem, merciless in his need to bring her more pleasure than she'd ever dreamed of.

The force of what came over her was like nothing she'd ever imagined. Caitrina felt the sensations build and build inside her until they had nowhere else to go.

The quiver between her legs where he touched tightened

into a frantic pulsing. She didn't know what to do. Her hips moved against his hand, seeking pressure. It felt as if she were reaching for something that hovered just out of her reach.

Frustrated, she writhed in his arms. "Please . . . Oh, God."

"Let go, my sweet. Don't fight it."

She couldn't if she wanted to. Not with the magical way he was touching her.

And then she felt it take hold, a feeling unlike anything that had come before, a feeling as close to heaven as she had ever thought to experience on earth. She cried out. Her entire body clenched. For a moment she thought her heart had stopped, then everything shattered and the spasms of release crashed over her.

When it was over she sagged against him, drained by the power and wonder of what had just happened.

Her heart stalled. *By what had just happened.*

She opened her eyes, seeing Jamie Campbell holding her in his arms. Restraint pulled tautly across his handsome features in the hard flex of his jaw and the fierce intensity in his eyes. She felt his body against her, the hard length of his manhood throbbing against her hip, the furious pounding of his heart that had yet to slow. The stark reality of what had only a few minutes ago been cloaked in passion hit her with the force of a thunderbolt.

Dear God, what have I just done? Shame crawled over her as she was forced to acknowledge the intimacy of what they'd just shared. She'd allowed Jamie Campbell to touch her in places and do things to her that belonged only to a husband.

Pushing him away, she staggered out of his arms, her eyes burning with humiliation.

He tried to take her arm to steady her, but she flinched away.

"There is no shame in what just happened to you, Caitrina." His voice was soft and soothing, so understanding.

But she didn't want to hear it.

"How can you say that?" she cried, her voice tight with the ball of emotion lodged at the back of her throat. She gazed down at her breasts bared over her stays and loosened gown, her nipples tender and rosy from his wicked kiss. Mortified heat spread across her cheeks. Turning, she made quick work of covering herself, trying to restore some semblance of modesty.

Despair drained through her as she recognized the truth: Some things would never be restored—like her innocence and illusion of indifference.

When she turned back around, she avoided his gaze but noticed that all vestiges of passion had been erased from his face. His expression was once again implacable. She hated his control. That he could be so unaffected when her world had just shattered seemed somehow all the more devastating. What would it take for this man to *feel*?

"Everything will be all right, Caitrina." He tried to take her hand, but she yanked it away. There was nothing he could do to comfort her. "I will speak to your father—"

"No!" Her eyes flew to his in panic. "You will do nothing of the kind."

His steely gaze bored into her, and he drew himself up to his full height—which was imposing indeed. "I will, of course, offer for you."

She shook her head. "There is no need—"

"Yes"—he caught her arm, this time not letting go—"there is. I want you."

Her chest squeezed: *possession.* "You don't want *me.* I'm merely another battle to be won. Something you saw and decided you had to have. A pretty decoration to keep by your side. You don't even *know* me."

His jaw clenched. "I know all I need to know. You are

clever, beautiful without artifice, strong, and care deeply for those you love. I've seen the way you look after your father and brothers."

"Because I *love* them. You can't think that I'd ever feel the same—"

"No," he cut her off curtly. "I'd not expect that of you, but after what just happened, you can hardly claim that you are indifferent to me."

God, it was true. How could I have succumbed so easily? Hot pressure built in her eyes and throat. He'd warned her that she was naïve. . . . Caitrina stiffened. Her eyes searched his face for signs of duplicity. Had he used her innocence against her?

She felt like such a fool. "And whatever the Highland Henchman wants he takes, is that it? You knew I didn't want you, so you tricked me. You are every bit as cruel as they say, not stopping at anything to get what you want."

Tiny white lines appeared around his mouth, the only sign that she'd penetrated his steely armor of control. "Have care, Princess," he said roughly. "I've already warned you that I'm not one of your mealymouthed suitors you can wrap around your little finger. You are wrong about my motives. I took nothing that was not willingly offered. Deny me if you wish, but at least be honest with yourself."

She knew he was right, but she didn't want to hear it. "I don't want to marry anyone." Her voice shook, she feared with a twinge of hysteria. "And I especially don't want to marry you. I hate you for what you did." *For what you made me feel.*

There was something so intense in his gaze, she had to turn away.

"Hate me if it makes you feel better, but it doesn't change the fact that you want me. What we have together—" He stopped. "It is not common."

He was only saying that. She clenched her fists at her side, fighting for control. "You may have succeeded in proving that I desire you, but it does not change anything. You are still a Campbell and still Argyll's toady—the sword arm of a despot."

"I'm my own man," he said flatly. "I make my own decisions. If you took the time to look beyond the golden gates of your castle, you would see the truth plain enough. My fight is with outlaws and men who stand in the way of law and order."

"You are a thug and a brute," she said, her voice laden with scorn. "And a fool if you think I'd willingly marry a man who is feared and reviled as the devil. Who is no more than a hired murderer."

The silence was deafening. His face was stony, but for a moment she glimpsed the cold fury in his eyes. Caitrina realized that she'd gone too far. But it was too late to take it back, even if she wanted to.

He took a menacing step closer, but she stood her ground.

"You claim to have such a definitive understanding of my character, and yet you do not appear frightened?"

He was right. Looking at him with all she knew, by all rights she should be terrified. Standing there, his handsome features hard and forbidding and six feet plus of rippling muscles with hands that could crush her in an instant. She'd seen his cold, merciless rage against MacNeil . . . yet he'd touched her with nothing but tenderness. She lifted her chin. "Should I be?"

His gaze met hers, deep and penetrating, seeing things she didn't want him to see. "Perhaps you should be."

She *was* scared—not of him, but of herself.

Caitrina's chest squeezed. The tears that she'd fought to control spilled down her cheeks. "Just go away and leave me alone," she choked.

He flinched. Or maybe she'd just imagined it, because when he met her gaze, his eyes were like ice. "You shall have your wish. But your scorn is misplaced, and you will regret your refusal of my offer. One day, Caitrina, the brutal reality of our world will find you—and I guarantee it won't be pretty dresses and fancy slippers."

Chapter 7

❖❖❖

It wasn't over. Not by any measure. Jamie turned and left her in the woods, not looking back, the hot rush of anger pounding through his veins. Caitrina Lamont was his. She might not realize it yet, but she would.

But right now, he was so furious that he didn't want to tarry a minute longer than was necessary. As soon as he returned to the castle, he gathered his men and with a quick word to the Lamont left Ascog and the maddening lass behind him.

After what they'd just shared, her scornful refusal stung. He'd thought she was softening toward him, thought that she, too, felt the passionate connection between them. Perhaps he'd erred in forcing her to confront her desire, but nothing could have felt more right. The feel of her coming apart in his arms would not be something he would soon forget.

He'd never felt like that before with a woman. Ever. The strength of his emotion and the force of his response had shocked him. It was the closest he'd come to losing control. The urge to take her, to slide into that delicious heat, had been unbearable. And when her release took hold, the surge of heat in his loins had turned excruciating. The pressure had been so intense, it had taken everything he had not to let go.

He shook his head, recalling her accusations. She thought he'd tricked her, but in fact it was the opposite. He wanted her for his wife, but he would not compel her.

He'd actually hoped she might come to him on her own. But it was clear that her prejudice against him ran too deep. She wouldn't even try to see him as anything other than a monster—a figment of tales and exaggeration. And Jamie was done trying to explain himself. He'd not grovel to any woman—least of all a cosseted lass who had no conception of the danger surrounding her.

His thoughts returned to his mission—where they belonged. Despite spending the better part of a week searching the surrounding area and keeping his ears open for any talk, Jamie had not found the proof he sought to substantiate his suspicions. But it did not dissuade him from his belief that the MacGregors were availing themselves of the deep bond of hospitality forged with the Lamonts.

Jamie understood the Lamont's quandary—and even sympathized with him. The bond of hospitality was considered a sacred obligation in the Highlands, and if the MacGregors had invoked the old obligation, Caitrina's father would feel honor-bound to give them shelter. But honor would not change the fact that he was harboring outlaws and, in doing so, breaking the law and putting himself directly in the way of the king's rage. King James wanted the MacGregors eradicated and would give no quarter to those who helped them. The Lamont would pay a price, though Jamie intended to do what he could to help him.

Jamie and his men left Ascog and traveled north to Rothesay harbor. If the Lamont was hiding something, he'd want to make sure Jamie and his men were long gone before revealing himself. So Jamie had taken the precaution of removing his warriors from the area, but they would circle back later. He didn't think they were being followed, but he wouldn't take any chances.

They crossed the Kyle of Bute, landing in Cowal just west of Toward point. He could just make out Toward Castle in the distance—the stronghold of Caitrina's kin, the Lamont of Toward. From there, Jamie headed north up the

Cowal Peninsula to Dunoon alone, instructing his men to wait until dark and then to return to Bute and Rothesay Castle. Rothesay had been taken by the Earl of Lennox over fifty years ago but had lapsed to the Crown on his death. From Rothesay, which was less than a dozen fur-longs from Ascog, they would watch the area and wait. Jamie would rejoin his men as soon as he'd reported back to his cousin.

Night was falling, and mist off the Firth of Clyde had begun to thicken as he wound up the hill to the castle gate. It was said that a keep had been on this point for over a thousand years. Dunoon, or *Dun-nain,* meaning "Green Hill," was located strategically on the western shore of the Clyde on a small promontory, providing an excellent van-tage from which to repel attackers—except on murky nights like tonight, where it was difficult to see his hand in front of his face. Jamie's approach, however, had been no-ticed.

He expected that Argyll, anxious for news of his search, would find him soon. But it wasn't his cousin who greeted him. It was his brother. Argyll was the keeper of the royal castle of Dunoon, but Jamie's brother Colin—as chieftain of Campbell of Auchinbreck—was its captain. Jamie had barely finished tending to his horse before his brother inter-cepted him as he crossed the yard to the keep.

Colin's sudden appearance surprised him. To his regret, they had never been close. When Jamie was young, before the death of their father, it had been Duncan he'd always looked up to. *Duncan.* He stiffened. Even after all these years, the bitterness of Duncan's betrayal was still raw. After Duncan fled Scotland, it had been Argyll—or Archie, as Jamie had called him then—who had taken his place. Jamie was as close to Argyll as any man could be to some-one in his position, but power and authority were a lonely companion. Something that Jamie had learned only too well.

As Jamie's role as Argyll's second in command had grown, creating a barrier between him and his childhood companions, it would have been nice to have a brother to rely upon—to trust. But he and Colin, it seemed, had always been at odds. Part resentment, Jamie suspected, and partly because of his brother's character. Colin wasn't close with anyone.

"I heard you arrived," Colin said. "Seems your gut was wrong this time, little brother."

Though there was some similarity in their features and coloring, Jamie refrained from pointing out that at nearly four inches taller and at least two stone worth of muscle, "little brother" sounded ridiculous. But the quick-to-take-umbrage Colin was unlikely to see the irony.

Jamie hadn't missed the slight smugness in his brother's voice. "I'm in no mood for your guessing games, Colin. If you've something to say, say it. Either that or get out of my way so I can find the earl."

"He's not here. He's been delayed at Inveraray, though he is expected soon."

Jamie frowned. "Nothing is wrong?"

Argyll had lost his countess last year following the difficult birth of his heir and had taken it hard. The troubles with the MacGregors hadn't helped matters any. The king held him to blame for their continued disobedience.

Colin shook his head. "The nursemaid hired to care for young Archie ran off, so he had to find another."

Jamie paused at the top of the tower stairs and looked at his brother. "So what is it that you are obviously so eager to tell me?"

Colin smiled. "I'm surprised you haven't heard by now," he said nonchalantly. "It seems Alasdair MacGregor isn't anywhere near the Isle of Bute. He's been spotted near Loch Lomond."

Jamie frowned. "How can you be sure it's him?"

"The MacLaren chief wrote Argyll and asked for help in

defending his lands against repeated assaults—he swears it is none other than Alasdair MacGregor who has been attacking his people. There have been numerous incidents on the road near Stirling, and 'tis rumored MacGregor has returned to the Braes of Balquhidder."

It would make sense, Jamie thought. It wasn't the first time MacGregor had sought to make his home on the MacLaren's lands. But it had seemed too obvious. Jamie had been sure MacGregor had gone to Bute, but he felt a surge of relief. For Caitrina and her family's sake, he was glad to be wrong.

He wasn't the only one. Colin took obvious delight in having Jamie proved in error. His brother resented Jamie's place at Argyll's side, a place that he believed belonged to him by birthright.

"So it seems your journey to Ascog was a waste of time," Colin added, conveniently forgetting that it was he who'd urged Argyll to send troops to Ascog without waiting for proof of Lamont's complicity. Having crossed the *barmkin,* they walked up the forestairs to the keep. "How did you find the Lamont's daughter? As beautiful as they say?"

Jamie stiffened, knowing what delight his brother would take in knowing the truth—that he'd asked the lass to marry him and been harshly refused. "Fair enough," he said, and then, switching the subject, "I'll leave tomorrow morning."

"You don't want to wait for our cousin to arrive?"

Jamie shook his head. "Not while the trail is hot. I'll leave him a note."

As they entered the tower and passed through into the great hall, Jamie looked around, right away noticing the subdued atmosphere. Ever since Colin's wife had died a few years ago in childbirth, the place had felt like a tomb. Though Jamie could smell the peat, the air was cold and damp. Only a few candelabras had been lit, and there was little sign of life about the place. With Lizzie's arrival, he'd expected to see her feminine touches livening up the place a bit. He frowned, noticing something else. Lizzie was usually the first person to greet him. "Where's Lizzie?"

Colin frowned. "At Castle Campbell. Where else would she be?"

Jamie felt a flicker of unease. He shook his head. "She wrote me a few days before I left that she was coming here." He met his brother's gaze, neither wanting to give voice to their thoughts. "She should be here by now."

Colin's face hardened with anger. "He wouldn't dare."

"There is not much that Alasdair MacGregor would not dare," Jamie said grimly. "He is a man with nothing to lose." He turned, striding for the door he'd just entered, not wanting to delay another minute.

Colin cursed and followed after him. "I'll go with you."

"No," Jamie said, his thoughts already on the journey before him. "You must be here when Argyll arrives. I'll go. But I will need men. Even now, mine are on their way back to Bute."

Colin looked as if he might argue but seemed to realize someone would have to stay and explain things to Argyll and nothing would turn Jamie from his course. "Take whomever you need. I'll have Dougal ready the provisions."

Jamie was already halfway down the stairs when his brother called after him. "And Jamie . . ." He turned. "Bring me his damn head on a pike."

Colin had always been the bloodthirsty one, but for once Jamie was in perfect accord. "If MacGregor has touched one hair on Lizzie's head, you can be sure of it."

Shaken by her argument with Jamie and the events that precipitated it, Caitrina took her time in returning to the castle. But when she entered the great hall and caught her father's questioning gaze as he spoke with a few other chiefs, she knew right away that her wish had been granted: Jamie Campbell was gone.

Just like that. As if what had happened between them had never occurred.

She felt a jolt of something akin to panic as she fought to stem the unwelcome tide of emotion. This was what she'd wanted. It was only the shock of him leaving so quickly—on the heels of such a cataclysmic event—that made her feel such an overwhelming sense of loss.

She'd dreaded the explanation to her father, but he'd accepted her decision to refuse without question. He wrapped her in his arms and placed a kiss atop her head, telling her that she must do whatever made her happy.

But she was anything but happy. The guests who had descended on Ascog for the gathering had departed, but rather than the sense of peace she'd expected, it felt unnaturally quiet—like the calm before the storm. Her father seemed distracted—almost worried—by something, and her brothers were no better. They were hiding something from her, but she knew they would never share it, and she resented being kept in the dark.

But what bothered her most was that since Jamie's abrupt departure, she couldn't seem to get him—or their passionate interlude—out of her mind. In his arms she'd felt safe and protected, and when he'd kissed her she'd felt a connection unlike anything she'd ever experienced before.

Worse, she realized that she'd acted unfairly. He'd come to her rescue not once, but twice. She shivered. If he hadn't come along when he had, who knows what MacNeil might have done?

She still couldn't conceive of marrying a Campbell, but there was no question that she'd welcomed his kiss. And more. Yet she'd lashed out, accusing him of seducing her, when she knew deep in her heart that he'd done nothing of the sort. It was just that she'd been angry at him for making her want something she shouldn't.

For pity's sake, he was the Campbell Henchman. The favored cousin of her clan's most hated enemy. Just because he was handsome and strong, commanding and intelligent, and nothing like the monster she imagined didn't change the facts—not all the rumors could be wrong. He claimed to want justice, to see order restored to the Highlands, but wasn't that just a convenient excuse to justify his actions?

Caitrina never doubted that despite her undeniable attraction to the scourge, she was right in refusing him. That is, until the morning three days after he'd gone, when she found Mor upstairs in the tower garret, sobbing at the bedside of a young serving girl.

"Mor, I—" Caitrina stopped. She took one look at the poor girl's beaten face and had to bring her hand to her mouth to stifle a cry. The girl's face was swollen beyond recognition and covered with welts and cuts where she'd been struck. Dark bruises mottled her freckled skin. She'd lost her kertch, and her long red hair was clumped with twigs and mud. The sleeve of the sark that she wore under her *arisaidh* had been nearly torn off. "Dear God, what has happened?"

Mor's voice was thick with tears. "She was attacked in the woods on the way to the village of Rothesay to buy some cloth."

Caitrina was dumbstruck. "But who would do such a thing?"

Her old nurse shook her head. "She didn't recognize them. But from her description, they've the sound of broken men."

"On Bute?" Caitrina asked, shocked.

Mor gave her an odd look. "There are outlaws everywhere, child. We've been more fortunate than most, but no place is immune."

You are a cosseted girl who lives in a glass castle. Jamie's words came back to her with growing horror.

Mor wiped the girl's brow with a damp piece of cloth, but the light touch made the girl jerk with pain. The sound she made brought the sting of tears to Caitrina's eyes.

It seemed the world that Jamie had warned her about had just made its brutal appearance. His objective to clear the Highlands of outlaws no longer rang so false. Dear God, what else had she been wrong about?

Chapter 8

❖ ❖ ❖

The vicious attack on the serving girl Mary brought the problem of rampant lawlessness in the Highlands home to Caitrina in full force. The sanctity of Ascog had been violated, and never again would she feel completely safe and secure. It seemed that in the space of a few hours, her world had shifted. Outlaws were no longer an amorphous problem; they were a very real threat.

Caitrina had never seen her father so angry. He took the attack on one of his clan as a personal offense and immediately dispatched a team of warriors to track the outlaws; but his men returned the next day, unable to find any sign of them. For the first time, he forbade Caitrina from going into the woods near the castle without an escort.

Jamie's warning haunted her. That his prediction had come true so quickly made her wonder whether he knew more than he had let on. It also made her question her judgment of him. He saw himself as a force of law and order and claimed to be trying to rid the Highlands of outlaws. For the first time, she realized there might be a need for such authority.

Argyll was the devil and clan Campbell his spawn, but was the truth perhaps more complicated than that? Had she judged Jamie Campbell too harshly? Had she wrongly accused him of brutality when he was only trying to bring order to the land? She'd seen him simply as a Campbell and closed her eyes to what was before her, choosing to listen to rumor instead. He was a hard man and a fierce warrior, but never once had she seen any signs of cruelty or unfairness.

But what did it matter? After what she'd said to him, she doubted she would ever see him again. The realization filled her with a deep sense of regret and a dull ache in her chest that would not quiet.

Finally, a few days after the attack, Caitrina realized that she had to do something. Her father had urged her to consider Jamie Campbell's offer, and she intended to find out why. Not for her clan, but for herself—though she realized it might be too late.

She'd just entered the great hall in search of her father when she heard the cry go out to drop the yett. Her blood ran cold. Closing the gate in the middle of the day could mean only one thing: trouble.

Heart pounding, she raced to the window in the great hall just in time to see the guard who was manning the gate tumble over the curtain wall, an arrow protruding from his back. She didn't need to look down to know that attackers were already inside. Another guard attempted to lower the yett but took a hagbut shot in the stomach for his efforts.

Chaos reigned as her clansmen fought to take control against the surprise attack. She froze at the window in horror, watching helplessly as a considerable force of men—numbering at least a few score—stormed through the gate and swarmed the *barmkin*. They'd obviously come prepared for battle; the steel from their helmets and mail gleamed in the sunlight. They carried swords, but a good number were armed with guns as well. This was no ragged band of marauding outlaws, she realized. These were well-outfitted soldiers, which perhaps explained how they'd virtually walked right in. They did not wear the regalia of the king's guard, leaving only one possibility—her heart dropped—Argyll.

A sick feeling twisted low in her stomach as she picked through the crowd of armored men near the front, looking

for one in particular. *Please, not him.* She was able to identify the leader right away by the way he was issuing orders,
and she breathed an uneasy sigh of relief. The man wasn't
tall or broad enough to be Jamie.

The fighting was over before it really started. There was
nothing her father's men could do. Once the soldiers had
breached the gate, the battle was already won. To Caitrina's great relief, she realized that the invaders didn't appear intent on attack but seemed to be looking for something. They'd obviously come with a purpose.

What did they want? And where were her father and
brothers?

Her gaze swept the courtyard. There. At the far side of
the yard, just coming into view, her father and a score of
his guardsmen, including Malcolm and Niall, were rushing
from the armory. They'd not had time to properly outfit
themselves for battle, wearing the leather jerks and plaids
they wore for practice rather than mail or cotuns, but at
least they'd taken the time to put on steel knapscalls to protect their heads. And they appeared to be well armed.

She heard her father's voice ring out in anger as he confronted the Campbell leader. The two men argued back
and forth, but it was difficult to hear what they were saying. At one point, she heard the Campbell say clearly: "We
know he's here. Tell us where he is or suffer the consequences."

Who were they talking about?

The Campbell pointed up to the tower and said something, turning his face toward hers. Her brows drew together. It was strange. He seemed familiar somehow.
Whatever he said, however, had enraged her father, and his
guardsmen clasped their claymores threateningly behind
him.

Her pulse raced, knowing that the situation was deterio-
rating fast.

The commotion must have alerted the castle servants

that something was wrong. The great hall started to fill with people, and thankfully, Mor, ever the voice of reason, appeared to stem the rising panic.

Like a veteran general, the old nursemaid started issuing orders. "Hurry," she said to a few young kitchen maids. "Run to the kitchens and bring up the wood used for cooking and the oil for the lamps." To another she said, "Bring me all the linen you can find."

Caitrina's chest clamped, knowing exactly what Mor intended. It was something her father had drummed into Caitrina's head countless times: If they were ever under attack and the gate was breached, set fire to the stairs.

No! The reaction was visceral. Father, Malcolm, and Niall were out there. She ran up to Mor and clutched her arm. "Stop. We can't do it. They will have nowhere to go."

Mor took her by the shoulders and gave her a hard shake. "Your father and brothers can take care of themselves. They can flee into the hills and hide in the caves if necessary. But they will never leave if you are not safe."

She shook her head. She couldn't do it. "But—"

"They are doing their job, Caitrina. You must do yours." She lowered her voice to a whisper and with her eyes indicated someone across the room. "Think of the lad."

Brian.

She sucked in her breath, looking around frantically, and found him emerging from the tower stairwell, holding an enormous sword that her father kept in the laird's solar. It would have been funny if it wasn't so terrifying. He darted across the room toward the door. Guessing what he was about, Caitrina shot after him and caught him by the arm. "Stop, Brian, you can't go out there."

He tried to pull away. "Let go of me, Caiti."

He looked far older than his two and ten years. She read his mulish expression and thought quickly, knowing his young man's pride was at stake. "We need you in here. If you leave, there will be no one to protect us."

His gaze swept the room behind her, seeing the dozen or so frightened women and children. At this time of day, most of the men were busy outside, practicing their battle skills. Those who weren't fighters fished in the loch, tended to the livestock, or cut peat.

"Please," she begged.

He nodded, and Caitrina wrapped her arms around him, hugging him tight in gratitude and relief. The serving girls had returned with the wood, cloth, and oil, and for the next few minutes they were kept busy wrapping the oil-soaked cloth around the wood like torches.

Brian had positioned himself near the doorway, keeping vigilant watch on what was happening outside and readying the stairs by dismantling the rope and nailed-in pieces of wood that kept them in position. It had been necessary to open the door, but as soon as the stairs were loose, they would set fire to them and bar the door. Caitrina could see he was having trouble. Time and age had rusted the iron, making the nails difficult to remove, and the knots in the rope were so tight, they could not be worked loose. It had been a long time since such drastic measures had been necessary, and never in her lifetime.

She moved to the door, intent on helping him, when she heard Brian cry out, "No!"

A shot fired, and mayhem erupted outside with a giant uproar. Brian lurched forward through the doorway, and Caitrina lunged after him, grabbing his arm to prevent him from running down the stairs.

"Brian—" Her words died when she saw what had provoked his reaction. A strangled cry rose in her throat. "Father!" Stunned, she watched in horror as her father clutched his chest, blood turning his hands crimson. He staggered and then fell back into Malcolm's arms—his eyes open but unseeing.

She couldn't breathe. Couldn't think. Pain gripped her chest, and hot tears sprang to her eyes. This couldn't be happening. But the faces of the clansmen told her it was. Shock had turned to rage. Led by Malcolm and Niall, they went berserker, attacking with a ferocity that proved what she'd seen was true: Her father was dead.

It was only the instinct to protect Brian that wrenched her from her trance. He was struggling to break free, but she wouldn't let go. Mor must have seen what had happened because she suddenly appeared at Caitrina's side and helped her pull Brian back safely inside.

"Let go of me," he cried. "I must go to him."

The anguish in his voice mirrored her own. She grabbed him by the face and forced him to look at her. "There is nothing we can do for him now, Brian." Her chest twisted. The truth was almost too much to bear, but she needed to be strong for Brian. *Don't think.* "We need you. We have to set fire to the stairs."

His eyes were bright and wild; she didn't know whether she'd gotten through to him until he nodded.

Mor had already started to instruct the girls on where to place the lit torches; they didn't have any more time to waste. It seemed to take forever, though it was only a few moments before everything was in place and the torches were lit. They stood by the door, watching and praying for the wood to flame. The torches burned, but the stairs only smoldered and smoked.

Mor cursed behind her. " 'Tis the wet weather the past few days," she said. "The wood has not dried out enough."

Caitrina could hear the shouts from below and knew that their effort had not gone unnoticed. Nor had she. She felt the eyes of their leader on her but ignored the chill of foreboding. A few of the attackers started to work their way up the stairs, her father's men doing everything they could to prevent them. Knowing there was nothing more they could do but pray the stairs burned quickly, she closed the door and lowered the bar.

Caitrina didn't need to look at the frightened faces

around her to know what they all were feeling—it was what she felt: absolute terror and disbelief.

Mor grabbed her by the shoulders. "Take your brother upstairs and hide in the ambry. No matter what you hear, do not come out."

"But what about you and the others?"

"We must separate." She paused. "It's not servants they want."

"Who do they want?" Caitrina asked, recalling the Campbell's words to her father.

Mor gave her a kiss on the forehead. "I don't know, child. Now go." To Brian she said, "Take care of your sister."

He nodded grimly, his expression hard and determined beyond his years. Her sweet young brother would never be the same. Neither of them would ever be the same.

Caitrina hesitated and then threw her arms around the old woman, resting her cheek one more time against the familiar shoulder. Mor gave her one last squeeze before gently urging her away. Caitrina took Brian's hand, and together they ran across the great hall toward the stairs. She had to force herself not to look out the windows. All they could do at this point was pray that her father's men would prevail—that strength of heart would defeat strength in numbers.

When they reached her solar, Caitrina hurried to the ambry and threw open the doors. She groaned.

"We'll never both fit in there," Brian said, echoing her thoughts.

The ambry was stuffed full with gowns. If they tried to remove them, it would only make their hiding place more obvious—though at this point, Caitrina realized there wasn't much they could do to prevent discovery. She fought against the rising panic, but the desperate nature of their situation was making it difficult to think. What could they do? Ascog Castle was not a particularly large or complex castle; there were few places to hide.

The sound of an ax striking the door below made the hair at the back of her neck stand up. They were out of time . . . and options.

Brian pushed her toward the ambry. "You hide in there, I'll go under the bed."

There was no time to argue—nor was there a better choice. She nodded and climbed in. If the soldiers were already trying to come through the door, that meant . . .

No. She forced her thoughts away from the battle below. She wouldn't let herself think about Malcolm and Niall. She had to close her eyes to fight back the tears. *They had to be all right.*

Time crawled forward. It was warm and dark in the ambry buried between all the heavy wool and velvet gowns. All of her senses seemed heightened, homing in on the sounds below. Every small noise made her heart skip. Her heart drummed unnaturally loud in her ears.

The waiting was interminable, though it was probably only a few minutes before she heard the unmistakable sounds of men clambering up the stairs.

"Find the lass!" a man shouted.

Me. Merciful Mary, they mean me.

The door to her solar opened with a bang, and she held her breath. The helplessness of their situation, the futility in trying to hide, came rushing forward in full fury. How long would it take before they found—

"Let go of me!"

Her heart lurched. *Brian. Dear God, they had Brian.*

"What have we here?" a man said. "The Lamont's whelp, I'd wager? What's left of them anyhow."

Caitrina stifled a cry, her nails digging into her palms. *It can't be true.*

"The lass has to be around here close," another man said.

The sound of Brian's struggles as he tried to distract the men from finding her was more than she could take. She pushed through the smothering stacks of hanging gowns and burst through the ambry door. All she could see was the wide backs of two mail-clad warriors, one of whom had Brian by the neck.

"Let him go," she yelled, jumping on his back and hitting him hard enough on the temple so that he cried out in pain and dropped Brian.

She would have wrapped her arm around his neck, but she found herself yanked from him and clasped in the steely embrace of a tall, heavyset man. In her haste to reach Brian she hadn't noticed that there was a third man in the room.

His face was red, puffy, and sweaty below the rim of his helmet. "I found the lass," he shouted in the direction of the doorway.

"Let go of me!" She tried to wrestle free.

His hand tightened around her arm until she thought it might break. He gave her a lecherous once-over and smiled. The look in his eyes chilled her to the bone. It was the look of a man intent on reaping the spoils of victory. "Not yet," he said.

Out of the corner of her eye, she saw a movement. "Brian, no!" But it was too late.

"Get your filthy hands off my sister!"

Brian had somehow managed to slide the claymore from under the bed and came rushing toward the man holding her. But the weapon was too heavy for him to maneuver, and he managed only a few steps before one of the other men caught up with him from behind. Time seemed to stand still. She saw the silvery flash of the blade as it descended toward her brother's head. She lurched forward with a sudden burst of strength, but she wasn't able to tear herself from the man's arms.

Brian's eyes, wide with shock, met hers as the force of the

blow temporarily stunned him, before he crumpled to the floor like a rag doll. The cry that tore from her lungs was surely not her own. She went mad with rage, lashing out at the man holding her and managing to rake her nails across his face before he backhanded her across the cheek with such force that she stumbled to the floor. Her jaw exploded in pain.

"What's going on here?"

The man she'd seen before, the one she'd assumed to be their leader, stood in the doorway.

"We found the Lamont lass," one of his men said.

His eyes fastened on her. "So I see."

Tears were streaming down her cheeks as she rose to her feet, cradling her injured face, but her eyes reflected her hatred for this man who had brought death and destruction to her home. "What kind of *man* makes war on women and children? Only a Campbell would have so little honor."

"Proud as well as beautiful? You have spirit, lass, but use it wisely. Tell us where he is and no one else needs to get hurt."

She looked over at her brother's still form, blood streaming down his face from the gash on his head. As if he knew her thoughts, the leader crossed the room and stepped between her and Brian, preventing her from going to him. "Who?" she croaked, her voice raw. "Who is it that you seek?"

"Alasdair MacGregor."

She gasped. *My God, this was all some horrible mistake.* She shook her head. "You have come to the wrong place. Alasdair MacGregor is not at Ascog."

The man's expression turned hard and unforgiving. For a moment, he reminded her of Jamie, but this man had a cruel edge that Jamie did not possess. "It is you who are wrong. MacGregor was seen in the area with your father yesterday, and he's likely been hiding here for weeks."

That was impossible. Her father wouldn't be so bold—or foolish—in defiance of the king. Harboring MacGregors could get you . . . killed. But then she remembered the bond between the clans. Her chest squeezed with pain. "You lie."

His mouth tightened. "And you test my patience. Tell me where he is and I may be persuaded to let you go." His eyes slid down the length of her. "Before or after I let my men have some fun with you. It's your choice."

She refused to show him her fear, though it wrapped around her like an icy noose. "I cannot tell you what I do not know."

He gave her a long look and shrugged. "Then you are of no use to me." He turned to one of the men. "Get rid of the lad."

"Brian!" She tried to go to him but was restrained by the man who'd struck her earlier. Instead, she watched helplessly as Brian was dragged unconscious from the room.

The leader's eyes were on the trunk at the foot of her bed where she'd carefully folded the plaid that Jamie had lent her the day he'd rescued her from the tree—which she'd neglected to return to him. He gave her a calculated stare and seemed about to say something, but then an odd look came over his face. "Find out what she knows," he said instead to the man holding her, "but be quick about it. The place is already on fire. If MacGregor is in the castle, we'll smoke him out."

Her father. Her brothers. Her home. This man had taken everything from her for nothing. Something inside her snapped. With her hand balled into a tight fist, she took aim at his face and hit him with all the hatred and anger burgeoning inside. She'd never hit anyone before, but her punch landed squarely on his nose and she heard the satisfying crunch of bone. His head jerked back with the blow. When he looked back at her, blood gushed from his nose.

There was a moment of stunned disbelief, before retaliation came hard and swift. His hand met her temple. A burst of pain, and then everything went black.

Caitrina couldn't breathe. She was dreaming of a man on top of her, the heavy weight of mail crushing her chest. The stench of sweat and blood filled her nose, and bile rose in the back of her throat. She groaned and struggled against the weight crushing her. Rough hands gripped the tender skin of her thighs, trying to pry open her legs.

It wasn't a dream. Her eyes fluttered open. A man was on top of her, one arm flat across her chest to hold her down, the other lifting up her skirts. She opened her mouth to scream, but she wasn't sure whether anything sounded before she felt another burst of pain across her cheek and her eyes closed again.

Darkness beckoned like the sweet song of a siren. She wanted to stay asleep, to escape to the safety of her dreams. But something wouldn't let her. She had to wake up. She couldn't let this happen. She had to fight.

She opened her eyes. The man's face swam before her gaze. Everything was fuzzy.

Suddenly, the weight crushing her chest was gone. She took a deep breath, wanting to fill her lungs with air, but inhaled choking smoke instead. Her body racked with coughs.

She thought she heard a man curse, but it was so difficult to hear with the ringing in her ears. She was lifted from the bed and cradled against a warm, hard chest. For a moment, she was confused; she felt safe. But then she remembered. The man started to carry her away. She flailed against him, but he held her firm, soothing her with gentle words. The voice was familiar but hovered just beyond the edges of her consciousness.

It was so hot. She opened her eyes, but they burned and filled with tears. She couldn't see through the thick smoke. She wanted to know who held her, but his features blurred.

He looked like Jamie Campbell. Her eyes fluttered again. *Jamie. It was Jamie. He's here.*

She relaxed against him, feeling a moment of elation before the sliver of a memory filtered through her consciousness: Campbells had attacked Ascog. And Jamie was a Campbell. *No.* She didn't want to believe it, but why else would he be here?

You will regret your refusal of my offer.

"You—" she choked; her throat felt stripped bare. "You did this," she cried, feeling as though her lungs were being shredded apart. "Campbells." She couldn't get the words out, she felt so horribly weak and tired. "Why?" The pain moved from her lungs to her chest, precariously close to her heart. She didn't hear his reply. The fight had left her, and she gave over to the pull of darkness.

Chapter 9

❖❖❖

Toward Castle, Cowal Peninsula, Three Months Later

A sharp wind blew across the moors, sending long strands of Caitrina's hair flying across her face as she made her way down the steep path from the castle toward the small beach. Even the sturdy heather that blanketed the countryside with its soft purple flowers was not immune and leaned with each gust. Gathering her tangled curls in her hand, she adjusted the wool plaid scarf farther over her head to better ward off the wind and cold. An autumn chill was definitely in the air. With Michaelmas behind them and winter approaching, the days—like the heather—would soon darken, turning shorter and colder.

She sighed. The changing of the seasons left her with a strange melancholy. Time passed whether she wanted it to or not. Part of her wanted to hold on to the past, afraid to sever the connection with all that she had lost. Another part, the part that remembered the loss of her mother, knew that time would lessen the sting, if not the ache.

She didn't think anything could be worse than losing her mother—how wrong she'd been.

Father, Malcolm, Niall—her heart squeezed—even her beloved Brian . . . gone. Along with so many others. She blinked back the sudden swell of tears, the pain still raw, though over three months had passed since that horrible day the Campbells had wreaked their particularly virulent brand of destruction on her clan.

In the space of one afternoon, her clan had been deci-
mated. First in battle and then in the fire that followed.
Over forty Lamont warriors had lost their lives defending
Ascog. Those who'd survived had fled into the countryside
to evade the bloodthirsty Campbells. All that remained of
her home was a burned-out stone shell. The life, the love,
and the happiness she had known there was a fading memory.

All because her father had been suspected of harboring
MacGregors.

The injustice was difficult to fathom. Most of what happened that day was lost to her, locked away in a dark place
that she dared not try to open. But sometimes, as now, the
memories would flash before her eyes in snippets. Her father's murder. The Campbell soldier's face hovering above
her. The flames.

Her brothers were said to have perished in the fire. All
she had to remember them by was her father's chieftain's
badge and a scrap of plaid she wore bound around her
wrist.

As for the other . . . Caitrina didn't think the Campbell
scourge had raped her, but she couldn't be sure. Her virgin-
ity seemed laughably unimportant after everything that
had happened.

But there was something, or rather *someone,* she remembered clearly. A bone-deep chill cut through her as it always did when she thought of Jamie Campbell.

*You will regret your refusal of my offer. One day, Cait-
rina, the brutal reality of our world will find you.*

Words that were cruelly prophetic or possibly something
more?

When she'd first realized that Campbells were attacking
Ascog, she'd wondered if Jamie were involved. It had been
a relief to discover he wasn't. She hadn't wanted to believe
he could be so cruel or that she could have given herself so

intimately to a monster. Was she a fool for not wanting to believe she could be so wrong?

But it turned out that she was wrong. He *had* been there. But why? Could he really have wrought such destruction on her clan? Had her harsh refusal of him had anything to do with the attack? If she had heeded her father's warning—done her duty to her clan—and accepted Jamie Campbell's offer, would her family still be alive? More than anything, these were the questions that haunted her.

But even if she couldn't be sure of Jamie's role in the attack on her family, it was clear his clan was responsible. If she'd hated the Campbells before, it was nothing compared with what she felt for them now. Her hatred had festered like an open wound, leaving it burning and inflamed. She vowed that they would pay for the murder of her family. It was this fierce determination to see justice done that had wrenched her from the bog of her own grief.

If it took her last breath, she would see Ascog returned to her kin. The remaining members of her clan were all she had left, and she vowed the Campbells would not profit from the blood of her family.

At last she reached the beach and picked her way across the rocky shoreline, the pebbles poking her feet through the thin leather soles of her shoes. Ignoring the cold, she stood at the edge of the water, the waves lapping at her toes, inhaling the salty tang of the sea air. She lifted her face to the icy spray, letting it wash over her as she'd done many times before. The sea drew her, as if she could find absolution in its frothy blue depths. But its cleansing power was illusory and all too fleeting. She loved the desolate and remote feeling of standing on the very tip of Cowal, looking across the blue sea to the Isle of Bute—to home.

Hearing a sound behind her, she jumped. Frayed nerves were another lasting reminder of the attack. It was only Bessie, an old washerwoman and one of the handful of servants who'd come with Caitrina from Ascog. She rushed over to her. "Here, let me help you with that, Bessie," she said, taking the basket of clothing from her. " 'Tis too heavy for you."

The old woman spread her lips into a wide grin devoid of a few teeth. "Bless you, mistress. Though Mor will have my hide if she sees you helping me again."

Mor couldn't understand why Caitrina chose to spend her days with the servants outside rather than with her aunt and cousins in the keep. But Caitrina didn't feel comfortable with her Toward kin. Her clansmen from Ascog were all the family she had left and her one connection to the past.

Caitrina gave Bessie a conspiratorial smile. "Well then, it shall have to be our secret."

The old woman chortled. "Ah, it's good to see a smile on your bonny face, mistress."

Caitrina nodded, acknowledging her kind sentiment, if not the underlying reference to her change in temperament. In the long dark days following the attack at Ascog, Caitrina hadn't been sure she would ever laugh again. Everything she once knew—her happy, carefree life as the beloved sister and daughter—was gone. Dead.

Toiling alongside Bessie for the better part of two hours, she scraped and rubbed the linen until her hands were raw from the lye in the soap. But she hardly noticed the discomfort, finding solace in the hard work. *Work.* The concept had been foreign to her a few short months ago, and now it was her saving grace.

When they'd finished with the washing, they bundled the sodden clothing in the basket and Caitrina helped Bessie carry it back up the path to the keep, where it would hang to dry.

Mor must have been watching because as soon as Caitrina entered the courtyard, her former nursemaid was there with a pack of serving girls to relieve them of their burden. Ever since the attack, Caitrina hadn't been able to blink without Mor knowing about it. Before, Caitrina would have found her hovering stifling, but now she found it oddly comforting.

She owed her so much.

It was Mor and the handful of servants left from Ascog who'd secreted the injured Caitrina into the caves while the Campbell soldiers were still scouring the hills for her father's remaining clansmen and the MacGregors. In addition to the smoke that had filled her lungs, making it difficult for her to breathe, the blows to her head had done some damage. She'd flitted in and out of consciousness for days. When she'd recovered enough to travel the short distance across the Firth of Clyde, they'd taken refuge at Toward Castle with her uncle, Sir John Lamont of Inveryne, who'd welcomed her dispossessed clansmen into his family without question.

Mor waited for the others to leave before clasping Caitrina's hands and turning them over to reveal her red palms and ragged fingertips. Her gray brows wrinkled. "Look what you've done to your beautiful hands! This must stop, Caiti Rose—"

Caitrina froze, the flash of pain nearly unbearable. *Caiti Rose.* It was what her father had called her.

Not realizing the unintentional hurt she'd inflicted, Mor continued, "It's not right, you working alongside the servants all day. I hardly recognize you." Mor's gaze traveled down the length of her. "Though you won't see fit to wear any of the gowns your aunt has generously provided, you are still the daughter of a chief. What would your father think to see you like this? A year ago, you would have used that gown as a rag."

Caitrina ignored the reference to her father and sighed; they'd had this conversation before. She glanced down at the worn plaid she wore over her plain sark and kirtle, knowing that Mor was right: She was barely recognizable from the pampered girl who'd delighted in beautiful gowns

and shoes. A few times she'd caught herself looking long-
ingly at the pretty velvets and brocades offered by her aunt,
but Caitrina just couldn't bring herself to don fancy clothes
and pretend nothing had happened. Such finery was a
painful reminder of a charmed life that no longer existed.

"A year ago, many things were different."

Mor gave her a sad look. "I know, lass. I would give anything to be able to ease your suffering. But it might help if
you talked about it."

Caitrina stiffened. *No, it wouldn't.* Keeping a tight rein
on her emotions was all that kept her on her feet. "There is
nothing to talk about," she said firmly. "Nothing will bring
them back. I just do not want to be a burden on my aunt
and uncle." What wealth she had left was in their lands—
lands that were now in the hands of Argyll. As if he hadn't
taken everything from her already. But that would change.

"They don't see you as such."

"Which only makes it worse. I'll not take advantage of
their kindness, they've done so much for us already."

Mor paused and gave her a long look. "You'll not be
able to hide here forever, Caiti. Eventually, someone must
know that you survived."

Her pulse quickened with a flash of fear. She knew her
uncle couldn't keep her hidden forever. He'd questioned
her more than once about why it was so important that he
not let it be known where she was. But how could she explain that she feared the man who'd been responsible for
her clan's destruction might not be done? Though it had
been difficult communicating with any other survivors of
the attack, it was said Jamie Campbell had been like a man
possessed after the attack, searching for her.

She looked up at Toward Castle, the thick stone walls of
the rectangular keep so reminiscent of Ascog, and felt the
grip of panic—as if the walls were closing in. She couldn't
breathe. Spinning around, she headed back to the sea.

"Where are you going?" Mor asked, her voice laden with worry.

To the only place she felt safe. "I'll be back before the midday meal," Caitrina said. "I've something I must do."

He'd waited long enough.

Jamie Campbell approached Toward Castle, knowing that months of effort and restraint would finally be rewarded. He did not deceive himself as to what Caitrina's reaction would be; he'd seen the horror on her face when he'd carried her from that fiery hell and knew what she thought. He'd had nothing to do with the attack on her family—though the same could not be said of his clan. Damn his quick-tempered brother to hell. But she'd disappeared before he'd had a chance to explain.

It turned out he'd been right in his suspicions after all. Two days after Jamie had left for Castle Campbell to check on Lizzie, one of his guardsmen stationed on Bute had arrived at Dunoon with the proof they'd been waiting for: Alasdair MacGregor and his men had been spotted in the forest near Ascog. Jamie's men had followed but had lost them in the hills.

Colin had seen his opportunity to further himself in the eyes of their cousin and decided not to send for Jamie but to take matters into his own hands and lead the mission himself. If only Jamie had found the MacGregors initially, this all could have been avoided.

Thankfully, Jamie's loyal guardsman had decided to track him down at Castle Campbell near Stirling. Lizzie had indeed been attacked on her way to Dunoon but had been rescued by some Murrays. Jamie had just finished ensuring Lizzie's protection by ordering the hiring of extra guardsmen for Castle Campbell, where she would be safe until the MacGregors were controlled, when his man arrived. Immediately guessing what might happen with his hotheaded brother eager to impress their cousin, Jamie rode at breakneck speed for Ascog. Alas, by the time he'd arrived, the battle was well under way.

He'd carried Caitrina from the burning keep and ensured her safety before he'd gone to help bring the battle and fire under control, in an attempt to salvage what he could of the black day. But by the time he returned, she was gone—spirited away by her loyal clansmen, leaving him no opportunity to explain.

Aye, there would be difficulties ahead, not least of which was his brother's role in the death of her family, but he was determined to see this through.

Still, he was anxious. He'd been searching for her for a long time. He'd scoured the hills around Ascog for weeks after the attack, to no avail. It was as if she'd disappeared off the face of the earth. But he'd known that she'd survived and had refused to give up.

Of course, he'd thought to look for her at Toward Castle, but her uncle had adamantly denied knowledge of her whereabouts until faced with proof he couldn't ignore, courtesy of the spies Jamie had thought to keep watch on the place. But negotiations with the Lamont of Toward had dragged on for too long, and Jamie's patience was at an end.

The short ten-mile ride from Dunoon seemed interminable.

Horse and man crested the brae of Buachailean, the hill that lay just north of the castle. Reining in his mount, he paused, appraising the castle and surrounding area before riding in alone. He was expected, but it never hurt to be cautious.

Nothing appeared out of the ordinary. A group of fishermen were returning a skiff to the docks, sheep were grazing on the hills, a group of young lads were playing shinty on the moors, villagers passed back and forth through the castle gates unheeded. A solitary serving woman wandered along the beach, collecting shells.

His gaze snapped back to the woman, catching a glimpse of long strands of black curls tossed around her face by the wind. His heart hammered in his chest. Squinting into the bright sunlight, he was unable to make out her features from this distance, but deep in his gut he knew who it was.

The lass was no serving woman.

Jamie's long wait was over. He'd found Caitrina Lamont.

Caitrina lifted two corners of her wool *arisaidh* together, forming a makeshift basket out of the wool, and placed another shell in the fold. Perhaps she'd make a necklace for Una? The little girl loved to pretend that she was one of the *Maighdean na Tuinne*. Caitrina had long stopped believing in mermaids, but watching Una lightened her heart. She admired the child's ability to laugh and play, even though it was clear that Una—like the rest of her clan who'd come with her to Toward—desperately missed her home.

Caitrina sighed, knowing Mor was right. She couldn't hide forever. As much as Toward had become her refuge, it had also become a place to hide. She needed to find a way to return Ascog to her clan, and she couldn't do that by remaining at Toward Castle with her kin.

For a young woman without resources, there was only one thing she could do: She must find a powerful husband to help her win back her home.

A wistful smile played upon her lips. Strange that she could think of marriage without a flicker of emotion, when only a few months ago the very mention of finding a husband had roused such fervent response. She'd avoided marriage because she couldn't imagine leaving her family. She'd just never expected them to leave her. Her chest squeezed and she closed her eyes for a minute, taking a steadying breath.

Her throat thickened as she knelt in the sand, cradling the shells in her lap, and began to dig. When she'd made a small hole about a foot deep, she carefully unbound the swatch of plaid from around her wrist. The muted browns and oranges were faded and the edges frayed, but the plaid was unmistakably that of her father's *breacan feile*. Her chest tightened as she slid her fingers over the soft wool plaid and then brought it to her cheek.

A few days after the attack, while Caitrina was still unconscious, a few of the servants had snuck back to see what remained of the castle and to see to the burying of the dead. The fire had made it unnecessary. In the ashes, they'd found a few items that had escaped the Campbells, including the badge and scrap of plaid.

No longer able to hold back the tears, she folded the fabric in a neat square and set it at the bottom of the hole, then covered it with sand. It was the burial denied her by the fire, her injuries, and the need to seek safety. For the first time since she'd recovered and realized that her family had been killed, the emotion poured out of her and she gave over to the powerful storm of grief.

When the deluge abated, she dried her eyes and, cradling the shells against her, rose to her feet, feeling oddly stronger. The life she'd had before was gone forever; it was time to look to the future—one that she would rebuild for her clan. They were her responsibility. And she'd be damned if she'd let the Campbells win. One way or another, justice would be done.

Hearing the muffled sound of hooves in the sand, she looked up to see a man approaching. At first she thought it was one of her uncle's guardsmen and lifted her hand in greeting.

She tilted her head. There was something familiar . . .

The blood drained from her face, and the carefully gathered shells scattered at her feet, forgotten.

No.

But it was him. She recognized the broad shoulders, the dark brown hair laced with strands of red gold, the hard, fiercely handsome face, and the cool, slate blue eyes that gazed at her with such intensity. The wide mouth she'd kissed with such hunger. And there was that air of confident command that she'd never seen replicated in another man—of absolute power and authority.

Jamie Campbell had found her.

The ache in her chest was unbearable as memories of the attack and the pleasure they had shared collided. Touching him. Tasting him. The intimacy of the moment when she'd shattered in his arms.

And his retribution for refusing him.

She'd known the kind of man he was but had been foolish enough to succumb to his masculine allure. Even now, when she should feel nothing but revulsion, she felt an unmistakable pull.

It hurt to look at him. How could something so beautiful be so black? Could she really have thought he was anything but a cold, ruthless enforcer?

Their eyes met. Emotion cut through her like a jagged knife as she gazed into the piercing blue eyes of the man who'd destroyed everything she'd loved.

The memories came back to her in pieces. His face. The fire.

Unconsciously, she took a step back. Her voice shook with emotion. "Stay away from me."

The look on Caitrina's face cut Jamie to the quick. He'd wanted to see her so badly, and here she was, finally, but with fear in her eyes. After months of searching for her, of wanting to make sure she was safe and protected, it was a surprisingly sharp blow. He hated that she would think the worst of him, though what else should he have expected? It would be too much to hope that she'd remember his part in her rescue and in putting an end to the battle.

After sliding from his mount, he approached her cautiously. "I mean you no harm, lass."

She shrank back, and it felt as if he'd been socked in the stomach.

"God, how can you say that?" she cried. "After what you've done?" She put her hand up as if to stop him and took another step back. "Stay away from me. D-Don't come any closer."

He halted, but he was close enough to see her tearstained face and the other transformations wrought by tragedy. She looked wan and tired and much thinner than he remembered. Her luminous eyes seemed to dominate her face, but there was a hard edge to her gaze that hadn't been there before—of wariness and distrust. The spirited, brazen girl who'd challenged him without thought was gone, and in her place was a forlorn young woman of heart-wrenching fragility.

He ached to hold her in his arms and wipe away the hurt, feeling an overwhelming urge to protect her and ensure that nothing ever harmed her again.

"I only wish to speak with you," he said gently. "Nothing more."

"How can you think I'd ever want to lay eyes upon you, let alone speak with you again?"

He looked into her eyes. "I had nothing to do with what happened to your clan, Caitrina. That is why I am here: to explain."

"You were *there*." She emphasized the last word with damning finality. "I saw you. Do you deny it?"

He shook his head. "Nay. I came as soon as I could, hoping to prevent a battle. But I was too late."

"You expect me to believe that?" she said, scorn dripping from her voice.

Her anger was a relief. She was undeniably fragile, but not broken. He hoped like hell that he would never have to see fear in her eyes again.

"After what you said when you left?" she continued.

"Should I believe it wasn't a threat when you told me I would regret refusing you? You told me I knew nothing of the real world and that one day it would find me."

The tears that rolled down her cheeks ate like acid in his chest. She looked up at him, her eyes sparkling in the sunlight, and he caught a glimpse of the strength that still burned inside her.

"Well, you were right, I know now that the world is a cruel place. You've made your point brutally clear, now leave me be."

Her accusations rang with more truth than he wanted to acknowledge. He *had* wanted her disillusioned, to see his side—but not like this. "I spoke out of anger," he said, taking a tentative step closer. God, he could smell her. The sweet flowery scent made him yearn to bury his head in her neck and hair. The urge to touch her was overwhelming. He took a deep, controlling breath. Right now he needed to make her understand. "I'm sorry for your loss, lass. You must believe that I had nothing to do with the attack on your clan."

Slowly, he reached down and put his hand on her cheek, bracing for her rejection, more relieved than he could imagine when she didn't flinch away from his touch. He wiped the tears from her face with his thumb, savoring the touch of her baby soft skin. Her mouth trembled and he ached to taste her, to wipe away her confusion with his kiss. He tilted her chin with his fingers, forcing her to meet his gaze. "I would never hurt you."

For a moment, it looked as though she wanted to believe him, but her eyes hardened and she turned her face from his hand. "So the timing was just a coincidence? You had nothing to do with the attack? You knew nothing of the charge leveled against my father that he was harboring the MacGregors?"

He hesitated. "I did not order the attack on your clan."

"And as to the other? That Argyll believed my father was giving aid to the MacGregors? You had nothing to do with that as well?"

He held her stare, not shying from the truth.

She gasped. "You did know." He watched her work it out in her mind. "You didn't come to Ascog for the gathering or to woo me, you came to spy on my father." She gazed at him accusingly, eyes wide with hurt. "God, you used me."

"No," he said roughly, his arms flexed rigidly at his side. Every instinct clamored to take her into his embrace and force her to understand, force her to deny what crackled like wildfire between them. Even with the waves crashing and the wind snapping all around them, he was aware of nothing but her. "My mission was to find proof that the MacGregors were at Ascog, but what happened between us had nothing to do with Alasdair MacGregor."

Her eyes scanned his face. "Why should I believe you? Why would I believe anything you say?"

He held her gaze. "Because it's the truth." He studied her face, wondering how much she remembered of what had happened. He tensed, thinking of the soldier. He'd never forget the feeling when he'd seen her unconscious, her face bruised, blood running down her pale temple, and one of his brother's men trying to force himself between her legs. If he'd been a few minutes later . . . The primal explosion of rage had been unlike anything he'd ever experienced. He'd wrapped his arm around the bastard's neck and broken it with one satisfying snap. Jamie didn't regret the loss of life, only how quickly the scourge had found it. If she did not remember, he would not be the one to remind her. "You were in and out of consciousness. Do you remember nothing of what happened?"

Confusion clouded her gaze. "A little."

He probed carefully, not wanting to cause more pain by

dredging up memories of the soldier. "I carried you from the tower. It was burning. There was smoke everywhere."

She started—as if she'd suddenly remembered.

"I wasn't there to hurt you, Caitrina."

Their eyes met, and something passed between them—something significant and for a moment heart-stopping.

She believed him.

But it wasn't enough.

"Even if what you say is true, it was your clan who attacked my home and murdered my family."

Jamie dragged his fingers through his hair. He dared not point out that it was worse than that—that the man who'd led the attack was his brother.

He dreaded this conversation, but it must be had. "Your father refused to comply with repeated requests to give over the MacGregor."

"How could he when he didn't know where the MacGregor was?"

Jamie drew a long breath. "Aye, lass, he did."

Her eyes blazed with anger. "You lie! The soldiers tried to say the same. How dare you spread falsehoods about my father to justify the actions of a bloodthirsty tyrant!"

Jamie clenched his jaw, not about to defend his cousin's actions to her—not when she was of no mind to listen. Jamie did not blind himself to his cousin's faults. Argyll could be ruthless in doing what needed to be done—then again, much the same could be said about Jamie. But his cousin was the best hope for the Highlands against a king who sought to marginalize his "barbarian" subjects.

The king wanted the lawlessness in the Highlands curtailed, and Argyll was one of the few Highlanders with the power to see it done. If Argyll didn't, it would be Lowlanders who did. The old ways of the clan chief's authority were fading. Troublesome clans like the MacGregors only succeeded in making the rest of the Highlanders look like barbarians and made the king's policies harsher. One day, Jamie hoped he could make her see that.

"We found proof that your father had been protecting outlaws by giving them food and shelter."

The blood drained from her face. "No. My father wouldn't do that. He would have told me."

"Would he?" Jamie watched her as she grappled with the implications. "Did he take you so much in his confidences, then?" She flinched, and Jamie knew he'd hit upon a tender spot. "Surely you know the bond between the MacGregors and the Lamonts—the old tale of hospitality." Her eyes shot to his. *She did.* "You noticed nothing amiss in the weeks before the games?"

She shook her head furiously, but then uncertainty eroded her adamancy. He had shaken her with his pronouncements, but her pride was fierce. She didn't want to see gray where there was black and white. "I don't believe you. You'll say anything to defend your clan."

He hated having to hurt her, but he could not let this stand between them. His brother had been overzealous, but Campbells would not shoulder all the blame for what had happened. "I regret their deaths, and might have been able to prevent them had I been there," he said. "But your father was not without blame. He chose to fight rather than produce the rebels. This is the Highlands, lass, he knew the consequences of his defiance. He knew that blood would be shed."

At that moment, she hated him. Caitrina wanted to close her eyes and cover her ears so she wouldn't have to listen to his Campbell lies.

But deep in her gut, she knew he spoke the truth about the MacGregors. She thought back to that week before the gathering, thought of her father's odd behavior, and it made horrible sense. She knew her father—he was honorable to the core. He would not refuse to give them shelter.

He couldn't. But, dear God, to take such risk when everyone knew the lengths Argyll would go to see the MacGregors destroyed.

But no matter. She straightened her spine. It did not justify what had happened. "So my father's death and those of my brothers and clansmen were justified? Merely a minor inconvenience in Argyll's witch hunt for Alasdair MacGregor?"

"It was a noble sacrifice that I hoped—and tried—to avoid. I sympathize with his quandary, but your father broke the law, Caitrina, and he well knew what would happen if he was caught. I warned him myself."

"And that makes it right? You think the deaths of over forty men is fair punishment for harboring a few outlaws?"

Tiny white lines appeared around his mouth, the first outward sign that she'd gotten to him. "The most wanted outlaws in the land."

"The MacGregors are our allies and not all thieves and murderers as you say."

"It depends on your perspective. Many of my clansmen and the Colquhouns would vehemently disagree."

She had only a vague understanding of what had happened at the battle of Glenfruin, but she did know that the MacGregors had been accused of—though denied responsibility for—what amounted to a slaughter, including the stabbing of forty men who'd been taken as prisoners. Whatever the truth, the MacGregors had taken the blame. But she knew that there were always two sides to a story. Her father had thought the MacGregors worthy of protection; she would not second-guess him. "You're a Highlander—unless you've forgotten."

His eyes narrowed. "What is that supposed to mean?"

"A *Highlander* would understand the sacred obligation of Highland hospitality. If what you say was true, my father was honor-bound to shelter the MacGregors."

His jaw flexed. "I understand the obligation well enough, but 'tis no defense for breaking the law, Caitrina."

"Have you no compassion? Or does your cousin's law not allow for that?" His face was a mask of stone, hard and unyielding. "God, do you have any emotions at all?"

He took a step toward her, and she could tell he was holding on by a very thin thread. "Unfortunately, I do," he said, but his steely voice belied his claim. "Though right now it pleases me no more than it does you."

She felt a jolt of awareness at his admission and turned away, not wanting him to see how he affected her. Did he feel something for her?

It didn't matter.

Then why did something deep inside her yearn for it to be true?

"Just go away," she said furiously. "If it's absolution you seek, you will not find it from me."

He grabbed her arm and spun her back to him; she felt the warm press of his fingers through her sark like a brand.

She knew he hated when she dismissed him, but nothing could stop her from provoking him—from making him as angry as she. But it wasn't just him; she was angry at the invisible force that seemed to draw them together, that would not let her ignore or forget him as she wanted, that made her deeply conscious of him and the strange physical awareness that seemed to drench her body with heat: his warm masculine scent; the shadow of stubble along his square jaw; the wide curve of his mouth that made her think of kissing. It was so unfair. He'd been battered by the past few months as well, but it only served to make him more ruggedly handsome.

"I did not come for absolution," he said tightly.

"Then why did you come?" All of a sudden it dawned on her. *Me. He's come for me.* She scoffed with outrage. "You can't honestly think I want anything to do with you?" His eyes flared at her tone, but she did not heed the warning. "I *despise* you. When I see you, I will always see a Campbell. The clan responsible for the death of my family. Nothing you say will ever change that."

His face was drawn in taut lines, and anger radiated from him. His vaunted control was wavering.

"You want to hate me." He put his hand on her throat, covering the frantic pulse at her neck, and she froze. "But you don't hate me at all, Caitrina." He lowered his head, and she could smell the warm spice of his breath. His hair spilled forward on her cheek, silky and warm from the sun. Her breath hitched and her heart raced wildly in her chest. "Even now you want me," he drawled, sliding his finger down her neck to the swell of her breast, singeing a path of heated sensation in his wake. Her nipples hardened in anticipation of his touch, throbbing when he dropped his hand. "The fire coursing through your veins right now is for me," he whispered in her ear. "And only for me. No one else will ever make you feel like this. Try to deny what is between us."

Her body was shaking; she was excruciatingly aware of every inch of his powerful body, so close to hers. She shook her head, holding on so tight that she dared not try to speak.

"Tell me you don't want me to kiss you." He lowered his mouth to hers until only a hairbreadth separated them. Her heart pounded in her ears. She couldn't breathe. Every nerve ending flared. The wind whipped across her face, but all she could think about was the silky texture of his lips and how he'd tasted on her tongue.

"I don't want you to kiss me," she managed, her voice wobbling.

"Liar," he growled, then murmured something about her being damn stubborn before his mouth fell on hers.

It was as if something exploded inside her. All the emotions she'd fought so hard to contain broke free. His kiss was everything she remembered. Hot, wet, and demanding as his mouth moved over hers with swift possession. The taste of him was like the darkest, richest wine, pouring into her soul until she was drunk with pleasure.

She sank against him, surrendering her breath, her mouth, her body, in one heart-stopping moment. She couldn't deny this if she wanted to.

His finger caressed her jaw in soft entreaty. She opened willingly, taking him deep in her mouth, savoring the erotic sensation of his tongue sliding against hers. He stroked deeper and deeper, as if he couldn't get enough of her.

She kissed him back, twining her tongue with his, meeting him stroke for stroke. He groaned, pulling her snugly against him, letting her feel every hard inch of his powerful body. Her body flushed with heat where they touched. God, he was magnificent. She wanted to touch his bare skin, to run her hands over the thick, bulging muscles of his arms and chest to feel his strength under her fingertips. She molded to him, melting into his heat. She wanted the comfort that only he could bring. To feed the starving emptiness in her soul.

His kiss turned a little rougher and more insistent. He opened her mouth wider, so he could sink deeper. The rough stubble of his chin scraped her skin as his tongue thrust faster and faster in a wickedly sensual beat. It was wet and hot, and deliciously erotic. The licking. The stroking. The fire.

Desire flooded her body, the memories of how he'd touched her making her pulse with anticipation. Heat rushed between her legs; she pressed against him, seeking friction, and felt his heavy erection straining against her.

For a moment, she tensed. The memory of the soldier hovering over her flashed before her eyes, but she pushed it away. *Jamie would never hurt her.* She knew it with a certainty that shocked her. Lust would never control him.

But would it control her?

It was as if she'd been doused by a bucket of icy seawater. She was passionately kissing a man in broad daylight—and not just any man, but her enemy.

A sick feeling curdled in her stomach. How could she betray her family like this? For a moment in his arms, she'd forgotten all that stood between them. She pushed against his chest, freeing herself from his embrace. Without thinking, she pulled her hand back and brought her open palm as hard as she could against his face.

The slap rang out as loud as a musket shot.

His face had barely flinched from the blow, but the imprint of her hand showed stark crimson on his cheek.

She covered her mouth with her hand, stunned by the violence of her actions, knowing that it had been as much a reaction against her own response as it had beeen to him.

What power did this man have over her?

Her breath came hard between her lips as she fought for control, fought to quiet the powerful yearnings still firing inside her. She looked into his eyes and the intensity there shook her to her core. His gray blue eyes bored into her, as if he could see right inside her—to her deepest secrets.

"You've made your point," she said hoarsely, her breath ragged. "I hate you, but my body lusts for you. If it was your intention to humiliate me, you've succeeded."

His face was a mask of cold implacability. Looking at him, you would never guess that such passion existed under his steely reserve—but she'd felt it. Moments ago, he'd been kissing her with more emotion than she'd dreamed possible. As if he wanted her more than anything in the entire world. As if she mattered.

"I assure you," he said evenly, "humiliating you was the furthest thing from my mind."

The possessive way he looked at her told her exactly what he'd had in mind. He wanted her, and the worst part was that she wanted him right back.

For a moment, her defenses fell and she gave him a pleading look. "Please, just leave me alone to find what peace I can."

He shook his head. "We both know that is impossible."

And because she feared he was right, she ran.

Chapter 10

❖ ❖ ❖

She raced away from him as if the devil were nipping at her heels. In a way, Jamie supposed he was. But she would never be able to outrun what burned between them.

He let her go—this time.

He shouldn't have kissed her. It was too soon. For months she'd blamed him for the death of her family; he should have given her time to accept what he'd told her.

He stared after her, unable to turn away. Though changed, her beauty was still magnetic. She moved with natural agility and grace as she scrambled up the pathway to the castle, hair streaming behind her head like a silky black veil.

The old plaid she wore had come loose, and she'd gathered it up in her arms. He felt a pang of regret. The plain sark and kirtle she wore was a stark contrast to the fine gowns he was used to seeing her in. The things that had once given her pleasure were barely spared a thought.

Princess, he'd called her then. Now, the comparison seemed cruel.

She'd changed, and not just in her choice of adornment. No, the changes went far deeper. Where there had once been naïveté and innocence, there was now wariness and sorrow—but also a hard glint in her eyes that hadn't been there before.

One thing, however, hadn't changed. She still possessed an uncanny ability to make him lose control. The harder she tried to push him away, the more he wanted to force her to acknowledge what was between them. It seemed the only thing she couldn't deny was her passion.

She thought it was lust. But lust was a simple emotion, and there was nothing simple about the blistering attraction and steely connection that seemed to bind them together.

He whistled for his mount, and the powerful black stallion clopped quickly to his side. After gathering the reins in his hand, he started toward the keep, troubled by how much she'd changed.

Hell, he'd never wanted to see her brought so low, he'd only wanted her to understand that the world was more complicated than she thought. He hadn't wanted her to suffer like this or see such brutality.

If he hadn't been so damn angry by her refusal, he might have been able to protect her. But pride stung, he'd kept his intentions to himself. If he'd told his cousin or brother Colin of his plan to marry her, her family might have been spared. She might have been spared.

He would never be able to give her back the family she'd lost, but he would do what he could to make things right.

He gazed up at the keep as he drew closer, remembering her parting words. A less determined man might do as she asked. But Jamie couldn't walk away and leave her as she wanted. Caitrina Lamont had gotten under his skin in a way no woman had before. Even though she'd been through hell and back, she was still fiery, passionate, stubborn, and proud. What he'd once dismissed as spoiled had reflected strength of character that ran much deeper. She was unlike any other woman he'd ever known.

She belonged to him, and he would not—could not—let her go.

Caitrina's heart was still pounding as she entered the dark stone staircase of the old keep and wound her way up to the small chamber that had been set aside for her in the garret.

It was no more than a servant's room, but for her it was perfect. The low, sharply angled ceiling of the small space made her feel safe. And because the chamber was at the very top of the tower, too high to climb, there was a large window for her to look out of onto the Clyde. Her uncle had offered her a more sizable room below to share with her two young cousins, but Caitrina preferred the solitude and quiet—the girls, though sweet, were but twelve and fourteen and prone to chatter. *Like Brian*. The memories were too painful.

She crossed the small corridor outside her chamber in a few steps, pulled open the door and quickly slammed it closed behind her, as if he might be following her. But a tiny voice at the back of her head warned her that if Jamie Campbell wanted her, a simple wood plank door wouldn't stand in his way. She shivered. *Nothing* would stand in his way.

Resting her back against the door, she closed her eyes and tried to catch her breath, waiting for the hard rise and fall of her chest to slow.

Caitrina had thought that she'd put what had happened between them and her irrational attraction to Jamie behind her. His involvement—or that of his clan—in the attack on her family had erected an insurmountable wall between them. Or at least it should have, but he'd toppled it with words that made her question what she thought she knew.

She still wanted him. As much as she wanted to deny it, her passionate response to his kiss told otherwise. The weakness put her to shame. He should be the last man she was attracted to. If only it were as simple as physical attraction, but she feared something more complicated. She couldn't seem to think straight when he was near.

Her emotions were in turmoil with all he'd told her, but two things rang true: He had carried her from the burning building—she remembered the feeling of safety and security when he'd held her in his arms—and her father had harbored the MacGregors.

She'd known her father was sympathetic to their plight—as many in the Highlands were—but Caitrina still couldn't believe that he'd taken such a risk in sheltering the outlaws. Though she supposed, given the honorable and proud Highland chief that her father was, he would have felt compelled to shelter the MacGregors no matter what the risk. What really stung was that she'd known nothing about it. She had been kept in the dark. Ignorance had left her unprepared for heartbreak; she vowed never to be like that again.

In hindsight, she realized there had been warning signs, particularly with respect to Jamie Campbell. It was clear that her father had urged her to accept Jamie's suit knowing that they might be in need of his protection.

Guilt twisted inside her. Would things have been different had she heeded his request? Would Jamie have protected them?

Caitrina didn't know what to think, but one thing was certain: She needed to shore up her defenses against Jamie to withstand further attack. She might have gotten rid of him this time, but she knew he'd be back.

She needed to put herself out of his reach forever—which meant speeding up her search for a husband. Today, after the midday meal, she would speak with her uncle.

Her eyes flew open in alarm.

Midday meal. She glanced out the window at the sun on the horizon and muttered a curse.

She was late.

It took her only a few minutes to change her kirtle, splash some water on her face, and tug a comb through her hair before she was on her way back down the stairs. She exited the keep and hurried across the courtyard to the separate building that housed the new hall and kitchens. The great hall with its specially constructed fireplace had been hastily built over forty years ago, when Queen Mary had visited Toward Castle. To this day, the arched gateway between the chapel and guardhouse was called "Queen Mary's Gate."

She could hear the boisterous sounds of revelry as she drew near and felt a pang of guilt. With all that her uncle and aunt had done for her, Caitrina knew she should make a better effort to repay their kindness. Forcing a smile to her lips, she took a deep breath and walked into the great hall.

For a moment, the sounds of merrymaking and the pipes, the warm smell of peat, and the vivid panoply of color from the colorfully dressed clansmen filled her with a painful longing. It was so reminiscent of Ascog, she had to pause to collect herself.

Her eyes scanned the room, sliding over the sea of unfamiliar faces. Except for the dais, where her uncle sat with her aunt, cousins, and . . .

She stiffened with shock.

Only Jamie Campbell would be bold enough to enter the enemy's lair after what had happened at Ascog. She should have expected something like this. He'd certainly wasted no time.

But what she didn't understand was why her uncle would receive him. The Lamonts of Toward hated Campbells as much as their Ascog kin—if not more so. The fact that her uncle would sit at the same table with Argyll's Henchman after all that had happened made her prickle with alarm.

Something did not bode well.

Jamie read her shock when she entered the hall and noticed him sitting at the dais beside her aunt.

He stilled, seeing her hesitate at the entry as she decided

whether to come in or turn around. Had she changed more than he'd realized?

Only a few seconds elapsed before she straightened her spine and started purposefully across the hall—not sparing him another glance. Jamie relaxed his hand, not realizing he'd been gripping his goblet so hard. No, she was still the passionate girl who would not back down from a challenge. But as she drew closer, he could see the wariness in her eyes—wariness that pricked.

He took a long drink of *cuirm,* knowing that she was right to be worried.

There was an empty space on the bench beside him; he wasn't surprised, however, when she took a seat at the opposite end of the long wooden table—as far from him as was possible.

He was left to converse with her aunt Margaret on his right and her cousin John, Lamont's *tanaiste,* on his right. Both were aware of his purpose in coming to Toward. Though Margaret Lamont did her duty as hostess without fault, he detected disapproval in her manner. Her son was less subtle. John, a hulking, battle-scarred warrior of perhaps thirty years, didn't bother to hide his hostility, speaking in grunts and monosyllables and looking as if he'd like nothing more than to slip a dirk between Jamie's ribs.

It wasn't the first time Jamie had experienced stilted and awkward conversation over a meal. Though perhaps he was more anxious by what was to come than he wanted to allow, because it seemed to drag interminably.

Finally, the Lamont of Toward rose. It was time. "Niece"—he turned to Caitrina—"would you join us in the laird's solar."

Caitrina glanced in Jamie's direction, as if she might refuse. He kept his expression implacable. She stood, following her uncle's lead, her smile dutiful, albeit forced. "Of course, Uncle."

Jamie, Caitrina, Margaret Lamont, and John followed

the chief into the small antechamber off the great hall. Under normal circumstances, the Lamont's *luchd-taighe* guardsmen would join them as well, but Jamie had requested privacy, knowing that Caitrina was going to feel cornered as it was.

It will be for the best. He didn't shy from doing what it took to achieve his purposes, but that didn't prevent the twinge of disquiet.

The room was small and dark, large enough to hold a table and benches and not much else. A woven rug of blues and greens was strewn across the wood floor. The paneled walls were unadorned with paint or plaster—or windows. Indeed, except for a few sconces, the only decoration was a large silk banner embroidered with the badge of Lamont hung on the wall opposite the door. A simply constructed bookcase held what looked to be mostly the household account books. The simplicity of the room was odd in comparison with the richly appointed great hall that adjoined it, but this room seemed to fit the Lamont.

Tall and sparse, with a ruddy complexion and a shock of reddish grayed hair that managed always to look windblown, the Lamont of Toward was a quiet man of few words. In temperament, Jamie had always thought him more suited for the kirk than the battlefield. He glanced out of the corner of his eye at the dangerous John Lamont—unlike the Lamont's warmonger son.

Jamie took the proffered seat beside the chief and noticed how John and Margaret Lamont had taken the seats on each side of Caitrina, as if trying to protect her. It wouldn't do any good.

"Undoubtedly, you are wondering why I've asked you here," the Lamont chief said to Caitrina.

"Actually, I'm wondering what he is doing here," Caitrina replied. Her gaze fixed on Jamie. "I thought I made myself very clear earlier. I have nothing more to say to you."

"I think you'll remember my response as well," Jamie said evenly, noting the burst of angry color that appeared on her cheeks. "Listen to what your uncle has to say, lass," he finished quietly.

The Lamont cleared his throat. Jamie could tell he was uncomfortable. Hell, he didn't blame him. "Campbell here and I have been in correspondence for the past couple of months."

He heard her sharp intake of breath and a look of such betrayal in her eyes that it cut him to the quick.

Her aunt quickly clasped Caitrina's hand and eyed her husband impatiently. "You misunderstand, dearest, your uncle did not betray you."

The Lamont's eyes widened in alarm, realizing what she'd thought. "Your aunt is right. I told Campbell nothing of your whereabouts. He contacted me about another matter."

Caitrina seemed to relax, but only a little, and she waited for her uncle to continue. But the Lamont still seemed to be having trouble finding the right words.

Taking pity on the man, Jamie interjected for him. "Your uncle has served as something of an intermediary." He could see her confusion and explained. "While searching the forest near Ascog after the attack"—*for you,* he left unsaid— "I captured two of Alasdair MacGregor's guardsmen—one of whom happened to be his cousin Iain."

Her eyes widened a little. "And so my father's death was for nothing," she said bitterly. "You found the MacGregors and turned them over to Argyll anyway, or maybe there was no need to turn them over?"

Jamie's mouth tightened. Killing them was what he should have done—and no more than Iain MacGregor deserved. That he hadn't done exactly that was only because of her. If they were to have any chance, he knew that no more death could come from the attack on Ascog. His jaw clenched grimly. Iain MacGregor was one of the worst of the lot—a murderous scourge who'd burned and pillaged Jamie's clansmen for years. What others might have been driven to, he did for pleasure.

Alasdair MacGregor, on the other hand, had made a different impression on him. Though they'd crossed paths a number of times in the past few years, during the negotiations Jamie came to see him as a man bound by duty into becoming the unlikely leader of an uncontrollable group of brigands—as their chief, Alasdair would be held accountable. Jamie had come away almost feeling sorry for him.

Unexpectedly, the Lamont rose to his defense. "No, he didn't do either, Caitrina. As a matter of fact, Campbell has prevented Argyll from sending more soldiers into the area until an agreement for a peaceable surrender of Alasdair MacGregor could be worked out. As evidence of Campbell's good faith, while brokering the deal, he has kept the location of the prisoners a secret."

Caitrina's gaze fell on him. He saw her surprise. She realized the significance of what Jamie had done by withholding information from Argyll. Hell, it had surprised him. Never before had Jamie refused to follow an order from his chief. Proof alone of what she meant to him. Initially, his cousin had been furious. Only when Jamie had explained his purpose had Argyll been mollified.

He knew she wanted to ask why he'd done so, but instead she turned back to her uncle. "And has a peaceable surrender been negotiated?"

The Lamont nodded. "MacGregor and his men have agreed to turn themselves in to Argyll, and in return the earl has agreed to indemnify him for past crimes and to see him safely on English ground. Alasdair MacGregor believes that he will be treated fairly by King James in England." Undoubtedly, Alasdair MacGregor would die for his clan's crimes, but at least his blood would be on King James's hands.

She nodded but kept her gaze on her uncle. "It is more

than I would have expected from Argyll. But I don't understand what this has to do with me?"

The Lamont cleared his throat again. "To seal the bargain, Campbell has asked for your hand in marriage."

Her entire body went rigid. Jamie could see her knuckles
turn white as she gripped the folds of her skirts in her lap.
Fury and outrage radiated from her, but she kept her voice
surprisingly calm. "I'm afraid I've already refused the
laird's *generous* offer of marriage. In fact, I planned to discuss another match with you tonight."

Blood rushed through Jamie's veins, his reaction instantaneous. "Who?" His fists clenched. *I'll kill him.*

Her lips pressed together. "It is none of your concern."

The Lamont appeared flustered. "This changes everything. I was not aware that your father had arranged another match. I thought you had refused every offer. Who is
it, child?"

Color crawled up her cheeks. "Nothing has been
decided . . . exactly."

The Lamont gazed back and forth between the two of
them, sensing the tension and probably guessing the cause
for it. "You should hear his offer before you refuse him,
niece."

"There is nothing he can say that will change my mind."
Don't be so sure of that.

"I think you will want to hear everything, Caitrina," her
aunt said quietly, echoing his thoughts.

He sensed her rising panic. She turned to her cousin
John, but he nodded as well—although he looked none too
happy about it.

"Very well. What is this offer, then?" she asked impatiently.

Jamie saw the pity in her uncle's eyes when he answered
her. "If you wed Campbell, you can return to Ascog Castle
with your remaining clansmen under his protection."

She flinched as if from a blow, and Jamie knew he'd

guessed correctly. With the death of her family, her home and her clan were what were important to her. But how much would she be willing to sacrifice for them?

She'd lost her composure; he could see her hands shaking in her lap. "I see. So he offers that which rightly belongs to the Lamonts."

No one spoke, but they all knew that Argyll had laid claim to her father's lands. To encourage the capture of the MacGregors, the Privy Council had enacted laws giving a bounty for the head of any MacGregor, in addition to all the dead man's possessions. By harboring the outlaws, arguably the Lamont himself was an outlaw. As such, his possessions would be forfeit. With no male survivors, Caitrina would face a long, uphill battle, with little guarantee of success in the end.

"My cousin has agreed to give the land to me on our wedding." An arrangement that had taken some negotiating and hadn't pleased Colin, who felt it should be his. "Eventually, it will go to our second son."

At the mention of a child, she blanched. He could see the panic in her eyes and knew that she was close to losing her composure.

"Leave us," he said to the others.

The Lamont frowned. "I'll not have you force the lass."

Jamie checked him with a glare but forgave him for the insult, knowing that the chief spoke out of concern for his niece.

"Caitrina?" Margaret Lamont asked.

She nodded.

The chief escorted his wife, with John following, but when her cousin reached the door, he turned. "You don't have to wed him, lass. I'd not see you tied to a bloody Campbell." His eyes narrowed menacingly on Jamie. "Say the word and he'll feel the edge of my blade."

Jamie stood, his hand moving to the hilt of his dirk. "If you don't feel mine first," he said matter-of-factly. He was itching for a fight, and from the size and strength of him, John Lamont looked as though he might actually give him a good one.

Jamie started at the gentle restraint of Caitrina's hand on his arm. "That won't be necessary," she said. "Thank you, John, but I'm fine."

Her cousin shot one more venomous glance at Jamie and shut the door behind him.

Caitrina dropped her hand and turned to face him in the candlelight. God, she was beautiful. Just standing so close to her was an exercise in restraint. His nose filled with the bouquet of her delicate perfume. He ached to plunge his fingers through the silky smooth locks of her hair, to touch the soft, velvety curve of her cheek, and to taste the honey sweetness of her lips. But she didn't want comfort from him.

Would the day ever come that she would? He'd never pursued a woman, never had to. What if Caitrina never . . . *No,* she would.

"So this is your plan," she said, her voice low and full of emotion. "You are every bit as ruthless as I thought. You'd force me to marry you, not caring how much I hate you."

His muscles clenched. He knew she didn't hate him but didn't like hearing it all the same. "I'll not force you to anything. It's your decision."

She made a sharp sound of derision. "What kind of choice is that when you hold everything that I want in the palm of your hand? Why are you doing this to me? Is it because of what happened before? Is this some kind of revenge? I dared to refuse the great Jamie Campbell, so now you will bend me to your will and humiliate me."

"Is that what you really think? Is it so hard to believe that I want you?"

"No, that's not hard to believe at all," she said flatly. "But that does not require marriage. If that's all you want from me, then take—"

He grabbed her arm, his reaction instantaneous. "Don't," he said in a low voice. "Don't say it."

He was doing a horrible job of this. He dropped her arm and raked his hands through his hair. "That is not all that I want from you." He'd never tried to explain himself to a woman before. He didn't know how to describe what he was feeling. "I care for you."

"If you care about me, then don't do this."

"It's because I care about you that I am doing this." To get Argyll to agree, he'd had to take surety—to assume personal responsibility—for the conduct of the Lamonts. If they broke the law, he would be the one held accountable. "I'm trying to help you. Can't you see this is the best way to get your home back? And I can protect you."

"I don't need your protection."

"Don't you?"

She shook her head stubbornly. "No."

Unable to resist, he reached down and stroked the gentle curve of her cheek with his finger. "Would marrying me really be so horrible?"

He felt her tremble, but she didn't respond.

He held himself still, asking the question that he feared the most. "Is there someone else you wish to marry?" The very thought sliced like a dirk across his chest.

He felt her eyes on him, studying his face, as if she might have glimpsed a little of his torment. "I . . . ," she started, then hesitated. "No. There is no one else."

He took a step closer to her, looking down at the feathery fan of black lashes on her pale cheek. The faintest hint of a few new freckles dotted the top of her tiny upturned nose. He took a deep breath but didn't touch her. "Give me a chance. I will do my best to make you happy." It was as close to begging as he would ever come. Without thinking, he reached out and gently tucked an errant lock of hair behind her ear, his fingers sweeping the velvet of her cheek, startling them both with the tender touch.

After a moment he said, "You will consider my offer?"
She nodded.

She was wavering, but there was one more thing she had to know. He didn't want anything between them. "You should know something before you make your decision."

She tilted her head questioningly, caught by something in his voice. "What?"

"The man who led the attack against your father"—her eyes locked on his—"he's my brother."

"No!" But the cry strangled in her throat. The leader's face came back to her. There had been something that reminded her of Jamie, and now she knew why. Her mouth soured. Dear God, his brother had killed her father.

Just when she wanted to think something between them might be possible . . .

"I'd not force you to accept him, but I thought you had a right to know. He didn't know what you were to me—"

And what am I to you? But she couldn't ask that. "And that is supposed to be an excuse?"

Jamie shook his head. "No. But it might have made a difference. I'll leave you now. Send word to Dunoon when you have made your decision. Should you decide to accept, we can be married right away."

"But the banns—"

"The banns have already been proclaimed."

Caitrina felt the noose tightening around her throat. "You were so confident of my response, or was I even allowed to have one?"

"I only wanted to be prepared. I'd assumed you would be anxious to return to your home."

"It's gone. There's nothing left."

"It can be rebuilt."

"Not everything," she said quietly.

He gave her a long look that seemed to touch inside her. "I'm sorry for your loss, lass."

He was. She could feel his sympathy and understanding, and for a moment she let it wrap around her and give her comfort. He would be a rock to lean on if she wanted him.

He lifted her chin. "You're right; not everything can be rebuilt," he admitted. "But we can try to build something new."

It was an olive branch of sorts. One that she wasn't ready to accept. "I don't want something new"—*you*—"I want my family back." She thought he flinched, but he covered it so quickly, she wondered if she'd only imagined it. "Don't you understand? I can never replace them."

"I'm not suggesting you try. But right now, I'm all you have."

Caitrina watched the door close behind him, numb. He was gone. Tears burned in her throat. The decision was in her hands now.

She didn't know what to do. She needed to think. After opening the door, she forced herself to walk steadily across the hall and outside, not daring to meet anyone's eyes. Only when she reached the courtyard did she run.

The sun was sinking over the horizon, and the air was damp with cold. Wind tore her hair from her bindings and tears streamed down her cheeks as she stumbled down the path to the beach. Sinking to her knees in the sand, she put her face in her hands.

Vaguely she was aware of someone calling her, but it sounded so far away. Moments later, she felt Mor's arms wrap around her. The familiar scent, the pillowy soft chest, made her sob harder—the way she had when she was a child. What had she ever had to cry about then?

"There, there, lass. What is it that has you so upset?"

Caitrina managed to choke out the story in bits and pieces, enough for her old nurse to put it together.

She frowned. "So he claims he was there to put an end to the attack?"

Caitrina nodded.

"And you believe him?"

Oddly enough, she did. "Yes. But I wasn't there. Tell me what you remember."

It was the first time she'd asked Mor about that day.

Mor thought for a moment. "It was so chaotic when we were dragged from the keep, I had to fight to hold on to Una. Smoke was everywhere—and the bodies. Everywhere I looked there were bodies. I was so scared I'd see you and the lad." She shivered. "I was so relieved to see the Campbell Henchman carry you out of that keep—" She stopped, her voice tight with emotion. "He'd saved you, but I didn't know for what reason. I thought it was odd, though, the way he cradled you in his arms like you were a bairn, and kissed your forehead before putting you down." Her brow wrinkled. "He had the strangest look on his face, and then he said, 'Watch her for me, I'll be right back. I must see what I can do. There are still people inside.' " Mor paused. "I thought he was talking about his men, but maybe . . ." She shrugged. "I don't know. I didn't think anything of it at the time, but I did see him arguing with the other man." Mor's face hardened. "The man who shot your father."

"His brother," Caitrina said tonelessly.

Mor sucked in her breath. "Oh, lass."

"I can't marry him."

Mor stroked her hair. "Of course you can't . . . if you don't want to."

"I don't want to marry him. I despise him—he's a Campbell. How could you think . . ." Caitrina's voice fell off as she caught the older woman's knowing gaze leveled on her.

"Caitrina Lamont, I've known you since the day you were born. I've seen the way you look at the man . . . and the way he looks at you."

Caitrina felt the telltale heat of a blush rising on her

cheeks. She wiped her eyes with her sleeve and then lifted her chin. "I don't know what you think you have seen, but you're wrong."

"Am I?" Mor shook her head. "Ah, Caiti, we can no more control who we are a-wanting than we can order the rain to flow or the wind to ebb. There is no shame in what you feel for the man."

Caitrina felt something twist in her chest. Mor was wrong—her attraction to Jamie Campbell was a betrayal of her father and brothers. Nor did it change who he was. "How can you say that? You know who he is and what he did?"

Mor nodded, seeming to understand Caitrina's conflicting emotions. "The Campbells are a vicious, land-grabbing lot, and I'd see the men who attacked your father hung, drawn, and quartered and not lose a wink of sleep. But I don't think Jamie Campbell had anything to do with that. He's Argyll's man—a point against him, to be sure—but he cares for you. And that may work to your advantage. There is no denying what the man is offering you. The Campbells are a powerful clan, and perhaps the best way to protect the Lamonts is an alliance with the Campbells through marriage. Moreover, without this marriage you may not have another opportunity to reclaim Ascog."

As much as Caitrina hated to hear it put so bluntly, Mor was only giving voice to Caitrina's own thoughts. He had backed her into a corner, leaving her nowhere to run. If she refused him, she refused her duty to her clan.

Just as before. Her father had urged her to consider Jamie Campbell's offer, but she'd been too selfish—not wanting to leave the sheltering bosom of her family.

Would things have been different if she'd accepted his proposal? The question hurt too much even to contemplate.

She'd failed in her duty to her clan once before; she could not do so again. If there was a way to protect what remained of her kin and to reclaim Ascog without blood-shed, she had to take it.

Jamie Campbell knew that as well as she did.

Sensing Caitrina's anguished thoughts, Mor folded her gently in her loving arms. Caitrina closed her eyes, taking comfort there and feeling her resolve strengthen as the wind blew over her, the tangy scent of the sea following close behind.

Slowly, Caitrina pulled away, her gaze once again turning to the churning mass of dark blue waves and the shadow of the Isle of Bute slowly fading in the orange glow of the darkening sky.

"What will you do?" Mor asked.

"What I must. What else can I do?" Caitrina replied, her voice as hard as the glistening jagged rocks that lined the seashore like polished ebony.

She would do her duty, but one day Jamie Campbell would regret forcing her like this. She would give him her body, but she would never belong to him.

All that was left of her heart was buried deep in the sand with her father's tattered scrap of plaid.

Chapter 11

❖ ❖ ❖

They were married on Sunday four days later—two days after Alasdair MacGregor and his men, accompanied by Jamie and her uncle, surrendered to the Earl of Argyll at Dunoon.

As a condition of her acceptance, Caitrina was spared the presence of the earl and Jamie's brother at their wedding. The Campbell contingent consisted only of the score of guardsmen who accompanied him. The ceremony was held in the small chapel of Toward Castle located opposite the keep beside the new hall. The pews were filled by all that remained of her family—her aunt, uncle, cousins, Mor, and, even though it was unusual for them to be present for such an event, the handful of clansmen who'd accompanied them from Ascog.

Ignoring the protestations of her aunt, Caitrina refused the elaborate velvets and brocades and chose instead a simple dark blue woolen kirtle and a plain sark. The simple clothing seemed more in keeping with the somber occasion.

There was no joy in this marriage—only duty.

Caitrina steeled herself against the unwelcome twinges of awareness that preceded the event, reminding herself that this was a marriage of necessity only.

Still, when she entered the dark stone chapel and gazed down the narrow aisle to the sight of Jamie standing beside the minister, she felt a hard flutter in her chest.

It's only nerves. It was her wedding day, after all, no matter how unwanted.

But that did not explain the way her heart seemed to stop beating when their eyes met. She felt the intensity of his gaze all the way to her toes. It was as if he'd reached out across the room to claim her with his arms, so thoroughly did he possess her with that one long, penetrating look. For one instant it felt *right*—as if this were meant to be. Until she remembered how he'd compelled her to this.

She could not deny, however, that he looked magnificent. His hair was swept over his brow and shone burnished brown in the soft candlelight. The square jaw and hard lines of his handsome face appeared golden in the flickering shadows. Damp tendrils of his silky dark hair curled at his neck.

He stood tall and proud, towering over the minister and her uncle, who waited beside him. Although he was resplendent in his fine doublet and Venetians, the soft black leather could not tame the harsh masculinity of his wide shoulders, muscular chest, and powerful legs.

Slowly, she made her way toward him until she stood before him, close enough to smell the hint of soap that lingered on his skin.

He held out his hand to her. For a moment, the world stilled. In his open palm, she confronted her future. Callused from his sword, his hand was peppered with white lines of battle, giving unmitigated proof of his occupation. He might have the refined manners of a courtier, but there was no doubt that Jamie Campbell lived by the sword. He was a hard, ruthless warrior—Argyll's Henchman—and if she placed her hand in his, she would be his wife.

Her heart pounded in her chest. Trying not to tremble, she lifted her hand from her side and laid her palm atop his, feeling a shock of warmth that flooded her when he enfolded it in his.

He must have sensed her unease because he leaned down

and whispered, "Breathe." The warmth of his breath tickled her ear, sending a shiver running through her. "It will be
all right."

There was something in his voice that touched inside her,
that made her want to believe him. Nodding, she let out
her breath and turned to face the minister, repeating the
vows that would bind her to Jamie Campbell forever—or
until death parted them.

And then, before she could change her mind, his fingers
cupped her chin and he placed a chaste kiss on her lips,
sealing their vows. The kiss jolted her from the daze that
had surrounded her throughout the ceremony.

It was done, and she was his wife—a Campbell. She'd
become her own enemy.

Jamie sat at the dais beside his new bride, watching the
raucous clansmen deteriorate into drunken revelry and
bawdiness as the feast, hours long already, progressed into
the evening. Any wedding, even an unwanted one, was an
excuse for celebration and was expected as a matter of
course by the clansmen. Looking around, he found it hard
to believe this was anything other than a happy occasion.

Motioning to a passing serving girl, Jamie indicated for
her to pour him another glass of wine. It was utterly unlike
him, but there was no question: He was stalling. He turned
to his bride on his right. "More wine?"

Caitrina shook her head no, which was about the sum
total of their communication throughout the evening.

He could feel her growing tension as the night progressed and the time for their wedding night drew closer.
Awareness hummed between them, so thick it was nearly
palpable. Hell, he didn't blame her. He'd waited so long for
her to be his wife, it felt strange to have it be so in truth.
And as the time drew near for him to make her fully his,
Jamie felt his anticipation tempered by a burgeoning trepi-

dation. He wanted tonight to be perfect, but he knew his bride would be reluctant . . . to put it mildly.

The entire day, he'd felt as if he were leading her to the executioner. He hadn't quite known what to expect from her, but this stoic lass bravely doing her duty stung.

He'd hoped that she might feel something for him. That after consideration she might view marriage to him with some contentment, if not pleasure.

Obviously, he'd hoped for too much. For such a normally pragmatic man, it was an uncharacteristic display of idealism. She was marrying him to see her home restored to her clan, and that was it.

He was getting what he wanted, but he wondered at what cost. Would she ever forgive him? Was he doing the right thing?

Earlier when she'd first entered the chapel, he'd felt a twinge of uncertainty, seeing her wide blue eyes and pale, creamy skin. She'd looked so nervous—more fragile than he'd ever seen her. He'd tried to reassure her. Initially it had appeared to help, but it hadn't lasted. What he really wanted to do was touch her—to hold her in his arms and calm her fears—but he knew any attempt to do so would likely make it worse.

How could he prove to her that he was not a monster—that he wanted to protect, not harm her? It would take time and patience, he realized. Suddenly, it occurred to him that he would have to woo his bride. It was ironic: He'd never been in the position of having to woo a woman, let alone one who was his wife. He couldn't understand why he would be willing to go through the effort, except that he was. He could have just walked away, as she'd asked. Maybe he should have.

No. Whatever it took, he would make her happy.

He studied her over his goblet. The longer he looked at her, the more moved he was by her beauty. The plain clothing she'd chosen only seemed to emphasize rather than dull her radiance, as she'd probably intended. But there was nothing she could do to obscure her striking coloring—the flawless pale skin, deep red lips, dark blue eyes, and jet black hair.

Nor was there any denying the perfect symmetry of her features. Even in profile he could see the high curve of her cheek, the lush fullness of her lips, the feathery softness of her lashes, and the gentle slope of her tilted nose. But her true beauty seemed to come from within. It was the fire of her spirit that had always drawn him. The passionate, brazen girl with the flashing eyes that challenged him like no other. A woman who rose from the ashes of destruction ready to fight for her clan.

She must have felt his study, for he detected the faint pink edge of a blush crawling up her cheeks.

She turned to him, her eyes meeting his for the first time since that morning. "It's rude to stare."

Jamie smiled, irrationally pleased that she'd not lost her bold tongue. Her somber air had worried him more than he'd realized. He lifted a brow. "Was I staring?"

"You were."

He shrugged, unrepentant. "You are very beautiful."

The compliment bounced off her. "And a beautiful wife is important to you?"

He smiled. "It certainly doesn't hurt." His finger traced the rim of his goblet; he knew what she was getting at. "But if you are suggesting that it is only your beauty which drew me to you, then you are very wrong. I've known many beautiful women."

She wanted to ignore him, but curiosity apparently got the better of her. "Then why?"

He paused, searching for the right words. "You intrigue me with your boldness and spirit. I've never met a woman like you."

"You mean if I had been biddable and shy, I wouldn't have interested you?"

She looked so disgusted, he had to chuckle. "Probably. Perhaps you should give it a try."

Her eyes narrowed. "Ha! It won't work. You can be sure that you have found yourself a shrew for wife. You are worse than my broth—" She stopped, eyes wide, stricken by what she'd been about to say.

He caught her hand in his, pleased when she did not pull it away. "Your brothers used to tease you?" he asked gently.

She nodded, her eyes swimming with anguish.

His heart went out to her; he couldn't imagine what it must be like to lose one's entire family in a single day. That she had not succumbed to grief was testament enough to her strength. "You must miss them very much."

"I do," she said softly.

He would give anything to return them to her, but that was one thing he could not do. "I wish Lizzie had been here today. I'd like you to meet her."

"Your sister?"

He nodded.

"Where is she?"

"At Castle Campbell." His face darkened. "I thought it too soon, that she would be safer in the Lowlands." At her questioning glance, he explained. "When I returned to Dunoon after leaving Ascog, I discovered that Lizzie, who'd been due to arrive before me, had yet to arrive. I immediately left for Castle Campbell and discovered that the MacGregors attempted to kidnap her—to use her against me."

Caitrina gasped, not hiding her shock. "That's horrible. She must have been terrified."

Jamie frowned. She should have been, but strangely enough, his sister had proved surprisingly unaffected. It seemed odd, but he hadn't had time to contemplate it because his guardsman had arrived with news of the MacGregors at Ascog. "She was lucky. There were a group of men in the area who drove off the outlaws and foiled the attempt. Lizzie was scared, but unhurt."

Caitrina was silent for a moment. "This is the matter you were tending to when your brother and his men came to Ascog?"

He looked into her eyes. "Yes. It was only because the guardsman who delivered the message to my brother decided to track me to Castle Campbell that I was aware of what was happening at all. I only wish it had been sooner."

"So do I," she said softly, dropping her gaze.

He looked at her bent head, her silky hair like polished black ebony glistening in the candlelight. He wanted to tuck her head under his chin and tell her everything was going to be all right, but he knew, for her, it wouldn't be. Nothing could change that day and bring back her family. Nor could he change his clan's part in their death. But he could give her back her home—and if she let him, a new family.

At times like now and earlier in the chapel, he would feel a moment of connection, but they were so fleeting that he wondered whether he only imagined them. Still, it gave him hope of something to build on.

Of course, there was another connection that they had to build upon as well, and the time was drawing near for him to show her just how powerful a bond passion could forge. Their sexual attraction might be the best way for them to grow closer. Though he hated to upset the quiet truce they had established, he knew he could delay no longer. They were married, and he would be damned if it would be in name only. He'd wanted her since the first moment he'd seen her, and his wait was finally at an end.

"I will send for Lizzie soon. With Alasdair MacGregor's surrender, it should be safe enough for her to travel."

"You think the feuding will end?"

Jamie shrugged. "For a while. Without their chief and

most of his guardsmen, the clan will be disorganized. Lizzie will be well protected"—he paused—"as will you."

He read her shock. "You think I might be in danger?"

"You are my wife, and as you've pointed out numerous times, I have many enemies. Anyone close to me is a potential target. But don't let it concern you, I would never let anyone harm you."

"And yet you travel across the Highlands with only a handful of men."

Was she worried about him? The mere prospect warmed him. "I can take care of myself."

She looked as though she wanted to argue, but a serving girl approached with more wine. He waved her away. It was time.

"Your uncle has arranged a chamber for us in the tower. I will join you there in a short while."

She paled, and he could see the sudden flare of panic in her eyes. "Surely it is early yet," she said quickly. "The dancing has yet to begin, and—"

"If you would rather, we can go together now," he interrupted in a voice that boded no argument. Her maidenly reluctance was expected, but he would not be gainsaid. Their marriage would be consummated. He gave her a long look. "It's up to you."

If it was up to her, she wouldn't be in this position, Caitrina thought.

Dear God, her wedding night. Her pulse raced with a flash of panic. A thousand divergent thoughts flew through her head, slamming and bouncing off one another in a confused heap. The moment she'd been dreading was upon her. It seemed that once she'd agreed to marry him, she could think of nothing else. Too often, the memory of what they'd shared by the loch intruded in her thoughts. She remembered how he'd made her feel and wondered if he would touch her like that again—until her body softened and shattered into a sparkling sea of sensation.

Worse, she feared that if he did, the carefully constructed wall she'd erected would begin to erode.

Would he be gentle? Would it hurt? She'd see his hands and imagine him touching her, stroking her skin. She'd look at his mouth and imagine him kissing her, sliding his tongue in her mouth, making her knees weak for want of him. If only it were fear that she felt, but she couldn't deny that it was also anticipation. And that was the most troubling part of all. Liquid heat poured through her whenever he touched her.

She gazed into his eyes, seeing compassion, but resolve. If necessary, she suspected he would lift her in his arms and carry her up the stairs himself, like some Viking marauder of old. He was a ruthless man, and she best not forget it.

Mustering what courage she could, she straightened her spine and stood up from the table. "I will bid my aunt and uncle good night, then."

He nodded. "I will not be long."

"Take as long as you need," she offered carelessly, feeling anything but.

Caitrina lingered over her good-byes, but in the end she knew she could not put off the inevitable. She made her way back to the old keep, and Mor led her up the stairs to the chief's chamber. In honor of the day's occasion, her uncle had given them his room for the night. Tomorrow they would return to the Isle of Bute and Rothesay Castle, where they would stay as the king's guest while the repairs to Ascog began.

The room was large and sparsely furnished, with only the occasional needlepoint or stuffed velvet cushion to hint at her aunt's presence in the room. Though she specifically avoided looking in its direction, she was keenly aware of the four-posted bed with silk hangings looming large opposite the door. Tamping down the sudden spike of her heartbeat, she turned away, putting the ominous piece of furnishing behind her.

Mor fluttered about the room, chattering about the day's events and recounting the latest gossip from the servants—doing anything to avoid the topic of the coming night. The airy cheerfulness was so unlike her, Caitrina realized just how nervous her old nurse must be, and it increased her own apprehension.

Would it be worse than she thought?

When the basin had been prepared for her to wash, and the candles—from what Caitrina could tell, every one available in the room—lit, as she did every evening, Mor helped to remove her gown. But the ordinary and habitual had taken on an uncomfortable significance. With each piece of her clothing that was removed, Caitrina's nervousness and awareness of what was about to happen increased. So that by the time Mor dropped the silk nightraile over her head, Caitrina could barely hide her trembling.

Mor moved to the chest of Caitrina's meager belongings, which had been moved down to her uncle's chamber for the night. After removing a thick woolen wrap from the small pile of clothing, she handed it to Caitrina. "Put this on, my love. You look cold."

Caitrina slipped her arms through the wide sleeves and belted it tightly around her waist. "Thank you. Indeed, it's freezing in here." But they both knew it was not the temperature that was making her shiver.

Plucking the pins from Caitrina's hair, Mor undid the work of hours in minutes, and her long, heavy locks tumbled loosely down her back. Caitrina's nerves were so frayed and ragged, she nearly jumped each time Mor's knuckles accidentally scraped her back as she dragged the comb through her hair. As if she could hold back the inevitable with her ministrations, Mor combed her hair until every strand ran smooth and each curl lay in perfect symmetry.

There was something soothing in the repetitive motion, and Caitrina eventually found herself relaxing and the frantic rise of her pulse calming.

She would have been content to have her hair combed forever, but the moment of peace was suddenly shattered by the loud knock on the door.

She gasped, and Mor stiffened behind her.

The older woman placed the bone comb on the dressing table and slid her hands on Caitrina's shoulders, giving her a little squeeze of encouragement. "It will be all right. There will be some pain," she whispered gently, "but it will not last."

Pain? Caitrina nodded, not daring to meet Mor's eyes, frightened by what she might see there—the worry and sympathy would surely make her lose the tight rein she had on her emotions. The fear that she'd managed to keep at bay had suddenly rushed forward full force.

"The lad cares for you," Mor continued. "He will not hurt you unnecessarily."

Caitrina swallowed, but a large rock had formed in her throat. "I know," she choked. *I hope.*

Another knock upon the door, this one more insistent.

"I wish your mother were here to explain," Mor said. "But as she's not, you are stuck with the faded memory of an old woman. It's been a long time since I was a bride—or a wife, for that matter. Do you know what will happen?"

Caitrina bit her lip, her cheeks warming. "Yes." She'd been raised around livestock. And any lingering ignorance had been eliminated years ago when she'd discovered one of the kitchen maids in the stables with one of her father's guardsmen. The heavy pumping and grunting had left little to the imagination. It had seemed so . . . noisy.

And then there was the soldier. Bile rose in her throat as she remembered him prying apart her legs and fumbling with his breeches. Icy droplets of fear trickled down her spine before she quickly pushed the images aside.

Dear God, I don't think I can do this.

With one more squeeze, Mor released her shoulders and strode to the door, opening it to reveal her husband.

She drew in her breath. His sheer physicality seemed even more intimidating than usual. His tall, wide-shouldered form filled the doorway.

Ignoring the servant's forbidding frown, he gazed right at Caitrina, his eyes sliding down her form. Though her wrap was thick and made of heavy wool, she felt as if he could see right through it. Even though she'd worn far less the first time she'd met him, she was deeply aware of the sudden charge in the air, not to mention their changed circumstances.

She was no longer a stranger, but his wife. She belonged to him. He could do with her as he wished and there was no one to stop him.

Except for Mor.

Her old nurse stepped directly in front of him, toe-to-toe, preventing him from entering the room. With the top of her gray head barely reaching the middle of his chest, she was hardly a threat, but Mor didn't let such a small matter as size stop her.

"I don't care who you are or what reputation you have. If you hurt her in any way, you will have me to deal with." Mor gave a deceptively sweet smile. "Have I ever mentioned that I have a very *extensive* herb garden?"

Caitrina sucked in her breath. Had her dear nursemaid just threatened to poison him?

Jamie eyed the old woman carefully, seeming to take the threat seriously. They stared at each other for a long moment, neither giving an inch. Finally, he nodded. "I will keep that in mind. But your concern is unwarranted. I am not an untried lad; I'll have care for the lass's innocence."

Innocence. Was she innocent? Would he be angry if she wasn't? Her heart beat faster.

"See that you do." Mor moved back to allow him into

the room. She took a few steps toward the door before turning back to Caitrina. "If you need me, all you have to do is call."

Before Caitrina could respond, Jamie interjected with growing irritation, "Hell's fire, woman. I just told you she won't have need of you."

Despite Jamie's flash of temper, Mor still looked reluctant to leave. Not wanting the situation between the two to deteriorate further, Caitrina urged her old nurse away with her eyes. "I'll be fine, Mor," she assured her. "I'll see you in the morning."

"When I call for you," Jamie added sharply.

With one last scathing look, Mor closed the door behind her with a definitive slam that seemed to ring out like an alarm bell.

Caitrina was alone with her husband.

The air that had moments ago seemed chilled suddenly felt warm and sultry. The room that had seemed spacious and sparse now seemed small and crowded—with no place to run.

Perhaps sensing her unease, Jamie strode over to the table beside the fire and poured two glasses of claret from the bottle that had been left for them. He offered her one.

She shook her head.

"Take it," he insisted, pressing it into her hand. "It will ease your nerves."

"I'm not nervous," she protested instinctively, but she took the glass anyway. She was annoyed that he'd so easily detected her weakness.

"Then that makes one of us," he said, gazing into the fire as he tossed back the contents of his glass.

The admission took her aback. He always seemed so controlled and unaffected; the idea that he might not be as impervious as she thought was oddly comforting. She eyed him cautiously. "Truly?"

He shrugged.

"But why?" she persisted. "What have you to be nervous about? Surely you've done this before."

He let out a sharp bark of laughter. "Once or twice," he said soberly, but she could hear the lingering amusement in his voice.

The idea of his previous experience left her feeling distinctly irritated. A horrible thought sank inside her like a rock: Did he have a leman? If he did, it wouldn't be for long. Still, it didn't explain why he would be nervous about this.

She wrinkled her brow. "Then I don't understand."

He didn't appear inclined to explain. Instead, he removed his doublet and laid it over the back of the chair before taking a seat by the fire. She could see the powerfully muscled contours of his chest beneath the fine linen of his shirt, and it sent a shimmer of awareness low in her belly.

Nonetheless, Caitrina breathed a sigh of relief as he appeared to be in no rush to press himself upon her. Obviously, he'd decided to give her time to adjust to his presence. She took a seat opposite him, the gentle warmth from the smoldering fire bringing her a strange sense of peace. It wasn't as uncomfortable as she'd expected it to be sitting alone with him in her bedchamber. In fact, it felt disturbingly natural.

"Won't you tell me what you meant?" she asked.

His gaze met hers. "You are innocent, and I have no wish to cause you pain." His eyes darkened with intensity. "I want to bring you pleasure."

The sensual undertone in his voice sent a tingle running through her. "And my pleasure matters to you?"

His eyes turned hard. "Is it so difficult to believe that I might have care for your happiness?"

Though she knew she'd unintentionally angered him, she answered truthfully. "Yes, it is, when you've forced me into this marriage."

He tensed visibly; every muscle in his body went taut. "You had a choice."

"Did I?" she asked softly.

He held her gaze, his expression unreadable. But there was something in his eyes that made her wonder if she'd erred in questioning his motives. An intensity that made her suspect he wanted this marriage—and her—far more than she'd realized.

He didn't say anything right away but shifted his gaze back to the fire. Finally, after a few minutes, he turned back to her. "Perhaps I was wrong to think that you would ever accept this. I'd hoped that tonight might mark the start of a new beginning. I've never forced myself upon a woman, and I'll not start now." His voice was harsh and rough. "If you do not want this marriage, then leave."

Her heart stopped. He was giving her a way out, which was what she'd wanted . . . wasn't it? The seconds ticked by. Still, she couldn't force herself to walk away.

He waited, his eyes never once leaving her face. She stood from the chair, and the raw disappointment in his eyes cut her to the quick.

He thought she was leaving. But Caitrina didn't know what to do. She should walk to the door and leave him behind her, this man who had brought so much pain. But instead, she found herself walking until she stood right before him, knowing that she was about to make the most important decision of her life.

A decision formed on what she knew of him, not what she'd been told. He might have manipulated her into marrying him, but she'd begun to realize that his intentions had always been honorable. Indeed, there was a streak of honor in Jamie Campbell that defied his reviled name. Was it possible he did care for her and was trying to make amends?

A force had drawn them together, and she no longer had the strength—or will—to resist.

She took a deep breath. "I gave you my word. I'll not go back on it now."

He rose from the chair, towering over her. Only a few inches separated them. Heat surrounded her—from the smoldering peat and from the fire that radiated from his powerful body. She wanted to lay her hands on his chest, to feel the rock hard muscles flex beneath her palms. To press her cheek against his warm skin and inhale the dark, spicy scent that enveloped her senses. To find safety in his strength.

He reached out, sliding the back of his finger along the contour of her cheek with a touch so gentle, it made her shudder. "You know what you are saying?"

She nodded. She did. She wanted him, and there was no going back.

As if to test her resolve, he slid his hands to her waist and slowly worked the ties of her woolen wrap—his eyes never once leaving her face.

Locked in the heat of his gaze, she couldn't breathe.

Caitrina was used to servants undressing her, but Jamie Campbell was no servant, and the intimacy of the act sent a thrill of erotic anticipation shooting through her.

Slowly, he moved his hands to her shoulders and slid under the fabric, pushing back until the wrap slipped to her feet in a heavy pool. His big hands covered her body.

He drew in his breath, his eyes devouring every curve and contour of her shape revealed plainly under the gossamer ivory silk of her nightraile. The raw desire in his gaze threatened to overwhelm her, but she stood firm beneath its withering heat. Never had a man looked at her so, with possession, lust, and something far more dangerous and enticing.

His finger traced the sharp point of her nipple until it strained taut against the thin fabric. Heat flooded between her legs at his touch.

"God, you are beautiful," he said, his voice rough. He

pinched her lightly between his thumb and forefinger, and something leapt inside her.

She remembered his mouth on her and knew that he remembered it, too. She wanted to close her eyes and succumb to the burgeoning sensations firing through her body.

His thumb moved over her nipple in a soft caress, rubbing the silky fabric over the sensitive peak with wicked friction until she felt herself sway—her legs like jelly.

She thought he was going to kiss her, but he surprised her by lifting her effortlessly in his arms as if she weighed no more than a child and carrying her to the bed. Gently, he lowered her and she sank into the soft feather mattress.

He sat on the edge of the bed, his weight causing the bed to dip, and quickly removed his boots. After pulling the shirt from his breeches, he yanked it over his head in one smooth motion, then tossed it to the chair where he'd laid his doublet.

Caitrina sucked in her breath, mesmerized by the sight before her. He was beautiful. The hard lines of his chest and arms looked as if they'd been chiseled from granite. She could see the outline of every tightly formed muscle beneath his golden skin—its smooth surface marred only by the occasional jagged scar that marked him as a warrior.

His arms were like rocks, his shoulders wide, his chest a steely shield. Thin bands of muscle rippled across his stomach. He stood, loosening the ties of his breeches until they hung low on his hips. She could see the thick length of his manhood straining against the waist, his desire for her undeniable.

He must have noticed her study, but he misunderstood her shocked reaction. "There's nothing to be scared of," he promised soothingly.

She shook her head. "You don't frighten me."

He chuckled at that and sat back down on the edge of the bed beside her. "Don't let anyone hear you say that, you'll ruin my reputation."

Caitrina couldn't believe it: He was jesting with her. It was so sweet and unexpected. She returned his smile. "I wouldn't dream of it." Her eyes slid over him again, her body softening with awareness. He was so close. She could just reach out and touch him. "It's just that I couldn't help but admire . . . you are beautiful," she said, the words tumbling from her mouth before she could take them back.

He frowned, obviously not knowing what to make of her pronouncement. "I'm a warrior. Warriors are not beautiful."

He was wrong. There was undeniable beauty in the strength and power of his body. Slowly, she reached out to touch him, feeling him flinch as she spread her palms over the hard span of his chest. She could see the pulse at his neck begin to tick and knew her touch had pleased him. His skin was warm to the touch and surprisingly smooth over the steely hard muscles. Holding his gaze, she moved her hands to his shoulders, sliding them down over the bulging muscles of his arms, which flexed instinctively under her fingertips. *Magnificent.* "You are to me," she said softly.

Something flickered in his eyes, and he lowered his head to hers, covering her mouth with his in a tender kiss that spoke far louder than words. With his lips he touched her soul, claiming a part of her that had never been exposed.

He dragged his mouth over hers, teasing her with the quick flick of his tongue—slow and languid, as if he had all the time in the world. He kissed her jaw, sliding his mouth to the sensitive recesses of her neck and blowing across the damp skin until she shivered with desire. The scrape of his chin blazed a fiery path along her sensitive flesh.

He drove her mad with longing, drawing out the kiss until her nails dug into his shoulders from gripping him so tightly.

He was still leaning over her—their bodies not yet touching. She strained with need, wanting to feel the weight of his chest on top of her, her breasts crushed against the hard-muscled wall that she'd just admired with her hands.

He kissed her mouth again, this time harder. She opened against him, forcing him to deepen the kiss when she met his tongue with her own.

She moaned, unable to contain the burst of pleasure as their kiss grew wilder. Hotter.

He tasted like sin, dark and spicy with a hint of wine. Sweet intoxication. She could kiss him like this forever, where there was nothing between them but the hunger of their mouths and tongues.

But something was happening to her body. The restlessness that she remembered from before. Every inch of her skin was aflame, her nipples ached, the sensitive place between her legs pulsed.

When he finally covered her breast with his hand, she jumped. He plied the nipple with his fingers until she arched against him, silently begging.

He undid the ties at her neck, then opened her nightraile to reveal her breasts. She was beyond embarrassment, her desire masking everything but the pleasure and anticipation coursing through her body. Scooping the pale flesh in his hand, he lifted the pink tip to his mouth and sucked.

A needle of pleasure shot through her. His warm, wet mouth on her sensitive flesh sent wicked sensations shuddering through her. The passion he'd carefully wrought within her came perilously close to bursting.

His low growl of pleasure as he squeezed her breasts with his hands and sucked her with his incredible mouth sent heat washing over her. Her hips started to lift as the urgency between her legs grew unbearable.

Her obvious need seemed to shatter his control. His mouth grew more insistent as he sucked, his tongue circling and his teeth nipping lightly on the turgid peak until her entire body arched against him.

Finally, when she didn't think she could stand it anymore, he lifted his head from her breast and moved over her. He lowered his chest to hers, letting her feel some of his weight. The warm air hit her skin as he lifted her night-raile and slid his hands between her legs.

All of a sudden, she froze.

His weight suddenly felt suffocating as her mind filled with haunting images. His gentle touch suddenly felt rough and threatening. Bile rose in the back of her throat. The smoke. The soldier attempting to pry her legs apart.

She pushed against him, tears stinging her eyes, the beauty of the moment shattered by memories of the past. "Stop!" she cried. "Please stop! I can't do this."

Chapter 12

❖ ❖ ❖

Desire twisted around Jamie like a steel vise. He drew a long, ragged breath, every inch of his body primed for passion. Never had he so wanted to thrust inside a woman and relieve the agonizing pressure in his loins. His cock throbbed, pulsing with need. Every primal instinct clamored to take. Her kiss. Her moans. The sweet movements of her body. Her responsiveness had brought him to the breaking point. He held himself taut, fighting for control, until sweat gathered on his forehead.

He knew what he had to do, even if it killed him. Slowly, he lifted himself off her. "You have nothing to fear from me, Caitrina. I would never hurt you."

She looked ready to burst into tears. "It's just that I keep remembering . . ."

Jamie cursed his brother's guardsman. If the blackguard weren't dead already, he would be now.

"You don't understand." She looked at him wildly, tears streaming down her cheeks. "I think he . . . violated me."

He wiped a hot tear away with his thumb. She'd remembered more than he'd realized, but not all of it. "He didn't rape you, Caitrina."

"How can you be sure?"

"Because I prevented him from doing so."

Her eyes grew wide. "You did?"

He nodded. "You were unconscious, and I wasn't sure how much you remembered. I would have said something earlier if I'd known what you thought." His face grew grim. "But be assured the scourge paid the price for what he attempted."

He could see that she'd understood—the soldier was dead.

"Thank you," she said softly, lifting her eyes to his.

Though he knew she was relieved to discover she hadn't been raped, he also knew that her fears would not be so quickly forgotten. But he also knew that making love would bring them closer. How could he show her . . .

All at once, he knew.

He took her hand, drawing it up to his mouth to place a soft kiss on her palm. "You show me what you want." He saw her uncertainty.

"What do you mean?"

"I swear that I will not touch you unless you ask it of me." *Heaven help me.* "If you want to stop, just say so." She would be in control.

She looked at him uncertainly. "You would do this for me?"

"Aye." He lifted her hand to his mouth. "I told you, I want to bring you pleasure."

She blushed. "You were, until . . ."

He thought for a moment. Until he'd moved over her and slid his hands between her legs. The first could be solved easily enough; the second, well, if he did his part, she would be begging for his touch.

He lay down in bed beside her and rolled her on top of him, excruciatingly aware of every inch of her incredible body plastered to him. Her long, slim legs were entwined with his, the curve of her hip nestled against his manhood, her lush, round breasts crushed against his chest, and the delicate pink tips poked him erotically. The sensation of this delectable woman poured over him was so extraordinary, and so unlike anything he'd ever experienced before, that Jamie wondered if he'd been hasty in his vow not to touch her.

He said a quick prayer for strength and tried not to think about it—which was easier said than done with her molded against him.

When he looked into her eyes, he could see her surprise—but not, he was relieved to see, fear.

"Um . . . are you sure it can be done . . ." She bit her lip. "Is this natural?"

God, yes. He tried not to groan, thinking just how natural this position could be. He didn't want to think of his hands around her waist, her breasts bouncing against his hands as she moved up and down on his throbbing—

Hell.

Clearing the lustful images from his head, he answered, "There is more than one way to make love, Caitrina. And I promise to show you all of them."

The shy blush that rose to her cheeks was one of the most sensual things he'd ever seen, for he could see the eager curiosity in her eyes.

He held his hands firmly at his side, resisting the urge to slide them along the smooth curve of her back and cup the lush swell of her buttocks.

"I'm afraid I don't know what to do," she said, clearly embarrassed.

"Whatever you will," he replied. "I'm yours to command."

She considered for a moment, and the naughty smile that played upon her lips sent a chill of foreboding straight through him. The feeling, so foreign, could only be described as alarm. He, a man who'd made hardened warriors turn and run on the battlefield, was scared of a wee lass.

What in Hades had he done?

She looked at his mouth, unconsciously sliding her tongue along her lower lip. Heat rushed over him. "You mean if I kiss you . . ." She lowered her mouth to his until only a hairbreadth separated them. The succulent honey of her breath made his mouth water. "You will not kiss me back?"

His body went rigid as she placed a tender kiss on his mouth. He had to grip the bedcoverings to fight the hard swell that rose inside him, demanding a response. He wanted to kiss her hard, to have his tongue deep in her mouth as he devoured her senseless.

"Not if you don't want me to," he said tightly.

He felt her relax, her body eased against him, melting. It was pure torture.

She kissed him again, sliding her tongue between the crease of his mouth. His chest pounded, his cock jerking hard against her. *Where in the hell had she learned to do that?*

If it was instinct, as he suspected, he was in trouble—deep trouble.

But he didn't have time to contemplate the future because she kissed him again. Pressing her soft lips to his and sliding her tongue in his mouth in a slow, tender sigh.

Her soft hand held his cheek as she stroked him with her tongue as he'd so foolishly taught her. It was all he could do not to flip her over on her back and kiss her as deeply as she was begging for.

"Kiss me," she murmured.

He groaned with relief, circling his tongue against hers, sparring, delving, tasting her every bit as deeply as she had him. She was so sweet and hot, he couldn't get enough.

Blood was pounding through his body. His erection was so hard, he knew she must feel him. As if reading his thoughts, she moved her hips over him, wedging him firmly between her legs.

He couldn't breathe.

Unaware of what she was doing to him, she broke the kiss and trailed her lips along his jaw and neck, singeing a path of fire on his skin. Her hands fanned over his chest and arms, exploring every ridge and bulge of muscle with almost childish delight, as if she were a bairn opening a gift at Yule.

His heart pounded, his cock pounded, every instinct clamored to touch her, but he held still under her innocent scrutiny.

He counted to ten in his head, doing anything to keep his mind from what she was doing to his body.

What had possessed him to do this? She lifted her chest off him a little to slide her hand between them, her hand skimming his stomach as her tongue slid along his neck. Every muscle in his body tensed. Her fingers trailed across the rigid bands of his stomach, and the feathery touch so achingly close was almost more than he could bear. He had to grit his teeth to prevent another groan.

Her hand dipped lower, to the waist of his breeches, and her palm accidentally brushed over the throbbing head of his erection. His buttocks clenched as he fought the urge to thrust.

He must have made a sound because she lifted her mouth from his neck. He could see the uncertainty in her gaze. "Did I hurt you?"

He shook his head and said tightly, "Only because I want you so much."

She slid her eyes down to him, seeing how he strained against the leather of his breeches. If possible, it only made him harder. "Would it help if I touched you?"

"Yes," he lied, even though he knew it would only make it infinitely worse. But what she offered him was so tantalizing, he could not speak the truth. Her tiny hand wrapped around him . . .

He shook off the thought and steeled himself for her touch.

"What do I do?"

"Undo the ties." She did as he directed. He knew he shouldn't, but he had to watch her. Her eyes widened, seeing him in the flesh—all of him. He wondered if she would change her mind, but after a long pause she raised her eyes to his in question. "Circle me with your hand," he said softly.

"I'll try."

He closed his eyes and groaned. *Oh God, that felt good.* Her hand was soft and cool, and he was so hot. He jerked a little in her hand as a drop of fluid escaped from his tip. Her grip around him was tentative, but sweet . . . achingly sweet.

Because he didn't think he could speak, he covered her hand with his and showed her how to stroke him.

Flames roared in his ears as he gave himself over to the fire she wrought in his blood. Pleasure unlike anything he'd ever known rushed over him.

She stroked him faster, harder, until the pressure built to erupting, his body clenched, and he knew he was about to come.

He grabbed her wrist. "Stop," he said through gritted teeth. "You'll unman me."

His heart pounded as he fought for control. She looked at him questioningly. "I've been too long without a woman," he explained, though he knew it had nothing to do with that—he had always been a man of prodigious control even when it came to sex—but everything to do with *this* woman.

His explanation seemed to please her. She leaned down and kissed him again. "How long?" she murmured against his mouth.

He thought about it a minute and decided to tell her the truth. "Since I first saw you."

Caitrina didn't know why, but his declaration pleased her enormously. She wasn't exactly sure what his need to stop had to do with other women, but it didn't matter. He'd lain with no one else since he'd met her. It must mean something. Perhaps he did care for her.

She could tell from the strain in his body that what she'd done had pleased him. And pleasing him, she realized, had also pleased her.

She felt relaxed, confident, and most important, eager to continue.

She kissed him again, rubbing her body ever so gently against his. The places where they touched tingled with sensation. But it wasn't enough; she craved the weight and pressure of his hands.

She kissed him harder, trying to convey her wishes with her mouth. She could feel the passion stirring inside him but knew that no matter how hard she drove him, he would hold to his vow.

She would have to tell him.

Her mouth moved across his jaw, rough with stubble, to his ear. "Touch me," she whispered. "Please, touch me."

"Where?" he asked.

The heavy brogue of his voice seemed as rich and dark as molten lava, sinking deep into her bones. No man should have a voice like that—one that could seduce with a word. "Everywhere," she answered.

He moaned and cupped her breasts lovingly in his hands, pinching her nipples to taut peaks. "Like this, my sweet?"

She threw back her head, giving herself over to the exquisite sensations wrought by his powerful hands on her body. Hands that could wield a claymore with deadly strength but could stroke and caress with painstaking tenderness.

His mouth clasped over one nipple as he drew it deep in his mouth, tugging it between his teeth until her body—of its own accord—started to move against him. She felt his erection hot and throbbing against her belly. Like the rest of him, he was a big man. Though she'd felt him pressed against her body, she hadn't quite realized just how big until she'd released him from the confines of his breeches. For a moment, all she could feel was shock and not a wee bit of trepidation—until she'd taken him in her hand. She remembered how he'd felt—like velvet over steel. But most of all, she remembered how it had felt to harness all that raw masculine strength in the palm of her tiny hand. *She* had the power to make him weak with pleasure, and the knowledge was both thrilling and emboldening, giving her confidence she would have thought impossible.

"I want you naked," he said, and his eyes bored into her with a passion that was almost frightening in its intensity. It wasn't merely lust, but something far deeper. Something that wrapped around her like a warm, fuzzy plaid. Something that she'd never thought she'd feel again: secure.

She nodded, and he deftly pulled her nightraile over her head, depositing it on the floor beside the bed. She was no longer on top of him, but stretched out beside him.

She didn't have time to be embarrassed by her nudity because he was sucking her breasts again, lifting them to his face and nuzzling between the deep cleft. The scratch of his whiskers was a welcome friction against her fevered skin.

Never had she felt so cherished. He worshipped her with his mouth and tongue. As if trying to memorize every inch of her, he sculpted her with his hands, leaving nothing unexplored. The long, slow drag of his callused palms across her feverish skin made her prickle with awareness. It was exquisite, beautiful in its torture. Every touch, every move he made, was calculated for her pleasure. Desire gathered between her legs in a heated pool. She was warm and soft and desperate for his touch.

His lips covered hers again in a wet, openmouthed kiss that was dark and carnal. His fingertip skidded along the inside of her thigh. Her breath caught in anticipation.

"Tell me," he whispered. She nudged toward his hand, but all he did was gently sweep over her with the tip of his finger. "Do you want me to touch you here, Caitrina?" She was in such anguish, her entire body shuddered from the feather-soft touch.

"Please," she begged, pressing against his hand, craving pressure.

She moaned when he finally slid his finger inside her, bringing her to the very peak of pleasure with his deft stroking. He was pulling her down a long, dark tunnel of sensation where all she could think of was releasing the pressure building between her legs.

He murmured wicked encouragements in her ear, driving her wild. She was so close. . . .

But she wanted more. She wanted to share her pleasure with him. Instinctively, she reached out to take him in her hand, her fingers wrapping around his hot, velvety skin. "Show me," she said.

His hand went still. His gaze met hers. "You're sure?" She nodded.

Taking her by the hips, he gently guided her on top of him so that she straddled him with her legs. The feel of his thick, heavy column between her thighs gave her a moment's pause, but all was forgotten when he moved her over his tip. Her body started to quiver as he nudged gently at her opening with the smooth, round head. She spread her legs wider and slowly lowered her body over him.

He made a sound that was almost pained as she sank down, taking the heavy head inside her. She stopped when she felt a bit of resistance and allowed her body to get used to the sensation of being stretched around him, trying to decide whether it hurt.

He held himself perfectly still, not moving an inch, though she knew that he was holding himself by a very thin thread. She could see the grim determination on his face, the muscles in his neck and shoulders drawn as tight as the string of a bow.

"It doesn't hurt so badly at all," she decided.

He made a sound that was like a strangled laugh. "I'm afraid we're not quite done yet, my love."

Love. She knew it was a turn of phrase, an endearment

uttered in the heat of the moment, but it did not stop the pang of longing in her chest. "We're not?" she asked.

He shook his head.

She tried to sink down a little more and stopped. "I'm afraid this is as far as I can go, you are simply too big."

This time he managed to smile. "Words to warm the heart of any man, my sweet, but I can assure you it will work. I must break through your virgin's barrier. I can make it go fast, but I'll not lie to you, it will hurt."

She nodded. Before she could reconsider, his hands grasped her waist, and holding her gaze, in one smooth motion he thrust up high inside her. Deep inside her. She felt a sharp pinch and cried out.

"I'm sorry," he said, his voice tight with restraint.

Her body fought the invasion and her first instinct was to lift off of him, but he held her firm.

"Give it a minute," he urged. "Try to relax. God, you feel incredible."

He started to massage the tip of the opening between her legs with his thumb, and slowly her body softened. The sweet drowsy feeling spread over her again.

"That's it," he groaned, rubbing her a little harder. He was right: It did feel incredible, unlike anything she'd ever imagined. She never thought she could feel this close to someone. He seemed to fill her, his manhood providing all the pressure she had craved—and more.

Her body began to move, lifting up a little and sinking down on him again. She fell into a natural rhythm. Never had she felt so free.

She knew from the look of rapture on his face that she must be doing something right.

As her pulse started to race frantically, he clasped her hips and helped move her faster over him. Churning, plunging, harder and harder. Faster and faster. Until . . .

Her body contracted in the tight grip of pleasure and

started to pulse. It must have been all that he'd been waiting for, because she sensed him relax and let go.

"I'm going to come," he said tightly, and thrust one more time, penetrating to her very core. Their eyes met, and what she saw there made her heart squeeze. The tender emotion was a sharp contrast to his usual cold implacability; she knew he'd revealed a part of himself that she'd never seen before—that maybe no one had ever seen before.

He cried out as his body tensed and the hot rush of his seed exploded inside her.

And she rose up to meet him, arching her back and crying out as her own release swept over her. It was the same as before, only much more intense. The slow breaking apart, the sharp pinnacle of sensation, the brief moment where her heart stopped and her soul seemed to touch the heavens. But this time, she was not alone.

I'm not alone.

She wanted it to last forever and clung to the sensations as long as she could, riding each wave until the last tingle of sensation had ebbed.

Breathing hard, she slumped forward onto his chest, their skin pleasantly slick with the sheen of perspiration.

Her cheek was pressed to his chest. Listening to the frantic beat of his heart begin to slow, she closed her eyes.

Jamie heard the soft, even sounds of her breathing and knew she slept. He breathed a sigh of relief. He didn't have words to describe what he was feeling and was glad for the time to collect himself.

What the hell had just happened?

It was like nothing he'd ever experienced. He'd known their attraction was strong, but it did not explain the connection he'd felt when deep inside her. A connection that had far more to do with sating his soul than with sating his lust. Never had a woman so completely penetrated his iron-forged control. She'd revealed a part of him that he hadn't known existed.

He stroked her hair, contemplating the strange tightness in his chest. The overwhelming feeling of tenderness for the tiny woman in his arms. His wife. He'd thought that would be enough, but it wasn't. He wanted more, much more. He wanted her love, trust, and respect. For without the latter two, the first was impossible.

But what if she could never give it to him?

He was inextricably tied to his cousin—a man she could not abide—and his own brother had destroyed her clan.

How long would it be before she asked him to choose between her and his family—his duty?

He dreaded the day, though he knew it would come. For there were some things he could not—would not—do. He nestled her more firmly under his arm. Even for her.

Chapter 13

❖ ❖ ❖

A knock at the door stirred Caitrina awake. It took her a few moments to realize where she was and that she was alone. She didn't know whether to be disappointed or relieved—probably a little of both. In the stark light of day, the memories of what they'd shared last night took on new meaning, and she was more than a little embarrassed by her passionate response to their lovemaking.

If she needed a reminder, all she had to do was look down at the sheeting twisted around her naked limbs to recall exactly how bold she'd been. Her cheeks heated. Quickly, she bent over to pluck her nightraile from the floor, then dropped it over her head, fastened the ties at the neck, and bade the person at the door enter.

It was Mor. She bustled into the room, a stack of drying cloths piled to her nose. "The laird bid me wake you so you had time to bathe before breaking your fast." She placed the linen atop Caitrina's chest and began to stoke the fire. "He wishes to leave within the hour."

Caitrina stretched lazily, reluctant to leave the cozy warmth of the bed. "What time is it?"

Her old nurse walked to the windows and tore open the shutters. Blinding rays of sunshine poured across the polished wood-planked floor. "Nearly midmorning."

"Already!" Caitrina exclaimed, suddenly wide awake. "We were supposed to leave for Ascog at daybreak. Why did someone not wake me?"

"The laird instructed me to let you sleep." Mor didn't

seem to be any more happy to take his orders in the morning than she had in the eve. She gave Caitrina a pointed look. "He said you needed your rest."

Caitrina turned so Mor would not see the telltale blush creeping up her cheeks.

"You are all right?" Mor asked hesitantly. "He was not too rough—"

"I'm fine," Caitrina said hurriedly. Better than fine. She'd never felt so . . . fine. She could still see the frown on Mor's face, so she reached out to clasp her hands and look into her worried eyes. "Truly, Mor, I'm well. He was . . . gentle." Surprisingly so. Completely at odds with the fierce, implacable warrior she thought him to be. Last night, she'd seen a side of him she hadn't expected, and she didn't know what to do with her newfound knowledge.

She still couldn't believe what had happened. He'd surprised her on so many levels. First by his sensitivity to her lingering fears from the soldier's attack and then by his ceding to her complete control in their lovemaking. Never could she have imagined that he would give her such a gift when his sheer physical strength, his natural authority and command, and the sexual virility that exuded from him all spoke of dominant male. And her confidence that he would stop at any point had calmed her fears like nothing else— he'd known what she needed even before she did. Had she once thought him cold and ruthless? Perhaps to his enemies, but to her he'd been understanding, tender . . . almost loving.

Satisfied by Caitrina's response, her old nurse nodded, and she was saved from further conversation by the arrival of the wooden tub.

While she was relaxing in the warm water, her thoughts drifted more than once or twice to her husband. Instinctively, she realized that something had changed between them, but what? Would it be uncomfortable to see him? Would he pretend nothing had happened? *Had* anything happened? She half expected him to open the door at any minute, but it wasn't until after she'd broken her fast that she saw him.

He entered the great hall with her uncle, and her heart jumped. She tensed, waiting for his reaction. His eyes found hers and, perhaps sensing her uncertainty, he smiled.

He took her breath away. And with that one simple gesture, perhaps a little of her heart as well.

It should be a sin to be so handsome. With his eyes twinkling, his dark ruddy hair slumped over his brow, and his sensual mouth curved in a wide grin, there was no one who could compare. He looked more at ease than she'd ever seen him. She'd never realized how much he was always on guard.

But there was something else. . . .

She drew in her breath. His clothing. For the first time since she'd met him, he was wearing the traditional *breacan feile* of a Highlander—the belted plaid was worn over a fine linen shirt and secured at the shoulder with his chieftain's badge. If anything, the garb made him look even more impressive. She recognized the plaid as similar to the one he'd lent her the first day they'd met. She was so used to seeing him in court clothing, but it reminded her that despite his worldly Lowland ways, he was, in fact, a Highlander.

She couldn't help wondering if it meant something.

He strode toward her and took her hand, lifting it to his mouth. "I trust you slept well?"

Aware of the eyes on them, she still couldn't prevent the heat that rose in her cheeks. "Yes, thank you."

"My pleasure," he teased.

Mortified, she stumbled, "I didn't mean—" She stopped, seeing the laughter in his eyes. "Wretch," she murmured.

He laughed and drew her hand into the crook of his arm. "If you are ready, we can bid our farewells."

It was strange. Standing beside him side to side, her hand

resting against the hard muscle of his arm, she felt connected. They were connected, she realized, as man and wife. She could never have her old life back, but maybe, just maybe, she could make a new one—not better or worse, but different.

Saying good-bye to her uncle, aunt, and cousins was more difficult than she'd expected. She owed them so much and knew that she could never repay their kindness.

It wasn't until her cousin John pulled her aside while Jamie spoke privately with her uncle in the laird's solar that reality intruded on the dreamlike spell woven by their passionate wedding night.

"It won't be easy for you, lass, married to a Campbell. You've made a great sacrifice for your clan, but if you find it more than you can bear, send for me."

Caitrina lowered her gaze. *Sacrifice*. It wasn't half the sacrifice it should be. Still, her cousin's concern—even if misplaced—touched her. She felt a jab in her chest. It was something Malcolm or Niall would have done. "Thank you, John, but it won't be necessary. I'll manage well enough."

He gave her a hard look. "Don't be deceived by the pleasure of the marriage bed, lass." John's blunt—and too accurate—appraisal of the situation took her aback. "He wants you, but Jamie Campbell is every bit as dangerous and ruthless as they say. I've seen him in action. He'll never allow himself to be swayed by a woman. His first loyalty will always be to his cousin. Don't let the costume fool you," he said, referring to Jamie's choice of clothing. Apparently, she hadn't been the only one to notice the change in attire. "He's a Campbell through and through—and as such, will never be a friend of ours."

Caitrina tried to cover her embarrassment. Was she so transparent? Was her fascination with her husband so easy to see? She thought of her vow to stay distant, of her vow for revenge against the Campbells, and was shamed by her weakness. How easily she'd succumbed. But never had she imagined he could be so tender . . . sweet . . . almost loving. Pride forced her chin upward to meet her cousin's gaze. "You don't have to remind me. I know well whom I've married." *And what I've become.*

"There will be grumbling," he warned.

Her cousin was right. Those who remained of her clan would not like what she'd done. She felt a flicker of unease. Jamie would never tolerate disloyalty or disrespect—how would he bring them in line? "They will see that it is for the best."

They had to. She would not suffer the same heartbreak of her mother: to be cast out from her clan for marrying the enemy.

Out of the corner of her eye, she noticed Jamie and her uncle come back into the room. He headed right for her with a dark glower on his face, almost as if he could guess what they were talking about.

John gave her another long look, this one almost pitying. "For your sake, little cousin, I hope you are right."

The short journey across the Clyde from Toward to Rothesay proceeded without event, and by midafternoon, Caitrina found herself ensconced in Rothesay Castle, the luxurious former Stewart stronghold with its unique design of circular towers that would serve as her home until Ascog could be repaired. It was far grander than any place she'd ever lived and took some getting used to—as did having a husband.

Over the next few days, they established a tenuous truce. One forged in the darkness of the night, where nothing could come between desire and passion. He'd come to bed late, take off his clothes before the smoldering fire, slip into bed beside her naked, and wait for her to come to him. As he'd done the first night, he never let her forget it was her choice—*she* was the one in control. And like a moth to the flame she was helpless to resist the primitive calling.

In the darkness, where no one could see her need, she reached for him. Sliding her hands over his big powerful body, savoring the strength flexing under her fingertips, she gave free rein to her desire. She told him with her passion what she could not say with words—of her hunger, of her wanting, for him. And with a tenderness that she would have thought impossible for such a powerful man, he fed that hunger, giving her pleasure beyond anything she'd ever imagined.

But as tender and loving as he was in bed, and as much as Caitrina had learned of his body, in many ways her husband was still a stranger to her. The light moments of intimacy they'd shared after that first night had not returned. He cradled her in his arms, but he never tried to talk to her, never shared his thoughts. They spoke in gasps and groans, in quickness of breath, and in tightening of muscles—the language of pleasure—sharing the secrets of their bodies but not of their hearts. She knew how to take him in her hands and milk him until every muscle in his body clenched with the need to find release, how to tease, how to touch, but nothing of his feelings for her.

And in the morning when she woke, sore and sated, he was gone. It was as if he'd sensed her subtle retrenchment and had decided not to press her.

She almost wished he would.

Watching him organize the men to begin the repairs on Ascog, she wondered whether she'd imagined those brief moments of lightheartedness. He was every inch the chief—every inch the commander. Every inch a Campbell.

Only in the dark, wrapped in his arms, did she wonder if there was something more.

By unspoken agreement, they assiduously avoided any mention of his family—or of hers. But it hung between them: his cousin who ruled the Highlands with an iron fist and his brother who'd killed her father and destroyed her home—not to mention Jamie's own fearsome reputation.

As her cousin John had suspected, Caitrina had been overly optimistic in her kin's understanding of her predicament. She knew Mor and the other servants who had been with her at Toward had done their best to explain the situation to the others, but the Lamonts would never welcome a Campbell into their midst, and the resentment toward Jamie and his men by her Lamont kin who descended on Rothesay Castle once it was known that she had returned was palpable. They took his orders, too intimidated to do otherwise.

His power was undeniable. As she'd noticed from the first, it seemed to surround him. He held himself with the bearing of a king. They were all aware that there was not much he couldn't do; he was limited only by his own forbearance. His authority might be unquestionable, but it was deeply resented.

It wasn't until the third day when she'd finally made her way to Ascog, however, that she realized just how precarious the situation could be.

The morning was already half gone as she strolled along the short path that led from Rothesay to Ascog—nary a half mile separated the two castles. The sun was masked by a heavy layer of clouds, and an autumn chill permeated the air. Her step slowed as she drew near. Though returning to her home had been all that she could think of at Toward, it had proved much more difficult than she'd expected. It was, after all, the place where her father and brothers had lost their lives only a few months before, and she wasn't sure she was ready to confront the emotions that seeing the destroyed castle would provoke. Seeming to understand her turmoil, Jamie had not pressed her but told her that when she was ready, she should send for him.

But when she woke this morning, finally ready to face the ruins of her home, he had already gone. Though she knew he slept beside her, he'd seemed to make it a practice to leave before she woke, further driving a wedge between the closeness they had in the night and their distance during the day. Instead of sending for him, she'd decided to go on her own, wanting to be alone when she viewed the ruins for the first time.

Her heart pounded as she crested the hill that served as the majestic northern backdrop to Ascog Castle. She drew in a sharp breath and tears burned her eyes as the charred shell of Ascog came into view. Streaks of ash had turned portions of the gray stone black. All that remained in the inner *barmkin* gate was the stone tower—bereft of its wooden roof. Indeed, everything made of wood—all the small outer buildings that circled the courtyard—was gone.

Despair mingled with relief. It was a ghostly shell of the place that she'd loved—but like her, it was still standing.

Her gaze swept over the *barmkin,* seeing the swarm of laboring men removing the ashes and debris. Her eyes blurred as memories of a happier time spun by. She could almost see Brian running after one of his dogs or Niall and Malcolm trying to clobber each other as they practiced with their *claidheamhmórs*. A single tear slid off her cheek and dropped on her *arisaidh*. God, how she missed them.

The weight of all she'd lost dropped over her shoulders. Loneliness and sorrow swept over her.

The work that it would take to restore the castle to its former glory was nearly overwhelming. Responsibility, duty—things that in her old life had always belonged to someone else—hit her full force. It belonged to her now, and she could not turn back. Wiping the tears from her cheeks with the back of her hand, she drew a deep breath and started down the hill.

Though some of the debris had been cleared, there was still much to be done, and she intended to be there for every step of the rebuilding. As she'd assumed Jamie would

be. But when she passed through the gate into the courtyard, she was surprised to find no sign of him.

The men, most of them former servants or tacksmen of
her father's, stopped their work and eyed her warily. Their
reticence stung, but she plastered a wide smile on her face
and spoke to one of the men she recognized.

"It's good to see you, Callum."

"And you, mistress," he replied, returning her smile. But
then he sobered. "We're sorry for your loss, lass. Your father was a great chief."

She nodded, a ball of emotion lodged at the back of her
throat. "Thank you," she managed. "I miss them very
much."

She made her way through the crowd, greeting others by
name and asking about their families. Sensing the lighten-
ing of spirit, she broached the subject of repairs. Callum
stated that they had a few more days of clearing the debris,
but by the end of the week, they expected to start cutting
the trees that would be used in the rebuilding. With wood
scarce in the Isles, they were fortunate indeed to have the
forest nearby with a ready supply of timber.

Another man stepped forward, this one not much older
than her, and asked the question that was apparently on
everyone's minds. "Is it true, my lady? Were you forced to
marry the man who killed your father?"

"No," she answered, startled. "I mean, I did marry, but
my husband had nothing to do with the attack."

"But he's a Campbell," Callum said angrily. "And Argyll's Henchman."

"Yes," she hedged. "But . . ." Her voice dropped off. But
what? What could she say? This was worse than she'd
imagined. Lamonts would never welcome a Campbell as
their leader. All she'd thought of was reclaiming her home
for her clan. But she knew that was only the partial truth.
Jamie had forced her hand in this marriage, but she'd not
put up much of a fight. On a base level that she could not

explain, she wanted to believe in him. She met Callum's gaze fully. "Now he's also my husband." She looked around, still surprised that she'd yet to see him. "The laird," she ventured. "Has he gone to the forest to see to the timber?"

One of the men spat in the dirt. " 'Tis not timber the Henchman seeks, but men."

Caitrina frowned, instinctively rebelling at the use of the nickname, though realizing that she'd called him worse. She felt a strange urge to defend her husband but knew that to do so would only alienate her clan further. "I don't understand."

Another man spoke. "He's clearing the forests of your father's men, rounding them up for Argyll."

No. The breath was knocked out of her. "There must be some mistake."

But there was no mistake, because at that moment she turned, hearing the sound of horses. And riding through the gate, leading a handful of bound men, was her husband. She recognized the bound men only too well as some of her father's former guardsmen.

Jamie wiped the dust and sweat from his forehead and dismounted. Despite the cool morning, he was hot and tired from chasing Lamonts since dawn. About the last person he wanted to see was his beautiful wife.

His beautiful wife, who was staring at him with silent accusation in her eyes.

The past few days had worn on him. He was doing his damnedest not to press matters between them, but his patience had been stretched to its limits. Passion wasn't enough, damn it. He wanted all of her.

After their wedding night, he'd hoped it might be a new beginning for them. But whatever her blasted cousin had said to her that morning had cured him of that notion. He'd sensed her withdrawal, her subtle pulling away.

Their closeness at night only served to make it worse. It gave him a small taste of how things might be. If only she would give him a chance. But he was beginning to wonder whether that would ever happen. How could it, when every venomous look directed at him by her clansmen widened the chasm between them?

"What are you doing?" she cried, running up to him. "These are my father's men." She turned to one of the bound men and threw her arms around him, not caring that he was layered with dirt and grime from months of living in squalor. Her overt display of emotion for her father's guardsman when she could barely manage to look at Jamie in the daylight ate like acid in his chest. "Seamus," she said softly. "I thought you were—"

"It's good to see your bonny face, lass," the older man replied. "We feared the same of you. It was only with news of your *marriage*," he sneered, "to Argyll's Henchman that we were sure you had survived."

"I'm so happy to see all of you," she said, touching the face of another man—this one far younger—with such tenderness that Jamie felt as if she'd just slipped a dirk between his ribs.

He wanted something from her so badly, he could almost taste it.

But when she turned to look at him, there was no sign of affection or tenderness on her face—only betrayal and distrust. "Release these men at once."

Jamie stiffened but otherwise ignored her demand. He felt his temper—something he hadn't known he had before meeting her—rise. Cool rationality gave way to hot emotion.

A kind of hush descended over the crowd as they waited for his reaction. How would the most feared man in the Highlands react to being ordered about by a lass?

Seamus moved in front of her. "I'll protect you, lass."

"From what?" Caitrina replied, completely oblivious.

That was some consolation, Jamie reflected, though admittedly small. Unlike these men, she knew he would never hurt her. Not that she didn't deserve a good tongue-lashing. But right now he didn't trust himself not to say something he couldn't take back.

"I thought I told you to send for me when you wished to come to the castle," he said, not bothering to mask his annoyance.

"There was no need—"

"In the future, *wife*," he said with emphasis, "you will do as I say."

Her cheeks burned with indignation, but wisely she chose not to argue. He was thinking only of her safety, but damned if he would explain himself again.

He heard the grumblings of her clansmen but also sensed their grudging admiration. By all rights, he could have done much worse. He was laird, and his word was law—and hardly subject to the dictates of a lass. Even one who was his wife. Her clansmen might not like it, but they would not interfere. Pride reigned supreme for a Highlander. No Highlander worth his salt would stand for his lady questioning his decisions before his men.

Perhaps realizing that she'd overstepped her bounds, she moderated her tone. "Please," she said. "What cause have you to bind these men?"

"None," Seamus replied. "Except that he's a rot Campbell bastard who burns and pillages people from their homes to fatten the pockets of a tyrant."

"Enough!" Jamie boomed. It wasn't his fault the men were bound in the first place, but they'd refused to surrender under the conditions he'd granted. He turned to the captain of his guardsmen. "Take these men back to Rothesay. Perhaps after a few days in the dungeon they will change their minds."

Caitrina gasped. "No! You can't—"

"Yes," he said with deadly calm. "I can."

"Don't worry, lass," Seamus said. "The Henchman doesn't scare us."

Jamie met the older man's stare with such intensity that he dropped his gaze, proving his lie.

Her husband addressed the rest of the men who'd gathered round to watch the proceedings. "Return to work, all of you." After issuing a few specific instructions to the two men he'd designated as foremen, he allowed his gaze to settle again on his wife. It almost hurt just to look at her. "If you would like to return to Rothesay, I can have one of my men escort you."

"I don't need—"

The furious look on his face stopped her.

"Please," she said, moving in front of him. She placed her hand on his arm. Already on edge, every nerve in his body leapt at her touch. "Will you not speak to me? In private."

He turned his gaze, not daring to look at her hand. "I'm busy."

"A few minutes are all I ask. Surely you can spare a few minutes?"

Though he wasn't sure he wanted to have this conversation in his present mood, he nodded stiffly and motioned her toward the gate. They walked down the path to the loch in silence. When they reached the edge of the water, he turned to her, his face expressionless. "What is it you wished to say?" Or accuse him of, which was probably more likely.

"Will you not explain to me why you have imprisoned my father's men?"

Tired of her thinking the worst of him, he was tempted not to, but the soft plea in her voice tugged at the part of him that still sought her understanding. "I believe I told you when we married that I'd taken surety for your clan— making me responsible for their actions. I've been charged with clearing Bute of outlaws, and I damn well intend to do so." He'd shocked her with his language, but he didn't care. She thought him a brute, so be it.

She studied his face as if looking for a crack. "I thought you'd come here to help rebuild Ascog."

"I did. But I have other duties." He gave her a long look. "Just what is it you think I do, Caitrina?"

"I . . . ," she stammered, eyes wide.

He took her elbow and pulled her against him, his body a mass of gnarling tension. He couldn't be this close to her, breathe in her seductive scent, and not want to take her into his arms and kiss her. To claim her body, even if she was determined to give him nothing else. "If men break the law, it is my responsibility to see them brought to justice."

He was not ashamed of what he did; without men like him, there would be anarchy and chaos.

He could feel the pounding of her heart. No matter what else, she was not unaffected by his touch. "But what have they done?" she breathed, her voice shallow.

"Do you mean after giving shelter to the MacGregors? They tried to attack my men and relieve them of some silver that I'd given them to purchase materials for the rebuilding of Ascog."

Clearly, he'd shocked her. "I'm sure they didn't know."

"I'm sure they didn't, but is that an excuse?"

"No, but couldn't you give them a chance? Once they know that you are only trying to help."

He gave her a hard look. "I did. I offered them a reprieve if they would agree to surrender and swear to me as their laird."

"Truly?" Her face lit with happiness. "That is wonderful."

"Your father's men refused."

Her face fell. "Oh." She swallowed thickly. "I see."

And he could tell that she did. She'd misjudged him and knew it. He released her, but she didn't move away.

"So what will you do now?" she asked.

"If they do not reconsider, I will send them to Dunoon."

"No!" Her horrified gaze flew to his. "You can't do that."

He clenched his jaw, a reaction to her again telling him what he could and could not do. "It is your father's men who give me no choice."

"Please," she said, putting her hand on him again—this time on his chest. It burned like a brand over his heart. She had to dip her head back to look at him. "Please. You can't. They'll be hanged."

Blood pounded through his body. He was achingly aware of the subtle persuasion of her body. He knew what she was doing, but damn her, it was working. Something stirred in his chest. He wanted to stay aloof, but he was not immune to her pleas. Would he ever be? And that perhaps more than anything angered him.

"Let me talk to them," she pleaded. "I can make them see reason."

It was what he'd sought all along. He had no more wish to send her father's men to their death than she. He nodded. "See that you do." His own weakness where she was concerned made his voice sound harsher than he intended. "But, Caitrina, this is the last time. Do not try to interfere with my duty again."

He wondered for whose benefit he said it. Their interests had jibed this time. But he knew it wouldn't always be so. This woman would stretch his duty to the breaking point because he'd do just about anything to please her.

All at once she dropped her hand, seeming to realize what she'd been doing—touching him, entreating him with the press of her body.

Caitrina had never seen him like this. He was furious with her. And worse, she knew it was not without justification. Once again, she'd jumped to the wrong conclusion.

But when she'd seen her father's men bound and then later heard his orders to send them to the dungeon, tact had flown out the window and all she could think of was his fearsome reputation.

Given what her father's men had done in waylaying his men, Jamie had been more than fair. And she'd not given him even the barest benefit of the doubt.

Instead she'd made demands, ordering him to release them without waiting to hear his explanation—and in doing so questioned his authority in front of her clan. And when that hadn't worked, she'd unconsciously fallen back on the one thing neither of them could deny to try to get through to him: their attraction.

He was not as impervious to her as he wanted to be, and there was something heady in the knowledge that she held sway over this fierce warrior.

But clearly, he wasn't happy about it. It had worked, but at what cost?

He'd turned and started back up the hill toward the tower. She felt a stab of panic, scared that if she let him walk away, it might be too late. "Wait." She rushed after him. He turned slowly and looked at her, his slate blue eyes giving no hint to his thoughts. "I'm sorry. I didn't mean to interfere. It's just that those men . . . you can't understand what it means for me to see them after all these months of not knowing whether they'd lived or died. Some of them I've known my whole life. Seamus used to sit me on his knee before the fire and let me play with his beard while regaling me with countless tales of our ancestors. I didn't mean to shame you by questioning your actions before my clansmen, but it's only natural that I would feel loyalty to them."

"Your first loyalty should be to me."

She felt a stab of guilt. He was right, but it wasn't that simple. "You're asking me to forget years of hatred and distrust between our clans." *And what I know of you.*

"No, I'm not. I'm asking you to trust me."

But could she? At times she wanted to. But her uncertainty must have shown on her face.

"What cause have I given you not to trust me?" he challenged. "Have I hurt you? Lied to you? Done anything to earn your distrust?"

She shook her head. On the contrary, he'd surprised her at every turn. And then there were those glimpses of tenderness, the side of him that he kept hidden but at times would reveal to her. "I want to trust you, but . . ."

"But what?"

She twisted her hands, not knowing how to explain. How could she explain that in trusting him, she feared she would lose some of her past forever? That it would feel as if she were cutting herself off from her clan? "It can't change overnight. Everything has happened so fast. I don't know what to believe." She gazed into his eyes, silently begging for understanding. "I'm confused."

"And yet you don't seem confused at night. You give me your body willingly enough."

Her chest squeezed and heat burned her cheeks. "That's different."

"Is it?" He arched a brow. "How? You trust me with your body, but not with your heart."

She stilled. Was that what he wanted from her? It was impossible.

Blood pounded in her ears. How could she explain that at night it was only the two of them? That the problems of the day did not penetrate the darkness? Why was he pressing her like this? He asked for something she was not ready to give. "It's my duty to give you my body," she blurted helplessly.

His face was a mask of stone, yet somehow she knew that she'd hurt him. Maybe it was in the sudden flex of his jaw or the small white lines that appeared around his mouth. His eyes pinned her. "It doesn't feel like duty when

you moan, taking me deep into your body. Over and over."
He took an intimidating step closer, and she could feel the
anger radiate from him. "Riding me until you come."

She flinched from the brutal honesty of his words.
"How dare you!" Hot shame crawled up her cheeks. Her
passion—her hunger—for him embarrassed her. It was all-
consuming, wild, and unencumbered.

"There is nothing to be ashamed of," he said more
kindly. "I love your passion."

But how do you feel about me? She wished she could
read his mind. It was clear he was angry with her for not
trusting him blindly. But what did she really know of him
other than in bed? She barely saw him during the day. He
kept himself so detached from her—except for that morning after they wed. Then, she could almost believe . . . She
turned away, emotion thickening her voice. "What do you
want from me? I married you, I come to your bed willingly,
isn't that enough?"

He drew back as if slapped. "No. I don't think it is."

This was all coming out wrong. How could she explain
that she did trust him, just not as completely as he wanted?
"What you are asking for doesn't happen overnight. It
takes time."

"Of course." The chill in his voice could have frozen a
loch in midsummer. "Perhaps we both need more time."

What did he mean by that? She watched him go, his
broad, muscled back retreating up the hill, and didn't know
what to do. She wanted to call him back but didn't know what
to say to make it right.

After a few minutes she followed him, spending the rest
of the day following the progress of the cleanup and carefully avoiding her husband. When it was time for her to
return to the castle, she found herself escorted by a few of
his men.

At the evening meal, he was polite, if more distant than usual. She didn't realize just how distant until later.

That night, for the first time since they were married, Jamie did not come to her bed.

Clutching the empty pillow beside her in her fingertips, she told herself it didn't matter, that she was grateful for the time to think; but the dull ache in her chest told differently.

Had she succeeded in pushing him away for good? Or was he simply giving her the time that she'd claimed she needed but now wasn't sure she wanted?

Chapter 14

❖ ❖ ❖

A few days later, Caitrina knelt on the floor of the great hall, trying to keep her eyes fastened on the soot-stained stone instead of what was going on above her as the men lifted the giant timbers that would support the new roof. Long planks of wood had been positioned atop the stone corbels and would eventually support the upper-level floors, but right now they were being used as makeshift scaffolding. By means of a series of ladders and ropes, the beams were being hoisted about thirty feet to the top of the open tower.

She couldn't help but be anxious—even though she was on solid ground. Fortunately, the stone floor of the great hall—built atop the kitchen vaults—had escaped significant damage. Not even the fragrant smell of fresh-cut wood could calm her unease. It was dangerous work, and she couldn't stand the thought of anyone getting hurt. Working side by side with her clansmen the past few days, she'd come to know so many of them, and the thought of anything happening . . . she didn't want to think about all that could go wrong.

But with winter fast approaching, they needed to work fast. The short days coupled with the off-and-on periods of misty rain made working conditions less than ideal.

In the back of her mind was the knowledge that Jamie was doing this for her. Normally the rebuilding would have been put off till spring, but he knew how much she wanted—nay, needed—to see Ascog restored to its former glory. If they could get the roof on and make the castle watertight, they would be able to continue the work inside throughout the winter.

Turning back to her work, she dipped her hands into the bucket of lye beside her to wring out the cloth. But the linen didn't look any cleaner when she finished, as the water had turned completely black. She stood with some effort, feeling like an old woman. Her knees were stiff and achy from being pressed against freezing cold stone for the better part of the day. Scrubbing the soot from the floors and walls seemed to be a never-ending proposition. She'd been at this for two straight days with no end in sight.

"Here, let me get that, mistress," said one of the young serving girls, moving toward her.

"That's all right, Beth, I need to stretch my legs." After picking up the bucket of filthy water, Caitrina walked to the window—now more of a hole in the wall without its shutters and glass—to toss it outside before going down to the well in the courtyard for fresh water.

She glanced down to make sure no one was below and stopped cold. Or perhaps she should say stopped hot, as heat flooded her body. There was just something about a big, strong man swinging an ax that made you look twice, and that something turned mesmerizing when it was Jamie. Despite the chill he'd removed his plaid, and his shirt was molded to the rippling muscles of his back as he swung the ax in a wide arc over his head and let it fall with a resounding chop.

She drew in her breath. As if sensing her eyes on him, he looked over his shoulder, and their eyes locked for one heartstopping moment—their separation stretched between them—before she quickly ducked out of the way. With her back pressed to the stone wall, she fought to catch her breath, feeling like a fool. Both for having been caught staring and for her reaction. How could he affect her so? It wasn't as if she'd never seen a man swing an ax before—although admittedly not one with such sheer physicality. Sheer physicality she was intimately familiar with.

That was the problem. She'd seen him naked, knew what it felt like to have her hands on all those warm, hard muscles. Knew what it felt like to have all that heat and strength surging inside her body. She missed that connection. She missed him.

She started to move away when she heard a shout go up followed by the deep shout of Jamie's voice: "Watch out!"

Her pulse spiked with panic, and she returned to the window, fearing the worst. But as her gaze shot to the direction of the disturbance, she saw that the situation was already under control. It appeared that two of her young clansmen had been balancing a huge pile of wood planks on either end, but as they'd tried to go up the new stairs, the weight had shifted back on the lower man.

What could they have been thinking? It was far too much wood for two men to carry. The lad would have fallen, or worse, been crushed by the heavy timber, but Jamie had stepped in to lend a strong arm. A very strong arm. His muscles flexed to bear the brunt of the weight of the shifting wood. Her eyes drifted from his arms down the strong torso and flat stomach to his powerfully muscled legs clad in dust-covered leather breeches.

She was doing it again. Staring.

But it wasn't only physical awareness that drew her. Since their confrontation a few days ago, she'd found herself watching him—nay, studying him. He was like a puzzle that she was trying to figure out . . . albeit in the dark. He gave no hint to his thoughts, treating her as he always had, with consideration and attentiveness. True to his word, he was giving her time, even spending more time around her in the day. But there was something missing: him in her bed. She longed for those moments of intimacy that they'd shared at night—which was undoubtedly his intention in removing himself.

How could she long for something she'd known only such a short time?

It made no sense.

Or maybe it did. Perhaps she cared for him more than she'd realized. And after observing him these past few days, she'd begun to wonder if maybe it wouldn't be so wrong.

She didn't think even her own father could have managed this much in such little time. Under Jamie's tutelage and management, the progress in repairing the castle had been nothing short of spectacular.

His authority had never been in doubt, but she'd come to admire his leadership. He led by example, not by decree, never asking anything of his men that he was not willing to do himself. As in battle, he was out in front, the first man to face the enemy. He drove them hard but worked himself harder, always the first to arrive and the last to leave the castle.

It was clear Jamie and his men had some experience in construction—not surprising, considering the vast number of castles held by the Campbells—but the depth of his knowledge impressed her. His mind was quick with numbers, measurements, and plans, giving her a glimpse of the cunning and intelligence behind the vaunted warrior. Indeed, his skill as a commander was evidenced by the uncanny way he seemed to be aware of where the men were positioned and what was happening around him. As her father had said, there was much more to Jamie Campbell than physical prowess, and she was certainly seeing proof of it firsthand.

Her clansmen, unlike the Campbells, had never done work on this scale and Jamie had shown remarkable patience—even when, as now, the mistake could have been costly.

With her husband's help, the two young clansmen managed to get the wood to the top of the stairs and stacked it along the side of the far wall of the great hall. Not wanting him to catch her staring, Caitrina turned back to her bucket and tossed the filthy contents outside. Beth and the two other serving girls who'd volunteered to help were watching the incident with more than casual interest, and all of a sudden Caitrina realized why those lads had been carrying so much wood—they'd been well aware of their audience and had sought to impress the young serving girls.

Jamie had grasped the situation as well and appeared to be giving them a stern lecture from across the hall. Whatever he'd said had worked, because the two shamefaced lads nodded in earnest and hurried down the stairs without a backward glance.

Jamie, however, looked back in her direction, and from the expression on his face, he wasn't happy to see her. He pierced her with a glowering look, giving her every indication that he was about to storm over and vent his displeasure. She smiled sweetly, which seemed only to outrage him further. But fortunately (as she had an inkling of what might be behind that dark look), he was prevented from coming over by a voice calling from outside.

"My laird!"

He looked back over his shoulder at the men in the *barmkin* below to respond and after a quick exchange, with one more irritated glance in her direction, retraced his steps down the stairs to the courtyard.

It amazed her how quickly her clansmen had come to depend on him. She doubted they even realized it themselves and probably would be horrified to have it pointed out. Old prejudices would take a long time to die.

It struck her that Jamie was in a very difficult position, straddling both sides of the Highland line—a Highlander who was sympathetic to the Lowland government. Embraced by neither and distrusted by both. On one side there were Highlanders—unwilling to relinquish the unfettered authority and way of life they'd enjoyed for hundreds of years. On the other was the king—made increasingly powerful with the added strength of England behind him. In trying to bring the two sides together, Jamie had distanced himself from both. It was a difficult—and lonely—path he'd chosen. But vital, Caitrina realized. Without men like Jamie to negotiate the treacherous road of change, they could all end up like the MacGregors. It was a sobering thought.

Beth and the other serving girls had gathered around her and looked visibly relieved when Jamie departed the hall.

Caitrina could see from their faces that they wanted to say something. "What is it, Beth?"

The girl hesitated, blushing a little as if she didn't know quite how to put it. "We just wanted to say that . . . uh . . . we all admire you, mistress, for what you have done. And for your, uhm, bravery."

Bravery? "What for?"

Beth lowered her voice, her eyes darting to the doorway where Jamie had just disappeared. "You know, for marrying the Henchman. Did you see how he yelled at poor Robby and Thomas? They were just trying to help."

"He was right to speak to them so; the lads could have been hurt." She didn't want to point out that the young men had been trying to impress them in the first place. But it was clear the girls hadn't seen it the same way she had.

If only they would give Jamie a chance.

She stopped, stunned by the direction of her thoughts and by how closely she'd allied herself with her husband. He'd done so much for her; why was she realizing it only now? Not just in rebuilding Ascog, but in seeing it restored to her clan in the first place. She knew his brother had wanted it, yet Jamie had risked Auchinbreck's displeasure *for her.* And that hadn't been the first time. When he'd heard of the attack on Ascog, he'd raced back and tried to stop it. Then later, he'd risked Argyll's displeasure by withholding the location of the MacGregor until he could negotiate his surrender, knowing what his safety had cost her father. He could have killed the MacGregor, the man he'd been hunting, but he hadn't. He'd done this for her, as a show of good faith, and what had she showed him in return? Suspicion and distrust.

The truth hit her hard. If she wanted her people to accept Jamie—to give him a chance—it had to start with her.

He was her husband. It was her duty. . . .

No. It had nothing to do with duty, but everything to do with the confusing tangle of emotions she felt for him. Emotions that she feared had taken hold and would not be easily dislodged.

"And the way he looked at you. It frightened me near to my toes." Beth shivered. "If he'd looked that way at me, I would have turned and run."

The other girls nodded furiously, and Caitrina smiled at their dramatics. "Oh, he's not so bad."

All three girls looked at her as if she were daft.

"No, he's worse," a man said. "And you'll do well not to forget it, lassie."

Recognizing the voice, Caitrina turned at the interruption to see Seamus carefully making his way down a ladder. As one of the few men with experience in construction, he'd been given the task of overseeing the necessary supply of wood for the construction. Jamie had honored him with the responsibility, not that you would know it by Seamus's resentment.

As promised, Caitrina had talked her father's guardsmen into submitting to Jamie, though she almost wished she hadn't. Seamus was stirring up trouble.

"I've not forgotten, Seamus," she said quietly. "But you can't ignore the good he's done around here. He's given me no cause to distrust him." She turned back to Beth and the other girls. "Nor is he the ogre people have made him out to be. We need to give him a chance." When they didn't look convinced, she pointed out, "He is our laird now."

"Not for long, God willing," Seamus said.

He wore a certain look on his face that sent a chill of foreboding through her. She frowned, hoping she had misunderstood his intent. "It will be some time before we have a son old enough to become laird, Seamus."

At the rate they were going, a child would be a miracle. Jamie had just reentered the hall and was heading straight for Caitrina when he overheard her unexpected defense of him and experienced a flare of hope.

It was the first sign he'd had in the almost week since they'd been at Ascog that she might be softening. He'd begun to wonder whether he'd done the right thing in removing himself from her bed. He'd wanted to give her time, to make her realize that what they had was special. To miss not only their lovemaking but him. The long, cold nights, however, had begun to chafe. He worked himself almost to the point of collapse every day to take his mind off his lovely bride, but her constant presence was like a burr under his saddle.

He was too damn aware of her and found himself watching her at the most inopportune times. His only conciliation was that he knew she watched him, too. It felt less that they were man and wife and more like two cagey lions circling each other.

At times, he felt as if he were watching a completely different person from the one he'd first met. Gone was the pampered and indulged lass dripping with silks and laces, and in her place was a determined young woman who swabbed floors all day long in a gown not fit for a servant.

For a girl who'd once dressed like a princess, the change was startling. Despite his repeated offers of new clothing and jewels, nothing she wore bore any signs of wealth. Her hair, which had once been twisted in elaborate arrangements, was now tied back simply at her nape with a thin, tattered black ribbon and had lost its lustrous shine.

But the changes went far deeper than appearance. At one time he'd thought her oblivious of what was going on around her, but nothing could be further from the truth. He was surprised by how perceptive she was of her people's needs. From organizing the men to aid the women who'd lost husbands in the attack with their fields or livestock to offering a hug or the squeeze of a hand in comfort—Caitrina was there.

The open display of love and affection he'd once witnessed her shower on her family had transferred to her clan.

Yet rightly or wrongly, Jamie craved it for himself.

The destruction of her home and family had forced her to grow up and take on more responsibility. He could admire the woman she'd become, but not all the changes were welcome. She'd been disillusioned, and there was nothing he could do to give her back her youthful naïveté. He would do anything to see joy in her eyes, untainted by sadness and loss.

But his more immediate concern was her health. He could see the signs of weariness on her pale face and knew she was probably getting as little sleep as he. She was working too damn hard, and he wasn't going to sit around and let her drive herself to exhaustion.

She'd claimed once that he'd wanted her as a possession, as a pretty ornament to have by his side. If there had ever been a hint of truth in her appraisal, there wasn't any now.

He would be proud to have her by his side, not for her beauty, but for her strength and resilience. For her spirit and passion. For the drive that matched his own. And for the compassion he'd witnessed countless times this past week with her clan. It was she who comforted, even though she had lost more than anyone.

His desire for her had nothing to do with possession and everything to do with how she made him feel—she'd touched a part of him he hadn't even known existed. Feeling. Emotion. Sentiment. All these things had been alien to him until he'd met Caitrina.

He'd never noticed how alone he'd been.

The very first time they'd made love, he'd known she was different. He'd lusted for many women, but none had ever made him want to hold her in his arms forever. Never had passion and emotion been entwined. When he came inside her, he felt not just physical pleasure, but pleasure that claimed every part of his body and soul.

At least that was the way it had been for him.

Her claim that she'd come to him out of duty still stung. *Duty.* How could one word wield such a powerful blow?

The irony, of course, was that duty was the tenet he held most sacred. Duty to his chief, to his clan, to his family. To his wife.

Never had he expected it would be wielded against him with such devastating effect.

He didn't want her duty, he wanted her love and desire. He wanted her of her own free will—because she wanted to, not because she had to.

He'd been angry with her a few days ago, impatient with her for not seeing him for what he was. But she needed time. After losing so much, naturally she would be scared to love again.

He'd vowed to hold out until she came to him, but with each day that passed, his temper was getting progressively more strained—at any moment ready to explode. He felt like a bear roused in the middle of winter. Hungry.

He drew closer, but they'd yet to notice him.

Seamus answered her, lowering his voice. "A babe is n—" He stopped midsentence, sensing Jamie's presence, and turned to meet his gaze.

Jamie arched a brow. "Don't let me interrupt. You were saying?"

Seamus smiled. "I was just commenting that we will all

look forward to the day when a Lamont rules again over Ascog."

That wasn't what he was going to say at all, but Jamie was already on his guard where the Lamont's embittered guardsman was concerned. "A day that will be a long time in coming," Jamie countered. "And one that might never come if we don't get this roof on."

Seamus took the hint. "Aye, my lord," he said, and climbed back up the ladder to oversee the men moving the wood up the tower.

Jamie didn't miss the subtle dig—the English "lord" rather than the Scots "laird"—and neither did Caitrina. She looked as if she were going to say something, but Jamie took her arm. "Don't. I can handle him."

"But—"

"It's what he wants. His taunts do not anger me. I'm just as much a Highlander as he is, though he might like to pretend otherwise."

The young serving girls Caitrina had been standing with had quickly made themselves scarce, but not without first peeking at him as if he were the devil incarnate.

Their fear appeared to upset Caitrina.

"Doesn't it bother you?" she asked.

He shrugged.

"It must."

He sighed, having learned something of his wife's persistence this past week. She would not stop until he answered. "Long ago I stopped trying to change people's minds. They'll believe what they want. Whether I'm a villain or a champion depends on whose side you are on."

She wrinkled her nose. A tiny, not-so-crooked nose that was currently smudged with soot. "I never thought about it like that."

"Not everyone despises me, Caitrina. I do have my admirers," he said dryly.

Her eyes narrowed. "What kind of admirers?" He shrugged. "The female variety, by any chance?"

He grinned at her expression, realizing she was jealous. "Oh, there's lots of variety," he teased, and laughed when her mouth drew together in a tight line. He ached to soften that mouth with his lips and tongue. "One day I'll take you to Castleswene to meet a few of them."

He waited for her reaction. He'd spoken of a future, though it wasn't at all clear whether they had one.

She nodded, and he let out the breath he hadn't realized he'd been holding.

He took a step toward her. "Caitrina, I . . ." He dragged his fingers through his hair, not sure what he wanted to say.

"Yes?"

How could he tell her he wanted her back in his bed? He'd vowed to give her time. . . . Oh, hell. "We need to speak," he said instead.

The edge of wariness in her eyes told him he was right not to press. "About what?"

He took her hands in his and turned them over, palms up. They were red and dry, with angry-looking blisters and jagged scratches. "About this." She tried to pull her hands away, but he held firm. "It has to stop," he said gently. "You are working yourself to the bone. If you don't slow down and get some rest, you are going to collapse."

She turned her eyes from his gaze, and he could see the stubborn set of her mouth. "I'm fine."

"You are my wife, not a scullery maid."

"Is that what this is about? Appearances? There is work that needs to be done, and it doesn't care by whom. This is my home. You'll not force me to sit by and let others work while I embroider and play the lute."

The picture of domesticity sounded fine to him. He would love to hear her play for him. But he did not think she would appreciate his honesty at this point, so he tried a different tack. "It's not safe with all the dangerous work on the roof going on. You could be hurt."

She lifted her chin a little higher and met his gaze, not giving an inch. "If it's safe enough for the others, it's safe enough for me."

His mouth fell in a grim line. "I don't—"

He stopped, stunned by what had been about to come out of his mouth. *Love. I don't love the others.*

Was that what he felt for her? At one time, Margaret MacLeod had accused him of not knowing what the word meant. Perhaps she'd been right, because he'd never felt this irrational intensity of emotion for anyone. He'd never had to fight to keep such a tight rein on his emotions, because emotions had never been a factor for him at all. Until he met Caitrina.

She must have read the shock on his face because she was giving him a strange look. "You don't what?"

He knew she would not welcome his feelings. They would terrify her. Send her running from him like a startled hare. Masking his expression, he shook off his disturbing thought and said, "I don't want to have to order you back to Rothesay."

Her eyes sparked like wildfire. "You wouldn't dare."

"Wouldn't I?" She would soon find out that he could be every bit as stubborn as she was.

The mutinous expression on her face said it all, but wisely she chose not to give voice to her thoughts.

He gave her a long look, taking in every inch of her tousled, tired appearance. "I'm willing to be reasonable."

She uttered an unladylike snort. "How gallant of you. And what, pray tell, is your definition of reasonable?"

"You are the lady of the keep, and you will act accordingly. You may supervise, but that does not mean you will be on your hands and knees scrubbing floors. And," he said, looking pointedly at her dress, "you will gown yourself as befitting your station as my wife."

She was furious. "So you can chop wood like a common laborer, but I am not accorded the same privilege."

Privilege to scrub floors? He couldn't believe they were arguing about this. He took a step closer. "I saw you watching me."

She blushed to her roots. "I wasn't watching you," she huffed. "But you still didn't explain why it is fine for you and not for me."

"It's different for men."

She took a step closer to him, close enough for him to feel the points of her nipples brush his chest. Heat rushed through him. He ached to take her in his arms, knowing exactly how all that lush softness felt against his skin. This was the closest he'd been to her in days. Her delicate floral scent wafted up to his nose, tempting, despite her obvious temper.

"That is the most pigheaded, ridiculous thing I've ever heard. It makes no sense."

"Nonetheless, it's the way of it."

"And that is all the explanation I am to receive?"

"I already gave you the one that matters most." He wiped the smudge of soot from her nose, looking into her eyes. "Can't you see that I'm only thinking of you? I want to keep you safe."

Some of her anger melted away with what he'd revealed. "Didn't you accuse me once of being too safe? Of being cosseted and protected from the real world? Now you are trying to do the same. Don't you understand that I'll never be that girl again?"

His finger slid along the gentle curve of her jaw to rest under her chin, then tilted her head back to meet his gaze. "I never meant for this to happen, Caitrina. Surely you know that now?"

She looked a little dazed but nodded.

"I know things will never be what they were, but I only want to keep you safe. You can't go on like this."

"All I want to do is help."

"And you shall, but not by working yourself to the point of collapse."

"You'll not ban me from here?"

He could hear the edge of desperation in her voice. "No, not if you do as I ask." He reached in his sporran and pulled out a small leather bag of coins. "Here, take this. I want you to go to the village and purchase some cloth or a dress if it can be found. I will send to Edinburgh for some finer gowns, but this will have to do for now. Today, Caitrina. You will go today."

She looked as though she wanted to refuse, but she took the bag and slipped it in her skirts. She bowed her head and curtsied with a great flourish. "As you wish, my laird."

His mouth twitched as she started to walk away, but halfway to the door she spun around and started back toward him.

"I forgot my bucket."

"I'll get it." He took a few steps to the side and reached down to pick it up as Caitrina stopped right where he'd just been standing. He heard a crash, then a shout.

He looked up and didn't think but just reacted. Diving for her, he snaked his arm around her waist and pulled her to the ground underneath him, shielding her with his body.

He braced himself. The impact from the falling wood slammed into him, tearing a groan from his lungs. Though he'd avoided most of it, the jagged edge of the beam struck his shoulder with enough force to rip through his shirt and tear a gash in his arm. He could feel the warm rush of blood running down his arm.

He rolled off her, fighting the blazing roar of pain in his shoulder. Pain that engulfed him in a haze. The hall exploded in chaos. He heard yells from above and screams from the serving girls. Everyone rushed around, but he had eyes only for her.

Caitrina was safe. Thank God. His enemies claimed ice

ran in his blood, that nothing ever penetrated his deadly calm. They should see him now. His heart was pounding like a frightened hare. He'd never been so damn scared in his life.

If anything had happened to her . . . Something hot and tight lodged in his chest. If there had been any doubt before, there was none now.

This was love, and he loved her with every fiber of his being.

She was leaning over him, her face deathly pale. "Oh, my God! What happened?" She looked down at his arm; blood gushed from the open wound, turning his sleeve red. "You're hurt." Tears sprang to her eyes and her face seemed to crumple.

She's crying. For me. But it was the look in her eyes that penetrated the black haze of pain like nothing else. It was a look he'd never seen before. Raw. Exposed. As if he were seeing into her heart.

His shoulder hurt like hell, but it was the most beautiful sight he'd ever seen. For there in her eyes, in the delicate fall of a tear, she gave herself away.

It wasn't just duty that bound them together.

Chapter 15

✤ ✤ ✤

Caitrina paced around the laird's chamber, doing her best to stay calm and out of Mor's way, but the wait was torturous.

Blood. There'd been so much blood. The rough-hewn beam that had fallen on them had been at least twelve inches thick. Thick enough to kill.

She closed her eyes and took a deep breath but couldn't calm the frantic beat of her heart. Panic had taken hold and had yet to let go.

Dear God, Jamie could have been killed. Taken from her as quickly as her father and brothers. In that split second when she'd realized what was happening, and what he'd done in saving her, her heart slammed into her chest and stripped away all pretense from her consciousness.

Enemy. Henchman. Campbell. None of that mattered.

She cared for him. Deeply. She didn't want to try to put her feelings into words—not when they terrified her. Caring for someone made her vulnerable. If she lost him, too . . . Fear laced itself around her heart and squeezed.

She couldn't stand it; one more minute of not knowing and she'd go mad.

Twisting her hands in her skirts anxiously, she approached the bed and attempted to peek over Mor's shoulder. Jamie was on his side, facing away from her, as Mor tended his wound.

"How does it look?"

"The same way it did five minutes ago, though it's hard

to tell with you blocking my light," Mor clipped. Caitrina quickly backed away from the flickering candlelight. Though it was just after midday, the small windows provided little illumination. "But it will look much worse if I don't finish stitching it up."

"Are you sure he'll—"

Two voices cut her off this time.

"He's fine."

"I'm fine."

Jamie's voice was steady and strong, giving her a moment's relief. "Are you sure you don't need any help?" Caitrina ventured, only to be cut off again.

"No!"

"No!"

If she weren't so upset, she might find Mor's and Jamie's uncharacteristic agreement amusing. Instead, she moved back to the other side of the room as Mor finished stitching the wound. A few servants hurried back and forth at her nursemaid's command, bringing fresh water, cloth, and herbs.

Never had Caitrina felt so useless—or helpless. How could this have happened? It was a horrible accident . . . or was it? She hadn't missed Seamus's pale face. She didn't want to believe it, but his words not long before seemed damning in light of what had happened.

Finally, after what had seemed like hours, though it was only a few minutes, Mor pushed back from the stool. "You can come see him now, Caiti."

She rushed back to the bed and at last got a good view of her husband. He'd sat up, leaning his back against the headboard. His naked chest gleamed, and the tight bands of his stomach muscles rippled in the soft light. He still wore his breeches and boots, but his ruined shirt and plaid had been tossed on the chair beside the bed.

Thankfully, Mor had cleaned away the blood, but there was a thick, jagged cut that she'd laced up his shoulder, and a dark, mottled bruise had already started to form from his collarbone to his elbow. It looked ghastly—and painful.

But he was alive. Her entire body sagged with relief.

She sat beside him on the edge of the bed and tentatively closed her hand over his. "How do you feel?"

One side of his mouth curved up in a roguish half-smile that shot straight to her heart. "I've experienced far worse on the battlefield. I don't think anything is broken." He glanced at Mor for confirmation.

"Nothing broken, though it will feel like it for a few days," the old woman said. As if anticipating the kind of patient he would be—disagreeable—she cautioned, "But you'll have to take care not to open the wound or it will fester. I'll send up a draught for the pain."

True to form, Jamie shook his head. "I don't need it."

Caitrina looked at Mor, silently telling her that she would give it to him—even if she had to pour it down his throat.

The old nursemaid harrumphed and bustled out the door, muttering about fool lads and their pride, leaving Caitrina alone with her husband.

She bit back a smile and looked at Jamie, who seemed to be doing the same. "I don't think she cares much for your manly display of fortitude."

Jamie chuckled. "I think you are right, but that is not why I refused her medicine. I don't like how it makes me feel. I'd rather bear pain than lapse into a drug-induced stupor."

Always on guard, she thought. After what had happened today, she could hardly blame him.

Alone now and safe, she was suddenly hit by the reality of all that had happened. Worry had propped up her composure, and now that she knew he would be all right, she was unable to hold her emotions in check. She needed him. Needed to feel his solid strength against her. Needed to assure herself that he was still here. Needed to blot out the moment of gut-wrenching fear that she would lose him, too.

Careful not to jog his shoulder, she laid her cheek on his bare chest, savoring the warm smoothness of his skin and taking comfort in the steady beat of his heart. She'd startled him with her touch, but only for a second, and then his body relaxed under her. "I was so scared," she confessed tremulously. "God, you could have been killed."

He stroked her hair, the strong hands that could wield a weapon with deadly purpose as gentle and comforting as a mother to a babe. "But I wasn't. Though it would have been a price I would willingly pay."

She sat up, eyes wild. "Don't say that! Don't ever say that. I can't go through it again. My father, my brothers . . ." Tears slid down her cheeks. She'd loved her family so much, and they'd been taken from her. How could she risk that heartbreak again? She knew what he did, the constant danger he faced. It filled her with icy terror. "I can't lose you, too. Promise me—"

"You won't," he soothed, dragging her back down against him.

They were quiet for a moment, with only the sound of her uneven breathing and occasional sniffle as her tears abated to fill the silence. It was a promise they both knew he couldn't keep. They lived in a world where death was a way of life—especially for a warrior.

"It matters to you," he said after a minute, "my safety?"

She stilled, not knowing what he wanted from her. "I . . ." She was scared. Scared that giving voice to her fragile feelings would somehow put him at risk.

Did he care for her? His voice gave no hint to his own thoughts. "Yes," she said instead. "More than anything."

It was enough. Her answer appeared to satisfy him, because he hugged her a little tighter. The frantic race of her pulse had calmed, but the accident played over and over in her mind. "It happened so fast."

"Aye, if I hadn't heard the sound and looked up . . ." Never had she heard such emotion in his voice. Jamie Campbell, the most feared man in the Highlands, had been scared—for her. He cleared his throat. "When I find out who was responsible . . ."

The dark edge in his voice chilled her. "I'm sure it was only an accident."

He held her gaze, and she knew he shared her suspicions. "I'm sure no one had any intention that *you* would be harmed."

He'd chosen his words with care, leaving her no doubt that he suspected someone had tried to kill him. She prayed Seamus hadn't been behind it, but her loyalty to her clansmen could be stretched only so far and it stopped at attempted murder. If Seamus was responsible, he would pay the price.

"I haven't thanked you," she realized, looking up at him. "For saving my life."

"You don't need to thank me. I told you I'd always take care of you, and I meant it." He drew her under his uninjured arm, wrapping his arm around her waist and holding her tight against the length of his body. She nuzzled her head under his chin and laid her hand on his chest, the hard muscle solid and reassuring beneath her fingertips. She smoothed her hand over the rigid plane, sculpting the familiar contours of his chest, wanting to hold on to this moment forever. With all that had happened in the past few months, she'd never thought to feel like this again—safe and content.

She didn't need to say anything. She sensed that he knew what she was thinking because he felt the same. A falling beam of wood had done what neither of them had been able to do, strip away the layers of pretense to reveal the truth. Only when faced with the horrible fear of losing him had she accepted what he'd come to mean to her.

"I've missed you," she said, speaking her thoughts aloud. Yet she had no wish to take them back.

He stilled. "And I you."

"I never should have said what I did. You've never given me cause not to trust you. I do trust you, it's just . . ." She searched for the right word but was only able to come up with "complicated."

But somehow, he seemed to understand. "Aye. I can't promise there won't be problems."

"I know." But whatever their problems with her clan's acceptance of him, she was no longer willing to allow it to take her from his bed.

Her hand slid down his stomach, absently tracing the taut bands of muscle. His arousal rose hard against his breeches. For a moment, she wanted to cover him with her hand, feel the steel rod under her fingers. But then she remembered he was hurt.

She jerked her hand away. "I'm sorry." Her cheeks burned. "I wasn't thinking." She sat up and attempted to move off the bed. "I should leave you to rest—"

She gasped when he grabbed her arm and pulled her back down on top of him. "No." His voice was dark and insistent. He took her chin and lifted her mouth to his, placing a tender kiss on her lips. "Stay. I need you."

"But your shoulder . . ."

"I assure you, the pleasure you will give me is the best draught for the pain." He looked deep into her eyes, his gaze soft and liquid, and smoothed a lock of hair from her brow. "Take my pain away, Caitrina." She looked at the bandage on his arm, but he turned her chin. "Make me forget," he whispered, and kissed her again.

She heard his plea deep in her heart. She wanted to forget, too. Forget the accident that had nearly taken him from her forever and the foolish days they'd spent apart. He drew her lips apart, sliding his tongue deep in her mouth with a long, sensual kiss, before releasing her.

Her breath came hard and fast. "You don't fight fair."

He grinned. "It's been too long."

She shook her head. "It's been three days."

"Almost four."

She laughed. "You're incorrigible."

He kissed her again and slid his hand down the curve of her spine to rest on her bottom, pressing her against his heavy erection. "No, I'm a desperate man. Have pity on me, lass."

He looked so in earnest, she had to laugh. "How am I to fight such a heartfelt request?"

He grinned and pulled her into his arms. "You aren't."

In truth, it was just what she desperately needed as well. Not until she was in his arms again would she feel perfectly safe.

She feigned severity. "Very well, but there will be conditions."

He quirked a brow. "I'm listening."

"You have to stay still."

A very naughty grin played upon his lips. "I'll do my best. What else?"

"You'll tell me if it hurts."

"If what hurts?" he asked innocently.

She gave him a playful tap on his chest. "Your shoulder, you wretch."

His attempt to appear contrite was ruined by the boyish twinkle in his blue eyes. "I promise."

Sometimes she forgot how young he was. His authority and battle-hardened exterior made him appear much older than his seven and twenty years.

God, he is beautiful. The hard, masculine lines of his face lightened by playfulness. His eyes even crinkled at the corners when he smiled. The effect was utterly devastating.

He took her breath away.

She stood up and moved to the door, sliding down the

metal bar so they would not be disturbed. She could feel his eyes on her every step of the way.

"There are a few problems," he said.

It was her turn to look at him questioningly. "Such as?"

"Our clothes." He sat back against the pillow with a wide grin on his handsome face. "I'm afraid my arm hurts too much to be of much help in removing them."

Her eyes narrowed. "Is that so?"

He nodded solemnly. "I guess you'll have to do it on your own."

"And what will you do?"

"Why, watch, of course."

"Of course," she said dryly. With her back to him, she removed her *arisaidh* and folded it carefully on the chair. She looked over her shoulder, catching him staring at her bottom. "I don't suppose I could bother you to help me untie my laces."

"I might be able to manage."

She returned to the bed and stood with her back to him as he unlaced her kirtle and then her stays. His fingers seemed to caress her skin as he worked the ties, lingering at the sensitive small of her back, sending a shiver of awareness down her spine.

When he'd finished she shrugged the gown off her shoulders, letting it fall to the ground. The stays were loose enough for her to shimmy them over her head.

Though she wore only her sark, the room seemed to be getting warmer, and she could feel a flush spread over her skin.

She could hear the hitch in his breath as each piece of clothing hit the ground and knew that watching her—even from the back—had aroused him. She started to work the ties at her neck, but he reached out to clasp her wrist.

"Let me see you, lass," he said, all playfulness gone from his voice.

She turned around to face him, cheeks burning. She

might be embarrassed, but she couldn't claim to be unaffected. There was something deeply sensual about undressing before a man knowing his eyes were on your every move.

Slowly, she untied the sark at her neck, then bent down to slide off her slippers, giving him a view of her breasts swaying from behind the open neck of her sark.

He swore, and she hid a smile, savoring the moment of feminine power.

He sucked in his breath as she slid her sark up to her thigh and rested her foot on the edge of the bed, taking her time sliding her stockings off her legs.

Her body dampened, knowing what he was thinking, knowing how badly he wanted to see her there.

Her eyes met his. His gaze was hot, burning with intensity. "Take it off," he hissed.

She slid the edge of the sark higher, still giving him a view only of her thigh, then higher to expose the curve of her bottom, moving the fabric up her sides and over her breasts as she lifted it over her head and let it drop in a puddle beside her bare feet.

She peeked from under her lashes and saw his gaze slide over her breasts, her stomach, her bottom, and then down her legs.

"God, you're beautiful."

"Except for me crooked nose," she teased.

He laughed. "*Especially* because of that crooked nose."

And under his appreciative stare, she felt so. She lifted her eyes to his and moved her foot to the ground. He lowered his gaze to between her legs, and she swore she tingled as if he'd touched her.

Her need for him was primal. She reached for him, sliding her hand along his stomach as she untied the waist of his breeches, releasing his straining erection from behind the tight confines of fabric. She moved over him on the bed, straddling him as she slid her hands behind his taut buttocks and worked the pants down his legs, desperate to have him inside her.

His hands were on her breasts, kneading and squeezing, pinching the taut tips as she worked. She rubbed her aching mound over his thickness, needing to feel him between her legs.

She was so wet and hot, throbbing for him, but she wanted to prolong the sensations pulsing through her body.

"Oh God, you're killing me. I need to be inside you."

He covered her breast with his mouth, pulling her nipple between his teeth and sucking hard. Demanding. Her head fell back as she arched against him, and she rubbed a little harder, sliding over him until the area grew slick with need.

He touched her with his thumb, caressing the most sensitive part of her, and she exploded, contracting against him as she cried out her pleasure.

While the spasms still rocked through her, he took her hips and thrust inside her, taking her so deep that she cried out again. There was nothing like this feeling of utter connection, a feeling that she now recognized was based on something far deeper.

She could feel it rising again, filling her, the desperate craving . . . he pulled her down hard against him so that their bodies touched and rocked, and the friction, the exquisite pressure, sent her flying over the edge again as the sweet contractions rippled through her body.

She was so beautiful like this, her naked body flushed and trembling with the force of her release, her face transformed with ecstasy. He could watch her come forever. It stirred something deep and savage inside him. An emotion so base and primal, he didn't have a name for it. Except that she belonged to him. Heart, body, and soul.

The last tremors ebbed, and he felt her go slack, weak as a newborn lamb from the force of her release.

Mindful of his injury, he rolled her under him, careful not to crush her by propping himself up on his good arm.

He was still inside her and aching to move. To unleash the storm of passion he'd fought to control. But ever mindful of her fears, he studied her face. "You're all right?"

A lazy smile played upon her sensuous mouth. Unable to resist, he caught the plump lower lip between his teeth and nibbled gently.

Her gaze was unfocused as she looked at him. "Better than all right."

"My weight doesn't bother you?"

Her eyes sharpened with sudden realization. "You promised to stay still."

He tugged her lip again, murmuring against her mouth, "I lied."

"But your shoulder."

"It's fine." Actually, holding himself off her with one arm was harder than he'd thought, but he had an idea.

He kissed her again, sliding his tongue in her mouth and circling until she strained against him. Reluctantly, he pulled out of her slick heat, feeling the unwelcome blast of cold air.

"But—"

He pressed his fingers against her lips. "Trust me."

He stood beside the bed and slid her toward him so that her buttocks rested just at the edge of the mattress—at the perfect height.

He throbbed in anticipation, anxious to get back inside that wet heat.

Holding her gaze, he scooped her legs up under her knees and held them on either side of his hips, running his hands along the warm, velvety skin of her thighs. Her legs were beautiful—long, slim, and creamy white. He couldn't wait to have them wrapped around his waist.

Slowly, he positioned the head of his cock at her opening. She was so moist and soft and pink . . . and waiting for him. He nuzzled the sensitive round head against her, and she moaned.

Her hips lifted just the sweetest amount. But he wanted her dripping. He dampened his finger in his mouth, then dragged it along her cleft. She jumped from the heat. He smiled devilishly. His pleasure could wait.

He bent over her, kissing the tiny pink nipples that strained to the ceiling, and then dragged his tongue down the soft ivory plane of her belly.

He heard her breath hitch and resisted a chuckle.

His mouth dipped lower, to the tender skin of her thighs. She tasted like honey, and he wanted to taste every delicious inch of her.

"What are you . . .?"

"Trust me," he whispered, his voice husky with lust. He blew against her, and she trembled. He inhaled her delicate feminine scent, the most powerful aphrodisiac, and blood rushed to the head of his cock. He pulsed hard, feeling as if he could come right there. He nuzzled his mouth at the top innermost portion of her thigh and felt her stiffen with anticipation.

Dripping, he vowed.

He moved his mouth above her and caught her half-lidded gaze, holding it as he placed a tender kiss at her very core.

Her hips bucked and she cried out. He slid his hands under the soft curves of her buttocks, lifted her to his mouth, and tasted her fully. A long, drawn-out kiss of pure pleasure. He circled her with his tongue and probed inside, licking and sucking, until she was deliciously wet and hot. Until she pulsed.

She writhed on the bed, circling her hips against his mouth, and he pushed her harder, driving her closer and closer to the edge as his tongue flicked at her most sensitive spot. He knew she was close. He broke the intimate kiss, stood up, lifted her legs again, and sank into her. Watching his cock sink inch by glorious inch into her body.

When he was all the way inside and their bodies joined, he closed his eyes and leaned his head back, savoring the sharp intensity of sensations ripping through his body.

He felt electrified, more complete than he'd ever felt in his life. This was heaven. This was what it felt like when a man met his mate, the woman he was meant to be with.

She lifted her hips, demanding more, and he let go. Plunging in and out, driving deeper with every stroke, his entire body tight and fraught with need. He loved the feeling of being inside her, of filling her, of making her his.

She clutched him with her feminine muscles, milking him with her body, and he lost all hold. Never had he felt like this. Consumed. Out of control. Wild with passion. Completely free.

His hips pounded with the primal rhythm, and she met him stroke for stroke, her beautiful lush breasts bouncing with each drive. He wanted to take them in his hands and squeeze, to flick his tongue over the pink tips and watch her skin prickle with passion.

But he couldn't think. He was on fire. Every inch of his body focused on holding on until . . . He heard her moan. Heard the soft cries of pleasure as she reached her peak, and finally he let go, exploding deep inside her with a guttural cry that tore from his very core.

He held her against him until the last shudder, the last drop of pleasure, left his body. When it was over, all he could do was drop down on the bed beside her, pull her under his arm, and wait for his breath to steady enough to say something.

But what was there to say? What else was there to be said between them? Words seemed insufficient and trite after such a cataclysmic experience. He loved her with every bone in his body and every fiber of his being. Till his dying day.

He couldn't give her back her family, but he would do whatever it took to make her happy. And maybe one day he would be enough. He vowed nothing would ever tear them apart again.

Perhaps it was the injury or perhaps the result of their lovemaking, but even though it was only the afternoon, when Jamie closed his eyes, he slept.

Chapter 16

❖ ❖ ❖

"But surely it is too soon?" Caitrina tugged the coverlet up over her breasts and stared at her husband, unable to keep the anxiety from her voice.

He deflected her question with an easy grin. Her heart tugged as it always did; his smiles seemed to come so freely now.

"I hardly think that is necessary," he said, indicating her attempt to cover herself. "There is no part of you that I have not explored in intimate detail and consigned to memory forever."

She blushed. Despite their very thorough lovemaking over the past few days, old habits—like modesty—died hard.

The same could not be said for Jamie. There was not a modest bone in his body—his incredibly gorgeous body. He was always so sure of himself; it was one of the things she most admired about him. There was an ease and confidence that came from position, wealth, and power. She'd noticed it from the first. His command and authority had always set him apart.

He'd just bathed, and the damp drying cloth clung to the tight muscles of his buttocks and hung loose around his hips. The linen dropped to the floor, and she sucked in her breath. He reached for his shirt and lifted it over his head, the muscles of his chest and back rippling in the soft morning light.

Wretch. He'd tried to distract her, and it had worked.

Well, two could play that game. Allowing the coverlet to drop, she slid out of bed and began her own morning preparations. She'd barely slipped her sark over her head before she gasped, feeling his hard body behind her. He wrapped his arm around her waist from behind, and she sank against him, the warmth of his breath teasing her neck as his mouth pressed kisses on the pulse below her ear.

She supposed this was one way to keep him in bed.

"It won't work, you know," he murmured in her ear.

She wiggled her hips against his burgeoning erection. "It won't?"

"No." He slid his hands over her breasts and hips. It was the possessive, comfortable touch of a lover. Liquid heat washed over her body. The sensation of his big, strong hands covering her body never ceased to thrill. And when he released her, the disappointment was acute.

She sighed and turned to face him. "But it's too soon for you to resume your duties. Your shoulder—"

"My shoulder is fine," he clipped in that authoritative, brook-no-argument voice that he used with his men but rarely with her.

"But—"

"No more, Caitrina." He gave her a sharp glance. "I took your blasted draught, didn't I?"

Her mouth twitched, recalling their wee battle. Getting him to drink Mor's medicine had indeed taken some persuasion. It was amazing what she could accomplish with her hands.

Still, it had been only a few days since his injury. "Yes, but—"

He stopped her protestations with a shake of his head. "I promise to have care, but I will return to my duties today." He reached out to caress the curve of her cheek. "We can't stay in here forever, Caitrina."

Hiding. She lifted her eyes to his, hearing the unspoken admonition. "I know." He was right. It wasn't simply his wound that worried her, it was the intrusion of reality into the oasis they'd carved out together in this room. What they had here was not complicated by clan loyalties and duty. Here, nothing could come between them. She was a coward, but she wanted to keep him to herself for a little bit longer.

She sat back on the bed and watched him finish dressing, securing the *breacan feile* at the shoulder with his chieftain's badge. His *Campbell* chieftain's badge, she realized, recognizing the boar's head symbolizing their fierceness in battle.

When he was finished, he pulled her to her feet and tipped her chin, forcing her to look up at him.

"You trust me, don't you, Caitrina?"

"You know I do." Many times over the past few days, she'd wanted to try to give voice to her feelings. She was tempted to do so again now, but the words tangled in her mouth. Her emotions were still too encumbered by fear. The scars of the past had yet to heal. And though it was obvious he cared for her deeply, she was not yet sure about the strength of his feelings. She was unwilling to complicate the delicate balance they'd achieved in the past few days.

It was too soon.

"Then we will get through this together."

She wanted desperately to believe him, but she did not delude herself that it would be easy. She prayed their new bond was strong enough to weather whatever storm life had in store for them, for she feared it would be a big one.

The rain began to fall not an hour later.

Caitrina had just popped the last bit of oatcake in her mouth from breaking her fast when she heard the cry go up that a messenger had arrived. As it was not an unusual occurrence, she hardly paid it any mind.

But as Jamie had just departed the great hall on his way

to Ascog, she was surprised to see him reenter the hall a few minutes later. From the grim look on his face, she knew something was wrong. Terribly wrong.

She stood from the table and rushed to him, heedless of the disapproving glances of Seamus and his men—their resentment palpable. Her newfound intimacy with her husband had not gone unnoticed.

She clasped his arm, feeling the tension coiling under her fingertips. "What is it?"

His face was hard and unyielding, a mask of fierce control. It was the fierce expression of a man going into battle. He looked every inch the leader, every inch the feared enforcer of a king.

"I must leave," he said without preamble. "Immediately."

Her heart sank. "But why? Where are you going? Who has sent for you?" All of a sudden she had a terrible thought, one that could explain his reaction. "Is it your sister? Has something happened to Elizabeth?"

He shook his head. "It's not Lizzie. The missive was from my cousin."

Argyll. Her heart sank a little deeper. "Oh."

"I'm afraid I cannot delay. I must go right away."

"But you are not fully recovered."

"I'm well enough. This cannot wait." He wasn't even looking at her. His mind was already on whatever was taking him away from her. She'd never seen him like this— distracted, impatient . . . remote. She hated Argyll, but never more than now. She hated that he could take Jamie away from her to do his bidding at a moment's notice.

"Won't you tell me what—"

"When I return."

His impatience stung. The intimacy they'd shared was seemingly forgotten. She took a step back from him. "Then I will not delay you any longer."

Perhaps sensing her hurt at his curt dismissal, he bent

and kissed her forehead—just as her father used to do. Never had she so resented it. "I will return soon and explain everything."

But Caitrina was not so easily pacified, no longer content to be kept in the dark. Danger and death lurked in ignorance. He'd started to turn away, but she clutched his arm. "You won't be in any danger?"

One side of his mouth lifted in an enigmatic grin. "I ride to Dunoon, Caitrina. That is all."

It wasn't until after he'd left the hall that she realized he hadn't really answered her question.

Once she'd recovered from the shock of Jamie's sudden departure, anger took over. Dirt and mud sprayed her skirt as she stomped along the path to Ascog, but she paid it no mind. It would serve him right to have her go around in mud-spattered "rags."

As if departing without explanation weren't enough, she'd been informed when she'd tried to leave this morning that he'd confined her to the castle for the duration of his absence. She was not even permitted to walk the short path to Ascog to watch the progress of rebuilding.

It had taken her precisely a quarter of an hour to disobey his orders—long enough to find a plaid to cover her head and a group of servants to join as they passed through the castle gate. She'd picked up a bucket and acted as if she were one of the women on her way to work at Ascog. Apparently, it had never occurred to him that she would defy his bidding, because no one was paying close attention to the maidservants leaving the castle.

Not trusting herself to control her anger at her husband, she'd fallen back from the other servants as they walked.

Jamie Campbell was going to face a severe tongue-lashing when he returned. If he thought she would be a complacent wife who meekly followed the bidding of her "lord and master," a wife who waved good-bye with a handkerchief in her hand and welcomed him back with open arms and a smile, he was in for one rude awakening. If he cared for her, he would show her the respect due his wife, his partner. *Partner.* Yes, she liked the sound of that. She wanted to know everything and refused to be kept in the dark again. When she thought of how he'd kissed her on the head . . . of all the overbearing, patronizing, loutish—

"It's good to hear you come to your senses, lass."

The voice from behind startled her. It took Caitrina a moment to realize it was Seamus.

Apparently, she'd been speaking her thoughts aloud. Not pleased by the interruption, she said sharply, "Senses? What do you mean?"

"We feared we'd lost you."

"I don't understand."

"To Argyll's Henchman."

She stiffened at the sobriquet, but as she was in no mood to argue her husband's finer points, she didn't jump to his defense—an exercise in futility with her father's old guardsman as it was. Instead she asked, "Did you wish to see me about something, Seamus?"

"Aye. That I do, mistress. I've been trying to tell you for some time, but the Henchman never lets you out of his sight." He looked around, as if someone might jump out from behind a tree. "Even the castle has ears."

Caitrina gave her father's old guardsman a measured look. "It is the laird's duty to keep himself apprised of all that is going on in the castle. Perhaps caution on his part is warranted given the accident that nearly took both our lives."

She'd yet to speak with Seamus about what had happened, but Jamie had done so first thing this morning. Her father's old guardsman claimed that while he'd been hoisting one of the large beams into position, a rope had slipped, knocking another piece of wood off the platform. The knocking was the sound that had alerted Jamie to danger and saved their lives. To a one, her clansmen swore that it had been an accident. Unfortunately, Jamie's men had not been in position to prove otherwise.

Without proof, Jamie had been reluctant to further stir up the Lamont clansmen's resentment by punishing Seamus, but he'd warned the older man that if there were any more "accidents," he would find himself with a rope around his neck—"proof" or not.

"Aye, that was a terrible mistake," Seamus said with unabashed sincerity. Caitrina couldn't tell if it was an admission and he was attempting to offer some sort of apology.

She held his gaze. "Seamus, promise me nothing like that will happen again. I know it is difficult, but we must try to adjust—"

"No!" The vehemence in his voice took her aback. "We'll never accept a Campbell as laird. It pains me that you would say so, lass."

How could she explain that she'd done what she'd thought best under the circumstances?

"If you had anything to do with what happened—"

"Not now, lass. It will all make sense soon enough. But hurry, we don't have much time. Follow me."

He tried to take her hand and drag her into the trees toward the mountains, but she dug in her heels, refusing to budge. "Where are you taking me? What is all the secrecy about?"

Seamus looked around again and lowered his voice. "I can't explain now, it's too dangerous—one of his Campbell guardsmen could come along at any moment—you'll have to come see for yourself. But trust me, lass, this is something you don't want to miss."

Caitrina hesitated, not feeling right about traipsing after Seamus into the wilderness. After what had happened . . . something in her urged caution. And then there was Jamie's order for her to stay at the castle. She bit her lip. She hadn't given much thought to its purpose but merely reacted against the presumption. What if he had a reason beyond his general protectiveness? A prickle of guilt needled at her. "I don't think it's a good idea. Perhaps tomorrow—"

A disembodied voice, coming from behind one of the trees deeper in the forest ahead of them, cut her off. "God's wounds, Caitrina, must you always be contrary? Haven't I told you repeatedly that men prefer biddable women?"

The hair on her arms electrified as shock froze every bone, every muscle, every nerve ending of her body.

Her hand went to her throat as she stared wildly in the direction of the achingly familiar voice. She shook her head. *Dear God, it can't be.* "No. . ."

A man stepped out from behind a tree, his tall, wide-shouldered body silhouetted by the low light and trees. "I'm afraid so, little sister."

The blood drained from her body. *Niall.*

She was seeing a ghost. It was too much to believe. The rush of emotion to her chest was too much to take.

"Catch her," he said, taking a step forward. "I think she's going to . . ."

But Caitrina didn't hear the rest as darkness rose up to swallow her.

Ouch. Someone was slapping her cheek. Caitrina twisted her head and batted the hand away. "Stop that!"

A man laughed. "I'd say she's fine. Looks like the blow to the head didn't soften her temper any."

Caitrina opened her eyes and gazed into familiar blue depths. She drank in every inch of his handsome face. It was lean and weather-beaten and bore a few new scars, but there was no mistake. Tears welled in her eyes as she placed her hand on his rough-whiskered cheek. "You're real."

A smile curved his mouth into the roguish grin he'd perfected many years ago—well before it had proved so devastating on the village lasses. "Aye, love. As real as they come."

She threw her arms around his neck and sobbed into the dusty leather of his heavy quilted cotun. Niall. Dear God, it was really him. The happiness she felt at having her brother returned to her from the dead was unfathomable. She felt as if a light had just shone on the dark corner of her heart she'd thought closed off forever.

And now he was here. Her irritating, teasing, cocksure brother was alive and by all appearances well. But she could see that, like her, he'd changed. He was harder, sadder, angrier.

The hot ball of emotion lodged in her chest exploded into a torrent of choking tears. Niall held her, smoothing her hair as he murmured soothing words. "Shush, Caiti, it's all right, I'm here."

She pulled back, blinking the tears from her eyes, feeling as if she'd just woken from a terrible dream. "But how?" Her eyes narrowed with sudden realization. "Why did you not tell me?" She swatted him on the arm. "How could you let me think you were dead for so long?"

He chuckled. "Now there's my sister. I'd begun to fear the sweet sobbing creature in my arms was someone else." His eyes swept over her meaningfully. "You look different, Caiti. I almost didn't recognize you." He took in her dirty gown and worn *arisaidh*. "What's happened to you, lass?"

A wry smile played upon her mouth. "I've changed."

"So I see. The damn Campbells have made beggars of us all."

Niall's anger made her wish she'd purchased the new cloth Jamie had insisted upon, but now was probably not the time to point out that Niall and Jamie were in agreement on the subject of her clothing. Instead she asked, "Where have you been, Niall?"

"I'll explain everything, but first come with me." He stood up and held out his hand to help her up.

She looked around and for the first time realized they were not in the forest, but in a cave. The tunnel of stone was dark and musty, the air cool and damp. "Where are we? How did I get here?"

"We're in a cave near Ascog, and as for how you got here, I carried you." Niall rubbed his back. "For such a wee lass, you sure weigh a lot." She swatted him again, and he laughed. "After you fainted . . ."

Now *that* demanded an immediate response. Her spine straightened at the affront. "I don't faint."

"You do now." Niall grinned again, and she thought if she weren't so happy to see him, she might shoot him.

She opened her mouth, intending to give him a few choice words on the subject, but he cut her off.

"I think, under the circumstances, it is understandable." He called over to one of the men guarding the mouth of the cave. "Isn't that so, Seamus?"

"Aye, Chief, very understandable."

Chief. Caitrina met Seamus's gaze with dawning understanding. Of course. Niall was Chief of the Lamonts—or would be, if it were known he was alive. Seamus's attitude suddenly made sense.

"Come . . ." Niall took her hand and led her deeper into the cave. "Come see why I have brought you here."

They walked about fifteen feet in the semidarkness and reached a fork.

"Be careful," he warned. "It's easy to get lost in here."

Caitrina clutched his hand a little harder and ducked as they entered a tiny chamber. A few torches had been secured to the walls, and on the dirt floor there was a makeshift pallet with a large deerhound laid out at its foot. It looked almost like Boru. One of her father's guardsmen was bent over. . . .

And there in the flickering torchlight, Caitrina had the second biggest shock of her life.

"Brian!" She ran forward and dropped to her knees, gathering his limp body in her arms.

"Caiti!" He coughed weakly. "I knew you'd come. Just like Boru. He was waiting for me when I returned."

Realizing how ill he was, she released him gently. Her eyes traveled over him, taking in every detail of her brother's bedraggled appearance: the thin, dirty face, the arm in a sling, the bloodstained bandage wrapped around his head.

She turned to Niall. "What's happened? What's the matter with him? We must get him help."

Niall shook his head, indicating he didn't want to say anything in front of the lad.

Caitrina looked back down at Brian, but his eyes were closed. A pang struck in her chest. Seeing her must have sapped him of his strength. She adjusted the plaid around his shoulders, making sure he was warm, and then leaned down to place a kiss on his head.

Tears glistened in her eyes again. Her throat grew thick with happiness. It was unbelievable. Niall and Brian both alive. She looked around, half expecting to see . . .

Her eyes met Niall's. He must have guessed her silent question and shook his head sadly. "I'm afraid not, Caiti. Malcolm fell not long after Father." His face hardened, becoming unrecognizable. "At the hand of Campbell of Auchinbreck: your husband's brother."

A chill went through her. The happiness she'd found with Jamie suddenly felt wrong. His eyes pinned her as if challenging her to deny it. She winced at the silent accusation. "Niall, I can explain—"

"You will, but not here."

She took a few more minutes with Brian, simply savoring the sight of him. Though weak and clearly dangerously ill, he was alive. She smoothed her hand across his warm, clammy forehead. God, how she'd missed them.

Knowing that there was nothing more she could do for him right now, she gave Brian another kiss on the head and followed Niall back toward the larger chamber near the mouth of the cave.

Niall pulled up a dried-out log they'd been using for a stool. "Sit."

She did as ordered, and he took a seat beside her.

"I know you have many questions, and I'll do my best to answer them. But then you will answer some for me."

Caitrina swallowed, not liking his tone. She lifted her chin. He had much to answer for himself. For months she'd suffered, thinking them dead. How could he not have sent her word? "Very well."

Niall cleared his throat and began recounting his version of what had happened the day of the attack. "After the first wave of fighting, it was pandemonium. The Campbells had taken the castle, and women and children were pouring out of the keep. Father and Malcolm had fallen, and I was trying to organize what was left of the men." He paused. It was clear that remembering what had happened that dark day was difficult for him. "At that point, I knew there was no chance we would retake the castle; my main concern was saving as many of our people as we could, leading them into the hills, and regrouping to fight another day. But before I had a chance to come after you, we were attacked again and I lost even more of my men. By that time they'd lit the fires." He looked into her eyes. "I can't tell you the agony I felt when I realized you and Brian were still inside."

Caitrina felt tears burning her eyes, remembering as well.

Niall continued, "It was a living hell. I've never seen so much blood. My men were being slaughtered left and right. Auchinbreck gave no quarter, intent on taking no prisoners. Knowing we would all die otherwise, I ordered the rest of my men into the hills and decided to go after you and Brian myself. I was doing my best to stay out of sight when I saw a couple of soldiers dump Brian on a heap of dead bodies they were piling in the *barmkin* to burn. They were laughing and joking, and I heard your name. They said it was a shame they hadn't had a chance to"—he caught himself—"violate you before you'd died."

An anguished sound escaped her.

Niall's gaze turned harder than she'd ever seen it. "It was the last thing they ever said."

Caitrina nodded, understanding. After a minute she said, "So you thought I was dead?"

"Otherwise nothing would have made me leave you. The tower was aflame, I never thought anyone would get out of there alive."

Yet somehow Jamie had managed it.

"Brian was in a bad state, barely breathing when I got him out of there. The blow to the head nearly killed him."

"Did you hide in the hills with the MacGregors?"

He shook his head. "Nay. I knew the Campbell scourge would be hunting us—and I'd seen the Henchman riding in as we left. If we led them to the caves, we'd lead them right to the MacGregors. What was left of my guardsmen sailed in *birlinns* to Eire. We thought it would be safer for those left behind not to have to hide us."

She couldn't hide her amazement. "You went all the way to Ireland?"

"For a while. Until Brian and the other injured men recovered enough to return. My men were anxious to have word of their families. Some had been forced to flee before they'd learned of their safety."

"When did you come back?"

"A couple of weeks ago, when word came that Alasdair MacGregor was going to surrender, we knew it was safe to come back. We took refuge in the hills near Loch Lomond."

MacGregor country. "Why didn't you return home to Bute?"

"I wasn't sure what I would find. I suspected Campbells would have overtaken the place." He gave her a grim look.

"I was right. What I didn't expect was my sister to be leading them in. How could you marry him, Caiti? How could you marry the man who killed our father and brother?"

The betrayal in his gaze cut like a knife. She tried not to wither under its icy edge. "Jamie had nothing to do with the attack."

He looked at her as if she were a fool. "You believe that? The only reason he came to Ascog all those months ago was to hunt the MacGregors."

"A fact that I could never have known since no one elected to tell me that we were harboring outlaws," she reproached him. "Surely Father knew the danger? He had to know what would happen if it was discovered."

Niall flexed his jaw. "He had no choice. The obligation of hospitality is absolute. You know of our debt to the MacGregors—of the history that binds us together. Honor demanded he give them shelter. And Father was sympathetic to their plight."

Caitrina sighed. "I know." Though his motives had been noble, it was still hard for her to accept the futility of her father's death. "But you are wrong about Jamie's part in the attack. He had no knowledge of his brother's coming to Ascog. Indeed, Jamie came to help as soon as he found out. It was Jamie who pulled me from the fire and prevented my being raped by one of his brother's men."

He studied her face. "You're sure about this?"

She nodded. "I remember him carrying me out."

Niall shifted his gaze, staring back into the darkness of the cave. "Well, then I'm grateful for that, but you did not need to marry him. Hell, Caiti, he's not just any Campbell, he's Argyll's bloody Henchman."

How could she explain? She twisted her hands in her skirts, trying to find the words. "He's not like that. I didn't know what else to do." She relayed the events that had led up to his proposal, including her escape to Toward and the attempt to communicate with the rest of their clan at

Ascog. "I thought I was doing what was best. He and our uncle had been working for the peaceable surrender of Alasdair MacGregor, and Jamie offered marriage as a way for me to reclaim our home for the Lamonts. Our uncle not only supported but brokered the union. I had no idea that you and Brian had survived. So many weeks had gone by. Why didn't you get word to me?"

"I would have, but I only learned of your survival when news of the banns reached me near Balquhidder. By then it was too late to stop the marriage. Seamus has been trying to tell you ever since you arrived at Rothesay, but you are rarely alone and it's too dangerous to make our survival known."

"How did you evade capture with Seamus and the others?"

"I had nothing to do with that. Brian and I arrived only yesterday. The rest of my men are still in the Lomond Hills, but Seamus came to Bute to tell you of our survival. Brian's injury is the only reason I've risked bringing him here."

"What happened to him?"

"The fool lad wouldn't listen. I told him to stay out of the fighting, that he wasn't old enough, but he's as stubborn and proud as Malcolm and wouldn't listen. He reinjured his head in the fighting."

"What fighting?" She was almost too scared to ask. If her brothers were fighting in MacGregor country, that could only mean they'd allied themselves once again with the proscribed men.

Niall looked at her skeptically. "You don't know?"

She shook her head.

"Alasdair MacGregor was hanged and quartered with eleven of his men a few days ago—including six men who'd surrendered as hostages and had no trial—at Market Cross in Edinburgh. More are scheduled to be executed in the next week."

Caitrina shook her head, dumbstruck. "No. You're

wrong. Jamie negotiated the MacGregor's surrender under the explicit agreement that he would be taken to England. It was one of the reasons for our marriage—a sign of good faith, if you will. Argyll promised to take him to England."

Niall's lips curled. "He did. Argyll took the MacGregor to the border, set him down outside the carriage so that his feet could touch the ground, and then returned him to Edinburgh for trial. Argyll kept his promise—fulfilling the terms, but not the intent of the agreement. Thanks to your husband's clever negotiating, Alasdair MacGregor is dead."

No. It isn't possible. Jamie wouldn't have deceived her so. He wouldn't have tricked her into marrying him, intending all along that the MacGregor should die . . . would he? Had he something to do with this? She felt a flicker of uncertainty that she quickly tamped down. No. Not the man she knew. He wasn't simply Argyll's strong arm, he was a good man. "If what you say is true, my husband knew nothing about this."

"I can assure you it's true. There have been risings from Callander to Glenorchy to Rannoch Moor in retaliation for the treachery of Argyll. Your husband is a hunted man."

A chill swept over her.

Niall looked at her as if seeing her for the first time and not recognizing her. He swore. "You care for him."

Heat crawled up her cheeks in silent affirmation.

"God, Caiti, don't you know what kind of man he is?"

Her eyes flew to his. "I do. He's nothing like what they say."

"You could wring more compassion from stone," Niall said flatly. "The Henchman is ruthless in achieving Argyll's pursuit of Campbell domination."

Caitrina stuck up her chin. "You don't know him like I do."

Niall laughed, and it wasn't pleasant. "You're a fool, Caiti Rose."

Caitrina stiffened at the insult. This wasn't how it should be. Her brothers had returned to her from the dead, and they were arguing. "What can I do to help Brian?"

It was clear their conversation had upset Niall as well, and he was grateful for the temporary change of subject. "He needs more care than I have knowledge for. He needs a healer. Can you bring one?"

"Here?" she said, aghast. "You can't mean for him to stay here?" He should be with her at Rothesay.

Niall's mouth fell in a hard line. "What else would you have me do? He would not last the trip to Eire again. Nowhere else is safe."

They are outlaws. Just like the doomed MacGregors they'd tried to protect. But it didn't have to be that way. "Let me tell Jamie when he returns. He can help. You are my brothers. You are chief by right. Perhaps he can get pardons—"

"You must be mad. Do you honestly think he wouldn't throw us right in the dungeon?"

"He released Seamus and the others, didn't he?"

"Because they had no claim to the land. He's a Campbell; he'll not willingly relinquish Ascog. And he need not look for an excuse. I'm an outlaw, Caiti."

"You don't need to be. What happened to Father, the attack on Ascog . . . Jamie never meant that to happen. I think if he knew the truth, we could trust him to be fair."

"You'd trust him with my life? With Brian's life?"

Caitrina bit her lip, ashamed for the shadow of doubt that crept into her consciousness. Niall's news about the MacGregor's death had shaken her but not changed her belief in her husband. She trusted him. "I do."

Niall paused and regarded her thoughtfully. "What if you're wrong?"

Caitrina met his gaze and swallowed hard. "I'm not wrong."

"Well, I can't trust him. Not yet, at least. You must promise to keep our presence here a secret, Caiti."

"But—"

"I'll leave here right now," he warned.

"No! Brian can't be moved."

"Aye, it's dangerous, but no more dangerous than relying on the Henchman's sense of justice."

Caitrina was torn. Loyalty to her husband warred with loyalty to her brothers—brothers she'd thought lost to her forever. She couldn't lose them again so soon. And she couldn't deny that news of the MacGregor's death had stunned her. What if Niall was right? Had his feelings blinded her to Jamie's dark side? No. But she would give her brother what he wanted—for a while. "Very well. But you will see when Jamie returns that he is not responsible for Argyll's treachery. You will see that he is a just man." If she knew anything, she knew that. Jamie was a voice of reason in the all too fractious disagreements between clans.

Niall looked at her as if she were sadly deluded, but he agreed. They turned their attention to Brian and bringing a healer to him as soon as possible. Caitrina would come to visit when she could, but she knew that she would have to be careful. If her disappearance was noticed, she could lead Jamie's men right to her brother. Once Jamie returned, it would be even more difficult.

For now she would see them when she could, content in the knowledge that part of her family had been returned to her. But in the back of her mind was the recognition that if he ever found out about her deception, Jamie would be furious and she'd be risking the fragile life she'd built out of ash.

Chapter 17

❖ ❖ ❖

The contents of Argyll's missive haunted Jamie on the journey from Rothesay to Dunoon:

"The deed is done. The Arrow of Glen Lyon hanged for his crimes in Edinburgh three days past."

Alasdair MacGregor dead *in Edinburgh*? What the hell had happened?

The MacGregor chief was supposed to be in London. Jamie had given his word to that effect. He could think of only one explanation: Argyll had reneged on his promise to conduct Alasdair MacGregor to England. And if he'd done so, he'd blackened Jamie's name in the process and unleashed a maelstrom of violence, giving the outlaws a martyr and even greater reason to rise in rebellion. Jamie didn't want to think his cousin so rash, but when it came to the MacGregors . . .

Damn.

He stormed up the stairs to the keep. Tired and dirty from riding all day, not to mention in considerable pain from his shoulder, Jamie didn't stop to rest or wash but headed straight for the laird's solar. Not bothering to knock or announce himself, he pulled open the door and strode right in.

The most powerful man in the Highlands sat behind a large wooden table surrounded by a retinue of about a dozen guardsmen, all poring over documents and maps. The Earl of Argyll glanced up, his sharp Gallic features frowning at the interruption. Seeing Jamie's dark expression, however, he quickly waved the other men out, bidding them take their piles of parchment with them.

"I hope you have a good excuse for the manner"—he looked down his long nose at Jamie's Highland garb—"and appearance of your arrival." Argyll prided himself on civility, distancing himself from the "Highland barbarians" and always dressing in the finest court fashion.

Jamie hadn't missed the subtle set-down, but right now he didn't give a damn. He'd known Argyll too long to be put off by the reminder of his authority. Though Argyll was only a handful of years older, after the death of Jamie's father and his brother Duncan's subsequent disgrace, Argyll had been more like a father to him, standing in for the man who'd lost his life fighting for Argyll. They were bound not only by family ties, but by something far stronger—honor, duty, and sacrifice.

His father had believed in Argyll enough to give his life for him, and Jamie did not take it lightly. Thus far, Argyll had lived up to his father's expectations, making the Campbells the most powerful clan in the Highlands. That power, however, could not be absolute or he would be no better than a despot. Jamie believed in justice even more than he believed in his cousin.

"You know damn well I do," Jamie said. "If this"—he slammed down the missive on the polished wooden table—"is true."

Argyll flicked his gaze over the piece of wrinkled parchment, sat back, and tapped his fingertips together, completely at ease. "Of course it's the truth." His eyes shone with triumph. "Alasdair MacGregor has been eliminated. The king will be delighted."

Jamie knew the extreme pressure his cousin was under to quiet the Highlands—and eliminate the MacGregor chief in particular—but it was no excuse. He struggled to keep his anger in check and met his cousin's gaze. "How can the

MacGregor have been killed in Edinburgh when he was supposed to be in England?"

One corner of Argyll's mouth lifted in a semblance of a smile. "He did go to England."

The answer took Jamie momentarily aback. His gaze turned on his cousin skeptically. "Explain how that is possible."

"My men took him to the other side of the border, set him down upon English ground, and returned him promptly to Edinburgh."

Jamie went rigid, disbelief mingling with an acute feeling of betrayal. The man he'd fought for, helped, believed in, had stabbed him in the back. When he thought of all the times he'd defended his cousin . . . Jamie more than anyone knew his cousin had his faults—including a reputation for wiliness. But never had Argyll so abandoned honor. He pinned the earl with his gaze. "God damn you, Archie. How could you? I'm not going to let you get away with this. You made a mockery of our bargain and of me." The hot rush of anger surged through his veins. He remembered his long negotiations with the MacGregor and the assurances he'd given him. His voice shook with fury. "I gave my word."

Argyll did not shrink from his rage, though Jamie could tell he was uncomfortable by the way he shifted in his chair. "Your word was preserved. The terms of the agreement were met."

Jamie planted his hands on the table and leaned toward his cousin, more furious with him than he could ever recall—and they'd disagreed plenty in the past. "But not the spirit. This trickery is not worthy of you. You are the representative of law, the king's justice general. If people do not trust in the rule of law—in justice—you are nothing more than a tyrant." He gave him a hard look. "And I will not support a bloody despot."

For the first time, a flicker of uncertainty crossed his cousin's face. "What do you mean?"

"What the hell do you think I mean?" Jamie seethed. "If this is how you intend to quiet the Highlands, I want nothing more to do with it. You will have to find someone else to fight your battles."

Argyll's eyes narrowed. "I'm your chief. You'll do what I say."

Jamie laughed in his face. His cousin was nothing if not opportunistic—he'd claim his Highland heritage when he had use of it. He leaned over, looking his cousin squarely in the eye. "Don't try that crap with me, it won't work. Intimidation might work for others, but I know you too damn well. I won't fight for a man I don't believe in, and I'll not serve a chief any more than an earl who has no honor."

Argyll's face hardened. "Have care, lad. You grow too bold."

The control he'd been fighting for let loose in an explosion of rage. "No, cousin, it is you who grow too bold. I've stood beside you all these years against recrimination because I thought you were the best choice for the Highlands. Up until now I believed we wanted the same thing: restoring law and order to the chaos created by feuding and outlaws, ensuring the prosperity of our clan, and protecting the Highlands against a king who wants to steal our land, crush our people, and see our way of life destroyed." He drew in a deep breath and spoke concisely so there would be no mistake. "But I'll be damned if I'm going to support you in your personal vendettas."

"I did what needed to be done to bring a criminal to justice," Argyll said defensively.

Jamie slammed his fist down on the table. "Alasdair MacGregor did not get justice, he got trickery and deceit. We might as well go back to feuding as a way of solving problems, living up to the barbarian name the king calls us. We are the men in charge. We have to show leadership.

Vendettas are exactly what I'm fighting against. If this is your solution to instilling law and order in the Highlands, I want nothing to do with it."

"It wouldn't have been necessary had *you* brought the outlaw to me in the first place." Argyll's mouth fell into a flat line. "As was your duty."

Was that what this was about? Jamie knew his cousin had been angry, but he thought he'd understood. "I explained to you why I felt it was necessary to negotiate with the MacGregor—after the disaster with the Lamonts."

Argyll dismissed the destruction of Caitrina's clan with a short wave of his hand. Jamie clenched his teeth. At times, his cousin's callousness annoyed the hell out of him.

"Your brother acted rashly," Argyll conceded.

An understatement if there ever was one. "And he did so in your name," Jamie pointed out. "You would have lost support of some of the other chiefs if amends were not made. Handing MacGregor over to the king was to remove any taint of his death from you. Alasdair MacGregor's blood would have been on his hands. Instead you've made it worse. God, Archie, don't you realize what you've done?"

"I've gotten rid of a notorious outlaw, a murderer, and a rebel."

"Aye," Jamie said through clenched teeth. "And with your deceit and trickery you've made him a martyr. This will unite the outlaws like nothing else. There will be renewed fighting."

"Bloodshed is to be expected. Your brother has gone to help our kinsman Campbell of Glenorchy in putting down the rising."

Well, that was some measure of relief. At least Jamie would not have to confront Colin while at Dunoon. They'd argued badly the last time they'd met over his attack on the Lamonts.

There was a gleam of satisfaction in Argyll's eye. "Every

one of the thieving, murderous vermin will be rooted out and put to death."

Argyll's irrational zeal and single-minded determination to see the MacGregors destroyed jeopardized Jamie's hopes of seeing a lawful society emerge in the Highlands. Not for the first time, he wondered what was behind his cousin's hatred—it almost felt personal. "Your hatred for the MacGregors has made you blind to anything else. With this one rash act you could well lose the support that we have carefully constructed over the past few years. It's not only MacGregors who will retaliate, but other chiefs will look at this as an example of what they can expect from you—and from me."

Jamie could tell his cousin was a little taken aback, perhaps realizing the truth of his words. "I don't know why you are so upset. It's not as if you exactly have a laudable reputation in the Highlands. Your name has been blackened before."

"Aye, for the sake of our mission I've been willing to be known as your ruthless strong arm, but I'm not willing to be known as dishonorable or deceitful. Up until now I've never been ashamed of anything I've done. But your clever play with words has impinged upon my honor and my word." Jamie shook his head. "I thought better of you."

The disappointment in Jamie's voice finally penetrated Argyll's defenses. He sagged a little in his chair. "Alasdair MacGregor has been a thorn in my side for a long time." He met Jamie's stare. "And I may have acted rashly in my eagerness to remove him. I can't say I'm sorry to see him dead, but I regret that doing so may have reflected poorly on you. It was not my intention. Surely you must realize that?"

Jamie arched his brow in surprise. His cousin rarely apologized. The acute feeling of betrayal was softened a bit by his cousin's words. He did believe him. "Perhaps it wasn't your intention," he pointed out. "But it was the effect."

"You've always had an appalling amount of integrity."

Though Argyll said it as if it were something to be ashamed of, Jamie knew that his integrity and loyalty were what Argyll most admired in him. Contrary to popular opinion, his cousin—known as "Archibald the Grim"—did have a sense of humor. "It's served you well," Jamie reminded him.

"Aye, it has." Argyll sighed. "We've been through a lot together." His face hardened. "When your brother . . ." He paused, searching for the word.

"Left," Jamie filled in, rather than "betrayed us," as they were both thinking. If anyone had been hurt more than Jamie by Duncan's betrayal, it had been Argyll.

"Left," Argyll continued. "I never blamed you or your brother and sister, though many urged me to do so."

Jamie nodded, knowing it was the truth. Many of the young earl's advisers had been eager to see the Campbells of Auchinbreck lose their favor. But instead, Archie had taken them in and rallied around them, showing the loyalty to their father that Jamie's father had shown him. "I've always been grateful for what you've done for us," Jamie replied. "And I've paid you back with years of service and loyalty—but my loyalty is not blind."

"You can't really mean to walk away," his cousin said. "Not after everything."

Though Argyll did not posit it as a question, Jamie sensed his anxiousness. If Jamie broke with him and laid down his sword, Argyll knew it would not bode well with the other chiefs—many of whom viewed him as a check on his powerful cousin, in addition to being his strong arm. "Give me one reason why I shouldn't."

Argyll looked him in the eye and said flatly, "I need you."

It was said with such honesty that Jamie couldn't help but feel some of his anger dissipate. "No more tricks, Archie. No more vendettas. If you ever—"

"No more," his cousin stopped him. "You have my word." The earl stood and walked to the sideboard, poured two glasses of claret, and offered one to Jamie. Argyll studied him appraisingly. "I've never seen you so angry before. This doesn't by any chance have something to do with your bride?"

Jamie swirled the dark liquid in his glass. "Of course it has something to do with my bride. Her acceptance of my proposal was predicated on the negotiations for the surrender of Alasdair MacGregor."

Argyll stroked the point of his beard and considered him thoughtfully. "So the lass refused you at first, did she?" Jamie clenched his jaw, provoking outright laughter from his somber cousin. Not a particularly handsome man, Argyll had always envied Jamie and his brothers' ease with the lasses. "I'd like to meet her."

"The sentiment isn't mutual. She has no great love for Campbells and blames you almost as much as Colin for the death of her family."

Argyll shrugged. "Perhaps she should look to her father as well. The fighting at Ascog was regrettable, but not without cause."

Jamie could tell there was something Argyll wasn't saying. "What is it?"

Argyll slid his finger around the rim of his glass with deceptive nonchalance. "Rumor."

"What kind of rumor?"

Argyll shrugged. "That not all the Lamont's whelps perished in the fighting."

The air sucked out of his chest. "What?"

"It's rumored at least one of the lads survived."

Jamie studied his cousin's face, but he appeared to be in earnest. *God, if this is true.* Excitement radiated inside him. If he could return part of her family to her . . .

"Has anyone been seen?"

Argyll nodded.

"Who?"

"I don't know."

"Where?"

"If rumor is to be believed, somewhere around the Lomond Hills."

The excitement Jamie had felt a moment ago at the prospect of earning his wife's eternal gratitude slipped. "Fighting?"

"One would assume."

Damn. If any Lamonts were fighting with the MacGregors, they would be outlawed. Though he was anxious to get back to Caitrina to explain before news of his alleged perfidy in the MacGregor's death spread to the Isle of Bute, he knew it would have to wait. Jamie met his cousin's gaze. "I'm going to Lomond."

His cousin didn't appear too surprised. "The lass means that much to you?"

Jamie met Argyll's bold stare with one of his own. "She does."

"What's she like?"

Jamie thought for a moment; how could he put in words the complicated woman who was his wife? How could he explain that from almost the first moment he'd realized she was different from any other? "Strong. Loyal. Caring. Spirited." He felt his chest tighten with a hot swell of emotion. "More beautiful than any woman I've ever seen." Passionate.

Argyll must have read his thoughts. "Never thought I'd see the day when you were smitten. Even when you asked me to intercede on Alex MacLeod's behalf a few years ago, I had the sense that it wasn't so much for Meg Mackinnon, but for yourself. But this is different, isn't it?"

Jamie nodded. "It is."

"And what will you do if you find them?"

He eyed his cousin with full understanding of the significance of his question. It was Argyll's not so direct way of
asking him whether he still had his loyalty.

Jamie realized that he did. He hadn't forgiven his cousin
for using him in his trick with the MacGregor, but though
his loyalty had been pushed to the limits, it hadn't been
broken. Despite his cousin's flaws, in the end Jamie still believed that Argyll was a better choice than the alternatives
and the best hope for the future of the Highlands. If Jamie
walked away, Argyll would suffer, but Mackenzie or
Huntly would be the beneficiary. There was also Jamie's
clan and Caitrina's to think about. Without Argyll, Jamie
wouldn't be in as good a position to help them. He needed
his cousin's influence as much as Argyll needed his.

Finally, he answered, "Whatever my duty requires."

"And if he is fighting with the outlaws?"

"I will arrest him."

Argyll smiled, well pleased.

"After all . . ." Jamie paused to return his smile. "I've
heard you have a mind to be lenient where the Lamonts are
concerned. Very lenient."

Argyll's smile fell, knowing he'd just heard the terms of
his recompense for the rash act that had jeopardized everything they'd strived for and maligned Jamie in the process.
He scowled and then said dryly, "Oh yes, I'm often regaled
for my leniency."

Jamie grinned and shook his head. "And people say you
are without humor."

Argyll's mouth quirked. He well knew his grim reputation. "And what if you don't find anything?"

"If one of my wife's brothers is alive, I'll find him."

They both knew it was only a question of when, not if.

"Just make sure you find him soon, before he does something I cannot undo. My 'leniency' is not without limits.
Remember, you are charged with clearing Bute of outlaws

and took surety for the Lamonts. Ultimately you will be held responsible for their actions."

Jamie nodded. The sooner he found any survivors, the better—before one of his wife's brothers put them all at risk. Argyll, he knew, could be pushed only so far.

Chapter 18

❖❖❖

A week later, Jamie rode through the gate of Rothesay Castle, exhausted and disappointed. He'd scoured the mountainous area north of Loch Lomond to no avail. If one or more of the Lamont's sons had survived, they'd ventured too far into the treacherous mountains for Jamie to find them now. With winter bearing down on them, he'd have to wait until spring and then try again. Assuming he wasn't chasing a ghost. There was always the possibility that the rumors of survival were unfounded.

The entire journey back to the Isle of Bute, he'd debated what to tell Caitrina. Should he wait until he had proof—or tell her what he'd heard, even if it turned out to be only rumor? Did he dare set fire to her hopes with so little? She was still so vulnerable and just coming to terms with their deaths. Would further disappointment send her catapulting back into the dark abyss of loss?

Hell, he still didn't know what to do—an unusual state for a man who prided himself on his decisiveness. Perhaps when he saw her the answer would come to him. He was also not looking forward to telling her about the MacGregor's death, assuming the news had not arrived before him. After over a week of separation, the closeness they'd shared before he left seemed tenuous and fragile.

Gazing around the *barmkin,* he half expected to see her. The closer he'd drawn to Rothesay, the more anxious he'd grown. He'd missed her more than he thought possible.

But there was no sign of her. He frowned. He'd hoped

she'd missed him as well, but apparently she wasn't eagerly awaiting his return.

He dismounted and tossed the reins to a waiting stable lad as his men filed in behind him. "Where is the lady?"

The boy shook, refusing to meet his gaze. "I–I do-don't know, my laird."

The lad's terror rankled; Jamie did not relish inspiring fear in children. His fearsome reputation, it appeared, had not lessened any with his marriage. He bit back his impatience and asked calmly, "Did my man not arrive with news of our arrival?"

"Y-y-yes, my laird. About an hour ago."

Seeing the boy's eagerness to leave, Jamie dismissed him and gave orders to his guardsmen to see to their horses before giving them leave to find food and drink. It had been some time since they'd had a regular meal. He intended to do the same after he'd spoken with Will, the guardsman he'd left in charge while he was gone—just as soon as he found his wife.

He entered the keep, and passed through the deserted great hall on the way up the stairs to their chamber. He opened the door and looked around inside, seeing no sign of her. A prickle of alarm coursed through him.

Where the hell was she?

Caitrina raced up the stairs, her lungs near bursting. She drew her hand across her forehead to wipe away the sheen of perspiration and gulped in air, her breathing hard and erratic. After Mor had appeared at the cave with news of Jamie's imminent arrival, she'd run the entire way back to the castle without stopping. His sudden return had caught her unprepared. He'd been gone for so long, Caitrina had begun to wonder whether he was ever coming back. And just her luck, he'd decided to do so when she was visiting her brothers in the caves.

Brian had shown some signs of improvement, but Caitrina wanted desperately to get him to Rothesay. Niall, however, was being stubborn. No matter how much she argued, she could not convince him that Jamie would not toss them in the dungeon or, worse, serve them up to Argyll.

Her slippers tapped on the cold gray limestone as she navigated the narrow staircase. Upon reaching the top floor, she crossed the corridor toward their chamber and paused for a moment to catch her breath and mutter a quick prayer that he hadn't been here long enough to search the keep.

Her step faltered as she walked through the doorway. A rush of emotion swelled over her as she took in the familiar tall, muscular form. Though she might fear his questions, there was no denying how relieved she was to see him safe and in one piece. The danger of his occupation was never far from her mind. Nor was the rampant hatred of the Campbells that made him a constant—and prized— target.

"You're back!" she exclaimed with relief.

He turned around and checked her with his gaze, taking in every inch of her bedraggled appearance with one glance, including the fresh spots of mud on her hem. Her pulse spiked as she read his suspicion.

Though he looked exhausted and his handsome face was weather-beaten from the cold and rain, he'd never looked more incredible. She'd missed him terribly. Yet something was different. . . .

The beard. A heavy shadow of stubble framed his hard, square jaw. She wagered he hadn't shaved since he'd left. Though she wasn't typically fond of whiskers, on Jamie there was no denying the primitive appeal. It gave him a dangerous edge that matched his ruthless reputation. If she'd met him looking like this all those months ago, she might not have been so trusting that he was a gentleman.

A wave of wistfulness passed over her at the memory of their first meeting. That day seemed like a lifetime ago.

She took a step toward him, but he stopped her with the forbidding clip of his voice. "Where have you been?"

She plastered a wide, welcoming smile on her face. "In the kitchens seeing to the preparations for your arrival." She felt a pang of guilt at how easily the lie slipped from her tongue. Cursing Niall for putting her in this position, she walked toward him, hating the need to deceive him. "I thought you and your men might be hungry."

He was not so easily put off. His gaze slid over her face. "Your cheeks are flushed."

Her smile grew stiff. "The fires in the kitchens were hot."

"You're out of breath."

She laughed carelessly and slid her arms around his neck, knowing she had to do something to stop his questioning. "I just ran up four flights of stairs." Before he could ask her anything else, she batted her eyes playfully and nestled up against him. "Is this the manner of your greeting, then? Are you going to question me all day, or are you going to give me a proper welcome?"

She lifted her mouth to his, and he did not ignore her none too subtle request. Her heart squeezed at the tender longing in his gaze as his eyes swept over her upturned face, before his mouth fell on hers, hot and hungry. The deprivation of a week demanded fulfillment.

She sighed against him. God, how she'd missed him. The spicy masculine taste filled her senses like a potent aphrodisiac. She opened, taking him deep in her mouth. His tongue circled hers, thrusting deeper and deeper in long, languid strokes that seemed to reach to her toes.

Heat spread through her limbs, as hot and heavy as molten lava. She sank into him. Her breasts crushed against his chest. She was achingly aware of the hard length of his arousal thrusting against her stomach. It had been too long since she'd taken him in her body and felt him filling her.

Distracting him had become secondary to sating the firestorm that combusted between them the moment his lips touched hers. With each stroke of his tongue, the tremors of desire rippling through her body grew more insistent.

It was madness. All he had to do was kiss her and she craved completion. How familiar he'd become . . . how vital.

The stubble shadowing his jaw scraped the sensitive skin around her mouth as his hands moved down her back, sliding over her hips to cup her bottom and bring her more fully against him. The subtle friction made her tingle with impatience as heat spread through every nerve ending, and she dampened with anticipation.

She felt deliciously soft and warm, her body dissolving against the hard steel of his muscular chest and legs. She would never grow used to the strength and power of his body. Her hands slid over the hard bulge of his muscled arms, savoring the raw masculinity that made her deeply conscious of her own femininity. At one time, his strength might have felt threatening, but now it gave her a feeling of safety and contentment that she'd never dreamed possible.

But it was more than that. It was the feeling that she had to touch him, that if she didn't, she would go mad. She ached to splay her hands on his hot skin and feel the flex of his muscles under her fingertips. She'd never thought that simply the sight and sensation of a man's body could rouse such wicked urges inside her, but his appeal was visceral—claiming every part of her.

Reluctantly, he pulled back, breaking the kiss. His breathing came as hard and uneven as hers. He swept his finger down the curve of her cheek. "I've missed you."

"And I you." She put her hand on his jaw and teased, "I almost didn't recognize you."

He looked embarrassed. "I'll shave when I have a chance to bathe later."

She shook her head. "Leave it for a while. It suits you." She liked this dangerous side of him. He looked nothing like the polished courtier, but every inch a powerful Highland warrior. And there was no denying the dark, sensual appeal in that.

As if he could read her thoughts, his gaze darkened with heat. "A proper welcome will have to wait. I've some matters to attend to, and then I must see to my men." His gaze grew intent. "But I was anxious to see you, and when you were not in the courtyard I grew alarmed."

Caitrina cursed inwardly. She should have known that he would not be so easily distracted. "I'm sorry. As I explained, I was in the kitchens and did not hear your arrival."

He challenged her with his unflinching gaze. "So you said."

Not liking being on the defensive, she had an idea of how to turn the tables. After all, despite their passionate embrace, she still had not forgiven him for the manner of his leaving—or for his "instructions."

"Where else would I be?" She smiled sweetly—too sweetly. "Did you not order me confined to the castle?"

He didn't even try to appear apologetic but simply shrugged. "A necessary precaution for your safety."

Caitrina bit back her rising anger. "And did you not think to ask my opinion on the matter?"

"Why would I do that?" he asked, genuinely perplexed. "You are my responsibility."

Her cheeks burned, and it wasn't from running. God save her from the obtuseness of men. It seemed not to occur to him that she might resent his high-handedness. "I am your wife."

Now he just looked confused and slightly wary—

apparently having the good sense to realize that he'd said something wrong but not knowing what. "Aye."

"Not chattel to be ordered around. If you wanted a meek, biddable wife, I'm afraid you are going to be disappointed." Her eyes locked on his. "Very disappointed."

Amusement hovered around his mouth. If he laughed, she swore he would regret it.

"Believe me," he said dryly, "I have no illusions in that regard."

Deciding not to be insulted, she gave him a short nod. "Good."

He drew his fingers over his chin, considering her. "And this truly upset you?"

"It did."

"But why? I was only seeing to your safety."

"It was the manner of your actions. Since it was my freedom at issue, don't you think you might have discussed it with me before giving your orders?"

He frowned. "That's what I do—give orders. I don't consult."

Caitrina pursed her lips and searched for patience. "Perhaps not with your men, but what about with your cousin or brother?"

He looked thoughtful. "Occasionally," he admitted.

"Is not the same courtesy due your wife?"

The notion appeared to startle him, but it wasn't altogether repugnant. "Perhaps."

"The next time, you will kindly inform me of your wishes *before* you leave." She smiled. "And I will do my best to change your mind if I don't like them."

At that he laughed. "I look forward to the challenge, lady wife, but I'm not easily dissuaded—particularly when it comes to protecting what I hold dear."

Her heart tugged at the tender declaration, but even if warmed by his motives, she would not fall back into the oblivion of her previous life. She was no longer content to be sheltered in the dark and allow others to make decisions for her. "And I can be a very persuasive woman."

"I don't doubt it," he said wryly. "Is there anything else on your mind before I see to my men?"

"As a matter of fact, there is."

"Why am I not surprised?"

She ignored the put-upon sarcasm. "The way you left, it was so sudden."

"I regret not being able to explain, but in this case it was necessary."

"Surely you could have spared five minutes?"

"What needed to be said required longer than five minutes."

"Be that as it may, the next time you try to leave with nary a fare-thee-well, I will not be so understanding."

He lifted a brow as if contradicting her claim of understanding. "I'll remember that."

"What was so important to take you from here like that?"

He sighed, dragged his fingers through his hair, and then gave her lopsided grin. "My duties, it appears, will have to wait." He strode to the fireplace and pulled out a chair, offering it to her. She took the proffered seat, and he pulled another chair opposite her for himself.

She could tell by the grave expression on his face that it was serious.

"You are not going to like what I have to say. But, please, before you say anything, hear me out."

Caitrina's heart thumped, suspecting what he was about to say.

"Alasdair MacGregor is dead."

She flinched from the blow. Dear God, Niall had been right. She hadn't wanted to believe it, but here it was straight from Jamie's mouth.

She sat stonily as he relayed the story of Argyll's treachery exactly as her brother had described it.

Please, she prayed. *Don't let it be worse.* "And what was your part in this, my laird?" she asked hesitantly. "Aside from negotiating the MacGregor's surrender?"

He took her hand and looked deep into her eyes. "I swear, Caitrina, I knew nothing of my cousin's plans. I thought he had every intention of handing the MacGregor over to King James. When I received Argyll's note that the MacGregor had been killed in Edinburgh, I knew something had gone horribly wrong. I also suspected the reason. That is why I left without explanation—I had none to give until I spoke to my cousin." His face darkened. "I was furious when I realized what he'd done."

Caitrina searched his face. He looked so sincere, and she wanted desperately to believe him. But could she risk it? Jamie had never shied from the fact that he was Argyll's man. His enforcer. Could he ever belong to her when his loyalty was tied to Argyll? Was Niall right? Was she a fool to trust him?

Her silence appeared to worry him. "Tell me you believe me."

His voice was insistent, but not pleading. She understood why. He was a proud, honorable man. When he answered, he'd told her the truth and would not beg for her to believe him. That was not his way.

The truth. It was the truth, she realized. "I believe you, but what you knew won't matter. You negotiated the surrender, and you will take the blame for what happened. It will be assumed that you knew what your cousin intended."

He grimaced. "Aye. I said much the same to my cousin."

His anger at Argyll seemed real enough. Maybe good could come of this after all—if Jamie broke with his cousin. "And what justification did he offer for betraying you like this?"

Jamie sighed. "I don't think he thought about how this would affect me at all. He's been under extreme pressure from the king to quiet the Highlands and Alasdair MacGregor in particular. These past few months, he's thought of little else. But no matter how justified the MacGregor's death, the trick was unworthy of him."

She couldn't believe it. "He still has your loyalty?"

His jaw hardened at the implied criticism. "He does. My first impulse was to turn in my sword, but I realized that to do so would be shortsighted. I'm well aware of my cousin's failings. Argyll isn't perfect, but I still believe that ultimately he is the best hope for the Highlands. Neither side is one hundred percent right, Caitrina, but eventually we all must pick one."

The observation struck her—he was right. It wasn't just a question of who was right and who was wrong. No matter how much she wished it were easy, eventually she would have to choose. This was what it meant to grow up. The ignorance of her youth had been deceptively simple.

"For me," he continued, "the balance still weighs strongly in favor of my cousin. He has the power to make change and wants the same things I do."

"And what is that?"

"Peace. Safety. Land for our people. Argyll has a blind spot where the MacGregors are concerned, but he's fiercely loyal to his friends and a fair chief."

"Fair? How can you say that after what he did to you?"

"That's just it, it wasn't to me at all." A corner of his mouth lifted. "You don't know him like I do."

Nor did she wish to. "What is this bond between you?"

He didn't say anything for a few minutes, then finally decided to answer her. "How much do you know about my father?"

"Very little." Only what Meg confided and what she'd picked up here and there.

"He died at the battle of Glenlivet, taking a musket shot meant for Argyll, barely a year after my mother passed. Elizabeth and I spent most of our time with my cousin and the former countess at Inveraray. Argyll has been like a father to me. My own believed in him enough to give his life for him, and that is not something I take lightly."

Caitrina knew there was much he was leaving out—about his eldest brother in particular—but the gist was clear. There was a personal connection between Jamie and Argyll that went far deeper than she'd realized. They were not simply chief and captain, but family bound by blood and sacrifice.

"And for his part," he continued, "my cousin has always looked out for Elizabeth and me. I was barely ten and eight when he made me a captain and not much older than that when he started having me represent him to the Privy Council. I owe him much for my position and fortune—he's provided me opportunities for advancement not common to a third son."

It sounded as though Argyll's indebtedness to Jamie's father had extended to the son. But it was also clear that the bond between Argyll and Jamie ran in both directions.

"His actions have stretched my loyalty to the breaking point, but it is still there. He wronged me," Jamie admitted. "Badly. And he knows it. But it won't happen again."

"How can you be so sure?"

"I am. That's all. You'll have to trust me. My cousin is not a perfect man, but I believe in him and what he is doing."

Could she do that? How could she reconcile the man she'd come to care for as the loyal captain of a man she could not abide?

"So that's it. You forgive him just like that?"

"No." He hesitated, looking as if he wanted to say something. "It's not that simple. When the time comes, my cousin will make amends."

"How? Will he clear your name and publicly absolve you of complicity with his treachery in the death of the MacGregor?"

A wry smile curved Jamie's mouth and he shook his head. "No one would believe him if he did."

The discussion with Caitrina had gone better than he'd expected. Jamie had been tempted to confess his bargain with his cousin, but in doing so, he would have to tell her the rumors about her brother and he still wasn't sure he wanted to do that.

She'd been upset by the news of the MacGregor's death but not shocked, which made him wonder whether she'd already heard about it. He would soon find out.

Jamie made his way down the stairs and across the great hall to the laird's solar, knowing his men were waiting for him.

What he would really like was a hot bath and food, but both would have to wait—as would a proper reunion with his wife.

His body hardened at the memory of their passionate kiss and how good it had felt to hold her in his arms again. Too good.

If he hadn't been in such a sorry state, he might have showed her exactly how much he'd missed her—not that his rough appearance had seemed to bother her any. His mouth curved. His wee princess apparently had a wild streak.

Princess. Odd that the old nickname had come back to him. He wondered why. Frowning, he realized it wasn't because she'd purchased the new gowns as she'd promised. His injury and subsequent orders to keep her confined to the castle had prevented that, but now that he was back he would see it rectified right away.

Nay, it was something else. A subtle difference that he couldn't quite put his finger on.

He recalled her sudden appearance and how his relief at seeing her had turned to suspicion. He could have sworn he'd smelled the wind in her hair and felt the chill of the cold on her ruddy cheeks. And then there was the fresh mud he'd noticed on her skirts. He was almost positive that she'd come from outside and not the kitchens. But she'd seemed sincere in her explanation. Perhaps he'd been mistaken.

Her passion and happiness to see him had certainly been genuine.

That was the difference: *She seemed happy*. The shadow of grief that had followed her since the death of her family had lifted. Though he would like to take credit for the transformation, he couldn't help but wonder if there was another reason.

He opened the door to the solar and strode in, seeing Will, the captain of his guardsmen, and a handful of his other men who'd stayed behind waiting for him.

They stood as he entered. "My laird," Will said, coming forward. " 'Tis good to see your safe return."

Jamie motioned for the men to sit and took his place at the head of the table. "You received my missive?" He had sent word of the MacGregor's death with instructions for his men to increase their vigilance—but to make no mention to the Lamonts.

Will nodded. "Yes, my laird. We've increased our scouting around the area, but there has been no sign of anything unusual or of any outlaws."

"And has word of the MacGregor's death spread?"

The guardsman shook his head. "Not from what we can tell, though the Lamonts have not been eager to take us in their confidence. Conversation tends to come to a sudden stop when we draw near."

Hardly surprising, given the tensions between the clans. Still, though communication was poor on the Western Isles and it could take many days for news to travel to Edinburgh, Jamie was surprised that word of the MacGregor's death had yet to reach them.

"Have you noticed any signs of unease or discord?"

"No more than usual."

The discussion turned to the status of the repairs on Ascog before returning to the Lamonts.

"You've kept a close eye on Seamus and his men?" Jamie asked.

"Aye," Will replied. "He's been remarkably quiet."

Jamie frowned, not liking the sound of that. Snakes were most dangerous when you couldn't hear them.

"He spends most of his day at Ascog, working on the roof," Will continued. "Including taking over much of the tree felling for himself."

Jamie's gaze narrowed. "In the forest?"

Will nodded. "We had the same concern, but he's been followed and nothing ever appears out of the ordinary. He's never absent longer than a few hours."

"I see."

"Did I misunderstand your instructions? The Lamont's former guardsmen are not prisoners?"

Jamie shook his head. "No, they are not prisoners. They can come and go as they please—as long as they are watched."

But he had the niggling suspicion that the old man was up to something, and he meant to find out what.

Chapter 19

❖ ❖ ❖

Caitrina held her breath as the last beam was lifted in place. The work on Ascog Castle had progressed well while Jamie was away and she was banned from its halls. In the two days since his return, even greater strides had been made. The roof was not yet weather-tight, but if all went well, it would be soon.

The heavy rainstorms on the mainland had lightened as they crossed the Kyl to Bute, bringing a dense, foggy mist and drizzle, but thankfully not enough to curtail the work.

Mindful of their agreement, Caitrina was careful to stay out of the way as the men worked, unwilling to test the limits of her husband's temperance. He wasn't pleased to see her around Ascog, she knew, but as she kept away from the danger by staying mostly in the kitchens and supervising rather than joining in the maidservants' work, there was little he could object to. Too many decisions required her attention, from what pots and dishes could be salvaged, to what furniture to purchase and what could be made, to where to build the new storage cabinets.

She'd come upstairs to the great hall to speak with Seamus about the rebuilding of the worktables and shelves for the cellars and had lingered to watch the momentous placement of the final beam. When it was secured, a great cheer went up around the hall and she joined in with enthusiasm.

Automatically, she scanned the room for Jamie, her heart catching as it always did when she caught sight of him. With his height and size, it was easy to pick him out among the other men, but it was the relaxed grin and twinkle in his blue gaze that made her pulse leap.

Feeling her eyes upon him, he turned, and their gazes collided. A moment of connection and shared accomplishment passed between them. She grinned back at him, feeling lighter, savoring the moment—until one of his guardsmen asked him a question and his attention was drawn away.

She sighed, regretting the loss. For an instant, it had felt as it had in those precious few days before he left. Though it was nothing that she could put her finger on, something had changed since he'd returned from Dunoon. On the surface, everything was as it had been before: At night he held her in his arms and made love to her with all the passion she remembered, and during the day he was more solicitous and attentive than she could recall.

But he was watching her.

Did he suspect something? Had she done something to alert him?

Perhaps she only imagined it. She bit her lip, the twinge in her chest belying that claim. Maybe it was her own guilt speaking?

Keeping something as important as her brothers' survival from her husband was tearing her apart. Caitrina wanted to share her joy; instead, it felt as though she were lying to him. *I am lying to him.*

To make matters worse, since Jamie's return she hadn't dared venture to the caves to see Niall and Brian—it was too risky. The reports from Mor were not enough. She missed them desperately and worried for their safety.

Jamie had been charged with clearing the area of outlaws—what would happen if he found them or discovered she'd kept them a secret from him?

Unable to find Seamus, she was just about to return to the kitchens when she caught sight of Mor trying to get her attention from across the room. She could tell from the anxious look on her face that something was wrong.

Dread sank over her. Her first thought went to Brian. No, it couldn't be him; he'd been getting better.

Caitrina hurried as quickly as she could toward Mor, doing her best not to give any indication of the turmoil burgeoning inside her. She didn't want to give Jamie any cause for concern.

She took her old nursemaid's cold hand in hers. "What is it?"

Mor's eyes flickered around furtively and she said in a low voice, "Not here."

Caitrina's chest tightened and her heart pounded even harder, having her fears confirmed: Something was wrong, terribly wrong. Knowing Jamie's eyes might well be on her, she forced a smile to her face and led Mor out of the great hall, down the stairs to the cellars. With too many people in the kitchen, they passed through the corridor into the buttery. It was cool and bone-penetratingly damp in the cellars. Caitrina pulled her *arisaidh* around her a little tighter, whether to ward off the cold or chill of premonition she didn't know.

She tensed, preparing for the blow. "Is it Brian? Did something happen to Brian?"

Mor shook her head. "No, my poor wee lamb, I didn't mean to frighten you. Your brother is as well as can be expected." Caitrina didn't miss the censure in her voice. Like her, Mor thought that Brian should be removed to Rothesay. Relief poured from every fiber of her body—until she heard her next words.

"It's your fool stubborn brother Niall who's going to get himself killed."

"Niall? I don't understand."

"I told him not to go."

Fear splayed like icy fingers across the back of her neck.

"Go?" She clutched Mor's arm, alarm slicing through her. "Where did Niall go?"

Mor's face sagged. The fine lines around her eyes seemed deeper, etched with trouble. "I don't know. He left with Seamus and the others, and you can be sure they are up to no good." She paused. "There was a strange man there when I arrived this morning. And the look on his face . . ." She shivered. " 'Twas feral and filled with such hatred as I've ever seen."

"This man . . . did they mention his name?"

Mor shook her head. "But I've no doubt he was a hunted man. If I had to guess, I'd say a MacGregor."

No. Niall wouldn't be so foolhardy . . .

Yes, she realized, *he would.* It was easy to see why he would identify with the MacGregors—he'd seen his home destroyed, his father and brother killed, and he'd become an outlaw.

Niall had changed. The teasing rogue still lingered on the surface, but there was a layer of cold steel in him that hadn't been there before. She sensed the bitterness and hatred lurking perilously close to the surface. But there was something else. She'd caught him more than once with a strange look on his face—as if he were a hundred miles away—almost as if he were yearning for something . . . or someone.

Oh, Niall! What have you done? "You said Seamus and the other guardsmen left as well?"

Mor nodded. "Aye, and the laird is sure to notice their absence."

She was right. Jamie would be searching for them now. All of a sudden Caitrina realized something else. "But what about Brian? Who will watch over Brian?"

"Niall said they would be back in a day or two. Brian is safe in the cave until then, being tended to by a lass from the village." Mor anticipated her next question. "She can be trusted."

Caitrina tried to think. Dear God, where would they go? Who was this man, and what had he said that would cause Niall to leave Brian—even if only for a short while?

But there was something else that caused her even more trepidation: What would Jamie do when he found out Seamus and the other guardsmen were missing?

Daylight was almost gone. Mist had descended like a heavy plaid, enveloping them in its icy dense fog. Jamie stood outside in the yard, a grim expression on his face to match the bleakness of the day. Seamus and the other Lamont guardsmen had been gone since morning, and the men he'd sent out after them had just returned—alone.

"I'm sorry, my laird," Will said. "We found no sign of them."

Jamie cursed. "Why weren't they followed?"

"They were. My man saw nothing out of the ordinary. He left them chopping wood this morning."

"And they weren't missed until the midday meal?"

"They did not usually return before then. I'm sorry, my laird, we should have kept a closer eye on them. But the old man had stopped his grumbling. Clearly he was loyal to the lady and seemed to have accepted the changed circumstances."

Jamie shook his head. " 'Tis not your fault." If anyone was to blame, it was himself. He'd suspected Seamus's acquiescence was too good to be true. "I took the man at his word." And had assumed, like Will, that he'd be loyal to Caitrina.

"Where would they go?" Will asked.

He could think of a few places, none of them good. "With the risings after the MacGregor's death, my first guess would be to the Lomond Hills." But what could have provoked the Lamont guardsmen to risk their lives? Would they risk so much for the MacGregors? Possibly, but there could be another explanation. He tensed. They would risk much for a Lamont.

Will frowned. "But why now?"

Jamie clenched his jaw. "I don't know. But I intend to find out." He spun on his heel and headed into the keep, his body hard with purpose.

He prayed that his suspicions were wrong. He didn't want to think that Caitrina had anything to do with this, but she was hiding something from him, of that he was sure. He tamped down his anger, not wanting to rush to judgment.

As there was still some time before the evening meal, he began his search for her in their chamber. She'd returned earlier than normal today from Ascog with her serving woman. He recalled thinking that the old woman had looked distressed about something, but as Caitrina appeared in good spirits, he hadn't given it much thought. Until now.

He'd survived this long partly because he didn't believe in coincidences.

He opened the door without knocking and froze, finding his wife had just finished her bath.

At the sound, she started. Her head snapped around, and he could swear he detected a flash of apprehension in her fathomless blue eyes—almost as if she suspected the reason for his visit. *Did* she suspect the reason for his visit?

The air was humid and sultry, heavy with the scent of lavender. She sat on a stool before the fire in her wrap, a serving girl combing out the long wet tresses of luxurious ebony hair—as thick and satiny soft as sable. The old woman stood protectively beside her, staunch as a guardsman.

His instincts flared.

He waved the two servants from the room. "Leave us. I wish to speak to your mistress."

Mor took a step toward him, shielding Caitrina from his view. "As you can see, we are not quite finished—"

"Now," he said in a voice that brooked no argument, meeting the old woman's gaze.

Mor stood firm, but the young serving girl dropped the horn comb. It clattered on the wood floor, unnaturally loud.

Caitrina stood and moved around in front of Mor, the full ripeness of her sensual curves displayed to lush perfection beneath the thin, damp silk of her dressing gown. His body heated, the power of her sweet feminine charms over him potent and undeniable.

His eyes slid over her, stopping at her breasts where the fabric of her wrap crossed to reveal the deep crevice between the gently rounded edge of her soft flesh. Her nipples were hard and tight, and clearly visible through the thin silk.

He stirred, his groin heavy with a lust that was even more powerful now that he'd tasted her passion. Passion that was open and honest—or at least it seemed that way. He wanted to believe it wasn't just lust between them, but something deeper. That he was not alone in these powerful feelings.

From the first moment he'd seen her, he'd known she was special and wanted her. He wished it were still that simple. But she'd changed, as had the complexity of his desire. At one time her body would have been enough for him, but not anymore.

He'd done everything he could to earn her trust, to show her that he was more than a name. But maybe he was a fool to believe that a Lamont could ever trust a Campbell.

But she was his wife, damn it.

Her welcoming smile didn't quite reach her eyes. Disappointment hardened in his chest.

"You're cold," Caitrina said, moving toward him. "Come sit before the fire." She looked to Mor and the terrified serving girl, who couldn't seem to lift her eyes from the floor. "I can manage from here," she assured them calmly.

The girl shuffled out as fast as she could, but Mor gave her a long look as if she meant to argue. At the pleading in Caitrina's gaze, she made a sharp sound of displeasure and left them alone, closing the door with an impertinent slam behind her.

"That old woman needs to learn her place," Jamie grumbled. He hadn't been taken to task so many times since he was a lad.

"Her place is by my side," she said. "You have to understand . . . when my mother died, Mor was there. She means no harm, it's just that she thinks she has to protect me."

"From who?"

Her gaze held steady as she met his. "From you."

Jamie's mouth drew into a tight line. Unrequited love burned in his chest. "I would never hurt you."

"I know, but when you are angry—"

"Have I cause to be angry?"

"You tell me. You are the one who came storming in here, ordering everyone out."

"Can a man not have some time alone with his wife?"

She arched a delicate black brow. "But it's something else, isn't it?" She walked toward him, the seductive sway of her hips all the more enticing because it was unconscious. Her hands slipped around his neck, sliding over the taut muscles bunched at his shoulders, feeling the tension.

She was so damned warm and soft. Her delicate feminine scent laced with lavender rose up to envelop him in its sensual vise. He ached to pull her against him and take her mouth with his, driving away the thought of anything else but the two of them. Alone. Where nothing could come between them.

Unable to think when she was so near, he took a step

back. She dropped her hands, and the wounded look on her face almost made him reconsider. Almost.

"Your father's guardsmen are gone," he said.

Something flickered in her gaze. "Gone? What do you mean, gone?" She sounded surprised. But was her voice just a touch high-pitched?

"I mean that they have not returned from the forest where they were supposed to be cutting down trees."

Caitrina's hands twisted in the smooth silk of her gown. "It's cold and difficult to see. Perhaps they simply took shelter from the weather."

Jamie shook his head. "They are gone. My men have searched the area."

The pulse at her neck ticked a little faster. "And what did you find?"

It was said with a nonchalance that he knew she did not feel. She was so anxious, he could almost taste it. "They covered their tracks well, but my men believe they've crossed the Kyle to the mainland. They swore to me as their laird, and they've broken their bond. I want to know why."

"If they've done as you say, which I hope they did not, I couldn't fathom."

He studied her face. She looked like an angel with her creamy skin, wide blue eyes, and red lips. Her innocent beauty seemed to taunt him. He took her arm, his fingers gripping her tight. "You don't know?"

"Of course not." She tried to pull her arm free, but he held firm. "Seamus and the others did not confide in me."

Her voice sounded so adamant, he had to believe it was true. Relieved, he dropped her arm. "I'm glad. I would not like to think that you were keeping secrets from me." He gave her a hard look. "Are you keeping something from me, Caitrina?"

Her eyes shifted ever so slightly. *Damn.* It was there

again, that look of unease. "What would I be hiding from you?"

It wasn't an answer.

"Why are you questioning me?" she demanded. "I've told you I knew nothing of Seamus's plans. What is it that you think I know?"

Jamie knew what he had to do. He hated the idea that he might cause her more pain, but she had a right to know. If she did not hear it from him, she might hear it from someone else. He took her hand and led her to a chair. "Sit."

Seeming to sense his seriousness, she did as he asked. He moved around in front of her so that his back was to the fire. He hated himself for thinking it necessary to see her face. "I've something to tell you. Something that might cause you pain, but I think you should know."

He could see her tense. Her eyes widened a little, and she swallowed. "What is it?"

Used to directness, Jamie was not very good at couching his words. It was probably better if he didn't try. He cleared his throat. "There are rumors." Her eyes lifted to his, the sooty thick sweep of her lashes as soft and feathery as a raven's wing against her pale skin. "Rumors that one or more of your brothers may have survived."

She froze, her face devoid of emotion. It was the look of someone who'd just experienced a shock—wasn't it? Or was it the look of someone who was frightened?

Her fingers gripped the carved wooden arms of the chair until they turned white. He swore he could see the tiny hairs on the back of her neck set on edge. Everything about her screamed brittle—as if she were glass that was about to shatter.

She stared at him, looking to him for answers. "Do you believe them? Is there any truth to these rumors?"

"I don't know."

"Tell me exactly what you've heard."

She was too calm. Too rational. He'd expected her to

race out the door and down the stairs to the courtyard, demanding a horse. He'd expected tears. He'd expected wild emotion. He knew how much she'd loved her family. How their death had destroyed her.

She knew.

He repeated what his uncle had told him and told her of his journey to Lomond to look for them and of finding nothing.

Instead of questioning him further, she gazed at him, eyes narrowed accusingly. "You've known about this for over a week and have not thought to mention it before now?"

"I did not want to raise your hopes without something more."

"You think of me as a child."

"No, as someone I wish to protect from further hurt. Can you blame me for not wanting you to experience more pain? You've only just begun to recover."

"Not recover," she said stonily. "Adjust."

"I know it has been difficult for you, but you cannot deny that you were happier the past few weeks."

"No," she said, turning away. "I'll not deny that."

"Then perhaps you can understand my reluctance."

But it was clear she didn't. "And you only decided to say something now because of Seamus's disappearance."

He nodded.

"I see." She stood and moved to the fireplace, standing stiffly, staring into the smoldering embers of burning peat. Was she simply angry or trying to avoid his gaze?

He hated the suspicion coursing through him, but every bone in his body told him that she knew more than she was telling him.

She tensed as he moved closer to her. He cupped her chin, forcing her to meet his gaze. The baby soft skin was like plush velvet sliding under his fingertips. "Did you know, Caitrina?" he said softly. "Have you had word from any of your brothers?"

The pulse at her neck fluttered like the wings of a trapped bird. He could slide his thumb over it and stop it with one soft press. His fingers tightened.

Her breath caught in her throat—hesitating. Her chin quivered under his fingertips. "No," she finally said. "I knew nothing of these rumors."

Her denial fell like a cold slap across his cheek. The blue pools of her eyes were like a stormy sea, tossing with emotion and turmoil. If she was lying to him, and every instinct told him that she was, it was not done without guilt—small consolation for the betrayal. He'd thought she loved him. *Fool.*

Her eyes pleaded with him for understanding, even as the lie slipped from her lips. The plump red lips with their sensual curve that brought him such pleasure. Her hair was drying in the warmth of the room, and tiny soft curls had sprung up around her temples, grazing the pink curve of her cheek.

God, she was beautiful. And he wanted with a gut-wrenching intensity for her to be his. But for the first time, he wasn't even tempted to take her into his arms and offer her comfort. She'd chosen to put her loyalty with her family and not with him. Perhaps he should have expected it. But what he hadn't expected was the hollow burning pain in his chest. If it didn't hurt so much, he might even be able to understand her divided loyalties. But it did. He couldn't do this anymore.

He dropped his hand. Perhaps he'd been hoping for something that was impossible.

He clenched his jaw, hardening himself against the truth, and turned to leave.

"Wait. Where are you going?"

He gave her a long, measured look. "To find your clansmen."

"What will happen to them?"

He heard the fear in her voice but was of no mind to offer assurances he wasn't sure he could keep. "I don't know." Her brother's future was just as uncertain as theirs.

Jamie had been gone for two days, and there was still no word from Niall. Caitrina had barely slept since he'd left. She kept playing over and over in her head the scene in their bedroom and knew that she'd made a mistake. She'd wanted desperately to confide in him, but her promise to her brother had smothered her instincts.

She should have trusted her heart.

The truth had been there for some time, but she'd been too scared to see it: She loved him. Loved his strength, his calm authority, his honor, the occasional glimpse of the carefree smile that he showed only to her, the tender way he held her in his arms and made love to her . . . and those not so tender times when he was wild with passion for her. She loved the way he challenged her to look beyond the surface. The way he accepted her for who she was.

She'd thought her heart was gone, buried with the scrap of plaid in the sand. But it had only been hidden behind a curtain of fear. Fear that loving meant losing. It seemed that she'd been hiding her whole life. First from what was going on around her and then from her own heart. But from the first, he'd never shirked from telling her the truth—no matter how harsh or unpleasant. His steadfastness, understanding, an indelible strength, gave her the courage to open her eyes and helped her to heal the wounds of the past.

She only wished she'd realized it before now. She needed to tell him her feelings. Needed to tell him how much she loved him before he discovered the truth. Had he believed her about not knowing where Niall was, or did he know she'd lied?

Early the morning of the third day, she heard the sound

she'd been waiting for. The call went out. Riders were approaching.

She gazed out the window, unable to see anything in the heavy gray mist. The weather had worsened to match her sense of doom.

Her heart pounded and her hands shook as she tried to wrap her *arisaidh* around her. Giving up, she simply tossed it over her shoulders and raced down the stairs to the hall. The men were entering as she came in.

At the lead was a tall, broad-shouldered man in full battle gear. He walked toward her, but she knew who it was and rushed toward him. "Jamie, I'm sor—"

The apology caught in her throat as he pulled the steel knapscall off his head.

The blood drained from her face. It wasn't Jamie.

It was his brother.

Chapter 20

❖·❖·❖

Colin Campbell of Auchinbreck, the man responsible for the attack on Ascog and the deaths of her father and brother, was standing in the hall not five feet away from her as boldly as could be.

Revulsion tugged at the back of her throat, but it was quickly smothered by the flames of hatred. She remembered so clearly the last time she'd seen him: in her chamber during the attack, hurting Brian and leaving his man to rape her. He still wore the same cold, ruthless expression on his face that he'd had that hideous day.

Seeing him again made her chest tangle with conflicting emotion: raw hatred mixed with the knowledge that he was brother to the man she loved. Now that she knew who he was, the resemblance to Jamie was even more marked—particularly around the mouth and eyes. His hair was darker, and though not quite as tall as Jamie, he was similar in stature and possessed the same air of kingly authority. But what was confidence in Jamie projected as arrogance in his brother.

Unconsciously, her hands curled at her sides, clutching the woolen fabric of her skirts instead of the dirk her fingers itched for. Never had she so felt the urge to kill someone. Colin Campbell was fortunate that she did not carry a weapon.

Though from all appearances, it looked as if he'd been locked recently in battle. His hands and face were streaked with dirt and blood. There was a dried cut on his forehead and a larger one on his wrist and right hand. But it was his eyes, wild with rage, that sent a shiver of fear whistling down her spine.

Caution urged her to take a step back, but she forced herself not to cower before him. She found courage in the knowledge that she was his brother's wife, and Jamie would kill him if he harmed her.

He scanned the hall and then demanded without preamble, "Where's my brother?"

The flat voice echoed in her consciousness, sending a shudder of horrible memories reverberating through her, but she forced herself to meet his gaze. She remembered with some satisfaction the punch she'd thrown in his face and could see that he remembered it as well.

"As you can see, he's not here."

His eyes narrowed at her impudent tone. "When will he return?"

"I don't know."

"Where did he go?"

Caitrina felt some of her old spirit rising inside her. How dare he burst into her home and question her as if she were one of his lackeys. Her temper flared. "My husband did not confide in me the details of his travel plans."

His cold gaze leveled on her. "Watch your tongue, lass. Unlike my brother, I do not tolerate disrespect from women. Even from family."

"You are not my family," she snapped, though she realized it was the awful truth. His smile only further infuriated her. Discretion escaped her. "I am the lady of this keep, and I'll thank you to remember it. Consider yourself fortunate that I don't have you tossed out of here after what you did."

If he felt any guilt, he did not show it, but he did moderate his tone. "Your father was harboring outlaws, he knew well the consequences of his actions." He paused, looking her over with a considered stare. "But I didn't realize what you were to my brother."

The concession surprised her. "Would it have made a difference?"

He shrugged indifferently. "I don't know. What's done is done. I cannot change the past."

And as much as she wanted to, neither could she. If she and Jamie were to have a future, somehow she would need to find a way to exist with this man. Though she hoped she would not be forced to endure his company for long. "Why are you here? What is it that you want?"

At first she didn't think he intended to answer her, but after a few moments he explained, "My men and I were attacked last night as we rode to Dunoon. If not for the timely arrival of some of my cousin's men, we would have been overwhelmed."

Caitrina couldn't help the feeling of disappointment that filled her. She would not mourn Colin Campbell's death. But disappointment swiftly turned to trepidation when she realized the significance of the timing of the attack. "What does that have to do with Jamie?"

"I've reason to suspect that he might have knowledge of the men who attacked me."

Ice trickled through her veins, but she gave no sign of how his words had affected her. "Why would you think that?"

"Because we followed some of the outlaws to Bute."

It seemed her fears had been realized: Niall had to be responsible. She dared not ask the question she most wanted to know: the toll of dead among the attackers.

"And why should my husband know about this?"

"Bute is his damn responsibility. He was charged with clearing this isle of outlaws, and if he can't handle it, I'll damn well do it for him."

Dear God, no!

"I'm sure you are mistaken," she said evenly, trying to calm her rising panic. "There are no outlaws on Bute."

"Is that so?"

His voice made her skin prickle with alarm. "Of course it's true."

"That's strange, since I swore I recognized one of the men as your brother. Your brother who is supposed to be dead."

She froze, fighting to control her reaction, but every bone in her body wanted to shake. "My brothers are dead," she said flatly. "You should know, as you were the one who killed them."

His mouth fell in a hard, flat line, and his eyes glimmered with anticipation. "I fear not well enough, *sister*. But it's a mistake I will soon rectify."

Too disturbed to maintain her composure any longer, Caitrina left Colin in the hall and retreated to her chamber to anxiously await Jamie's return. Colin, she suspected, was preparing to search the hills and caves, and she prayed Jamie came back before he did. If Colin found them first, her brothers and her father's men would have no chance.

What a mess. She should have trusted Jamie. If she had, maybe this could have been prevented. Justified or not, Niall had attempted to murder one of the most powerful men in the Highlands. After what Colin had done to her family, she did not blame her brother, but she wondered if something else had provoked the sudden attack. Something that had to do with the strange man Mor mentioned. None of that mattered—Niall would die no matter what the reason if Auchinbreck found him.

By midday, her prayers were answered. When the call went up, she rushed to the window in her chamber in time to see Jamie ride through the *barmkin* gate. Wanting to avoid another confrontation with Colin, she waited—impatiently—for him to come to her.

The minutes dragged on. Finally, after about half an hour, she heard the heavy footfalls tread up the stairs and cross the corridor. A moment later, the door opened.

Though the fire had burned low, the room heated with his presence. She could feel the anger radiating from him. Anxiously, her eyes flickered to his face.

His mouth was drawn in a tight line, and his visage bore the marks of his journey. She wondered if he'd slept more than a few hours since he'd left. His lips were chapped raw from the cold, and lines were imprinted around his eyes as if he'd been squinting into the icy rain. Soaked to the skin, he looked as if he'd slogged through bad weather for days—which he probably had.

She wanted to go to him, but the forbidding look on his face stopped her. "Jamie, I—"

"You know what has happened." His voice was hard and flat.

God, he'd never looked at her so coldly. She knew then that he realized she'd lied to him. Fear ripped through her. Surely he would understand? She'd been in an impossible situation, divided between two loyalties.

And you didn't choose him, a voice inside her head reminded her.

She'd always thought him imposing, but never had he seemed so unreachable. Never had he held himself so apart from her. She'd hurt him, she realized. *By not giving him my trust, I've made him think I don't care for him.* How would she explain?

He was waiting for her reply. "Yes, your brother informed me of his purpose for being here."

The mention of his brother seemed to trigger his conscience. "I'm sorry that you had to be here alone when Colin arrived. I'm sure it was difficult for you."

She lifted her chin, meeting his gaze. "It was."

"He mentioned that you threatened to toss him out."

Her cheeks burned, not sure what Jamie's reaction

would be. Colin might be the devil, but he was Jamie's brother. "I did," she admitted.

"I would have liked to see that."

For a moment, she thought she detected the shadow of a smile, but then his gaze hardened. "You know what this means, don't you? If your clansmen are found responsible for the attack on my brother, not only will they have broken the truce, but they will be charged with murder. My brother is out for blood, and their actions have put all of us in jeopardy."

"What do you mean?"

"When we married, I took surety for the Lamonts. I am responsible for their behavior, and my brother wants me to pay. Colin was furious that Argyll gave me Ascog when he thought it belonged to him by right."

The blood drained from her face. Niall's rash actions had put Ascog in jeopardy. Her dream of returning their lands to the Lamonts was slipping through her fingers. And what would become of Niall and Brian and the others? Her eyes shot to her husband. "You must do something."

"It's a little late to ask for my help now, Caitrina."

Her heart stopped, hearing the censure in his words. *Late.* Was he telling her it was too late for them? "I'm sorry," she said. "You must believe that I never meant for this to happen."

His eyes pierced her with accusation. "Is what my brother said true? Was your brother Niall with them?"

Did you lie to me? She heard the unspoken question. Her eyes burned as she met his gaze unflinchingly and nodded.

He let out a vile oath that shook her—the uncharacteristic loss of control proof of the extent of his anger. "When?" he demanded.

"Not long ago. I only discovered that they lived when you were called away to Dunoon."

"They?"

Her mouth lifted in a smile. Even in the circumstances,

the joy she felt at the thought of her brothers' survival could not be dampened. "Brian survived as well as Niall."

She explained how they'd escaped and what had happened after the battle—how they'd fled to Eire and returned only when news of the MacGregor's surrender reached them. She left out the part of them fighting with the MacGregors, but when she told him of Brian's recent injury, he no doubt realized how it had occurred.

The whole time she'd been speaking, he'd been watching her face carefully. "I'm happy for you, lass." She could hear in his voice that he was. "I know how much they mean to you. You must have been overjoyed."

She blinked back the tears. "I was. I am. I still can't quite believe it."

"If you'd told me the truth, I might have been able to prevent them from coming to any harm."

"I wanted to tell you, but Niall swore me to secrecy."

"I'm sure he did, but you should never have agreed, knowing that in doing so you would be keeping something like this from me."

"It's not that simple. Niall swore that he would leave if I did not agree—and Brian was so ill, I feared that it would kill him. He said that you would throw them in the dungeon."

"And you believed them?" His voice was deceptively even.

"No."

He gave her a measured look, challenging her claim with his cool, assessing gaze.

"At least I hoped you wouldn't," she admitted. "But I know how you feel about outlaws and your duty to the law."

"You are my wife," he said stonily.

She could tell by his voice that her lack of faith had hurt him. "I know that. But there's also your cousin to consider.

I feared what he would do if he discovered they were alive."

"Your fears, as it turns out, were misplaced."

"What do you mean?"

"If it was discovered that your brothers lived, Argyll promised to be lenient."

"But why would he agree to that?"

"He had much to account for."

She realized what must have happened. Jamie had exacted payment from Argyll for the wrong he'd done him in mercy for her brothers. "You did that for me?"

He nodded.

"You never told me."

"You never gave me the opportunity."

Because I didn't tell him the truth.

"Where are they, Caitrina?"

She hesitated a second too long.

"Bloody hell!" he exploded. "You want my help, but you still don't trust me."

"I do trust you, I do." She could sense him pulling away from her and clutched his arm. She had to do something. Tilting her head back, she looked deep into his eyes and somehow found the words that she'd been unable to voice but had been in her heart all along. "I . . ." Her voice lowered to a whisper. "I love you."

Something flickered in his gaze, and his muscles went rigid under her fingertips. "If only I could believe that."

"It's the truth."

"Why now, Caitrina? I know how much your brothers mean to you and that you'd say anything to help them. But it isn't necessary. I'd help them anyway."

Caitrina was incredulous. She'd finally found the courage to voice her feelings and he refused to hear her. "You don't believe me?"

"Love means trust. You can't have one without the other."

"You don't understand. I promised—"

"To hell with your promise." He took her elbow and shook her angrily. "Tell me where I can find them. If you don't tell me what you know, I won't be able to help them."

"But what about Colin?"

His face was grim, not hiding the truth. "You better hope that I find them first."

Her blood ran cold. He was right. The hills would be blanketed with Campbells in an hour. If Colin found her brothers, there would be no mercy. Of course, there was a chance that they would evade discovery, but it wasn't a chance she was willing to take.

She debated but knew she didn't have much choice. She had to trust that Jamie would help them. Still, breaking her word to her brother did not sit well with her. Niall would be furious. But what else could she do? She'd rather have them angry than dead.

Sensing her struggle, Jamie said gently, "I can protect them, Caitrina."

She looked deep into his eyes and saw only sincerity. "Promise you won't let Colin harm them."

"I'll do everything in my power to see that they come to no harm, but I can only do that if you tell me where they are."

There was no time left for indecision. Tears streaming down her cheeks, she nodded. *If I'm wrong . . .*

No. She trusted Jamie with her life. And now she trusted him with her brothers' lives as well. "Very well. I'll take you there."

"No," he said flatly. "It's too dangerous."

The overprotectiveness toward her was to be expected, but she would have none of it—not with something this important. "There is no other way. I would not be able to give you directions, and my brother and his men will be lying in wait. If they see you, they are liable to put an arrow in you. I'll go first and explain." *Lord knows what I will say.* "I've been many times before without incident."

His mouth tightened at the reference to her secret. "But not with my brother and his men roaming the hills. Someone else must know where they are. What about the old woman?"

Caitrina would not be dissuaded; Mor would not be able to explain. "I'm going. I need to be the one to explain." He looked ready to argue, but she stopped him. "Please, Jamie, I need to do this. I promise to be careful, and you'll be there with me."

He shook his head. "I don't want to see you get in the middle of anything."

"I'm already in the middle," she said softly.

He was silent for a moment, studying her face. "Please," she said one more time.

She could see the conflict war across his features. Finally, he swore. "Very well, but you must promise to do exactly as I say."

"You mean follow orders," she said dryly.

He didn't see the humor. "That's precisely what I mean," he snapped. "If I so much as blink in your direction, you'll listen. If I say jump, you do it." His voice grew more insistent. "I mean it, Caitrina. No arguments. No questions. Understood?"

Knowing he would not allow her to go otherwise, she agreed—albeit reluctantly. "What about your brother?" she asked.

"He rode out a short while ago. Let's hope in the wrong direction."

"Then we'd best not waste any time." She strode to the ambry and pulled out a heavy wool cloak to wear over her *arisaidh*. Tossing it around her shoulders, she hurried to the door that Jamie was holding open.

They were standing so close, yet the distance between them had never felt greater. For a moment, it seemed time stood still. They stood at the door, eyes locked in a silent struggle. She wanted to lift up on her toes and give him a kiss, to throw herself into his embrace and feel a moment of comfort—the knowledge that everything was going to be all right. That together they would get through this.

If only she could be sure.

To Jamie there was right and there was wrong, and by lying to him, she had betrayed him—or so he thought. He didn't see that she hadn't had a choice. Nor had he believed her declaration of love. Once her brothers were safe, she swore she would do whatever it took to convince him that she'd spoken in earnest.

Finally, he dropped his gaze and stepped through the doorway, allowing her to cross. Inexplicably disappointed, she started down the hall.

"Caitrina."

His voice stopped her in her tracks. She turned, seeing him still standing outside their chamber, watching her. "Yes?"

His eyes pinned her, hard and unyielding. "Don't ever lie to me again."

Though it was only late afternoon, twilight fell like a black curtain through the trees. With winter coming on strong, the days had shortened considerably. But in the dense forest, where it was difficult for light to penetrate in the best of circumstances, there was an eerie, unsettled feeling floating through the ghostly mist. Many Highlanders avoided the hills and forests, believing them to be the mystical domain of fairies.

It wasn't fairies that worried Jamie, but his wife.

Caitrina had led them to a tree-lined ridge opposite the cave. From here, they had a good view of the surrounding hillside but were far enough away to avoid detection by the Lamonts. Jamie scanned the trees, seeing the remaining two Lamont sentries posted beyond the entrance to the cave. They'd already captured the man who served as the perimeter warning, and Jamie's men had circled around to take the two others—waiting only for his signal to do so.

He'd promised to give her a few moments alone with her brothers to explain, but something didn't feel right. He should never have allowed her to come, but he'd seen the determination on her face and understood the source. Hell, he admired her for it. It wouldn't be easy to face her brothers' wrath.

Just as it hadn't been easy for her to face his. He'd been furious and frustrated, but most of all betrayed. For two days, he'd ridden nonstop across Cowal and Argyll, searching for any sign of her clansmen, hoping to prevent disaster. News of the attack on his brother had reached him in Dumbarton west of Loch Lomond, and suspecting those responsible, he'd ridden hell-bent for leather back to Rothesay. Finding Colin here had only made matters worse. His brother would demand retribution and wouldn't be happy to see the Lamonts spared. But Jamie had no doubt his cousin would keep his word—whatever Colin's demands.

And the whole time he'd been searching, trying to avoid this very scenario, his wife had been lying to him.

It wasn't simply the fact that she'd kept it a secret from him that stung, but that she could keep from him something that gave her such happiness. He'd hoped someday to garner that kind of loyalty from her, but the chance for that seemed to be slipping away.

He wanted to understand, but he couldn't escape the knowledge that ultimately she hadn't trusted him enough. Some part of her had believed what her brothers claimed about him. Jamie might want to toss Niall Lamont and the other guardsmen in the dungeon, to keep them out of trouble, but he would never do anything to hurt Caitrina. He'd thought that she'd understood that. And how could she ever think he would harm a child? Brian was barely old enough to hold a sword, let alone die by one.

When they'd married he'd made a vow—the Lamonts were his responsibility—his people as much as hers. But she still saw him as an outsider. Now that she had her brothers back, maybe she no longer needed—or wanted— him.

Despite his anger, his heart had tugged when she'd said she loved him. He'd wanted to believe it. For a moment something cracked in his chest, and it felt as though light were pouring in. But he knew she'd say just about anything to save her brothers, and he couldn't help but doubt her sincerity. Love meant trust, and her actions had said otherwise.

The hair at the back of his neck rose, and his skin prickled. He had the distinct feeling that he was being watched. Not wanting to take the chance that the Lamont guardsmen would alert them to their presence, he motioned to his men to take the remaining sentries stationed in the forest. Peering through the darkness, he could just make out the odd-shaped shadows behind the trees to his left.

"I know you're there, Colin," he said softly. "You might as well show yourself."

His brother stepped out from behind a tree about twenty feet away. "You've always had the most uncanny ability to sense danger."

Jamie quirked a brow, not missing his brother's choice of words. "Am I in danger, brother?"

Colin's eyes narrowed menacingly. "Not as long as you do your damned duty."

His brother's attempts to intimidate might have worked when they were lads, but those days were long past. "Don't presume to tell me my duty. I'm a chieftain in my own right. I don't answer to you."

Jamie could see his brother's face twisted with anger. "But as his captain, you do answer to Argyll, and I'll see these men hung, drawn, and quartered for what they dared."

"Perhaps, but you'll not see it here. These are my lands, and I'm responsible for the men on them. If you have a problem with that, take it up with our cousin."

"I will."

"Until then, I want you off my lands. Now."

Colin's jaw dropped. "You can't be serious."

"Try me," Jamie said with deadly calm.

The two brothers squared off, face-to-face in the darkness, their men gathered behind them. Though Colin had the strength in numbers, both knew that if it came to a fight, Jamie and his warriors' superior skills would win. And Colin would not willingly suffer that humiliation.

Jamie gave his brother an opportunity to salvage his pride. "But know that if I have to fight you, they will likely escape."

"Are you sure that isn't what you intend anyway? How can I be sure that you will not let these men go?"

"You can't," Jamie said flatly. "As I said before, this is my land and the people are my responsibility."

The hatred in his brother's eyes took him aback. Jamie knew that Colin would not soon forget this perceived disloyalty.

Colin ordered his men to their horses, which presumably had been tethered at some distance away so as not to alert them of their presence. He started down the hill but turned back to issue one parting shot. "I never thought I'd see the day that my sanctimonious brother took the law into his own hands and turned on his own. You grow more like our bastard brother every day. Your pretty little wife has gelded you."

Jamie's fists furled and unfurled at his side. He'd thought he was immune to his brother's taunts, but this one pricked. "Do you doubt my loyalty, brother?"

"To whom? Your wife or your clan?" Colin mocked. "You can't be loyal to both."

Yes, damn it, I can. But his brother's words were not without effect. His love for his wife had stretched his duty to the breaking point—challenging his deep sense of justice. Since his brother Duncan's treachery, Jamie had always seen the law as absolute—right and wrong. But for the first time, the question of what was right and what was wrong was not so easily answered.

He waited to hear the sounds of hooves in the distance and for the man that he'd sent to follow Colin and his men to return before ordering his men forward. They crept through the darkness toward the cave, only the sound of silence billowing in their wake. If all went according to plan, it would be over before it started.

Caitrina was a mass of tangled nerves when she finally entered the cave. Though she was confident that what she was doing was right, it didn't make it any easier. Nor did it ease the guilt.

It was dark and damp, with a deep chill that penetrated the heavy layers of wool right through to her skin. At least one good thing would come of this: Brian would be removed to safety and warmth. It took her eyes a moment to adjust, as only a single torch flickered near the back wall of the cave. No doubt they were being cautious, worried that more light might give away their hiding place.

Niall moved forward to greet her. He looked horrible—dirty and scruffy, like the outlaw he'd become. He looked as if he'd aged a decade since she'd seen him last. But there was something more. His expression was as hard and angry as before, but now it was tinged with an unmistakable air of sadness.

"What are you doing out here, Caiti Rose?" he said edgily. "It's dangerous."

"I know, but I had to come."

Despite his irritation, he wrapped her in a warm, brotherly embrace. "I'm glad to see you, lass, but you shouldn't have come. There are Campbells all over these hills."

She pushed back and looked into his eyes. "For good reason. Oh, God, what have you done, Niall?"

His eyes darkened with a pain so acute, it almost hurt to look at him. "What needed to be done. But I failed."

"Why? Why would you risk everything like this? You've put all your lives in danger. Auchinbreck will kill you if he finds you."

"He won't find me."

"So you will be an outlaw, when instead you might have taken your rightful position as chief? Your men would have been free. Now you will be living in the wild like broken men. And what of the rest of our clan? It's not only you who will suffer for what you've done. You've put everything I've done to reclaim Ascog for our clan in jeopardy."

His face was like stone that was ready to crack. "I'm sorry for it. But I had no choice." He looked into her eyes, his own as bleak as she'd ever seen them. "I had to, Caiti." His voice caught. "God, they raped her."

Shocked by his declaration, all Caitrina could ask was, "Who?"

"Annie MacGregor."

She searched his face, looking for the sign that she knew was there. "And who is Annie MacGregor to you, Niall?" she asked gently.

The intensity burning in his gaze told her even before he answered. "The woman I love, but was too damn proud to admit."

"Oh, Niall, I'm so sorry." She wrapped her arms around him. He stood there stiffly in her arms, yet she could feel the emotion—the pain and helplessness—surging inside, and her heart went out to him. To a man like Niall, a man who lived to protect, she knew he must be feeling that he'd failed the poor girl.

"It was Auchinbreck and his men," Niall said. "They left her for dead." His voice lowered. "She was like a broken bird." His eyes met hers, and the stark pain there made her chest squeeze. "God, she was scared of me, Caiti."

Caitrina sickened with sympathy for Annie, knowing how close she'd come to suffering the same fate. Though it was not uncommon in the times of old feuds to dishonor a clan by ravaging their women, an honorable man would never use a woman to fight his wars.

She could understand why Niall had done what he had, but it didn't make their situation any less precarious. "Give her time, Niall. She'll see that you would never hurt her in that way, but you'll be of no use to her if you go to prison." *Or die.* But she couldn't even put those horrific words in her mouth. "I won't let them harm you."

"Then you had better hope that your husband and his brother don't find me."

The guilt on her face must have given her away. "What is it, Caiti? You look pale."

"Niall, I . . ."

A noise at the entrance of the cave drew his attention. She could hear the successive cries of surprise as Jamie and his men stormed through the entrance. Niall's gaze shot back to her, and the look of acute disbelief and betrayal he sent her cut her to the quick.

His hands gripped her shoulders, and he jerked her around to face him. "What have you done?"

Panic rose inside her; she was terrified that she might not be able to make him understand. "You don't understand; Jamie will help you."

"He'll send me to the devil by morning."

She shook her head furiously. "No. He's promised to protect you."

"How? By handing me over to his cousin for some of his Highland justice?"

A sudden wave of unease churned in her stomach. "He wouldn't do that."

Niall pushed her out of the way as Jamie's men swarmed the small space. He slid out his dirk from the scabbard at his waist. "You're a fool, Caiti Rose."

"I'm trying to help you." But he was deaf to her pleas, caught up in the effort to repel the invaders. She wouldn't let Niall's certainty erode her trust. Jamie had sworn to protect them, and he'd never given her a reason to doubt him. But the enormity of the trust she'd placed in him hit her hard. *Argyll.* She shuddered. No, Jamie wouldn't betray her like that.

Her brothers had only just come back to her, she couldn't lose them again.

Chaos erupted around her as she sank into the stone wall behind her. It was so hard to see what was happening—with virtually no light and the small space crowded with large, mail-clad bodies. Everywhere she looked, men were fighting. With little room to maneuver, bows and claymores were impossible; it was hand-to-hand combat and dirks. It was the latter that she feared.

Jamie and his men easily overpowered the couple of guardsmen who'd been watching the entrance of the cave and worked their way toward the place where Niall, Seamus, and the other guardsmen would make their stand. She wanted to squeeze her eyes closed and block out the hideous sounds—the grunts of pain, the thump of fists slamming into flesh, the struggle. She just wanted it to be over soon with as little bloodshed as possible.

Thank God Brian was safe in the back chamber, Boru standing guard.

Although Niall and her Lamont clansmen were vastly outnumbered, the tight confines of the cave worked in their favor—at least for a while. There was nowhere for them to go; they were trapped with their backs to the cave, and eventually they would be overtaken.

Jamie was doing everything he could not to kill her brother's men, but she was terrified that if Niall fought back, Jamie would be unable to prevent something terrible from happening.

There were perhaps only half a dozen of her Lamont guardsmen flanking Niall when he and Jamie met, warrior to warrior, each wielding a dirk.

She held her breath, her worst nightmare about to be realized.

Niall showed no signs of backing down. She stepped out of the shadows, moving toward her brother. She clutched his arm, but he didn't look at her, his gaze fixed on Jamie. "Please, Niall, don't do this," she begged.

"Get out of here, Caiti," he said at the same time as Jamie.

Tears were streaming down her cheeks. "But—"

"You gave me your word, Caitrina," Jamie added. "I want you to leave . . . now."

I can't! she wanted to scream. Her feet wouldn't move. She had the horrible feeling that only if she stayed could disaster be avoided. She looked into Jamie's eyes, but it was useless—he would not budge. Every instinct clamored to argue, but she'd given her word. She dropped her hand and started to back away, her gaze fixed on Niall, who still refused to look at her. Her throat was thick with emotion. She shot a quick pleading glance at Jamie. "Please, don't hurt them."

"I have no wish—" All of a sudden, his eyes widened with alarm. "Caitrina, watch out!" He made a move toward her, but it was too late.

Chapter 21

❖❖❖

Caitrina was lifted off the ground, a heavy arm wrapped around her waist and the long sharp blade of a dirk pressed to her throat.

"One more step and she's dead."

Dear God, it was Seamus. The edge of the blade nicked the tender skin below her jaw and she cried out, more surprised than pained. Jamie froze in his tracks.

Niall's gaze darted back and forth between Jamie and the old guardsman. "What in Hades are you doing, Seamus?"

"Trying to get us out of here," the old warrior answered impatiently.

"By using my sister?"

"Who has betrayed us! It was she who brought the Henchman here."

Caitrina said, "I was only trying to help—"

"Shut up!" Seamus ordered, pressing the blade deeper into her throat. She gasped in shock, feeling a sharp sting followed by the wet trickle of blood sliding down her neck. Any hope that Seamus might be bluffing shattered.

Jamie made a sound of such animalistic rage, she felt it deep in her bones. Clearly, it had rattled Seamus as well, because his hand began to shake dangerously.

"Let her go," Niall demanded with deadly calm, though Caitrina could see that he was feeling anything but.

"No," Seamus said more anxiously. "He'll let us go as long as we have the lass."

Niall dropped his weapon and kicked it toward Jamie,

raising his hands in surrender. He shook his head sadly. "It's over, Seamus. Let her go."

"No!"

Caitrina could feel the old man's heart race against her back and knew that he was panicking—his rash plan hadn't gone as he'd anticipated. His arm tightened around her waist. She sensed what he was going to do but could do nothing to prevent it. Up until now it had almost seemed unreal, but for the first time she felt fear. His hand shook as he started to draw the knife across her neck.

She could hear the wild desperation in his voice as he turned to Niall, his voice laden with apology. "The lass is a traitor. It's all her faul—"

The sound of a blade whizzing through the darkness followed by a dull thud stopped Seamus cold. He stiffened with shock and released her as he fell back. The knife he was holding to her neck dropped, landing at her feet in the dirt. She glanced down and then jumped back, horrified. Her father's old warrior lay glassy-eyed, with Jamie's dirk planted deep in the side of his throat.

It was deathly silent as she processed what had happened. If not for Jamie's considerable skill with a blade, she might be lying there instead.

Regret washed over her. Jamie had killed him, but it was her hands that were stained with blood.

She felt herself swept up in her husband's embrace. "God, are you all right?"

She nodded mutely, and he cupped her head against his chest. She inhaled the deep masculine scent—savoring the warmth and safety of his embrace. He'd looked so calm a moment ago, but she could feel the frantic race of his heart against her chest. He squeezed her to him harder and pressed his mouth against her hair. He held her for a long moment, as if he didn't want to let her go. She wanted to thank him for saving her life but was too horrified by the one that had been lost in her place.

With some reluctance, he released her. His hand brushed the side of her face with aching tenderness. For a moment, in his eyes she saw the emotion he normally kept hidden. He tilted back her chin and looked at her neck. "Bring me some damn light." A man moved forward with a torch.

"Is she all right?" Niall asked.

"Aye, thank God 'tis not deep." She could hear the anger in his voice and knew he was blaming himself for allowing her to come. Jamie grabbed hold of the edge of her cloak and pressed it against the cut to stanch the bleeding. "Hold it like this," he instructed, "all right?"

She nodded again, and he ordered one of his men forward. "Take her back to the castle and see that the wound is tended to immediately. Don't let her out of your sight." His eyes met hers. "I'll be back soon." He leaned forward and dropped another kiss on her forehead.

"Yes," she managed, then looked to Niall hesitantly.

"Go, Caitrina," her brother said roughly. "See to your wound."

Numb, she allowed Jamie's guardsman to lead her out of the cave and back to Ascog, having no wish to see her brother's face as he was forced to surrender to her husband.

There was nothing left for her to do here; Caitrina feared she'd done enough already.

Jamie watched as Will led Caitrina to safety, his stomach lodged firmly in his throat. Only now that the danger was gone did the fear settle in as he realized just how close he'd come to losing her. It had happened so damn fast—he hadn't had time to think. Years of battle, of honing his instincts, had paid off. When the old warrior had turned, it had been the only opening he needed. He hadn't hesitated; seeing his target, he'd thrown his dirk with a precision born of a lifetime of practice.

"You really do care for her?"

Jamie turned, not realizing Niall Lamont had been watching him. His hands had been bound behind his back while Jamie's men cleared the tunnels of the outlaws.

"You are surprised? Do you doubt your sister's allure?"

Niall snorted. "Not at all, I've seen her charm even the most impenetrable heart. I just didn't think you had one."

Jamie's mouth tugged. He studied the other man. "She told you the truth. I mean to do what I can to help you."

"Why?"

"You need to ask?"

"But Auchinbreck is your brother."

"Aye. If she'd confided in me earlier, I might have prevented this. I had no wish for your father to die. I can understand your anger, but my brother had cause to attack your castle." At the look of outrage on Niall's face, Jamie added, "I didn't say I agreed with what happened, but it wasn't wholly my brother's fault. Had I been there, I might have been able to avoid a battle, but you know as well as I do that fighting is the way men settle disputes in the Highlands."

"Aye," Niall said reluctantly. "My father never backed down from a battle. But it wasn't only my father's and brother's deaths that I was avenging." Jamie watched as his face twisted with an emotion he could describe only as raw anguish. "He ordered the rape of an innocent woman." Niall met his gaze, his eyes glowing with rage. "My woman."

Jamie cursed. He didn't want to think his brother capable of such a despicable act, but he did not doubt Niall's word. "I'm sorry."

The apology seemed to surprise the other man, and he nodded in acknowledgment. After a moment, he asked, "What do you intend to do with us?"

"What I can," Jamie responded. "We'll stay the night at Rothesay and then tomorrow depart for Dunoon."

Niall's jaw hardened. "It was as I thought, then. We won't die by your hand, but by Argyll's."

"You won't die by anyone's hand. My cousin has promised to show you leniency."

"I can imagine," Niall said dryly. "Drawn, but not quartered?"

"I hope to have more influence than that," Jamie said with a crooked smile. Just then, his men came out of the darkness carrying a makeshift pallet with an enormous dog tracking after it.

Niall's demeanor changed in an instant. "Careful. He's hurt."

"Niall, what's happening?" Brian asked, his voice weak and delirious.

"Shush," Niall said. "We're taking you to the castle."

"But the Enforcer," Brian protested. He tried to lift up his head, but Jamie knew he couldn't see him.

He felt sick, hating the fear in the lad's voice.

"Don't worry, Brian. Caiti will keep you safe." Niall met Jamie's gaze as he spoke, and Jamie nodded.

At that, the boy seemed to relax and eased back down on the pallet as the men carried him out.

"I hope you won't make me a liar," Niall said.

"The lad will come to no harm. He was not involved in the attack on my brother, though when he is well enough to travel, he will have to account for the fighting with the MacGregors. I'll pay whatever fines it takes to see him cleared."

Niall nodded. With the cave cleared of Lamonts, Jamie led his prisoner out into the forest. Leaving them to his men, Jamie started toward the place where he'd left his horse.

"Campbell."

Jamie looked back over his shoulder.

"I know I've no right to ask . . ."

Jamie moved his head, indicating for him to continue.

"If anything should happen to me, when he's old enough you'll see that Brian takes his place as chief?"

The odd request took Jamie aback. " 'Tis the position that rightfully belongs to you. Would you not ask it for yourself?"

"You really think you can convince your cousin?"

"I do," he said confidently.

Niall paused, considering. "Still, I'd have your promise if you're willing to give it."

Jamie bowed. "Then you have it."

For the first time since Jamie had burst into the cave, maybe for the first time in months, hope flared in Niall Lamont's gaze.

Caitrina suffered the frantic ministrations of her former nursemaid, all the while worrying about what was happening with her brothers. She'd heard the men ride through the castle gates not long after her, and from the numerous servants who rushed back and forth fulfilling Mor's requests for herbs, salves, water, and clean linens, she'd learned that her brother and his men had been taken to the old, unused south tower. She admitted to a certain relief that Niall had been wrong and they'd not been imprisoned in the dungeon. She'd been right to trust Jamie.

Mor was about to send a girl on another errand—this time for more pillows—when Caitrina sat up, having suffered enough. " 'Tis nothing more than a scratch, Mor. Truly, I'm fine." The blade had sliced about a two-inch cut at the base of her jaw.

The old nursemaid put her hands on her hips and pursed her mouth disapprovingly. " 'Tis deep enough to scar."

"You've put your salve on it and bandaged it. Any scar that remains won't be visible."

"I'll know it's there," Mor said stubbornly.

Aye, and so will I. A lasting memory of my betrayal of

my clan. But she would wear the badge with honor if her brothers were spared.

The door opened again and another young serving girl rushed in.

" 'Tis about time," Mor said angrily. "What took you so long? I sent you for those herbs hours ago."

More like a few minutes ago, Caitrina thought wryly.

"I'm sorry, mistress. The kitchens are in an uproar at the laird's bequest, readying everything for the morrow."

Caitrina froze, every instinct flared. "Tomorrow? What is happening tomorrow?"

The girl cast her a furtive glance, then looked to the floor. "I thought you knew, my lady. The laird is taking the prisoners to Dunoon."

Caitrina felt the blood drain from her face. *No!*
There has to be a mistake.

Not long afterward, Caitrina sat woodenly before the fire, staring into the dying embers of flaking ashy peat. The incident that had almost taken her life was far from her mind as she waited for a more painful blow to fall. She'd sent Mor and the others from the room, knowing that he would come to her soon—if only to check on her injury.

She fought the bitter swell of betrayal; she would hear his explanation first.

At last she heard the familiar heavy footfalls. Her heart pounded. The door opened and closed. She lifted her eyes to his.

He spoke first. "Your wound—"

"Tell me it's not true," she said, cutting him off, her injury insignificant in the face of what she'd just discovered.

He seemed perplexed by her tone. "What's not true?"

Her hand gripped the wooden arm of the chair. "Tell me that you have not arrested my brother and his men. Tell me that you are not taking them to your cousin."

He straightened, clearly taken aback. "I thought you understood. It's my duty—"

"Duty?" Pain seared through her. Caitrina wanted to wail like a wounded animal. The affirmation of his betrayal cut more deeply than she could imagine. She'd trusted him with what she held most dear, and he'd betrayed her. "I don't care about your duty! I would never have told you where they were if I'd known what you intended. You swore you would help them."

His mouth fell in a tight line—a look she recognized when he was trying to control his temper. A temper that seemed to exist only around her. "I will help them. Brian will stay here until he can recover, but Niall and the rest of the men must go to Dunoon to face the charges against them."

This couldn't be happening. Her chest squeezed so badly, she couldn't breathe. "You'd help them by turning them over to the hands of an executioner? Dear God, Jamie, they'll die for what they've done."

His eyes leveled on hers. "I told you before that my cousin has promised to act fairly—and leniently—with them."

"I've heard Argyll's promises before," she scoffed. "Will he act as fairly with them as he did with Alasdair Mac-Gregor? Did you convince me to help turn them in so that Argyll can kill them also?"

He took her arm and lifted her out of the chair, pulling her hard against him. She could feel the tautness of his muscles and the heat radiating from his body. His face darkened with barely contained fury. "Damn you, Caitrina, you know I had nothing to do with that."

"Do I?" She turned her head sharply away, refusing to look at him. "I'm not sure of anything anymore."

He was silent, but she could see the ominous tick at his neck and knew he was furious. But she didn't care. She wanted him to feel as hurt and betrayed as she did.

His voice was low and forbidding. "I warned you once not to interfere with my duty."

She remembered: when he'd imprisoned her father's guardsmen. "That was different."

"Was it? You said you trusted me. I believe you even claimed to love me not so many hours ago."

How dare he throw her feelings back in her face with what he intended to do! "It's not that simple."

"Actually, it is." He took her chin in his hands and forced her gaze back to his. "Love can't be by half-measure. It's all or nothing. Either you trust me—and my judgment—or you don't."

He asked for too much. Heat gathered behind her eyes. "How would you know? You, who hold yourself so apart. You, who don't need anyone. What do you know of love?"

"Plenty." His voice snapped like the crack of a whip. "Though right now I wish I didn't."

Her heart faltered and then started to pound furiously. Her gaze raked his face, searching for a crack in that implacable façade. "What are you saying?"

"Damn it, Caitrina, don't you know how much I love you? So much that there is almost nothing I wouldn't do for you. But I can't change who I am."

For a moment, she savored the overwhelming burst of joy. *He loves me.* The words she'd longed to hear. . . .

But it wasn't supposed to be like this. When they confessed their love, it was supposed to be perfect—a moment of unparalleled closeness and intimacy—it wasn't supposed to make her feel more uncertain. Nor was it supposed to be spoken in anger and frustration.

Instead, it felt like a final offer. Blinking back tears, she turned her head from his hold. "I wish I could believe that."

"You can." He lifted her chin gently, examining the bandaged area of her neck, assuring himself that it was not bleeding. "Don't you know how I felt seeing you with a blade at your neck? I've never been more terrified in my life. I could have lost you."

"It's nothing," she dismissed. "No more than a scratch."

His jaw hardened. "I never should have let you go, it was too dangerous."

"I needed to be there. I needed to explain."

"Your brothers will understand."

"How can you say that?"

"Because I'm confident that it will all work out for the best."

She lifted her chin. "I don't share your confidence. It's my brothers' lives at stake." Her voice thickened with emotion. "I just got them back. Please don't take them from me again."

"I'm not taking them from you," he said with exaggerated patience, each word uttered with careful precision. It was clear he was near the edge, holding himself by a very thin thread. "I'm trying to protect them."

"How?" she asked, incredulous. "By arresting them?"

"While they are in my custody, Colin can't do anything to them. If I can clear their names, they'll be out of his reach for good. Would you rather I waited until my cousin was forced to send his men after them? Your brother and his men are outlaws—they can't stay here indefinitely. Eventually they will need to face what they've done."

Caitrina felt as though she were beating her head against a rock. The law. Duty. It was always the same. "Is that all that matters to you? The law?" She held his gaze, knowing where his rigid adherence to law and order came from. "You are not your brother, Jamie. Don't hurt mine to bury the memory of yours."

He flinched at the reference to Duncan. His eyes flared and she wondered if she'd gone too far. "You know nothing of what happened with Duncan. This has nothing to do with my brother, only with yours. I thought you wanted Ascog restored to Niall."

"I do."

"The only way that can happen is with my cousin's help."

She didn't want to hear justification—even if there might be an element of truth. "It's too soon," she said stubbornly.

His gaze bit into her. "I'm asking you to trust me."

If only it were so simple. "I do. It's your cousin I don't trust. After what he did to you, I can't believe you would trust him either. Dear God, what if you are wrong?"

"I'm not."

She heard the unwavering confidence in his voice, but it wasn't enough. "Well, it's not a chance I'm willing to take."

He stared at her with those slate blue eyes, hard and unyielding. "I'm afraid that it's not your decision to make."

Jamie knew his words were harsh, but she needed to understand. Caitrina was blind when it came to Argyll—understandable, perhaps, but if she was going to be married to him, she needed to accept his loyalty to his cousin. How could she claim to love and trust him and believe the man he gave his loyalty to a monster? He'd thought she'd started to believe in him.

Her accusation where his brother Duncan was concerned was misplaced, but it pricked nonetheless.

He had to get the hell out of here. No one could penetrate his defenses the way she could. Caitrina had an uncanny ability to make him feel raw, exposed. To make him lose control. She riled his anger with her accusations and persistent lack of faith. What more could he do to prove himself? He'd told her he loved her, yet it had barely seemed to penetrate.

He was confident that he was doing the right thing, though it didn't make him deaf to her heartfelt pleas. He just didn't know how else to explain.

"Please," she said, her eyes soft and beseeching. "If you care for me at all, don't do this."

Jamie looked at her, feeling his insides twist. The urge to please her was nearly overwhelming. He ached to take her into his arms and love her until she smiled at him again, until her eyes softened with tenderness.

She leaned closer to him. The innocent brush of her breasts stirred his already burning hunger—his blood fired from their argument and from the fear of almost losing her in the cave. His need for her rushed over him like a firestorm, blasting him with liquid heat. He fought the urge to bring an end to their argument in the most basic way, because he knew it would not be resolved. But damn, he was tempted.

What was she trying to do to him? Was this what being in love was supposed to feel like? Was it supposed to make him feel out of control? Was it supposed to rip him apart, pulling him in two opposite directions? Was it supposed to make him want to tear his hair out in frustration? If it was, he didn't need it.

"Care for you? Haven't you been listening to anything I said? I love you. Do you think I want to hurt you?"

Her eyes were bright with unshed tears. "I don't think you care who you hurt. Maybe they are right what they say about you, that you are a ruthless henchman without a heart."

Her barb had struck flesh. He snapped. His carefully tethered anger whipped around like a banner in a storm. He pulled her to him, not quite sure what he meant to do. "After all these months . . . is that what you really think?"

She seemed to realize that she'd gone too far. "I don't want to, but what else should I think when you won't listen to reason?"

"I am listening, but my duties and responsibilities cannot be ignored."

"What about your duty and responsibility to me? Do I not matter?"

Everything was still so damn simple with her—it had been that way from the first. She never probed below the surface. "Of course you do." He released her and took a step back. This was getting nowhere. He wondered whether they would ever be able to breach the barrier between them. He wanted to think that love would be enough but had begun to fear that it wasn't. "You said you didn't want me to treat you like a child, Caitrina. You wanted to see the real world in all its vivid complexity, where decisions aren't always so clear-cut and where loyalty can be divided. Well, this is it. I know you don't understand right now, but I'm doing this for you."

She shook her head, her chin quivering. "For me? You're wrong if you are trying to convince yourself that you are doing this for anything other than yourself and your precious duty to your cousin. No wonder you have been so alone. Nothing can come between you. I'll never understand how you can do this and claim to love me."

He clenched his jaw, fighting to stay calm, but it was a lost battle. "One has nothing to do with the other."

"Of course it does. You are choosing your duty to your cousin above your love for me."

"Dear God, what do you want from me?" he asked roughly.

"All of you." Her eyes locked on his. "What if I asked you to choose between us? Would you choose me, Jamie?"

He gave her a long, penetrating stare, furious with her game. "Aren't you choosing your outlaw brother above me? What if I gave you the same choice: your brother or me?"

As he'd expected, his ultimatum was met with silence. It was an impossible choice for either of them. Life—and love—was not that simple.

And if she couldn't understand that, to hell with it. He'd

hoped that it wouldn't come to this. That she would not ask something of him that he could not give her. That she would love him enough to trust him to do what was right for her brothers. He was done asking for her to believe in him, and he wasn't sure where that left them.

He felt stretched as taut as a bowstring, ready to fire. Not trusting himself to stay another minute longer, he said, "It seems, then, my lady wife, we are at an impasse." After giving her one long glance, he turned on his heel and headed for the door.

Chapter 22

❖ ❖ ❖

Caitrina's pulse raced with a sudden burst of panic. He was going to leave her. Desperation rose up inside her. She needed to do something to stop him.

"Jamie!"

He stopped before the door but did not turn around, his back stiff with resolve.

Feeling suddenly helpless, Caitrina twisted her hands in her skirts before she caught herself. She wasn't helpless. She hadn't survived the past few months to let everything fall apart now. She wouldn't let it come to this. She didn't want to lose Jamie any more than she wanted to lose her brothers. Surely they could find some common ground?

"Please," she said. "Don't go. Not like this."

Slowly he turned around to face her. "I'm tired of fighting with you, Caitrina. Leave it be, before we both say something we wish we hadn't."

She walked toward him, coming to a stop only when she stood right before him—close enough to feel the heat blasting from him like a firestorm waiting to envelop her in his sensual hold. Her body crackled with awareness as it always did when she stood this close to him, craving the balm of his touch. She wanted to run her hands all over his broad chest, to feel the warm velvet of his skin over the hard, chiseled muscle.

He was imprinted on her mind and body, and every instinct clamored to reclaim the intimacy, to seek refuge in the deep connection that could not be denied.

"I don't want to argue with you either." *I want you to hold me. I want you to tell me everything is going to be all right.* She leaned closer to him, drowning her senses in his sultry masculine scent. Lifting up on her toes, she slid her arms around his neck. "It doesn't have to be like this."

He stood stiffly before her, but she could feel his body react to her touch. Passion, restraint, and smoldering anger sizzled between them.

"It doesn't?"

She shook her head. "I love you, and if you love me—"

"I do, God damn it," he growled. "If only you knew how much."

Every muscle in his powerful body tensed with restraint, and she could tell that he was holding himself by a very thin thread. His nostrils flared when her mouth moved to inches below his. She hated when he was like this: the cold, ruthless warrior. The man who didn't need anyone.

She wanted him to need her as desperately as she needed him.

She wanted to slide her mouth along the hard flex of his stubbled jaw until it softened with desire. To drag her hand over the rigid bands of muscle on his stomach until she reached the thick column of his manhood and make him groan with need of her. Instead, she smoothed her hand over the soft wool of his *breacan feile* at his shoulder, noticing how the muted blues and grays of the plaid complemented his eyes. Her gaze was drawn once again to the Campbell chieftain pin he used to secure it—the boar's head a sharp reminder of all that stood between them.

Why did it have to be so complicated?

Maybe it didn't. Maybe in his arms everything would become clear—he would see that nothing should come between them. Maybe if he knew how much she loved him . . .

Sometimes words weren't enough.

"Then show me," she whispered. "Please."

She melted against him, her breasts crushed to his chest,

and he groaned. His mouth sank over hers, and passion exploded between them as hot and swift as lightning. It had been too long. There was a desperate, raw urgency to their movements, as if they were both fighting to hold on to something that was in danger of slipping away.

She returned his kiss with equal fervor, opening to take him deep into her mouth. The warm, delicious taste of him drenched her with heat—and hunger. The anguish and anger of a few moments ago slid away as the hard pull of desire drove everything else from her mind.

His hand slid down her back and gently cupped her bottom, lifting her hard against him as he sank deeper and deeper in her mouth. Heat rushed between her legs as she felt the thick steely column wedged against her.

Her legs grew weak, and she clutched his shoulders, sensing the passion straining under her fingertips.

His kiss was wild as his hands possessed her. He cupped her breast, her nipple hardening against the warm pressure of his palm. His tongue plied hers, hard and demanding. She met him stroke for stroke, holding nothing back.

Her breathing came in uneven gasps as her need spiraled out of control. He moaned into her mouth with each hungry thrust of her tongue.

Lifting her leg around his waist, he nudged her more firmly against his erection. God, he felt so good. So hard and full. Heat pooled between her legs. She was throbbing where they touched. The pressure was almost too much to take. She wanted to rub up and down over him until the clawing need subsided.

His mouth slid down her neck, mindful of her bandage, singeing a path of sensation in its heated wake. The wetness of his lips, the warmth of his breath, the flick of his tongue, made her skin prickle and sent a hard shiver running through her. Every nerve ending was set on edge, so that every stroke, every touch, seemed more intense.

And when his tongue slid beneath the edge of her sark,

circling the turgid peak of her nipple with moist heat, she thought she might fall apart.

Her head fell back in abandon as he took her nipple more fully in his mouth and sucked while his hand lovingly squeezed her breast. She cried out as a white hot needle of desire shot through her, and she collapsed against him, utterly boneless.

Her legs were swept up under her as he lifted her in his arms, carrying her toward the bed. Clasping her hands behind his neck, she laid her cheek against his plaid as she tried to catch her breath.

Carefully he set her down, and she sank into the pillowy feather mattress. Leaning over, he looked deep into her eyes—his own dark and hazy with unspent passion. "Are you sure about this?" he asked.

How could he ask such a thing? She held his face in her hands and pressed a soft kiss to his mouth, lingering at the rich, dark taste of him. "I never want you to doubt how much I love you. I don't want anything to come between us."

His lips curved in a smile that reached his eyes. "It won't, my love."

Happiness burst over her in a shimmering wave at hearing exactly what she'd wanted to: agreement. *I knew he would reconsider.*

With nothing left between them, he quickly removed his own clothing and then hers. When they were both naked, she didn't let him stop to look as he wanted to, but pulled him down on top of her.

Automatically, he tried to roll to the side, but she stopped him. "No. I want to feel you. All of you." Latent fears had no place in their bed.

He took her chin and dropped a tender kiss on her lips, then his eyes searched her face intently. "You're sure?"

In answer, she slid her hands over the wide span of his chest, gripped his powerful shoulders, and pulled him down on top of her—skin to skin. The feel of his weight pressing into her was incredible, the pressure exquisite. He was so heavy and hot, her skin flamed where they touched. They melded together in a pool of liquid fire.

He kissed her with a deep groan that tugged in her chest. It was a sound of raw pleasure and deep emotion that called to her in the most primitive way.

His mouth found hers again in a long, languid kiss that seemed to reach down to her toes. His lips were soft and coaxing as his tongue probed the deep recesses of her mouth and throat.

Their bodies slid against each other, the friction rousing her passion to a maelstrom. Her body dampened, deeply aware of his thick, hard erection hot and throbbing against her belly.

Unable to hold back, she clutched his back, his shoulders, the hard flanks of his buttocks, wanting him closer. Wanting him inside her.

Jamie wanted nothing more than to slide deep inside her and relieve their restlessness, but he didn't want to rush. He wanted to savor every moment of their joining.

Whatever qualms he'd had were appeased by her words of understanding. Their love was what was important; nothing else mattered. Her trust warmed him, and he was relieved that she'd recognized the truth before it was too late.

His lips dragged over her mouth, her chin, her neck. His hands caressed the baby soft skin of her breasts and hips. He loved feeling her under him, raking her hard nipples against his chest and rubbing her downy mound near the head of his cock.

It was ironic—they'd made love countless times, but never in this most basic position. It seemed the final surrender of trust.

He was deeply conscious of how small and vulnerable

she was. As if to dispel that notion, she lifted her hips against his in gentle entreaty. Blood rushed to his already throbbing erection as he circled her damp opening with his heavy head, teasing.

He bent his head and took one pink nipple in his mouth, nibbling and sucking until she writhed under him. Her skin tasted of honey and heat.

He forced her to slow, sliding his hands over her belly, down the insides of her legs, and up to the soft inner thigh. His finger brushed over her, and she shuddered.

She was so warm and soft, weeping for his touch. She tensed in anticipation. He slid his finger along her slick opening until she spread for him.

Releasing her breast, he gazed up at her face as his mouth slid down the pale curve of her belly. Her eyes were hot and heavy with desire, her breathing rough as she realized what he was going to do.

He could not wait to inhale her heat, to slide his tongue deep inside her. Holding both hands under her hips, he lifted her to his mouth. Then, holding her gaze, he pressed his mouth to her feminine core.

She cried out with pleasure as his lips nuzzled the delicate pink skin between her legs. As his mouth tasted her dampness. And then as his tongue probed deep inside her.

He loved to watch as ecstasy took hold. As her head fell back, her back arched and her lush red lips parted with hitched breath.

She pressed her hips against his mouth, finding that perfect spot of pleasure as her release shattered over her in wave after wave of pulsing pleasure.

It was too much.

He lifted his mouth and moved over her. He looked down between their bodies, his hard and stiff, hers soft and pliant, as he slid gently inside her and started to thrust with long, deep strokes.

She wrapped her legs around his waist and lifted her hips

to take him deeper as their rhythm built to a frantic beat that matched the pace of his heart.

He gave over to the primal call. Heat washed over him and blood pounded through his body.

She was so tight and soft, milking him with her body. Drawing him back even as he pulled away.

His eyes closed as the force of his release built inside him. He heard her own cries just as pleasure erupted from deep inside him. As the love he felt for her poured from his body in a powerful explosion that welled up from deep in his soul.

When the last tremor had died away, all he could do was collapse beside her, trying to find his breath and the words to express the happiness he was feeling.

He rolled to his side so that he could look at her. His chest squeezed with love. Her breathing was uneven, her cheeks flushed pink, and her lips red and swollen from his kisses. His fingers swept a strand of hair that had tangled in her thick, velvety black lashes. A tiny smile curved her lips. Her eyes fluttered open for a moment.

"I'm so happy that you decided not to go through with it," she murmured, sleep tugging on her lids.

Unaware that he'd stiffened beside her, that she'd just plunged a dirk in his heart, she drifted off into a happy, well-sated slumber.

Chapter 23

❖❖❖

Caitrina woke with a start at the sound of movement below her window.

God, what time is it? She rolled side to side a few times and pulled the pillow over her head, trying to drown out the clatter. The lull of more sleep tempted, but awareness hovered around the edges of her consciousness, forcing her awake.

She opened her eyes to a room still shadowed in darkness. But she didn't need light to know that she was alone. Sometimes it felt as if she were so aware of him, he'd become a part of her, as vital as air and food. And when he was gone, she felt his absence as acutely as a missing limb.

She frowned, wondering what had taken him from bed so early. She stretched her arms over her head and yanked them back again, retreating to the cozy warmth of the coverlet. The chill dawn had taken hold of the thick stone tower walls and wouldn't easily let go. Glancing to the fireplace, she realized the fire had died long ago.

He'd been gone for some time.

A slow, satisfied smile spread across her face as she recalled what had happened last night. Jamie was usually so immovable; she'd been terrified that she wouldn't be able to convince him not to take Niall to Dunoon. But love had won out after all.

The sounds of horses and raised voices returned her attention to what had disturbed her slumber. Something was going on in the *barmkin* below.

She lay back and contemplated the wood ceiling for a moment, but curiosity eventually overrode comfort. Taking a deep breath, she tossed off the warm bedcoverings, slung her bare feet over the side of the bed, and braced for the shock.

It didn't help.

She jumped, letting out a little yelp as she reached for her sark and then scurried to her slippers across wood planks that were about as warm and inviting as an icy loch.

Chilled to the bone, she dressed as quickly as she could manage with stiff, frozen fingers. When she'd finished, she grabbed a plaid from the bed, wrapped it over her shoulders, and hurried to the window. She pulled open the shutters, rubbed the fog from a pane of glass with the side of her fist, and peered down into the *barmkin* below.

The first rays of dawn were just starting to break over the horizon, and a cold, misty rain cloaked the morning sky.

For a moment, she felt entrenched in that fog as she took in the scene below. Men dressed for battle gathered around the courtyard, readying to ride out. At the head of the procession was her husband. He sat upon his great black steed, his chest plate shimmering over his yellow war coat. The jewel-encrusted hilt of the claymore slung over his back flashed like a beacon in the low light.

Her pulse leapt as comprehension began to dawn. A minute later, her fears were confirmed when Niall and the rest of her father's guardsmen were led out from the tower.

She didn't want to believe it. For a moment, she stood there in cold disbelief. Jamie had betrayed her. He was going through with it. But after what they'd shared . . . He'd promised . . . hadn't he?

Not wasting another second, she raced from the bedchamber, down the stairs, and across the great hall, exiting the tower keep just as the men had started to ride through the gate two abreast in a long line.

"Wait!" she cried out.

Jamie halted at the sound of her voice but ordered his men forward. Droplets of rain needled her face like tiny darts as she sprinted toward him. She reached the gate just as Niall was about to pass through. Heedless of the others watching, she grabbed her brother's leg, forcing the man leading him to stop for fear of crushing her.

"Niall . . ." She gazed up at her brother, tears streaming down her cheeks. The tightness in her throat made it difficult to speak. "I'm so sorry. You have to believe me, I never meant for this to happen."

"Let go of him, Caitrina," Jamie ordered, his voice devoid of emotion.

"It will be all right, Caiti," Niall said, carefully untangling her from his leg and stirrup. He took her hand and gave it a squeeze but was forced to release it as he was led away. "Take care of Brian."

Tears streamed down her cheeks as she turned on her husband, who'd pulled his mount up beside her. His jaw was set in a hard line, his expression unyielding and implacable. Every inch the Campbell Enforcer.

"How can you do this?" she cried. "I thought we had an understanding." Emotion balled hot and prickly in her throat. "We made love." She looked into his eyes but saw only the steely curtain of duty. "You said you loved me."

He held her gaze. "I thought we had an understanding as well. It seems we both were in error. You confused my love for you with bending me to your will, and I confused your method of persuasion with true emotion."

It took her a moment to realize what he meant. Her eyes widened with shock. "You're wrong." She hadn't planned it like that. She hadn't seduced him to try to persuade him. "I wouldn't do that." But even as she vehemently denied the accusation, she wondered if perhaps there was an element of truth to it. She'd been desperate, searching for any straw to hold on to. Had she unconsciously relied upon his desire for her? *No*.

"Wouldn't you?" He stared at her a moment longer. "It doesn't matter. As you see, it didn't work."

She looked out past the gate at the trail of men and horses, a cloud of mud and leaves splattering behind them as they galloped toward the sea. Her gaze flickered back to Jamie, seeing the resolve and determination etched firmly on his face. Immovable.

Her worst fears had come true. Her carefully rebuilt happiness was crashing down around her. And now she might lose her brother all over again.

She'd trusted him, and he'd failed her.

Rage born of helplessness took hold. She couldn't think. All she wanted to do was stop it from happening. "I'll never forgive you for this," she vowed, her voice reverberating with emotion. There was only one thing left—one more gauntlet to throw down between them. "If you leave now, if you take my brother from here, I never want to see you again."

Almost before the words were out, she wanted them back.

The raw emotion in his eyes burned a hole in her heart as her reckless ultimatum hung in the air between them. She wanted to think he wouldn't be able to do it.

But in her heart she knew he would. He'd warned her not to try to come between him and his duty again, but she'd done just that.

His eyes locked on hers, not letting go, but she didn't take it back. Finally, he bowed his head. "As you wish." And without another word, he pulled his destrier around and galloped out the gate. Never once looking back.

Maybe that hurt the most. That after what they'd shared, he could just cut her off without a moment's hesitation or remorse when her world had just been destroyed.

He wouldn't be coming back. To save her brothers, she'd gambled with her heart and lost.

There was nothing she could do. It was too late. Niall was gone. As was the only man she would ever love.

Desolation cut through her like a dull knife, the anguish unbearable. Her heart felt as though it were being ripped in two. She wanted to pour out her grief in a torrent of cries, but she was beyond the relief of tears. Dry-eyed, she watched him ride away, watched as his proud, strong back faded into the distance.

Gone.

A dry sob caught in her throat. Not again. She could not bear it. Never had she thought to feel this kind of pain again. Never had she thought to feel so alone.

Love had failed her.

She sank to her knees in the mud and dirt and bowed her head. Then an uncomfortable twinge penetrated her grief. Or had she failed love?

Jamie forced his gaze straight ahead as he rode away from Rothesay, knowing it would be some time before he returned.

It had taken every ounce of his strength to ride away, and he didn't know when he dared attempt to see his wife again. Being near her would be impossible; the pull was too strong. It would be easier to sever all connection.

As if cutting out his heart were easy. There was a hollow emptiness in his chest that ached more than any wound he'd ever suffered in battle.

He squared his jaw, hardening himself against the raw surge of pain and loss.

It seemed ironic, indeed, that a man who was virtually invincible on the battlefield had been felled by something as ordinary as emotion. He should have avoided the entanglement altogether, just as he'd done with his friendships. A man in his position was better off alone. He'd taken a chance with Caitrina, hoping it would be different, but it had been a mistake.

Disappointment ate like acid in his stomach. He'd wanted so much to believe that they could come to an understanding, but he'd mistaken sex for trust and love. It might not have been done consciously as he'd first thought—the shock on her face had seemed real enough—but clearly she'd not made love to him as a show of trust, as he'd assumed.

Apparently, she'd made some assumptions as well. It had taken her ultimatum for him to finally realize that no matter how hard he tried, he would never convince her to believe in him fully. He'd hoped that once she grew to know him . . .

No. Her family and his being a Campbell would always be between them. She would never see past the name and reputation to the man. He was better off alone. He should have stayed that way.

Love, it seemed, was not enough.

For a man who didn't allow for defeat, failure was difficult to stomach—especially with something he'd fought so hard for.

"My sister can be quite stubborn."

Jamie turned to Niall Lamont, who sat in the *birlinn* beside him, watching him, and from his contemplative expression, he'd probably seen more than Jamie wanted him to. He plunged the oar into the water and pulled. "Aye."

As Niall's hands were tied and he was unable to row, he'd made himself comfortable, kicking out his feet and leaning back against the edge of the wooden seat behind him. The relaxed pose was hardly that of a prisoner. "She's scared. I'm sure she didn't mean everything she said."

"I'm sure she meant every word." He leveled his gaze on the other man. "She thinks I've betrayed her by taking you to Dunoon to account for your crimes."

Niall lifted a brow. "Can you blame her? Your cousin is

not exactly known for his compassion to outlaws. And neither are you, for that matter."

Jamie couldn't deny it. But the very fact that he would ask his cousin to intercede on Niall's behalf should tell her how much she meant to him. He wanted to think she knew him better. That even if he wasn't known for his compassion, he was capable of it. Argyll would be facing pressure from Colin, but Jamie was confident that in the end Niall Lamont and his men would be spared the executioner's noose. His cousin wouldn't like it, but he would keep his word. "It's not my cousin I asked her to trust."

"It's not?"

Jamie pondered the rhetorical question for a moment. "You seemed to believe my avowal of leniency."

Niall shrugged. "What choice did I have? Were it my brother's or sister's life at stake, I can assure you I wouldn't feel the same way."

Reluctantly, Jamie admitted that maybe he had a point. Caitrina didn't know Argyll as he did—and what she did know he could understand might not instill confidence in his temperance.

But something about what Niall said had bothered him. Jamie studied the other man's face. His voice held the edge of a man who didn't care whether he lived or died. Of a man who'd lost faith with the world. Jamie remembered what Niall had told him about the ravaging of his lass.

He couldn't imagine what Niall Lamont must be feeling. If someone had harmed Caitrina like that . . . His entire body flooded with white hot fury.

He glanced at Niall's stoic face, knowing the rage that simmered under the surface. Rage that could drive a man to lawlessness. For the first time, Jamie realized what could make a man seek his own justice—outside the law. And it was Jamie's own brother who'd driven him to it. Twice.

He hated to think that Colin could be capable of such brutality against a woman, but he knew Colin wouldn't think of it as such. He'd think of it as the spoils of war, of a way to shame his enemy. Many men would agree with him.

Jamie clenched his mouth in disgust. *He didn't.* "I can understand your anger, but why the MacGregors? Why ally with them? Surely you know they are doomed. The king will not forgive them for the massacre at Glenfruin."

"The woman I mentioned . . ."

Jamie nodded solemnly for him to continue.

"Her name is Annie MacGregor."

Jamie swore.

"I'm aware that some MacGregors have been at times"—Niall cleared his throat—"less than lawful. But what choice have they had, driven from their land with nowhere to go? I, too, have felt the brunt of a Campbell sword."

Jamie's jaw hardened. The issue of land had been at the heart of the off-and-on feud between the Campbells and the MacGregors for hundreds of years—since King Robert the Bruce had granted the barony of Lochawe, including much of the MacGregor lands, to the Campbells. "The MacGregors are still clinging to a claim of land that goes back almost three hundred years. At some point they have to accept that they are not going to get it back. I sympathize with their plight, but feuding, reiving, and pillaging are not the answer."

"What choice have they had? You can't poke a snake and expect it not to bite."

Niall had a point, not that it would do the MacGregors much good. Even the law would not help them now. "It will not change their fate. They will still pay for what happened at Glenfruin."

"Just as my men and I will pay for attacking your brother."

"I will see that you have justice." Given Colin's part in the lass's suffering, maybe it was fitting that justice come from Jamie.

Justice. What was it in this instance? He'd always equated justice with the law, but this time the answer was not so clear-cut. Niall Lamont had not had an easy time of it—the choices he'd made under the circumstances seemed understandable. Caitrina's accusation came back to him. Had he unknowingly been driven by Duncan's betrayal and become rigid in his view of right and wrong because of it?

He'd never questioned Duncan's guilt, but he wondered now whether he should have. Had he judged his eldest brother too harshly? It was a sobering thought. One with implications that resonated far deeper than Jamie wanted to contemplate.

Niall was watching him. "You know, I almost believe you." Jamie rowed for a while longer before Niall broke the silence. "Give her time."

Jamie's gaze was shrewd and appraising, wondering at Niall's motives. "Why do you care? I would think you would be happy to have your sister rid of me."

"You're right. You are about the last man I'd wish to see my sister married to. But I'm not blind. I see how she feels about you, and I want her to be happy."

Jamie nodded. *So do I.* He just didn't know if he was the one to make her so. Because no matter what her brother said, it was Caitrina who needed to believe in him.

Chapter 24

❖ ❖ ❖

It took Caitrina less than an hour to make up her mind.
She would not sit back and allow her brother to be taken
from her—not again. Not while it was in her power to do
something. If Jamie wouldn't listen to her, there was only
one person left to whom she could appeal.

She gritted her teeth and fought back the wave of dis-
taste.

"Are you sure about this, Caiti?" Mor met her gaze in
the looking glass, putting the finishing touches on her hair.

Caitrina caught sight of her image in the mirror and
started, shocked at the transformation wrought by a new
gown and a few hairpins. For a moment, it was like looking into the past. But the girl who met her gaze in the gilded
mirror was nothing like the one that day last spring who'd
donned a beautiful gown and met a handsome knight in a
magical kingdom. That kingdom was gone forever—if it
had ever really existed. If you looked deeper, you could see
the changes. The girl was now a woman who knew what it
was like to lose everything and find the strength to live—
and love—again.

She would give anything to have her father and brother
back, but she didn't want to be the naïve, cosseted girl she
was before. Jamie had never withheld the truth from her
but treated her as an equal. No longer blind to what was
going on around her, she found that life was more complicated, but also richer and more meaningful. It was a
strange realization.

Her hand slid over the plush silvery blue velvet of her bodice, and her mouth lifted in a small smile. One thing hadn't changed: She still could appreciate a beautiful gown. Earlier, she'd sent Mor to the village with the bag of coin given to her by Jamie to purchase a new dress, if one could be found. Much to her surprise, Mor had returned with this fine court gown with its ivory satin underskirt and elaborately embroidered velvet bodice—only to discover that Jamie had sent for it some time ago. Her heart squeezed, realizing he must have meant to surprise her.

Her hair had been coiled into an elaborate arrangement and secured with a wreath of delicate seed pearls that Jamie had given her on their wedding day, along with a matching set of necklace and earrings. It was the first time she'd worn them. Ironic, perhaps, given the state of her marriage.

But she could not think of that now. The pain of losing him was too paralyzing; she had to concentrate on what she needed to do.

To that end, she stood up from the table and answered Mor. "Yes, very sure." She was determined to do whatever it took to keep her home and family safe. She would beg or bargain with the devil himself if it meant keeping her brother alive. In this case, the devil was the Earl of Argyll.

Fortunately, Jamie had not left orders confining her to the castle, but the captain of his guardsmen had insisted on accompanying her himself with at least a dozen men. "I'll leave as soon as my escort is ready and I've had a chance to check on Brian."

"The laddie is doing much better," Mor said.

It was a relief to hear so, but Caitrina needed to see for herself. A few minutes later, she opened the door to his chamber and was pleased to see her brother sitting upright in bed. He'd been cleaned up and a fresh bandage—thankfully absent of bloodstains—placed around his head. A healthy flush had returned to his cheeks.

"I've had enough broth," he said, waving the bowl away. "I'm starving. Can't you find just one wee piece of beef?" he pleaded, a plaintive expression on his face, trying to cajole the pretty maid at his bedside.

God, he looks like Malcolm. But if that roguish expression was any indication, he'd been around Niall too long. Her heart tugged, realizing how much Brian had aged in the months they'd been apart. He was three and ten now, but the passage of another birthday wasn't the cause. Like her, he'd seen death and the destruction of their clan, not to mention living as an outlaw for months.

He caught sight of her in the doorway, and a wide smile spread across his boyish face. "Caiti!" He turned his efforts to her. "I'm so glad you're here. Won't you tell Mairi that I need beef if I'm to get back my strength?"

" 'Twas Mor's orders, my lady. She said the laddie was too weak to have anything other than broth."

"Weak!" Brian protested indignantly. "Bah. I will be if I have nothing but boiled marrow and water."

Caitrina bit back her smile at the look of outrage on his face. A young warrior did not appreciate being called weak no matter what the reference. She sat on the edge of his bed and gestured for the serving girl to leave. "I'll talk to Mor and see what I can do about getting you something a bit more substantial, *if* you promise to stay in bed and rest until I get back."

All at once, Brian's expression changed to one of concern. "Back? Where are you going? And where's Niall? Why hasn't he come to see me? No one will tell me anything."

Caitrina debated whether to tell him the truth. Though it might be difficult for him to hear, she knew from experience that a pat on the head and being kept in the dark would not protect him. And with what he'd been through the past few months, he'd earned the right to know. "Niall has been taken to Dunoon. I'm going after him."

He paled at her disclosure but did not otherwise react. Her heart tugged again at the proof of how much the past few months had changed him. Her young brother was old beyond his years. But his controlled reaction also told her that she'd been right to tell him. She wanted to smooth her hand over his brow and assure him there was nothing to worry about, but Brian was no longer a little boy—and she didn't want to give him false hope.

Instead she added, "I'll be back as soon as I can."

"I don't understand how this happened. Niall was so certain we wouldn't be discovered."

Caitrina bit her lip. "You weren't," she admitted. "It was I who told Jamie where to find you."

His eyes widened. "You told Argyll's Henchman where to find us? But he's a bloody Campbell. Our enemy."

"He's not like that." The instinct to defend him was automatic. She hated the Henchman epithet. Jamie wasn't a cold-blooded killer or a man who killed without thought on the orders of his chief. He was doing what he thought right. "He's one of the most honorable men I know. He's restored our home to our clan and treated them like his own even when our clan did not welcome him."

Brian didn't seem inclined to believe her, not that she expected him to. He had, after all, spent the last few months as an outlaw because of the Campbells. "But why now? Why did you think it necessary to tell him where we were?" He paled. "It wasn't because of me?"

"No, no," she assured him. She explained how Auchinbreck and his men had arrived at Rothesay followed by Jamie. "I couldn't take the chance that his brother would find you first. I thought my husband would protect you."

"But you've changed your mind?"

"No, I—" She stopped, realizing what she'd said. *No.* She hadn't changed her mind. Even after what had passed between them, she still believed that Jamie would try to help her brother and clansmen; it was his cousin's mercurial ruthlessness that she feared. How could she explain? "It's complicated," she hedged.

Brian studied her. "You don't think he holds enough influence over his cousin?"

His shrewd appraisal of the situation took her aback. At that moment, he reminded her so much of their father.

She considered his question. Jamie claimed that Argyll had promised leniency. Though every instinct warred against trusting Argyll, it was clear that Jamie still believed in him—Argyll's deception of Alasdair MacGregor notwithstanding.

If she believed in Jamie, did that mean she must believe in Argyll as well? The very idea was abhorrent, but uncomfortably true. She knew the type of man Jamie was: Was it possible that his loyalty and duty would extend to a despot? Jamie was right: At some point, she had to choose a side. She was either for Jamie and his cousin or she was against them. It wasn't a simple matter of black and white, but a complicated shade of gray. Whom did she believe in more?

She knew the answer in her heart but was too scared to admit it when doing so might mean she'd made a grave error. "Jamie has influence, and he's promised to speak on behalf of Niall and the others. But I'm not sure it will be enough. Too much is at stake for uncertainty. I never would have told him where you were if I'd known what he intended."

"I should have guessed," Brian said disgustedly. "He tricked you into telling him, then?"

"No, of course not," she defended automatically. "He would never do that. He just assumed I would realize what he had to do."

"You tried to convince him otherwise?"

She nodded. "He wouldn't listen." Even when she'd thrown down the ultimate gauntlet. The panic and fear of the moment had made her grasp at anything. "He said it was his duty."

"What did you expect him to do, Caiti? He's Argyll's bloody Henchman. Even a Campbell has to abide his laird."

God, it was clear even to her thirteen-year-old brother. Unease penetrated the veil of betrayal that had blinded her to anything else when she'd discovered what Jamie had meant to do.

She'd asked him to put his duty to her before that to his cousin, and he'd refused. It had seemed so simple, but when he'd put the same choice to her, she'd realized it had been anything but. Love wasn't an either-or proposition, but she'd made it one by issuing threats and ultimatums.

His duty and loyalty to his cousin were the very things that bound him to her; they couldn't be tossed off at will.

As she'd done.

A pit of despair settled low in her belly as understanding dawned. She'd driven him away, left him with no choice when he'd done so much for her.

The more she thought about the past few months, the worse she felt. He was one of the most powerful men in the Highlands, yet he'd married her when she'd had nothing. Without him, her clan would have fallen apart. He'd not only helped her reclaim their land, but had poured his own gold into rebuilding Ascog—the progress of which was incredible. They never could have done it without him. She didn't have his experience or leadership. The Lamonts might not like him, but they relied upon him. And they still needed him if Niall hoped to reclaim his lands.

But it wasn't just her clan. *She* needed him. As a woman needs a man, as a soul needs its mate. He was a part of her. He'd brought love back into her life, making her feel safe and happy when she never thought she'd feel that way again.

Brian's question came back to her in a rush of guilt. What had she expected him to do? "I don't know. I hoped to have some time, but he said that Niall and the others would eventually have to face what they had done and it was better now than later."

She could see Brian's frustration. He liked the idea of Niall and the others in Argyll's clutches no better than she. "We have no choice but to go along with it. As long as Argyll is the law, your husband is right." He gave her a considered look. "I suppose he must truly care for you to put your brother before his own."

Caitrina started. She hadn't thought of it like that, but Brian was right. Auchinbreck would be out for blood, and because of her, Jamie intended to stand in his way.

"And he must have been very certain of his influence to refuse you."

"Aye," she realized. He must have been.

She swallowed hard, a ball of emotion lodged in her throat, feeling the twinge of shame that came with a bit of perspective. Perspective that had been sadly lacking only a few hours ago. Had she been wrong not to give him her trust? She feared she knew the answer, and it might be too late.

"What do you think you can do by going after them?" Brian asked.

She leveled her gaze on her brother. "I don't know. But I have to do something." Both for Niall and for herself.

Caitrina felt as if she were racing against a burgeoning sense of doom. Every second of the journey seemed to toll against her as the certainty that she'd made a mistake grew.

She'd failed him. She'd gone to him for help, put him in an impossible situation between two conflicting duties, demanded something of him that he could not give, and then refused to trust him. Once she'd told Niall that she trusted

Jamie with their lives, but when it came down to it, she hadn't. She'd had a right to her anger, but she'd tried to use their love to bargain with his duty, and she deeply regretted her harsh words.

She couldn't imagine life without him. She couldn't forget that he was a Campbell, but neither could she forget what he'd done for her and her clan. Campbells and Lamonts might never like each other, but her love for him was strong enough to overcome the clan hatred. Was his?

Unable to shake the fear that he might have taken her at her word and would not want to see her again, she pressed forward in the saddle, urging her mount a little faster.

"How much longer?" she asked the dour captain.

Despite the growing darkness, she could see William Campbell's frown. It was clear he disapproved of her last-minute journey across Cowal but hadn't wanted to risk the displeasure of his laird's lady. They'd set out shortly after midday and had made their way across the Firth of Clyde to Toward, where they'd exchanged the *birlinn* for horses and ridden about eight miles up the Cowal coast to Dunoon.

"Only another furlong or so. We should be there before nightfall."

Her nerves, already frayed, set on edge. It wasn't only Jamie's reaction twisting her stomach in knots. She was nervous about coming face-to-face with Argyll as well.

She might not like him, but there was no disputing the fact that Archibald Campbell was the most powerful man in the Highlands. It was easy to hate him, but what if the truth was more complicated? Would he confirm her fears or lessen them?

She would soon find out.

Her pulse spiked when the path turned north and the shadow of an enormous keep came into view. The monolithic stone fortress poised on the hilly promontory overlooking the Firth sent a shiver of trepidation running down her spine. Trepidation that only increased as they drew near. Beyond the *barmkin* wall, the thick stone walls of the keep, crudely built hundreds of years ago, dominated the skyline and up close seemed all the more formidable.

Like its keeper.

The sight of the castle had tested her resolve. She felt a flicker of uncertainty. What was she going to do, throw herself on his mercy? That assumed he had some.

It didn't matter. She would do whatever it took.

With a determined set to her shoulders, she dismounted and turned to the nearest guard before she could reconsider.

"Take me to the earl."

Another man, who appeared to be in charge, was marching toward them and had heard her request. He greeted her, identified himself as the porter, and then said, "We were not told of your arrival, my lady. I will have a chamber readied for you and then will let the earl and your husband know that you are here."

"Thank you, but I have no need of a chamber. I need to see the earl immediately. What I have to say cannot wait."

The man looked uncomfortable, obviously not used to a lady insisting on seeing his lord and unsure what to do about it. "I'm afraid he's in a meeting with his men and cannot be disturbed."

Her heart raced, fearing the subject of that meeting. "Is my husband with him?"

"Aye."

That was all she needed to hear. She started up the stairs, with the porter following close after her.

"Wait!" he shouted after her. "You can't go in there."

But Caitrina wasn't taking no for an answer. She turned her most dazzling smile on him. "Oh, I'm sure he won't mind."

The poor man was flustered witless. "But . . ."

Caitrina was already crossing the great hall. There were two doors on the opposite side of the entry, and she was guessing that one of them—she opened the first door and smiled—was the laird's solar.

About a dozen pairs of eyes stared at her as if she were an apparition. The nervousness she had felt on the ride to Dunoon was nothing to what hit her now, but she was determined not to let it show. Plastering a confident smile on her face, she floated into the room as regally as a queen—or, she thought with a wave of bittersweet memory, a princess.

"What is the meaning of this?" A sharp-featured man seated at the center of the table addressed the porter, who'd come rushing in behind her. Caitrina quickly scanned the room, disappointed not to see Jamie. Despite their current state, his presence would have provided some much needed support at the moment, but it appeared she would face the devil alone.

The Earl of Argyll wasn't quite what she'd expected. Though dressed like a king—his clothing and jewels as fine as she'd ever seen, befitting his role as trusted courtier to King James—there was an unmistakable glint in his eyes, a toughness to his appearance that bespoke his Highland origins. His dark features were sharp and angular, his mouth thin, and his expression every bit as grim as his sobriquet, Gillesbuig Grumach, attested. But he looked older than his thirty odd years, which probably wasn't surprising given the troubles of his youth. His father had died when he was only a boy, and he'd faced early attacks—even attempted murder—by those supposed to take care of him.

"I'm sorry, my lord," the porter apologized profusely. "The lady insisted."

The earl's gaze narrowed as he looked her over with unflattering scrutiny. "And who is this *lady*?"

Caitrina took a deep breath and stepped forward. "Caitrina Campbell, my lord. Wife to your cousin."

If he was surprised by her announcement, he did not show it. "What do you want?"

"A moment of your time, if you please, my lord." When it appeared he was going to deny her, she added through clenched teeth, "I apologize for the abrupt manner of my arrival, but it's a matter of the utmost importance."

She waited, heart pounding, sure that he was going to deny her. Instead, she was surprised when he waved away his men.

She felt a small burst of accomplishment that deflated quickly when he motioned her forward. She stood before the massive table, trying not to twist her hands and shift her feet, feeling like an errant child facing punishment. Suddenly shamed by her failing courage, she straightened her spine and lifted her chin to meet his gaze.

Argyll peered down his long nose, taking in every inch of her appearance, including the mud-spattered skirts and slippers. "It seems that bursting in on my solar is becoming a common occurrence in your family—although at least you are dressed appropriately."

She had no idea what he was talking about. "My lord?"

He waved his hand. "Never mind. What is it that has brought you here with such urgency?"

"My brother and his men. I know they are here. I've come to plead on their behalf. If you hear them out, I'm sure you'll see why they did what they did. But I would see them first, if you would take me to them."

Argyll took his time in responding, his dark eyes probing with an uncomfortable intensity. "You are aware of what your brother and his men are accused, and that your husband has brought them here for my judgment?"

Her jaw clenched, but she did not turn away. "I am. Jamie swore that you would show them leniency."

Argyll stroked his small pointed beard. "He told you all this and yet you are still here?"

She nodded, again feeling like a recalcitrant child—and a disloyal one at that.

Argyll drummed his fingertips on the tabletop, and the annoying click only increased her agitation. "Your brother's men are in the tower under guard, awaiting my punishment." His eyes met hers with cold calculation. "But I'm afraid you are too late. Your brother is already gone."

Chapter 25

❖ ❖ ❖

Gone. Caitrina felt as if she'd slammed into a stone wall, the breath knocked right out of her. She was too late. Niall was already dead.

For a moment, the bleakness and anguish of unbearable loss blinded her; it seemed as if her worst fears had come true . . . but only for a moment.

Something far deeper prevailed and pushed aside the flash of despair. *Jamie wouldn't have let that happen.* She knew it with a certainty that pervaded every fiber of her being.

She believed in him. Completely. She knew that the Highlands were a better place with him. Loyalty to his cousin notwithstanding, Jamie would do what was right.

And it had taken Argyll's trick to prove it. Was that what he'd intended? Her eyes narrowed on the most powerful—and despised—man in the Highlands. Trusting Jamie meant that she was forced to concede that Argyll was not the monster she believed. Jamie would not be loyal to such a man. Argyll must have some redeeming qualities—not that they were necessarily apparent at the moment.

Argyll was testing her. Did he not think her worthy of his prized cousin? Perhaps a few minutes ago he'd been right, but she would prove him wrong. "How unfortunate that I missed him," she said breezily, as if her brother had been making a social call. "Do you expect him back soon?"

Argyll arched a wiry brow. She thought she detected a

hint of approval in his gaze. "Jamie was to bring him here for my judgment; don't you care to hear it?"

Caitrina gave him an icy sweet smile. "I'm sure Jamie will tell me all about it."

"Tell you all about what?"

Caitrina's heart skipped a beat, hearing her husband's deep brogue behind her. She turned and took a step toward him, wanting to throw herself into his powerful arms and beg forgiveness for doubting him; but he stopped her cold.

"What the devil are you doing here, Caitrina?"

Her heart faltered, then crashed to her feet. Hope that he would be happy to see her was extinguished by the harsh greeting and the glacial expression on his face. He seemed to look right through her, as if she weren't even there. As if he wanted nothing to do with her ever again.

Jamie couldn't believe it when Will found him in the stables as he was preparing to leave and told him that Caitrina was here.

For a moment, he'd hoped that she had come after him to apologize—until Will told him she had insisted on seeing his cousin. Argyll, not him.

Knowing how much she despised his cousin—holding him partially to blame for what had happened at Ascog—Jamie realized the courage it had taken for her to confront him. He had to admire her determination to save her brother, even as her lack of faith in him was made more glaring.

Seeing her so soon was like salt on an open wound. She was so beautiful it almost hurt to look at her. But there was something different. . . . Then it hit him. The gown, the jewels, the hair. For the first time since the attack on Ascog, she had donned her finery. She looked like a princess again. Not a fairy princess, but a real one. A strong, confident woman who'd struggled and survived. Was it significant?

"It appears your new wife has come for a visit to see her

brother," Argyll said, taking up the slack in the conversation.

"I see," Jamie said tightly, his instincts confirmed. Disappointment curdled in his stomach. He wanted to get the hell out of here and ride as far from her as possible.

"I told her she was too late," Argyll said, giving him a meaningful glance. "That Niall was already gone."

Jamie shot his cousin a look. Argyll obviously had wanted Caitrina to think Niall dead, but her face bore no signs of grief. He turned back to his cousin, giving no hint of his impatience. He knew his cousin well enough to know he would not be rushed. What game did he play?

"Naturally, I expected her to assume him dead."

Jamie's gaze flickered to Caitrina, but she betrayed no reaction to Argyll's words. "Naturally," Jamie said wryly, his cousin's purpose having become suddenly clear to him. The betrayals of Argyll's youth had left its mark on his cousin—loyalty was of utmost importance to him. Obviously, Caitrina's sudden appearance had made him question hers. Jamie appreciated his cousin's sentiment, but he could fight his own damn battles.

Argyll gave him a look that said he knew exactly what Jamie was thinking and thought he was doing a piss poor job of it.

Caitrina finally spoke. "But I didn't believe him."

Jamie felt a dim ray of hope and looked to his cousin for confirmation.

"She seems to have a rather high opinion of you." Argyll's expression changed to one of barely concealed annoyance. "And assumes I share that opinion."

"I see," Jamie repeated. The sudden show of faith was something, he supposed, but not enough—and too late. He hardened himself against the soft pleading in her eyes and looked away.

"I was about to explain my recent disappointment when you came in." Argyll turned his attention back to Caitrina.

"It seems my normally diligent captain made a careless mistake on his way to Dunoon."

"He did?" Caitrina asked warily.

"Yes," his cousin said. "It seems your brother slipped away when they stopped to water the horses. Jamie and his men gave chase, but he disappeared." Argyll gave Jamie a sharp look. It was a look that said he knew exactly what Jamie had done but would never voice his suspicions—not when Jamie's actions in effect had made it easier on him. Argyll would not be held accountable. There was only one person Colin would blame.

"Niall escaped?" She turned to Jamie, incredulity written on her face. He could see the questions form, but wisely she kept them to herself—for now, at least. "And the others?"

"Free to return to Rothesay," Jamie said. "I was seeing to their release when you arrived."

Caitrina looked stunned. "I don't know what to say." Her eyes fell on Argyll. "Thank you."

"Thank him," Argyll said with a wave of his hand toward Jamie. " 'Twas he who paid the gold to see their crimes atoned."

"Jamie, I . . ."

Before she could say anything more, Jamie took her arm and steered her toward the door. "If you'll excuse us, I'll see my wife settled in her chamber."

"If you need anything else," Argyll said dryly, "just let me know."

Jamie threw him a quelling glance, but the amusement in Argyll's eyes only annoyed him further. Oh yes, his grim cousin was a regular court jester at times. Argyll might be satisfied by the display of loyalty, but Jamie wasn't.

The chamberlain had readied the third-floor chamber in the south tower—the one Lizzie used when she stayed at Dunoon. Fresh water had been brought up, and the few items that Caitrina had brought with her were laid out on the bed for night.

He quickly looked away from the bed and stood stiffly near the fireplace as the chamberlain closed the door behind him.

As soon as the man had gone, Caitrina moved to stand before him, her soft feminine scent clouding his senses. Would it always be like this—this clawing need for her? The inability to think when she was near? The feeling that if he didn't take her in his arms and kiss her, he would surely die?

"Jamie, I'm so sorr—"

"My men will see to your return to Rothesay in the morning," he clipped, cutting off her apology.

"Are you not coming with me?"

He heard the quiver in her voice but kept his eyes fixed on the wall behind her head, refusing to meet her gaze. The steel vise enclosing his chest tightened. "I believe you made your wishes quite clear. I will return to Castleswene. You need not fear that I will interfere with anything you wish to do." His meaning was obvious: They would lead separate lives. His gut twisted. The thought of her with another man . . .

"But . . ."

"But what, Caitrina?" he said harshly, finally looking at her. "Is this not what you wanted?"

The stricken look on her face hit him square in the chest. He took a deep, ragged breath and forced himself to look away. *I need to get the hell out of here.* It hurt too damn much. Hurt to know how much he loved her, but that it wasn't enough. She was grateful now, but he didn't want her gratitude. He wanted her love and trust—her heart and soul. He wanted her to believe in him. He'd never cared what anyone thought . . . only her. He turned to leave.

"Please, don't go." His heart jerked when she pressed

her tiny hand on the sleeve of his doublet. "It's not what I want."

"Maybe not now," he said roughly. "But what about the next time we disagree or my duty requires something of which you do not approve? What then, Caitrina?" He couldn't bite back his anger. Her lack of faith and quick dismissal of his love were not easily forgiven, but it was her response that had truly shaken him. "Will you send me away again?"

"God, I'm sorry, Jamie. I should never have given you an ultimatum like that. I was wrong to try to bargain with your feelings for me. I know that. But I was so scared at the thought of losing my brother . . . I didn't know what else to do. Can you not understand that?"

Aye, he supposed he could. Hell, he admired her passion, her openness, the unconditional loyalty and love she felt for her family. He just wanted it for himself. Nor did it lessen the sting of the moment when she'd cast him and his love aside.

He heard a sound and looked down. Damn. Not the tears. He could take just about anything but the tears. His hand itched to wipe them away, his arms to give her comfort, but he forced them to his side.

"What if it were your sister?" she said softly. "Would you have been so understanding if the situations had been reversed?"

His gaze shot to hers. His mouth clenched; he might be willing to concede her point, but not all of it. "No, I wouldn't have," he admitted. "But I wouldn't have asked you to choose."

"Didn't you? It felt like you were asking me to choose between my brother and you. Maybe if you'd told me of your plans, but I had to find out from the servants what you intended."

He grimaced. She was right. He was used to making decisions on his own. "I'm sorry for that. Perhaps I should have explained more. But why are you always ready to believe the worst of me?"

"Years of practice. I realized it would be difficult marrying a Campbell, but when I realized I loved you, I thought that would be enough. It isn't. Old tensions are not just going to die because I want them to, it will take work."

Her insight surprised him. He couldn't expect her to cast aside her prejudices just because she loved him. "What are you saying?"

He could see her hands stiffen at her side. "I want to know everything about you, Jamie. And if that means getting to know your cousin, I'm willing to try."

Jamie stilled, completely shocked. "You'd do that for me?"

She nodded. "I do have faith in you. It wasn't until your cousin tried to trick me that I knew how much. But it was always there."

He felt a crack, hearing the vulnerability in her voice and wanting desperately to believe her.

"I made a mistake," she continued. "And I'm sure I'll make more. But you hold those around you to a very high standard." He tensed, knowing she was referring to his brother. "I need to know that you'll be able to forgive me."

He felt the stirrings of a smile. "Are you saying that I can be rigid and uncompromising?"

Her mouth twitched. "Maybe a little." They shared a moment of understanding before her expression shifted again to one of earnestness. "I love you, Jamie. You brought happiness and love back in my life when I never thought to feel that way again. I was wrong to think I could ever make you choose between your loyalty and duty to your clan and to me when they are the same. I'll never do so again. Knowing that I have your love is enough." Her voice lowered to a shaky whisper. "If I still have it."

She lifted her face to his. "Do I still have it, Jamie? Please, tell me it's not too late for us."

Her mouth trembled, and his resistance shattered. His thumb wiped the dampness from her cheeks as he looked deep into her eyes. He'd hardened himself to a future without her, but he was relieved not to have to face it. "Aye. You have it, lass. You've always had it."

A smile broke through the tears. "Then that is all that matters. You have my love and loyalty forever. I vow to never doubt you again."

Jamie arched a brow. "Never?"

She bit her lip. "Well, hardly ever. And not about anything important."

He laughed and pulled her into his arms. It was good enough.

Caitrina lay in bed, luxuriating in the warmth and security of her husband's embrace. She nestled her naked backside against him, wiggling closer when he lightly squeezed the breast that he held cupped in his hand.

"You're an insatiable wench," he murmured against her ear, and the warmth of his breath at her ear sent shivers of desire down her spine that she would have thought impossible after their vigorous lovemaking of just moments ago. "I need my rest."

The hardening against her buttocks belied his words. She circled her hips against him. "Liar." He groaned, sliding his hands down her belly to between her legs, cupping her in his deft hand. "I've been thinking," she said, pressing her hips against his hand.

"So I gather."

"Not about that, you wretch." She tapped him playfully on the arm but admitted to a certain curiosity about their current position.

His mouth trailed hot kisses down her neck and nape that made her body soften all over again with the tingly rush of pleasure. He kissed her harder as he pinched her nipple lightly between his fingers. "About what?"

Her eyes opened. "You're trying to distract me."

"Hmm." He kissed her shoulder again. "Is it working?"

God, yes. She could feel the round head nudging between her legs from behind as his finger dipped inside her. Her head fell back against his shoulder as his deft stroking brought her to the very brink of yet another torrential storm of pleasure.

Heat poured through her veins, heavy and slow, as he brought her hips back so that her back arched gently to position himself at her opening. She teased him mercilessly, rubbing him with the dampness of her own body but not taking him in. The sensation was incredible, his erection so big and thick between her thighs. She could tell from the harshness of his breathing that her teasing was driving him wild.

Finally he grabbed her hips and gently pushed inside her, stretching her, filling her. She moaned at the sensation. *God, what wickedness.* His hands were on her breasts and between her legs, caressing her as he drew in and out with long, slow strokes—letting her feel every inch of him. The pleasure that gripped her was indescribable.

He pressed her back tightly against his body and thrust up high inside her, holding still. She gasped at the incredible sensation as her body tingled around him, as the tremble of release built. Just when she thought she couldn't stand it any longer, he slid a little deeper, holding her tight against him until she came apart in a slow, intense shattering that seemed to go on forever. He thrust high inside her again, bringing her hips against him hard in rapid succession as he cried out his own release.

Well after the last shudder had faded, she remembered what she'd been about to say before he'd so effectively distracted her. "You let him escape, didn't you?"

He went still behind her for a second, but it was confirmation enough. "Why do you say that?"

"You would never allow a prisoner to slip away."

"Your confidence in my skills is flattering, but I assure you I'm not infallible."

She snorted. "Tell me the truth."

He shrugged.

"But why? Did you have second thoughts about what your cousin would do?"

"No. Argyll wouldn't have liked it, but he would have kept his promise. I just made it easier on him by giving your brother a choice."

Caitrina couldn't believe it. "You mean Niall chose to be an outlaw rather than return to Ascog? But why would he do that?"

"I think he had other things he needed to do," Jamie said gently.

Caitrina swallowed. Because of what had happened, she realized. The fight had become personal, and Niall would never rest until someone had paid for what had been done to the woman he loved. Her heart broke for him, even as it did for herself.

"He loves you, Caitrina. I know it wasn't an easy decision."

She smiled, hearing the concern in her husband's voice. "I know, but thank you for telling me." As much as she wished Niall had chosen to return to Ascog, as much as she wanted to hold on to him and protect him, he had to make his own decision. But she also knew what it meant: Niall was an outlaw, lost to her and their clan probably forever. "He will never be able to take his rightful place as chief."

"Aye. Brian will be the next chief—when he is ready. I will hold Ascog for him until then."

She didn't know what to say. "You would do that?" Brian had the makings of a good chief, and under Jamie's tutelage and guidance, she knew he would grow to be a great one.

He nodded. "It's rightfully his."

"And Argyll?"

He grinned. "My cousin doesn't like to lose land, but in this case he agreed."

But there was one thing that she still didn't understand. "Why did you do it, Jamie? Why did you decide to let Niall go?"

He leaned up on his arm so he could look into her eyes. "Justice."

"And justice would not be served here at Dunoon?"

"Not in this case. The law will not help your brother."

She lifted an eyebrow, surprised to hear such blasphemy from his lips. "Is not the law the same as justice?"

"I thought it was."

"But now you don't?"

He grinned and dropped a soft kiss on her mouth, lingering for a moment before lifting his head. "I think there may be some room for interpretation. A wee lass once accused me of being driven by the past." *By Duncan.* "It turns out there might have been an element of truth to her assessment."

"Oh, really?"

His mouth quirked. "Perhaps a bit."

Her heart soared, realizing what Jamie had done for her. He'd compromised his duty to help Niall. She knew how he felt about outlaws after his brother's dishonor—yet he'd helped her brother even though he knew Niall was fighting with the MacGregors.

"What about the MacGregors?"

He shook his head. "You're as relentless as your brother. No amount of sympathy for their plight will atone for their crimes, but . . ." He paused. "I will do what I can to ensure that they—as any man—are treated fairly."

A wide smile spread across her face. How could she have ever doubted him? Argyll was fortunate to have a man like Jamie at his side. They both were. And Jamie, she suspected, was an important tempering force to his cousin. If Argyll crossed the line, Jamie would be there to do something about it. Caitrina bit her lip to keep from laughing. And if Jamie forgot, she would be there to remind him.

She'd made her choice and chosen her husband. She could trust him to do what was right for the future of the Highlands. The problems facing them were not easy ones. Jamie walked a precipitous line between the Highland divide, and she loved him for the strong, fair-minded man that he was.

Caitrina laughed, happier at that moment than she'd ever been in her life. All she'd ever wanted was standing right in front of her. Home. Security. Love. She would never forget the past, but she could make a new future. And she was ready to do so.

She looked deep into his eyes. "I love you, Jamie Campbell."

He placed a tender kiss on her soft lips. "And I love you. Although I never thought to hear those two words together."

"What?"

"Love and Campbell."

She grinned. "Get used to it. You'll be hearing them forever."

Author's Note

Jamie Campbell is based on a compilation of historical figures. Most significant: Sir Dugald Campbell of Auchinbreck (the captain of Castleswene and the man said to have convinced the MacGregor to surrender to Argyll, although some sources lay the blame for this on Campbell of Ardkinglas; Auchinbreck's father died fighting for Argyll at the battle of Glenlivet); James Campbell of Lawers (known as one of the most ruthless hunters of MacGregors); and Donald Campbell of Barbreck-Lochow (the natural son of Campbell of Calder, said to be the strong arm of Argyll and the keeper of Mingarry Castle). An interesting side note for readers of my first trilogy: One of Auchinbreck's daughters, Florence, married John Garve Maclean, the son of Lachlan of Coll and Flora MacLeod (from *Highlander Unchained*).

Caitrina and her immediate family are also fictional characters. However, the attack and razing of Ascog Castle was loosely inspired by an actual event—much more horrific than the one I described—that occurred about forty years later, in 1646, during the British Civil Wars. Then, the Lamonts were supporters of the Royalists and the Marquis of Montrose, putting them in direct conflict with the Marquis of Argyll (Archibald the Grim's son).

Following the defeat of the Campbells at the battle of Inverlochy in 1645 by James Graham, first Marquis of Montrose, the Lamonts ravaged Campbell lands. A year later, when Montrose had been defeated, Argyll sought his revenge, attacking the Lamonts at Toward and Ascog with "Fire and Sword." The Lamonts surrendered under an agreement of safe conduct. Instead, over one hundred (perhaps as many as two hundred) clansmen were taken to Dunoon. Thirty-six men were hanged in the kirkyard. There were even reports of men being buried alive. Today there is a memorial at Dunoon to the Lamonts who were killed that day.

Both Ascog and Toward castles were destroyed, leaving only ruins.

The massacre of Toward (and Ascog) would come back to haunt the Marquis of Argyll. The sister of Lamont of Toward, Isobel, apparently managed to smuggle out (in her hair) a signed copy of the "articles of capitulation" promising safe conduct. Sixteen years later, it was one of the pieces of evidence used to convict the Marquis of Argyll, who would eventually be sentenced to death.

Though the immediate cause of the dispute between Campbell and Lamont was the British Civil Wars, clan Lamont's bond with the MacGregors may also have been a factor. The tale of Highland hospitality between the Lamonts and MacGregors occurred sometime in the early seventeenth century. Significantly, the Lamonts are said to have repaid the MacGregors' hospitality by sheltering the MacGregors when they were proscribed—an offense punishable by death.

The story of Archibald the Grim, the seventh Earl of Argyll's "Highland Promise" in the death of the MacGregor, happened much as I described—albeit a few years earlier. Alexander MacGregor of Glenstrae, known as "the Arrow of Glen Lyon," was hanged and quartered in Edinburgh with ten of his men on January 20, 1604. Twenty-five MacGregors were executed in total over the next few weeks. As I alluded to in the book, following his execution there was a resurgence of violence by the MacGregors. One of the clans targeted by the MacGregors was the MacLarens—

mentioned in the story—a neighboring clan who occupied Balquhidder until they were ousted by the MacGregors.

I condensed the persecution and many of the prohibitions against the MacGregors into one period, but the campaign against clan Gregor spanned a number of years. The biggest push occurred in 1604 (the year following the battle of Glenfruin—the massacre of Colquhouns by the MacGregors) and then in a renewed assault in 1611. However, there is evidence that the clan was hardly subdued in the intervening years. A letter in 1609 from Sir Alexander Colquhoun of Luss to the king in London complained of the lack of progress in the campaign against clan Gregor.

The persecution of the ill-fated clan Gregor, the fabled "Children of the Mist," by the Earl of Argyll is well-known. Whether his motivation was simply land or something more personal, we'll never know. Though Argyll has been relegated by history as the "bad guy," it is clear that atrocities were committed on both sides.

The Duke of Argyll is still the hereditary keeper of the royal castle of Dunoon and pays the nominal rent of a red rose—last given to Queen Elizabeth II on her visit to the castle.

The Lomond Hills (so labeled on John Speed's map of 1610) referred to in the story are today better known as the broad area around the Trossachs.

For more on the Earl of Argyll and the MacGregors, please see the "Special Features" section of my website, www.monicamccarty.com.

Looking for more sexy Scottish adventure?

Turn the page to catch a sneak peek at the next
pulse-pounding book in
the Highland series

❖

*H*ighland
*O*utlaw

❖

by

Monica McCarty

Near Castle Campbell, Clackmannanshire, June 1608

Elizabeth Campbell lowered the creased piece of parchment into her lap and looked out the small window, watching the hulking shadow of Castle Campbell fade into the distance with a heavy heart. No matter how many times she read the letter, it did not change the words. Her time, it seemed, was up.

The carriage bounced along the uneven road, moving at a painstakingly slow pace. Recent rain had made the already rough road to the Highlands treacherous, but if they continued like this, it would take a week to reach Dunoon Castle.

Lizzie glanced across the carriage and caught the furtive gaze of her maidservant, Alys, but the other woman quickly shifted her eyes back to her embroidery, feigning a concentration belied by the ill-formed stitches.

Alys was worried about her, though trying not to show it. Hoping to divert her questions, Lizzie said, "I don't know how you can sew with all this bumping—"

But her words were cut off when, as if to make her point, her bottom rose off the seat for a long beat and then came down with a hard slam that rattled her teeth, and her shoulder careened into the wood-paneled wall of the carriage.

"Ouch," she moaned, rubbing her arm once she was able to right herself. She glanced at Alys, who'd suffered a similar fate. "Are you all right?"

"Aye, my lady," Alys replied, adjusting herself back on the velvet cushion. "Well enough. But if the roads do not improve, we'll be a heap of broken bones and bruises before we arrive."

Lizzie smiled. "I suspect it will get much worse. Taking the carriage at all was probably a mistake." They would have to switch to horses when they left Sterlingshire and crossed into the Highland divide and the roads narrowed—or, she should say, became more narrow, as they were barely wide enough for a carriage even in this part of the Lowlands.

"At least we're dry," Alys pointed out, always one to see the positive side of a situation. Perhaps that was why Lizzie enjoyed her company so much. They were much alike in that regard. Alys reached down and picked up the letter that had fallen to the ground with the tumult. "You dropped your missive."

Resisting the urge to snatch it back, Lizzie took it casually and tucked it safely in her skirts. "Thank you." She could sense Alys's curiosity about the earl's letter, about what was taking them to Dunoon Castle so suddenly, but she wasn't ready to alleviate it. Alys, like everyone else, would find out the contents soon enough. It would be no secret that her cousin the Earl of Argyll intended to find Lizzie a husband.

Again.

Apparently, three broken engagements weren't enough. It was her duty to *marry*, and marry she must.

Lizzie gazed out the window to distract herself from the

memories, the countryside rolling by in a vivid panoply of green. The heavy spring rain had reaped its munificent bounty, turning the glens thick with grass and the trees dense with leaves.

The light dimmed as the hours passed and they moved deeper into the forest, sending shadows dancing across the walls. The carriage slowed and an eerie quiet descended around them. It felt like they were being swallowed up. Like a sponge, the canopy of trees took hold, soaking up the noise and light. Unconsciously, her fingers circled the hilt of the small dirk she wore strapped to her side, as she silently thanked her brothers for insisting that she learn how to use it.

The coach jerked hard to the side, knocking Lizzie from her seat once again. But this time the carriage did not right itself, and they came to a sudden stop.

Something didn't feel right. It was too quiet. Like the still before the storm.

Her pulse quickened. Tiny bumps prickled along her skin and the temperature seemed to drop as the chill cut to her bones.

They'd come to rest at an angle so that both women had settled on the right side of the carriage opposite the door. It took a wee bit of maneuvering to get themselves up.

"Are you all right, my lady," Alys said, giving her a hand. Lizzie could tell from her quick, high-pitched tone that the maidservant was nervous as well. "A wheel must be stuck—"

A primal cry tore through the shrouded trees, sending an icy chill straight down her spine. Her eyes shot to Alys's in shared understanding. Dear God, they were under attack.

She could hear the voices of her cousin's guardsmen outside shouting orders back and forth, and then the name clear as day: "MacGregors!"

Lizzie couldn't believe it. *The outlaws must be mad to risk . . .*

Her blood went cold.

Or so desperate they have nothing to lose.

Fear started to build along the back of her neck. A whispery breath at first, then an icy hand with a tenacious grip. She fought to catch the frantic race of her pulse, but it kept speeding ahead.

A shot was fired. Then another.

The two women put their faces to the small window, trying to see what was happening, but the smoke from the musket shots was thick and the fighting seemed to be in front of the carriage beyond their field of vision.

The noise was deafening, but the most horrible part was imagining, trying to match the sounds with what might be happening. Unfortunately, there was no mistaking the sound of death. It surrounded them like a tomb in their small carriage, closing over them until the air was thick and difficult to breathe.

Lizzie had never been so terrified. It felt like every nerve ending, every fiber of her being was honed to a razor's edge on what was happening. Everything felt like it was moving too fast: her mind, her pulse, her breathing. But strangely, at this moment of extreme danger, she'd never felt more alive.

But for how long?

The handle to the door rattled, and she jumped. A menacing face appeared in the window and her heart lurched forward, slamming into her chest, and then came to a complete stop.

Alys screamed. Lizzie wanted to, but though her mouth was open the sound wouldn't come out. She couldn't breathe; all she could do was stare at the face in the glass. At the wildman. His hair was long and unkempt, his features hidden beneath the dirt and hair that covered his face.

All except for his eyes. They were glaring at her with hatred. It was like looking into the face of a feral animal. A wolf. A beast.

For the first time it occurred to her what these men might do to them if they were taken. The thought of him touching her . . . Bile rose at the back of her throat. She would slit her own throat first.

The door started to open. Lizzie grasped the handle from her side and pulled hard, finding an unexpected burst of strength as she engaged in a battle that she was sure to lose. "Help me!" she yelled to Alys.

But before Alys could move to do so another shot rang out, and the man jerked and froze in a state of momentary suspension. His eyes went wide, then wider, right before his face smacked hard against the glass with a horrible thud. As the dead weight of his body pulled him down, his nose and mouth dragged against the glass, stretching his features into a hideous mask of death.

The muscles she'd been clenching released. Her breathing was hard and quick as air once again tried to get into her lungs. The immediate threat was past, but Lizzie knew it was far from over.

Her heart was still racing, but her mind was oddly clear, focused on one thing: keeping them alive.

That an attacker was able to get so close to them did not bode well for their guardsmen. She looked out the window again, trying not to think about the dead man lying right below them, and weighed their options. They only had two: stay put or try to hide.

The carriage that had felt safe a few minutes ago now felt like a coffin waiting to be lowered into the ground. It was worth the risk. She turned to Alys. "We need to go."

Lizzie could tell that Alys was hanging by a very thin thread—ready to slip into panic at any moment. "Stay close and follow me." Taking a deep breath, she lowered the handle and pushed open the door. When it was wide enough, she poked her head out to get a look around. The acrid smell hit her first—of gunpowder and the unmistakable metallic scent of blood. It filled her nose and burned the back of her throat.

It was as she feared. The Campbells were outnumbered. The surprise attack had worked to immediately lessen her guardsmen's numbers, giving the MacGregors the advantage. She counted only a handful of Campbells and almost twice that many MacGregors who were easily identified by their Highland clothing and barbaric appearance.

Taking hold of Alys's hand, Lizzie carefully stepped out of the carriage. Anticipating Alys's instinct, Lizzie looked back at her and reminded her, "Don't look."

The ground was spongy under her foot with dirt and moss still damp from the earlier rain. The thin leather slippers she wore had little traction so she had to move cautiously. They stepped around the disabled carriage, heading toward the woods.

Neither of them had time to react before the riders were upon them. Warriors. Perhaps a half-dozen strong. But who were they? Friend or foe?

Her pulse raced as she waited to find out, horribly aware that their fate likely hung in the balance.

She could just make out their faces . . .

She sucked in her breath, her gaze locked on the man a few lengths in front of the others, tearing through the trees at a breakneck pace toward them. Every nerve ending prickled as she beheld the fearsome warrior. She prayed he was a friend. One glance was all it took to know that she would not want him as her enemy. The man had the look of a dark angel—sinfully handsome, but dangerous. Very dangerous.

The shiver that swept through her was not from fear but awareness. Awareness that made her skin tingle just to look at him. Enormous warriors armed to the teeth and clad in heavy steel mail did not usually provoke such a distinctly feminine reaction—except that he wasn't wearing mail. The hard lines of his formidable physique were all him. She sucked in an admiring breath, noticing the way the black leather of his doublet pulled tight across a broad chest and snugly around heavily muscled arms, tapering neatly over a flat stomach.

He was built for destruction, his body forged into a steely weapon of war.

But it wasn't just his physical dominance that set him apart from the others. It was the ruthlessness in his gaze, the hard, uncompromising bent of his square jaw, and the strength of his bearing. He wore a steel knapscall, his jet black hair just long enough to show below the rim. Thick and wavy, it framed his chiseled features to perfection. A strong jaw, high cheekbones, and wide, sculpted mouth were set off by deeply tanned skin. Only a nose that had been broken more than once and a few thin, silvery scars gave proof of his profession. He was a Greek god carved not from marble, but from hard Highland granite.

He met her gaze for an instant and a charge shot through her with all the subtlety of Zeus's thunderbolt. It rippled through her like a warm current from her head, down her spine, extending to the tips of her fingers and toes, shocking her with its intensity.

Green, she thought inanely. In the midst of the most terrifying experience of her life, she noticed the striking color of his eyes. Not the obvious skill with which he wielded his sword or the way he ordered his men with the barest gesture into formation or even—God forbid!—whether he intended to finish the job that the MacGregors started, but that his eyes blazed like the rarest emeralds sparkling in the sun.

He held her gaze for another moment, before the situation came back to her in a staggered heartbeat and she froze, waiting to see what he intended. One beat. Two. Her heart rose higher in her throat.

Relief washed over her, when an arrow shot by one of his men landed in the tree inches from the MacGregor's head. *A friend. Thank God!*